CW00404771

Flight into Darkness

and other stories

First Published in 2006 by;
Red Kite
PO Box 223
Walton on Thames
Surrey
KT12 3YQ
www.redkitebooks.co.uk

Illustrations by Mark Postlethwaite GAvA, Iza Bick and Paweł Bagiński
Some of the illustrations will be for sale via www.posart.com

© Tom Neil 2006

All rights reserved. No part of this publication may be reproduced, stored in a retrieval system, or transmitted in any form or by any means, electronic, mechanical, photocopying or otherwise without the prior permission of the publisher.

ISBN 0-9546201-7-8

Tom Neil
249 Sqn

Flight into Darkness
and other stories

by
Wing Commander Thomas F. Neil DFC* AFC AE

*For my wonderful wife, who also served, and our three sons
who are God-given rewards for those five
stressful years in a fighter cockpit.*

Contents

Author's Foreword

Throughout the Second World War, I had the privilege of flying fighter aircraft in both the Royal Air Force and the 9th United States Army Air Force. I engaged my first enemy aircraft in the spring of 1940 as a young officer of 19 and was still flying and fighting at 24, when the war ended in 1945.

In those six momentous years, I served and flew with hundreds of splendid men and women at home and overseas, whose courage I so greatly admired and whose bravery and devotion to duty I found humbling. I witnessed at first hand, death and the cruellest of injuries; I experienced the thrill and excitement of combat; the exuberance and joy of achievement; the stimulation borne of associating with young men and women, brilliantly successful in their various tasks; and finally and less comfortably, the sadness of consorting with others who faltered and fell below the levels of conduct expected of them.

The stories in this book describe many incidents and events I myself experienced or of which I had first hand knowledge. They involve many colleagues and friends with whom I flew but, in order to interpret their achievements more truly in terms of personal endeavour and human emotions, I have created imaginary situations and in some instances, more dramatic endings. In short, the stories here are fiction, though based on fact, and the main characters, whilst real enough to me, are creatures of my imagination.

In order to ensure a convincing measure of authenticity, I have referred now and then to actual wartime squadrons and the names of wartime airfields, some of which are still in existence. For the same reason, I have identified several well known senior officers and others, almost all of whom, alas, are now dead.

Finally, it is just possible that a few readers may recognise either themselves or their acquaintances in these various tales. If so, I crave their indulgence. All those I have written about, I hope and trust, have been dealt with fairly and without malice. My aim throughout has been to paint pictures of war as experienced by those who were active participants.

Tom Neil
Suffolk, April 2006

FLIGHT INTO DARKNESS

Flight into Darkness

This story deals mainly with events during the Battle of Britain.

Throughout 16 weeks of the summer and autumn of 1940, some 35 squadrons of the RAF - about 650 fighters - were deployed around London and along the south coast as far west as Dorset and pitted initially against a combined German fighter and bomber force of approximately 3,500 aircraft.

Each fighter squadron had on establishment eighteen aircraft, - mostly Spitfires and Hurricanes - divided into two flights of nine. These were flown by up to 24 pilots, - officers and senior NCOs - and serviced by up to 180 ground crew.

Several months earlier, during the spring of 1940, the RAF feverishly sought to increase its defensive strength by recreating units disbanded after the First World War. Mainly, the pilots posted in came straight from Flying Training Schools, a few via the limited number of Operational Training Units then available, plus several more experienced officers, transferred from existing squadrons. Overall, the average age of pilots in Fighter Command was 22, but many of them were no more than 19.

The quality and operational value of these young men varied considerably. As fighter pilots, some soon showed themselves to be manifestly brilliant, most others were of good average ability and a few were, and would remain, undistinguished. Such lesser pilots were usually weeded out fairly quickly and given different, less demanding flying roles in other squadrons.

This story is about two such young men posted to a newly formed squadron, one much more capable than the other. It reveals how their relationship developed during the Battle, and what occurred later.

Most of the flying incidents were exactly as described.

CHAPTER ONE

The following events occurred mostly at the beginning of the last war when I was a young chap of nineteen, or thereabouts. I say 'mostly', but not entirely. In fact it was a chance encounter only some months ago when I was visiting friends in America that led to these half-forgotten memories being dredged from the past and a sad, disturbing, conclusion to an incident which took place long before in 1940.

As I now look back, my feelings are mainly those of sadness and regret. Regret that, at the time, I had not been more perceptive; regret that I had lectured a lonely and unhappy man when I might have offered the sympathy, companionship and encouragement he so desperately needed. The indifference and inexperience of youth very often blinds us to the problems of others and it is sometimes only with the passing of time that their misfortunes are revealed to us and we see the true measure of our folly. So it was when I became involved in the affairs of Quentin Elliot, brother officer and companion in my first fighter squadron.

It was, as I recall, the second week in May 1940 when, having recently been commissioned at Cranwell, I was on leave prior to joining my first operational unit. I can see the telegram even now as it arrived at my parents' home in Hertfordshire, and the grey eyes of my mother, wide with concern, as she handed it to me. It was brief and to the point:

'Post Acting Pilot Officer P.A.E. Fitzgerald to 606 (S) Squadron, RAF Church Fenton, w.e.f. 14 May.'

The (S), I deduced, signified Spitfire but I had to turn out my old school atlas to find Church Fenton, tucked away obscurely in rural Yorkshire.

The following day, elated, but with more than a tinge of apprehension, I took leave of my family and headed north by train. After several changes on what seemed to be an endless journey, the station name-plate of Church Fenton slid slowly past my carriage window and the wheels of the train squealed to a standstill.

Stepping down I left my bags on the platform and, being in no particular hurry, walked forward until I was alongside the big, green Atlantic locomotive which stood radiating heat and blasting twin jets of steam into the heavens. I remember, as if it were yesterday, the faces of the driver and fireman as they leaned out of their cab and nodded to me amid the ear-numbing din, a little amused, possibly, that the elegantly turned-out youth in his smart new uniform with wings, cap and gloves, should show even a passing interest in anything so mundane as their sweating, grime-streaked engine. However, as a life-long steam enthusiast I watched with boyish fascination as, on a signal from the guard, they ducked back to their controls and the great coupled driving wheels were set in motion, heaving and clanking down the platform to the whoofing beat of the exhaust. The coaches then 'tack-tacked' past me, gathering speed, until after a time, with the rear of the train fast receding into the distance, I was left alone in the balmy silence of the Yorkshire countryside.

Returning to my luggage I saw that it appeared to be under the protection of a tall, thin youth dressed much as myself but with a greatcoat draped over an arm. As I approached he bobbed his head in a greeting - a rather unusual mannerism - before calling out to me.

"I saw you get off. If you're going to the aerodrome, I thought we might share a taxi."

We picked up our bags and equipment, he was humping an enormous camp-kit, and walked outside in silence to be faced by an ancient Austin 18 with the handwritten notice 'Taxi' pasted to the windscreen.

When we had installed ourselves with our luggage and the car had lurched into a grinding, rate-four turn around the station yard, my companion turned to me, 'My name's Elliot, by the way. Quentin Elliot.' Then, quite unnecessarily, he added, 'Named after an uncle somewhere or other - I've never known why.' After which he bobbed his head again and flashed me a Gary Cooper grin which quite transformed his face, making it most attractive.

I responded, giving my own name and where I had come from, after which we sat in silence, watching the hedges and cottages rumble by and looking ahead for signs of the airfield. During this brief interval, I was able to sneak several surreptitious glances in his direction and concluded that he was not only a remarkably highly-strung young man but also decidedly odd. He had a pale, angular face with deep-set blue eyes and a disconcerting habit of humming and nodding to himself as though carrying on a private conversation. I judged him to be about my own age - a year or so older, perhaps - and although around the same height, his bony frame made him seem very much taller despite a noticeable stoop. His tunic, though plainly new, fitted him badly and gave the appearance of still accommodating a clothes hanger in the shoulders with the result that his thin wrists protruded like skewers. But, most noticeable of all were his hands, large, veined and powerful, constantly on the move and always twisting, clasping, gesticulating.

After a time, he turned to me. "I say, are you 606 or 73?" Then, without waiting for me to reply, he went on, "73 haven't long been here. They were booted out of France, you know, and lost most of their aircraft. I'm 606, by the way. I hope you are, too." I replied that I was and that seemed to please him because his eyes lit up and he said in his Greyfriars schoolboy voice, "Oh, good show, I'm so glad." Then there was the bob of the head again and another of his delightful grins. After that brief exchange, there came a further pause before, with a suddenness I had almost come to expect, my companion said rather loudly, "I think I ought to tell you that I'm known as Camel." He looked at me with a measure of pathos and defiance in his eyes and, seeing the surprise on my face, went on, "I was given the name at F.T.S. - someone said that I rather looked like a Camel, and, well, the name stuck." When I made no reply, the expression of defiance returned before he added, a little lamely, "Well, there it is." The large hands clasped and wandered and he muttered almost to himself, "You'd get to know, anyway, so I thought I'd better tell you now." He was looking me sharply again, his eyes questioning, "D'you think I look like a Camel? Honestly, do you?"

By this time acutely uncomfortable, I felt a surge of compassion for the boy. However, before I had time to make a suitable response the taxi made a smart left-hand turn which had us both grabbing for support and we found ourselves approaching what was obviously an airfield. An orange-coloured windsock and hangars stood to our right, with the carefully manicured lawns and gardens of an Officers' Mess to our left.

We turned in through the ornamental gates and continued along the drive. A handsomely attired foursome playing tennis did something noteworthy and there were polite cheers and handclaps from a mixed group of onlookers sitting around several tables laden with the paraphernalia of afternoon tea. My new acquaintance, wide-eyed and solemn, exclaimed, "There you are, the British at war! Who can possibly beat them?" I glanced at him quickly, but there was no hint of a smile on his face.

The Officers' Mess at Church Fenton, built during the expansion period of the RAF in the mid-thirties, managed to retain the refined atmosphere of a gentleman's club in spite of being newly-built, modern in design, and comfortable. Elliot led the way through the tall glazed doors with eager strides and I followed him into the reception hall. In front of us was a long oak table set with silver, standing beneath the crests of squadrons past and present and a large painting of SE5s of the First World War, in combat over the wastes of Flanders.

Elliot launched forth again, "You'd better sign the 'Warning In' book first - they get frightfully snotty about that if you forget - and leave your card. You've got cards, I take it? Then, in a week or so, you'll have to call on the Station Commander's wife and some of the other wives, too." He bobbed his head in an embarrassed mannerism. "The Station Commander is a stickler for good form. However, his wife's really rather pretty, so it's not much of an ordeal. Some of the others, though - !" He pulled a schoolboy face, a look which did not require amplifying. I found myself looking curiously at him yet again. Most young officers would have commented on the ladies in question in rather more colourful terms, but Camel's face was without expression and I immediately assumed that he had in mind the rule that ladies, politics and religion were forbidden subjects in any Officers' Mess.

Whilst we had been talking an elderly servant appeared and, taking my bags, guided me to the East Wing and my quarters there. My bedroom - the first of a hundred I was to have during my Service career - was spacious, airy, and clinically clean, the decoration, bed-linen and wash-basin spotless, the light-brown lino like glass. The tall sash windows, half-open, looked out on to lawns, a rose garden, and an endless vista of open countryside and woods.

I stood and gazed, enraptured. In the foreground and to the left were the angular features of the camouflaged aircraft hangars, with the familiar orange windsock lying limply down its post as though exhausted. The sound of laughter from the tennis players and others drifted faintly to my ears. I filled my lungs with the deepest breath I could manage and experienced sheer, unadulterated joy. I felt secure and supremely happy. I belonged! This, above all else in my life, was what I had dreamed of.

Later, and somewhat nervously, I found my way downstairs and into the ante-room. With some relief I noticed that Camel was already there, standing at a table in the middle of the room, talking to an older man. He caught my eye and motioned me across, waving a hand in introduction. "This is Pilot Officer Fitzgerald. He's another one for 606. I met him at the station. And this is Flying Officer Vandenburg, the Squadron Adjutant. Referred to as Adj, or Van, but never sir - unless you need something!"

The man before me was of middle height and in his early 40s. He had about him an air of quiet authority and when he smiled, his light-brown eyes disappeared into a thousand crows-feet wrinkles. He held out his hand and I was instantly and warmly attracted to him.

"Welcome! The Squadron is reforming and you're the third new boy to arrive. With the CO and myself, that makes five here and about eighteen to come."

He nodded in the direction of the sideboard where two Mess servants were setting down tea, sandwiches and cake, towards which Camel was advancing purposefully.

"If you're wise, you'll have some tea before that young man wolfs everything in sight." He smiled tolerantly. "He bolts down food like a starving cormorant!"

I stood for some moments, waiting my turn in the tea queue, looking around. There were about a dozen officers disposed throughout the room in various black-leather settees and armchairs. All were in uniform and three, rather surprisingly, wore black calf-leather flying boots, a recent and fast-growing liberty, apparently, against which I had already been severely warned. There was almost no conversation, everyone appearing deeply engrossed in newspapers and magazines, a large variety of which lay on a separate table.

I glanced back towards the Adjutant, who was conversing with another officer, and saw that he wore the single wing of an Observer's brevet and the ribbon of the DFC, together with those of the Victory and General Service medals of the First World War. As I looked at him he raised his head and smiled, an expression I was to look for and appreciate many times in the months to come, a smile full of gentleness, tolerance and good humour.

I poured my tea and made my selection of food before returning to his side.

"I see that you were an Observer in the last war, sir." I hoped that my tone would convey something of the awe I felt. His eyes wrinkled. "Briefly, yes - but don't call me sir! I was on D.H.4s. Nice old cows, provided they didn't catch fire."

"Were you ever shot down?" I realised at once it was a childish remark and instantly regretted making it. He smiled patiently.

"No, not really, although the Huns frightened my engine into stopping a couple of times - we had the American Liberty in the D.H.4. Apart from those few moments of horror, I had a pretty easy time. In fact, I only managed six months in France. Then the Armistice came and we returned to England and disbanded."

"You were decorated, though."

He grinned. "Very little to do with me, old son. When you're an Observer, you do what the pilot decides. I just read the maps, aimed the bombs, and fired the gun when the occasion demanded. Anyway, they seemed to dish out DFCs to squadrons in rotation and it was obviously our turn. Nothing at all heroic, I do assure you." He smiled again and paused, signifying unmistakably that the subject had been exhausted.

I tried another tack. "You know Pilot Officer Elliot, I take it?"

"Indeed, yes. He's been here for several days - the first of you chaps to arrive, in fact. But, apart from that, I've known his family for a long time; since Quentin was a child, actually." He grinned. "He improves with age - but very slowly!"

At that moment, his gaze strayed over my shoulder and, lowering his voice a little, he added, "Here's the CO now, if you're interested. I think we might go and meet him, don't you?"

My first encounter with Squadron Leader James Denby was neither memorable nor even cordial. He was then a smooth, rather precious-looking young man of about 26, with dark hair brushed back from a prominent forehead to curl fashionably at his ears and neck. He was good-looking, in a faintly florid way, with an unusual but engaging high-pitched chuckle during which he showed very white and even teeth.

However, he was not in a chuckling mood on the occasion of our first meeting and he simply nodded when my name was introduced and asked me where I'd come from. When I explained, a little diffidently, that I was straight from Flying Training School with no experience other than on biplanes - Hawker Harts, Audaxes, and the like - he gave me a baleful stare and said that I had a lot of hard work ahead of me if I was to come up to scratch within the next six weeks. After which, having flattened me with that remark, he addressed the Adjutant on another subject entirely so that I was left alone not knowing quite whether to withdraw gracefully or remain in their exalted company until I was dismissed.

Whilst I was trying to make up my mind the Adjutant, sensing my discomfort, put a hand on my shoulder in order that I should feel part of the conversation. Then, after an interval, he gave me one of his very engaging smiles and said, "Look, old son, why don't you take young Elliot on at snooker?" He winked. "He's only allowed on the table in the company of an adult in case he should try to put a hole in the cloth."

Grateful for his intervention I smiled with relief and moved off, anxious to get away from Denby but also to avoid any further discussion which might produce the terrible admission that, having only played snooker once before in my life, I was no more to be trusted on the green baize than Camel.

The following two months were probably as memorable, if rather less dangerous, than any that followed, including the hectic days of what was later to be called the Battle of Britain. Other pilots arrived in groups of two and three and soon the Mess was full of new faces accompanied by laughter and loud talk, bent elbows, and a variety of small-bowled undergraduate pipes, puffed with inexpert vigour by ex-members of the University Air Squadrons. A few old hands were brought in from other units and the squadron divided itself formally, but comfortably, into two Flights; 'A' and 'B'. Later, with less formality but equally comfortably, there formed half-a-dozen cosy 'cliques' consisting of old-boy-net acquaintances and 'newly-weds'. It was the happiest of assemblies, everyone full of bubbling enthusiasm, boyish good humour, and Boys' Own Paper slang. There were 'wizards' and 'prangs' and 'good shows' by the score and, to the older set, it must have all seemed very juvenile.

The first four Spitfires arrived within a day or two of my arrival, together with an old Fairey Battle which was used to ferry several of the more experienced pilots to airfields around the country from which, in ones and twos, other Spitfires were collected. Meanwhile we all busied ourselves drawing flying kit - including the new oxygen mask which most of us had never worn before - signing vouchers, reading orders and books by the dozen, and studying silhouettes of German aircraft. In the most inappropriate places one would suddenly be asked the vital statistics of a Junkers 87 or a Heinkel 111 and out would be trotted wingspans, speeds, and load capacities, all correct to an inch and to a pound.

More than half of us had never so much as sat in a Spitfire and those who had come from Flying Training Schools equipped with Hart-variant trainers, had never even flown a low-wing monoplane. For us a new Miles Master was imported and, as privileged first arrivals, Camel and I headed the list of those to be converted to a boosted engine, a three-bladed, variable pitch airscrew, a retractable undercarriage, and flaps.

It was all shatteringly new and exciting. My Flight Commander, a red-faced stockbroker from one of the London Auxiliary Squadrons, endured three excruciatingly trying half-hour trips with me, during which I forgot to retract the wheels after take-off, throttled back when I should have been coarsening the aircrew pitch, lowered my flaps at speeds greatly in excess of the maximum limit, and bounced him around unmercifully in an aircraft 100 miles-an-hour faster than anything I had ever before experienced. A master of euphemism, he assessed my performance as 'promising'.

Having been judged inexpert but safe, I was introduced to a Spitfire - on trestles and in a hangar! There I sat with a blindfold around my face, going through the mnemonics of my cockpit drill and identifying as best I could all the controls and switches. Meanwhile the wheels went up and down, the hydraulics moaning and squealing; the flaps - which were operated by compressed air - hissed in and

out like enraged pythons, and all the time I listened, felt, pushed, and pulled. Up and down, in and out. A hundred times. I was there for a whole day.

Finally, the real thing! I was led out to my first Spit - letter D, as I recall - like a lamb to slaughter. My Flight Commander watched me strap-up before imploring me quietly and in the most cultivated of Oxbridge accents, not to 'prang the bloody thing'. After which, he strolled away, hands in pockets, comfortably snug in an aura of weary indifference.

Tied down and hemmed in by Spitfire - a cockpit full of instruments, two stubby elliptical wings, eight machine guns, and the sweet smell of new paint and high octane petrol - I sat there uncertainly. The nose stretched away dauntingly in front and I was suddenly stricken by the awful realization that I did not know how to start the engine - no one had ever shown me!

A senior NCO and two members of my crew were stifling yawns at the end of the wing, waiting for something to happen. They were waiting in vain! Totally abashed and thankful that my crimson cheeks were hidden beneath my face mask, I beckoned to the Sergeant and explained my predicament in a whisper. After that, like a couple of conspirators, we unscrewed the ki-gas priming pump, squirted six jets of fuel into the cylinders, set the throttle and everything else vital to the occasion, and pressed the starter and booster buttons. Ahead, the airscrew gave a clank and began to rotate against compression. Almost immediately the engine started with a bellow and a minor hurricane of air snatched away the Sergeant's hat like a leaf and left me gasping. After a few seconds of utter confusion I gradually regained my composure, after which all was plain sailing – comparatively!

I taxied out across the grass, bouncing and swaying, kicking the nose left and right so that I could see ahead and being especially cautious with the brakes to avoid standing the aircraft on its nose. Throughout, I left half an eye on the radiator temperature gauge - Spitfires were notorious for overheating on the ground.

At the far end of the airfield I turned cross-wind, braked to a standstill, and experienced a stomach-clenching moment of sheer, naked panic. The Spitfire, meanwhile, stood there like a trembling stallion at the end of a none-too-certain rein.

I opened the engine to 0 lbs boost and checked the ignition switches one by one. I then ran my hands and eyes quickly around the cockpit. Trim - elevator one notch down; rudder bias - full right; mixture - rich; airscrew - fully fine;

fuel - on and contents full; flaps - up; instruments - checked, compass and DI gyro set and uncaged; oxygen - on and flowing; harness - locked; hood - open and secure. I took a nervous breath and gave a last quick look around. Anything else? Then, I turned into wind and opened the throttle cautiously.

There were no half-measures about that engine. With the howl of a Dervish the Spitfire set off across the grass like an electric hare, the acceleration alarming. As it raced ahead, the curved wings dipping and rocking, I gently lifted the tail and found the controls growing lighter, the elevator as sensitive as a balanced needle. The wheels, a blur of motion now, tipped a rise . . . and again . . . once more . . . and then I was up and away, shooting skywards, the engine raging away in front of me at almost 7 lbs boost and 3,000 revs. My first solo in a Spit: Electrifying! Breathtaking!

Once airborne I changed hands on the control-column and raised the wheels, hearing first the rumble then the 'clunk' as they locked in the 'up' position. Gently I reduced power and, putting the airscrew into coarse pitch - constant speed airscrews came later - heard the engine note die to a more sober level. The wind howled around my ears - the hood was still open - but I was half afraid of committing myself to being totally enclosed for the first time in my life. So, I straightened out, throttled back, and watched the speed settle at 250 mph.

Like a skater on wafer-thin ice I then cautiously turned to the left and looked about. I was at 1,400 feet with the airfield below me and somewhere behind. I lifted the nose to climb away again and saw the needle begin to wind around the altimeter. What if the engine stopped now? What would I do? But why should it, for heaven's sake? It was roaring away throatily and, to my relief, continued to do so as I opened the throttle again. The speed fell to 180 in the climb as I felt for the hood catch behind my head, pulling it so that the perspex bubble slid forward and locked shut with minute thud. Silence! Well . . . not quite silence perhaps but far, far less noise. And no gale of wind, thank God! A little cramped, but quite comfortable! And, strangely, not as claustrophobic as I had feared. Everything roaring and vibrating minutely, I settled in my seat and felt my breathing return to normal.

I flew around, my confidence growing by the minute. What a wonderful, beautiful aircraft: such a sense of power, agility and strength. The nose stretched ahead of me a full furlong, it seemed, the engine hurled its raucous challenge to the world at large and the two elliptical wings rocked at my slightest touch.

I pushed forward and, momentarily, the engine hesitated; the exhausts gave

out a smudge of dark smoke and my backside rose majestically from its bucket seat. I pulled, and the universe dragged at my feet, reducing my sight to a mottled grey as gravity took its toll. Heavens! The elevators were feather-light and devastatingly effective. The wings were still there, though - weren't they? Thankfully, they were!

I climbed again until I was above a layer of cloud and at 10,000 feet. After that I dived, then flattened out, brushing the racing white fluff with my tilting wings and flicking joyously through a flimsy patch here and there before pulling back and soaring upwards, the white carpet falling away like a discarded mantle. Oh, the sheer joy of it! The aircraft was alive! The sky was my playground: My God, I could do anything!

I forced down the nose and watched the speed rise rapidly, 300 then 350, finally 400. Everything tight and the starboard wing dropping. Hard left aileron now - it must be the radiator under one wing! I trimmed her forward . . . more, then more, working the rudder bias at the same time. God, I'd never been so fast: 430! The needle steadying now with everything trembling and as vibrant as a bowstring - the Spitfire was alive, exulting in it, pulling hard like a wayward horse. I reined her in, picking the nose up gently . . . gradually . . . feeling the blood begin to drain again. My sight, greying first, faded into almost complete darkness, although all the time I was fully aware and faintly amused by this new phenomenon. Strange, most strange!

With returning vision, I was rocketing up . . . up . . . up . . . a flash of cloud and a brief but violent shudder as my aircraft rode a few corrugated strands of turbulence. Then I was curving skywards like a leaping salmon into a void of endless blue . . . and stillness . . . with the hard white line of the horizon tilting and falling away, tilting again, then rotating and leveling out magically until it was exactly and soberly where it ought to have been. Wonderful, sensible things horizons!

Intoxicated almost by the sheer joy of flying the aircraft, I suddenly became aware of time. Twenty minutes was all that had been allowed and I had already been up 25! I dropped the nose and began to search for the airfield.

I approached the circuit quietly and without fuss, tried first to open the hood at too high a speed and, not succeeding, dropped down to 180 and tried again. This time I forced it back along its slide, the slipstream buffeting my elbows and shoulders. Then down with the wheels; I moved the lever in the quadrant precisely and unhurriedly so that I should not risk jamming the rotating pins. The undercarriage legs fell away and, after a few seconds of apprehension, locked down, a single green light showing left of centre on the dashboard. The airfield, ahead and to port now, I curved towards it.

All clear. Down to 140. Then the flaps - I flicked down the flat disc and felt the flaps extend, the aircraft wallowing a little in protest, then steadying. Airscrew into fine pitch - the engine raised its voice - and I was trundling in nicely with 100 showing on the ASI and the tail settling. The hedge slid towards me then flashed underneath. I held off with the undulating grass approaching with deceptive stealth then, in a moment, racing past - a green blur. No, not yet! I porpoised slightly, holding the control column firmly to the rear. The nose way up now! Floating! Floating! Floating! God! I ought to be down by now! I should be . . . !

The port wheel hit and the aircraft bounced. Not much, just a trifle. A second touch, stick hard back, the smallest ballooning jolt and everything was rumbling and bouncing and jigging, the wings rocking, the exhausts crackling and spouting minute puffs of blue smoke. Straight! Keep her straight! STRAIGHT! I kicked hard and corrected as the nose began to wander, the aircraft wilfully testing my skill.

I was down! Safe! Whoa! Keep still, you brute! STILL! The mettlesome Spitfire, tamed at last, slowed to walking pace. I turned. And stopped. My first solo. I was down. In one piece!

I began to taxi in, relieved, breathless, and feeling like a king. The radiator! Crikey. I'd forgotten the radiator. I moved the lever that operated the flap. Mustn't let her boil!

My crew was waiting for me, climbing on to the wing roots with polite smiles. "Everything all right, sir?" I feigned nonchalance. "Fine! No problem. Everything went beautifully." I threw off my straps, climbed out, and dropped to the ground.

As I walked off, I heard raised voices and looked round. A Spitfire was taxying in, steam spouting from the front end. It turned suddenly and stopped. The engine, although obviously switched off, carried on stubbornly, the propeller jerking rhythmically until there was a series of expensive-sounding 'clanks' and the three-bladed airscrew set off in the opposite direction. After a time, everything quietened down and the pilot made to climb out. Still humping my parachute I walked towards the late arrival, which was still simmering like a kettle on a hob. Camel emerged from the vapour, frowning.

"What on earth happened?" I enquired.

"It boiled!" explained Camel succinctly. "It couldn't have been filled properly."

I was unable to restrain a snort. "Don't talk rot! You let it overheat. You probably taxied back too slowly."

"Back!" Camel's face showed outrage. "I was on my way out! I haven't been anywhere yet. It really isn't fair, you know!"

CHAPTER TWO

Under the tutelage of Flight Lieutenant Jonathan Oliver St John Garland, Camel Elliot and I formed the nucleus of 'A' Flight. This seemingly privileged and elevated status was in no way due to our being superior in any manner or degree, but merely stemmed from the fact that we were the first to arrive on the Squadron.

'Guinness' Garland, besides being incredibly old - about 35! - was a large, shrewd and beefy man with an agreeable, offhand manner and a remarkably even temper. A stockbroker by profession, he was an Auxiliary and therefore a part-time airman to whom the war represented an unfortunate interlude in an otherwise pleasant, indefinite and lucrative arrangement whereby he enjoyed cost-free flying at week-ends and much good fellowship. Although he was never heard to make such a remark in public, he regarded his appointment as Flight Commander in a newly-formed fighter squadron as a perfectly proper means of meeting his war-time obligation to come to the aid of the nation by training young pilots - such as me - to take on the enemy. I don't believe `Guinness' Garland ever had the slightest intention of fighting himself and, in the nicest possible way, he successfully manipulated some of his many contacts in London to see that he didn't. Indeed, with his pleasantly bovine temperament, I doubt that he would have lasted a week had he felt driven to take on a more active and warlike role.

Within a fortnight we pilots of 'A' Flight had settled-in comfortably and had been able to establish close personal relationships with colleagues who, only days before, had merely been names and faces. In total, they - we - were a splendid group of young men - average age 21 - and I think each of us experienced that most satisfying sense of well-being that comes from being engaged in an arduous and demanding endeavour of vital national importance. Of the 24 pilots in the squadron, nine were sergeants and the rest officers. However, regardless of rank, there grew up between us all a respectful, disciplined yet intimate association akin to that of a family.

Even so, though collectively a 'happy breed', each pilot developed a reputation of his own; there were the manifestly brilliant, others were good but either flamboyant or lacking in histrionic flair, some merely honest and workman-like, and a few - just a few - careful and hesitant. And, as in every squadron, one or two were - different! Quite different! Not so much in their ability to fly, but in their attitude to life in general, their response to the sort of problems and situations with which we were, even then, being confronted by and their natural tendency towards extremes of individuality bordering on eccentricity.

Quentin Elliot was one such person. With spectacles on the end of his nose, even at the age of 20 he could have undertaken the role of absentminded professor. He was totally unpredictable, agreeable but distant, quietly and amusingly nutty, and, from time to time, either childishly gay or owlishly solemn.

In the air he was always the chap who couldn't keep up with the rest and who, when everyone else turned right, as often as not turned left. If our Squadron Drill was in any way irregular, it was always Camel who formated too tightly or left a gap. In short, in any demonstration designed to prove to the world our squadron's efficiency, discipline and dash, Camel was invariably a downright embarrassment. Many were the times that quiet and despairing words were muttered to the effect that we would all be a damn-sight better off if Camel were fighting on the other side. And, on a more personal level, as Camel Elliot and I invariably flew together during the earlier parts of our training, we shared some memorable experiences and incidents.

The first arose from a practice dog-fight on which he and I were engaged, an exercise designed to give us confidence that we could handle our new Spitfires in any and every condition of flight. In fact we did many of these sorties, taking-off together and climbing to 15,000 feet, after which one of us would act as target whilst the other attacked from above and from the quarter.

After each attack there would follow a brisk exercise in evading and chasing which would leave each of us sick with fatigue - the early Spits did not incorporate the damping device fitted to the elevators of later aircraft of the type, so that we seemed constantly to be in the twilight zones of blacking-out or coming-to!

On this particular occasion I had grown weary of acting as target after his sixth attack and, on impulse, I whipped into a half-roll and plummeted earthwards, the Camel in hot pursuit. We tumbled down thousands of feet, twisting and turning at a very fair lick, until I saw that we were very close to the ground - much closer than I had ever intended - obliging me to pull out very firmly indeed. I remember seeing the Camel, obviously taken by surprise, charging past like a runaway mare and disappearing. Half a minute later he reappeared from under my port wing and joined up, after which we returned to the airfield and landed in a very calm and orderly manner.

It was only when we were relaxing in the crew-room some time later that 'Tommy' Thompson, our Engineer Officer, put his head around the door and, in his quiet almost apologetic way, asked for the chap who had last flown 'C', Charlie. When the Camel admitted to being the pilot, 'Tommy' informed him, with more than a hint of amused malice, that the squadron now possessed probably the only Spitfire in existence with about six inches additional dihedral on each wing and a set of wrinkles on the top surfaces which would put even a very old tortoise to shame.

Wide-eyed, we all trooped out to examine the damage. It was, incidentally, the only evidence of over-stressing on a Spitfire I ever did see in five years of combat, and found 'Tommy's' description to be no more than the truth. Camel had obviously manhandled the aircraft so violently that he had buckled the structure more than a little, requiring a new pair of wings and sundry other parts and adjustments, which put the Spitfire out of commission for more than a fortnight. Within the hour Camel had disappeared in the direction of the CO's office, after which we saw very little of him for four days - except at meal-times!

Then, a week or so later, with Camel back again in circulation, there occurred another incident which I have never forgotten.

One aspect of our training which never appealed to me greatly was cloud flying, possibly because 'Guinness' Garland's methods, effective though they may have been, were crude in the extreme. He adopted a kill or cure technique; flying us straight into the middle of the meatiest clouds he could find and woe betide us if we were not still in tight formation when we emerged.

In fact, cloud flying is less hazardous than it would first appear as, other than in the densest of murk, it is usually possible to pick out the outline of an aircraft flying in close formation. Therein lies the trick; close formation is the essential prerequisite for success provided also that, in the event of losing one's partner or leader, one flies immediately on a diverging course until daylight reappears.

On this particular occasion, Camel, by reason of seniority, was flying as No. 2 - on 'Guinness's' right - whilst I formated on the left, a position I never enjoyed as it always had me facing what I considered to be the wrong way. The RAF, in my view, was a left-handed organisation, a theory of mine I won't bother to expand on here.

After a series of plunges into clouds of varying thickness and density, 'Guinness' selected a mountainous, evil-looking Cu Nim, which towered like a precipice in front of us. My heart sank as we flew remorselessly towards its solid, cliff-like side.

I shiver, even now, as I think of it! It was like stepping into a blackened room, so that within two seconds of entering its stygian interior I had lost him. Horrified and clinging to the controls of my bucking Spitfire I flew on, deviating not one degree and being tossed around like a leaf in the upcurrents. My mind congealed with fear, until, after about 30 seconds of sweating apprehension, I shot out into clear sunshine the other side. To my relief and utter surprise, 'Guinness' was more or less where I had left him, but the Camel had vanished.

I then saw Garland's helmeted head turn towards me and do something in the nature of a double-take, because, there, tucked-in tightly on my left-hand side, was Camel's Spitfire, no more than six feet distant. Somehow, he had contrived to move across, either under or above us both, and had taken up a close formation position on my port wing, all at 260 mph and without being able to see a thing.

Back again on the ground 'Guinness', in rather pained but pointed tones, asked him why he had changed position at so dangerous a time; to which Camel blandly replied that he had simply obeyed the order, 'Echelon Port'.

The normally unflappable Garland, dropped his mouth in surprise before recovering admirably.

"Are you really trying to tell me that I gave the order Echelon Port in the middle of a Cu Nim?" His eyes were wide in disbelief although his voice remained coolly level. "My dear boy, you must be demented!" He turned away, shaking his head. "I suggest you get your ears washed out before you write off the whole Squadron."

Later, I pulled Camel's leg about his poor airmanship but he stuck to his tale and became terribly solemn and huffy. Nor did he ever admit his mistake.

We flew very hard between mid May and mid July, 1940 and my log book records 93 flights and 107 hours in Spitfires over one four-week period. Our immediate aim was to become 'operational within six weeks', which meant that we could then be employed against the Hun who was pretty active in small numbers in the Yorkshire area and off the coast. So there was no lack of endeavour, I need hardly say, and we were all bursting to 'have a go'.

Our work became so intensive, in fact, that even the more aggravating idiosyncrasies of a few pilots became trifling incidentals. Camel Elliot continued to pursue an individualistic course both in the air and on the ground but, there being no malice in the boy, even his more extreme gaffes were regarded as nothing more than amusing irritants. Vandenburg, the Adjutant, kept him very much in check on the ground and 'Guinness' Garland, in his own inimitable way, leaned on him pretty heavily in the air. Elliot wasn't at all a bad pilot, but his unpredictability knew no bounds.

About the second week in July it became necessary to carry out some night flying practice - we were laughingly called 'day and night' fighters in those days - and in order to enable us to do so without interruption, bearing in mind the Hun night raids on major towns in northern England, 'Guinness' Garland arranged that we should operate briefly from Prestwick, in Scotland.

It was decided that four of us should go; 'Guinness', Camel, Sergeant Davidson, and me. After several hours of preparation we all flew off northwards, three of us at least, glad of the break and change of scenery.

We arrived in the early evening after an uneventful flight of 50 minutes or so. There had been heavy rain and, with the sun low in the western sky, Scotland was at its most beautiful. The clouds, grim, solid masses of white on the horizon, had departed leaving the countryside bright and scrubbed-looking, an iridescent mosaic of gem-like greens and mauves and browns. To the west a calm and endless expanse of water shone like polished pewter out of which the Isle of Arran rose like a dark monster whilst, far away to the south, the mountains of the Lake District were visible only as muted tints. As we stopped to savour the freshness of it all, the air was cool and sweet with the peaty smell of early summer and the airfield a lush but deserted area of rolling pasture. The west of Scotland gave not the slightest hint of being at war with anyone.

We flew briefly the following day, carrying out essential air tests, and as the sun began to drop once more behind the dark silhouettes of the western islands, Sergeant Davidson and I paced out the flare-path. Half-a-dozen airmen, who had travelled up by road, helped to set the goose-neck flares at 100 yard intervals, their oily heads drooping with paraffin and ready for the flame. Not without difficulty we positioned the Chance light at the threshold of the grass runway and, after checking all the positions and equipment, I left to prepare for flying.

Prestwick, in those days, was far removed from its present shape and condition. In the early summer of 1940 it was a pleasant, concave, expanse of grass with very little in the way of navigation or radio aids. Once airborne a pilot was on his own, more or less, and was obliged to find his own way around the sky and back to base.

I went off first and climbed away to the west, into the wake of the disappearing sun, a solitary dot gradually losing substance. I wandered up and down the coast and over the Isle of Arran in the direction of Ulster until the light faded completely and the ground was lost in huge and merging pools of darkness. Soon, all vestiges of grey had disappeared and the stars were pinpricks in an indigo sky. It seemed that I, and I alone, was alive in the whole infinity of space. I, and one important companion, the roaring, beating engine ahead of me with its rows of glowing eyes. After an hour I returned to the airfield and, with navigation lights on, did a slow and careful circuit, aware of a quite unusual atmosphere of bleak loneliness and isolation. From down below and out of the night the green eye of the Aldis winked up at me, after which I put down my wheels and flaps and dropped gently onto the grass like a settling bird. It was good to be down; night flying always gave me a great sense of achievement. I taxied carefully back to our dispersal point across the black and featureless airfield, small pink-and-blue serpent's tongues flicking out contentedly from my engine exhausts.

Camel Elliot, who had been in charge of the Chance light and flare-path during my absence, joined 'Guinness' and me in the hut which served as a crew-room. After a brief exchange of information he kitted up and went out into the darkness whilst I walked off towards the runway. After some minutes I heard his engine in the distance and saw his navigation lights moving slowly towards me. He emerged into the pale gleam of the floodlight, lined up on the flares and took off, the noise of his Merlin shattering the silence, his port bank of exhausts a raging blow-torch of fiery energy. As his aircraft gathered speed and lifted off into the darkness, the pulsating din subsided and gradually dwindled into silence.

Sergeant Davidson and I exchanged resigned glances and began to stamp our feet and wander around in slow and patient circles, prepared to kill time until the Spitfire returned.

The hour passed quickly enough. The night was ink-black and brilliantly alive with stars. Davidson and I stood and watched, then chatted agreeably about this and that until the Sergeant suddenly motioned with his hand.

"There he is!" and, after a moment, I picked out Camel's navigation and downward identification lights moving across the sky.

I watched him turn and pass overhead, his engine well throttled back, the distinctive whistle of the early marks of Spitfire just audible above the murmur of a generator.

Davidson flashed a green signal from his Aldis before the big petrol-engined generator feeding the Chance light revved up in preparation for the landing.

With a crackle of elements the floodlight developed and a brilliant pool of white light rolled in a glaring tide up the flare-path. I walked across to where Davidson was standing and after some moments shouted in his ear. "Where is he? Can you see him?"

"Yes, sir." The man pointed. "He's on final approach now." I stared into the blackness but could see nothing.

We waited. The generator was making such a din that we could not expect to hear Camel's engine but, in a moment or two, the Spitfire would appear, bursting into the floodlight glare, to touch down and go careering down the flare-path, exhausts crackling and rudder wagging.

I waited . . . and waited. Seconds passed. But there was no sign of an aircraft. I was puzzled and fidgeted. Where in heaven's name had the man gone? I turned to the Sergeant.

"Can you see him?"

"No, sir."

"What the heck's happened to him?"

"Don't know, sir."

"You didn't see him overshoot?"

"No, he hasn't gone round again, I'm sure of that."

Another ten seconds passed. Then, in a moment, I knew something had happened and was galvanised into action. As I started running, I yelled, "See if you can turn the flood-light round. Follow me with it, if you can."

There was no defined end to the airfield, it just petered out into a field of grain which rose gradually into the first of a series of low-lying hills. I could see next to nothing in the darkness and soon found myself pushing into a waist-high crop of some sort - corn, oats, barley, I didn't know which - so that in a few moments I was wet to the thighs. I pounded on, my heart thumping, hoping I would not find Camel in the middle of an ugly wreck. On and on into the blackness and wet, clinging, earth until my tortured lungs were bursting.

Suddenly, I ran full tilt into something warm and soft yet angular and bony. It was so unexpected that a cry was knocked out of me and I was thrown to the ground, for a moment bemused and shocked. A cow? In a cornfield? Then, I heard some human and very aggrieved expostulations. Still dazed, I scrambled to my feet, conscious of wet mud on my hands and knees, and heard my own raised voice.

"Camel! Is that you?"

"Who's that?" A muffled croak came from the darkness.

"It's me! Fitzgerald!"

"Where am I?" It was Camel's voice - no mistaking it!

I calmed down, knowing him to be reasonably whole and live enough to knock me flat and still be able to talk. "You're in a cornfield, you ape! Five-hundred yards short of the flare-path!"

He said in slurred and confused tones, "Where?" and I knew immediately that he was heavily shocked.

I called sharply, "Camel, for God's sake! Where are you?"

I heard him rustling about in the darkness. At that moment we were illuminated by the thin glare of the floodlight that Sergeant Davidson had managed to turn around and I saw Elliot a few yards away, blinking like an owl, his face chalk-white but with a mess of blood around the nose and mouth.

I was immediately concerned. "Are you all right?"

"Yes . . . I think so."

"Where's the aeroplane?"

Camel turned away vaguely and said, as though in a dream, "I don't know. It's . . . it's around here somewhere - I suppose." Then he wandered off slowly in a circle, presumably to find it.

The tension broken, I burst out laughing. "Camel, for heaven's sake! Don't you know?"

I heard him muttering something in the darkness and, laughing still, followed the sound of him crunching about until, in a few moments, we were confronted by his Spitfire. It was almost in the flying position, two blades of its metal airscrew deep in the soil and the wheels and legs half collapsed and totally embedded. It looked very forlorn.

Elliot reached out to touch it and said plaintively, "This must be it. D'you think it is? I think I hit my head on the gunsight . . . or something. Look!" Bathed in the eerie gleam of the distant floodlight, he began dabbing his face with a handkerchief and looking at the blood. His hands, I could see, were shaking badly so I put my arm around his shoulders.

"Come on, Camel. Let's leave everything where it is and I'll get Sergeant Davidson to arrange a guard." I looked back in the darkness to the swathe that had been cut in the corn. "By gum! The farmer's not going to be pleased with you, old chum!"

Camel kept muttering but did not move, so I grasped him by the arm and began to pull him away. He resisted like a stubborn child and said petulantly,

"I think I ought to stay with my aeroplane, really I do." He was still very groggy.

I pulled harder. "Come on, Camel! Don't mess about. You're doing no good here and I, for one, am wet through. Let's get your face seen to and find something to raise your morale. Something large and neat, preferably!"

He began to pull again and, almost whining, said, "Fitzgerald, you know I don't drink."

Losing patience I gave him a push. "Tonight, Camel, I know nothing of the sort. You're going to darn well drink something if I have to spoon it down."

"Fitzgerald!"

"Shut up, for Pete's sake! And get a move on!"

The following morning we were sitting at breakfast in the Airport Cafe, Camel with a liberal covering of gauze and plaster across his nose and forehead. His lips were still puffy and he was very solemn.

"I still don't know how I came to be in that field. I was coming in quite nicely, then everything began to rumble and shake. So I opened the throttle, but the engine just . . . well, just, died away." He shrugged, his big hands working. "After that . . . nothing! Until I met you, that is."

I hesitated. I did not want to tell him baldly that he had totally misjudged his approach, undershot badly, and touched down 500 yards short of the aerodrome. Poor chap! He really had been a fool. But, how to put it?

My dilemma was soon resolved, however, when 'Guinness' Garland appeared in the doorway. Catching sight of us he walked across to our table. Possibly because he had been out since early morning in borrowed gum-boots, assessing damage and visiting a very aggrieved farmer on whose land Camel had intruded, he was in one of his less tolerant moods. He came straight to the point and addressed himself to Camel who was eyeing him warily.

"You, young man, have made a howling cock of things, as usual."

I saw Camel frown and, stung by the remark, made the mistake of answering back immediately. "I'm sorry, Guinness, but . . . !"

"But, my backside!" Garland's voice was a low and dangerous drawl. "You missed the airfield by a mile; you ran your wheels down a slope, carving up a whole field of barley - which His Majesty will have to pay for - and, if your engine did stop, it was only because you were fool enough to scoop four bushels of grain into the air-intake. All in all, you behaved like a thoroughly irresponsible clot.

What saddens me most, however, is that you never seem to learn. Which, in my book, is the hallmark of a complete ruddy half-wit!"

He turned to me. "I want to get away as soon as possible. We'll take off at 10.30, so tell the others."

Returning to Camel, he added, "You'll have to go home by train, my lad, and if I had my way, you'd walk!" He bent forward, his face within a foot of Elliot's. "And, Camel, try to resist pulling the communication cord. And stay right away from the engine. Because in your present accident-prone condition, you could well have the damn thing off the rails before it leaves the station!"

With a curt nod, he picked up his hat and left.

Limp with embarassment, I kept my eyes to the table so that it was only Camel's voice that I heard. His tone was full of compassion. "You know, Fitzgerald, I honestly believe the war's getting to old 'Guinness'. I really think he's beginning to crack-up, you know."

I stifled an incredulous sigh. I ought to have replied - but I couldn't!

Back home, Camel came in for a good deal of ragging about his accident and for a time was referred to as Farmer Elliot. He took it fairly well, for the most part solemnly, but occasionally he laughed with the rest of us, nodding his head in his peculiar way, his great hands twisting and turning. His relationship with James Denby, however, was less of a joke. He collected a seven day stint as Duty Pilot, a chore which each junior officer had to endure occasionally and which meant languishing for 24 hours at a time in the Watch Office, the primitive forerunner of the present Air Traffic Control. It was said that Denby was all for packing him off as unsuitable material for a fighter squadron but that the Adjutant, with his customary calming influence, had talked him out of it. So Camel sat alone in the Watch Office for more than two weeks and, apart from an occasional appearance at Flights, did next to no flying and had very little contact with the rest of us.

The business of preparing ourselves for the rough and tumble of combat proceeded apace and, in the third week of July, we were deemed 'operational' and very proudly we took our place with other frontline squadrons as fully-fledged defenders of the United Kingdom.

For the next week or so we sat at 'Readiness' from dawn to dusk, reading and hearing of the raids that were taking place down south and waiting hopefully for the enemy to turn up in our Sector. However, nothing substantial came our way and it seemed that at Church Fenton we were a little too far inland to be employed against the occasional Hun reconnaissance aircraft which made a habit of flying up the east coast. For whatever reason our services were not immediately required, a situation which delighted my parents, to whom I wrote regularly. It didn't stop us flying, of course, but I seemed to spend a lot of time booted and spurred, reading the novels of Denis Wheatley and James Hadley Chase to while away the hours, and playing endless games of Monopoly and L'Attaque, the latter quite a favourite among all squadron members.

Camel, meanwhile, came back into circulation, suitably chastened, and thereafter - in the modern idiom - maintained a low profile. It was something of a surprise therefore when, one afternoon, we had a 'Scramble' order and I was lucky enough to be one of the section of three involved.

We were airborne well within the statutory three minutes and, in a lather of excitement, climbed away, flat out, towards the coast, heading for Flamborough Head. It was a glorious summer's day with a fair amount of fluffy cumulus about. Camel, the third member of the section, and I were led by a recent addition to the squadron, a very solid and unimaginative Flying Officer neither of us knew at all well named Stuart; known, inevitably, as 'Sporran'. This time I flew on the right of the leader as No. 2 with Camel, possibly because of his recent inglorious performances, as No 3.

We crossed out over the coast at about 14,000 feet and, after being vectored due east and out to sea for some 15 miles, were turned on to 040 degrees and warned that there was a 'bogey' 10 miles ahead. By this time, of course, I was fairly hopping about in my seat at the prospect of intercepting my first Hun. Everything was perfect for it; excellent visibility, about half cloud cover and, hopefully, at the end of the trail a nice juicy Heinkel 111, or some similar not-too-belligerent aircraft.

We had barely received the last snippet of information from Control when I saw the Hun on the horizon, an elongated black dot, slightly below us and creeping northwards, presumably on a reconnaissance trip and after shipping. It was a sight I shall never forget; sighting a Hun at any time was always a breathtaking moment and for a moment I was transfixed.

Almost incoherent with excitement I fumbled with my old TR9D radio switch, completely forgetting my RT drill, gesturing, pointing, and beating on the hood with my gloved hand. To my fury and despair the phlegmatic 'Sporran' kept staring in my direction as though I had gone mad and I suppose we lost about 20 seconds before I made him understand that the enemy was in sight. Thereafter, things happened quickly enough.

The German aircraft, a Dornier 17 *Flying Pencil*, had obviously seen us at about the same time I had been able to goad the wooden Stuart into action but, instead of running for it, the Hun pilot had the experience and good sense to turn towards us. Diving as he did so, he flew underneath us, between our legs so to speak, whilst we reared up like pheasant chicks scattered by a dog, with 'Sporran' intoning as though he were in church, "Number one attack, number one attack. Go!"

Hurling my aircraft into the approved line-astern formation, I found myself desperately trying to avoid overtaking my leader, praying at the same time that he would get out of the way and allow me an uninterrupted shot at the Dornier which, by this time, was diving purposefully for the nearest cloud some 800 feet beneath. We tumbled down in pursuit, me wild with excitement and my Spitfire bucketing about in 'Sporran's' slipstream. In moments he was sufficiently close to open fire and I saw rippling trails of dark smoke appear from under his wings, before his aircraft upended itself almost viciously and veered off to the right.

My turn! I had about ten seconds before the Hun reached the cloud. The range bars in my gunsight showed me a little further away than the approved 250 yards, but close enough. The slim shape of the German aircraft was there - I see it now - sitting in the middle of my windscreen and sight as though I had arranged it by hand. All grey in colour, with a high wing, the two radial engines trailing faint streamers of exhaust smoke, visible testimony to the Hun pilot's keenness to get into cloud. There was even a suggestion of the black crosses I knew to be there; or was I imagining them? A German, anyway. A real live German! This was it. And it was mine!

My thumb had already begun to exert pressure on the gun-button when a pointed wingtip swerved quickly and as though by magic into my vision from the left, followed instantly by the rear view of a whole aircraft, not 20 yards in front of me. A Spitfire! Camel's Spitfire! It was close, so close indeed, that I thought for a moment we would collide.

Instantly I snatched at my throttle and, simultaneously, his slipstream caught me and whirled my aircraft off-balance. In a moment I found myself somewhere off to the right and above, looking down stupidly at the red and blue roundels in front of me - and the disappearing Dornier! For possibly five seconds I had a

grandstand view as the bomber flashed in an out of the fringes of the cloud then, very determinedly, duck its head - and vanish.

Forty and more years after the event I can still experience vestiges of the emotion, the frustration, and the sheer naked desire to kill Camel Elliot that flooded over me in those following few seconds. Yet again he had behaved like the mindless, unpredictable, clown he so clearly was. Why, oh why, in God's name did we have to put up with him? Our first Hun, and he had ruined everything! I would shoot him down, so help me God! That's what I would do - kill him!

But, as so often happens, the Lord, in his wisdom, took control. At that moment my aircraft shot into cloud with a lurch that jolted some of the venom out of me and I found myself obliged to fly on instruments with a toppled artificial horizon and a direction indicator that was a blur of motion as the result of my violent manoeuvring. It took me eight or more seconds to sort myself out, by which time I had shot out again into clear air, just in time to see the two remaining members of my section racing around the clouds trying to find the departed Hun.

I joined in immediately and, in retrospect, the sight of our three Spitfires behaving like Jack Russell terriers rushing around a rat-infested haystack must have amused those of the Divine audience privileged to witness our tantrums. But, of the Dornier 17, we saw not a sign and no doubt there are four German aviators to this very day, who can describe to their grandchildren the manner in which they fingered their noses at three RAF Spitfires in the early days of August 1940.

After 15 minutes, with the adrenalin still surging but with no additional information from Sector Control, we formed up disconsolately and returned to the coast and eventually to base. As it was a further 20 minute flight from the coast to Church Fenton, the extra time enabled me to bring myself more or less under control before landing. Even so, I was still in a highly emotional state when I tumbled out of my aircraft and ran across to where Camel Elliot was throwing off his straps.

I jumped onto the wing beside him. "Camel, for God's sake, what were you doing? What possessed you to get in the way just when I was about to open fire? Apart from the fact that it wasn't your turn, I damn near ran into your backside. What's more I finished up by not firing a shot."

Camel climbed down, dusting himself off and looking worried. "To tell you the truth, old chap, I didn't really see you."

My mouth dropped open. "You didn't see me? An aircraft not 20 yards away? How could you not see me? And fly right in front of me, just when I was about to open fire? You came within a split-second of being killed, you half-wit! Can't you understand?"

"Well, if you'll let me explain." Camel put on a hurt expression. "I was swinging into line, right? Then I suddenly saw I hadn't switched on my gunsight. So; by the time I'd persuaded the little red lines to pop up and got them all sorted out, I must have passed in front of you by mistake." He looked around warily. "Look, I'm sorry if mucked you up." He gave a nervous little giggle. "As a matter of fact, I thought I'd give him a quick squirt when he was disappearing . . . you know, just for fun. But . . . er, when I pressed the tit - !"

My eyes like stones I said, "You don't have to tell me. You'd left the damned guns on 'Safe'!" I turned away feeling nothing but contempt for the man. "Camel, for God's sake, pull your finger out! I could have had a crack at that Hun if you hadn't interfered. If in future you find you have to do your cockpit drill in the air, then go to the end of the bloody queue and let someone else do the shooting"

"Look, I'm terribly sorry, Fitzgerald. Really I am."

"Oh - !"   I stalked off, still fuming, but almost as cross with myself for losing my temper.

Within the hour, however, all was forgotten as later that afternoon the squadron was ordered south. The following morning I flew one of the 18 Spitfires which took off and headed towards the Channel coast and the titanic combat which later became known as the Battle of Britain.

CHAPTER THREE

Although Quentin Elliot and I were both involved, it is unnecessary for me to give a blow-by-blow account of the Battle of Britain. Suffice it to say that the squadron, despite its lack of experience, was thrown into action immediately, acquitting itself most creditably and claiming more than 70 German aircraft as 'Destroyed' and at least as equal number as 'Probably Destroyed' and 'Damaged' in the three month period of the Battle.

We flew, initially, from RAF Middle Wallop, which is just to the south of Andover, then Warmwell, in Dorset. Both were grass airfields in those days. Then we moved up to North Weald, on the northern borders of London, at the beginning of September.

For me it was a period of great excitement, considerable and gratifying achievement and - yes - paradoxically, wonderful, bubbling happiness; I have always counted myself fortunate to have been in the right place at the right time. I flew as hard as I've ever done and my log book shows 154 sorties and 165 hours flying, almost all of it against the enemy, between the beginning of August and the end of October 1940, when the Battle of Britain was deemed to have ended.

I was shot down almost at once, which, in retrospect, was a good thing as it taught me a lesson. On about my third major engagement I very stupidly flew into the centre-rear of a broad vee formation of Junkers 88 bombers which was moving towards Bristol, and collected the concentrated cross-fire of about six rear gunners. As I sat there firing at their leader I knew I was about to be hit, but foolishly continued the engagement while watching the tracer whipping and curling in my direction. I heard and felt the thuds as the bullets struck home and there followed moments of wild panic as my cockpit filled with a mixture of smoke, glycol fumes and heat. Thinking I was on fire I dropped out of the fight immediately and fell away below, prepared to bale out without further delay. Then, in an unusual moment of calmness for me, I realised that things were not as bad as I had first thought and that I had probably only been hit in the engine and/or among the pipes that led to the radiator. The engine by this time was showing ominous signs of lethargy and would not respond to the throttle, eventually giving up altogether and just idling and producing no power. So, I was obliged to glide down and land, wheels-up, on a hillside not far from Blandford.

I remember as though it were yesterday, sitting in that cockpit on the quiet, deserted hillside, limp with emotion and fatigue, wondering if I had broken my legs, my shins having crashed against the bottom of the dashboard during the rather lumpy landing. Later, when I had been hauled out by some not-too-gentle farm hands, I saw that my legs, even then, were a fascinating mixture of red, green and purple, and that I was bleeding from the thigh and right arm. Further investigation revealed that I had been wounded slightly by splinters but, such is the miracle of the human constitution, I had felt no pain at any time during the five or so minutes of madness. Within three days I was as good as new - almost! The wounds were trifling and I could walk about well enough, albeit a little apprehensively in case someone should thump me playfully on the shins - fighter pilots, aged 20, were apt to indulge in that type of heartless horseplay! In fact, I flew on the fourth day and soon forgot about the whole thing although I was never stupid enough to tackle Junkers 88s in quite the same way again.

The hard flying and incessant combat had, of course, a very significant effect on the squadron as a whole. Aircraft were lost and damaged fairly regularly but we were never short of replacements. And losses among aircrew were equally apparent. Over the three to four months of the Battle, six colleagues were killed or died of wounds and almost everyone was knocked down at one time or another, some twice or even three times. And, inevitably, a few fell by the wayside.

We had barely reached Middle Wallop when 'Guinness' Garland, not unexpectedly, was promoted to Squadron Leader and posted away to Headquarters, Fighter Command. 'Sporran' Stuart also disappeared, why and in which direction I never learned, although, frankly, his departure didn't interest me one way or the other. Several other faces also quietly vanished until we had a hard core of young but fairly experienced pilots - experienced, less in terms of length of service than in the day-to-day rough and tumble of combat flying.

Camel Elliot, by the end of August, had rather faded into the background, a strange remark for me to make, perhaps, considering there were only 24 pilots in the squadron. However, it becomes easier to understand when I explain that, on arriving at Middle Wallop, there was a reshuffle and Camel moved across to 'B' Flight, almost immediately thereafter going down with shingles, a complaint I had never heard of and which sounded to me something of a joke illness. Sick Quarters, however, took an altogether different view and, apparently concerned that others might become affected, packed him off home where he remained for three weeks. When he returned we were at Warmwell and about to move on to North Weald and, having seen a great deal of action in the meantime, we rather looked upon him as being out of touch. The result was that Camel spent most of his time ferrying damaged, but flyable, aircraft to Maintenance Units, Henlow included, collecting replacements and doing many of the dogs-body jobs around the squadron.

It was during this period that he came to be regarded as the local 'odd-job' man and I'm ashamed to say that most of us took advantage of him in later months, although on looking back he must have been something of a willing victim to have endured such indignities without complaining more strongly than he did. Even so, he did fly when required although he never gave me the impression that he regarded himself at all times a fully operational member of the squadron. Camel was with us in body more than in spirit; always an outsider, he never exhibited anything more than a spoken willingness to become involved so that not even his closest friend would have described him as an enthusiastic fighter pilot.

James Denby, too, made less of a contribution than he himself might have wished, being shot down very early on and obliged to bale out. As the result of this incident he damaged a leg and spent the next four months hobbling about on a stick until he, like 'Guinness' Garland, was promoted and moved on. My relations with Denby had improved steadily, if in stages, after our first rather frosty encounter, so that in the final months of our association I found him a warm and helpful friend. He was, in fact, a very engaging man who had the good sense to realise that besides being an excellent administrator, his congenial personality and his ability to talk, listen and mix were by far the most potent weapons in his not too impressive fighting armoury. He made it a duty almost to further his career in the RAF Club, operating there with a degree of expertise that could only be admired; moreover, his contacts within the Service were at least matched by those of his wife beyond the RAF. Jennifer Denby was an enchanting, wealthy, and well-connected young woman, and together, they made a formidable and very successful team. She it was who christened me 'Junior' - for reasons I need not go into - a name which followed me about for years and eventually became something of an embarrassment.

Of the rest, what can I say? Strangely, most of the original squadron members are still alive, supporting the belief that, in war, experience makes a great contribution to longevity. Some I still keep in touch with although I am not by nature a joiner of old comrades' organisations or one who hankers after the past - there is not much to be said for growing old and I like to think of them all as they were. Flying Officer Vandenberg, especially! Our dear old Adj! More than any other relationship I made during the war, my association with him remains by far the most vivid; which, considering the age difference of 20 odd years, is remarkable.

He was in no way a substitute father as I had loving parents of my own, but somehow he filled a gap, acting as a prop, encouraging me when it was necessary and being a constant source of strength in so many ways. I remember his serenity, his quiet determination, his understanding, and his support when we were all under great strain and too young fully to understand the reasons for our impetuousness, our tempers, and often, our outrageous behaviour. There were many times, I know, when I must have sorely tried his patience but I never once remember him as being other than sympathetic. I know, too, that he was the catalyst which enabled Denby and me to work together - without the Adj, I doubt that I would have lasted out that first, rather trying month.

I would also be the first to admit that he was as generous with his support for others, Camel especially. It was well known that he interceded for Camel on many occasions and that, but for him, Elliot would have left the squadron under any one of several clouds. But he was by no means soft with the young man; many were the times when I would have been greatly wounded had Vanderberg taken me to task as he did Camel. There was a humbling, remorse-provoking element to the Adj's dressings-down, although they were never noisy or vituperative, always calmly delivered, invariably hard-hitting, but seldom without a note of encouragement and never accompanied by sarcasm. I have known Camel reduced almost to tears on several occasions by his remarks, indeed I know of no one in the squadron who ever got the better of the Adj verbally, or, on the other hand, who resented his guidance or admonishments. He was respected by everyone, young and not so young, perhaps most of all by Denby who worked very closely with him and, in his own lofty way, revered him. A unique and memorable personality was the old Adj. I was devoted to him almost to the point of love.

Perhaps it was a measure of his regard for me that, when the squadron moved from Warmwell to North Weald, Vandenberg approached me and, with just a trace of shyness, asked if I would fly him to our new station in the Miles Magister, the one small trainer aircraft carried on the establishment of each fighter squadron. I was surprised and faintly irritated, to put it mildly. I had expected and, indeed, was down on the list to fly with the others in my own Spitfire.

A little put out, and totally lacking in tact, I pointed this out fairly succinctly and remember his smiling, apologetic nod and him saying that he quite understood. However, it didn't end there. Within minutes, James Denby had taken me aside and suggested, rather pointedly, that I might like 'to fly the Maggie and give the Adj a helping hand!' This time the message sank in and I agreed to do so with the best grace I could muster, childishly annoyed that my arm had been twisted and that, instead of a 30 minute flight as one of a brave, flag-waving formation of eighteen Spitfires, the journey would take me well over an hour in a wretched 'phut-phut' I didn't much care for anyway.

In the event I quite enjoyed the journey. It was a lovely day and with Adj goggled and helmeted in the front seat, we kept very low - I had no wish to run into a marauding Hun fighter - and wandered up the valleys to Salisbury at a steady 90 before 'Bradshawing' along the railway lines towards London and beyond.

Shortly after take-off Van asked if he could fly the aircraft and, when I agreed, did so very competently until we sighted the radio masts alongside North Weald airfield. I then suggested that he might wish to land it, but he declined with the excuse that if he pranged the aircraft it would be my fault. Which, of course, was true although I didn't think of it at the time. As we walked with our parachutes towards our new dispersal huts and the apparent chaos that was our recently landed squadron, I remarked that I had not been aware that he was able to fly. He gave a wink and a sidelong grin before adding that any fool could fly, but only the brightest and best submitted to becoming observers - or passengers in Maggies!

I shall remember always those last few days of August, 1940. And September!

Having arrived at North Weald and dispersed our aircraft and possessions on the western edge of the airfield (alongside the present M11 Motorway, incidentally) we were hardly permitted an hour to reflect or acclimatise. Our Spitfires had barely been refuelled when twelve of us were ordered off to counter a major raid against airfields south of London.

We clambered up steeply from our new base through layers of ragged cloud and over unfamiliar territory, looking down for the first time on the smoke and clutter of North London and the East End, and on the River Thames - a pale silver band tracing a winding, widening path eastwards to the estuary at Southend and beyond. It was a sight we were to witness four and five times each day for months to come and it remains a picture I can bring to mind even now in a flicker of a eye when I choose to reflect.

That first flight gave evidence of the development that had taken place within the squadron throughout the previous days and weeks. A fighting unit intent only on intercepting the enemy, we were more concerned with clawing for altitude and methods of attack and survival than with the niceties of station-keeping and close formation. Airframes and engines were pressed to the limit; as indeed were we. Our orderly and much-practised Fighter Command Attacks - numbers 1 to 12 - having been tried and found wanting, were discarded. Our new combat tactics were the cold, direct and deadly stuff of the professional - uncompromising and, more often than not, violent and shatteringly destructive. There was no gentlemanly period of adjustment; our blooding was instantaneous. Successes we had but casualties too; the days of training a mere month before were but fading memories.

Almost heralding our arrival, and within four days thereafter, our airfield at North Weald was heavily bombed - twice - on each occasion by around 30 Hun bombers escorted by drifting curtains of enemy fighters. The first attack coincided with my being in Epping on some trivial errand or other, so that I was obliged to leave my transport hurriedly and take shelter on the fringes of the Forest, from where I watched the bombs cascade down with a degree of fascination and excitement I was later almost ashamed of. The sight was awe-inspiring, the noise shattering, but the realisation that friends, colleagues, buildings and equipment were being mutilated and destroyed before my eyes was totally absent - strangely but totally absent. It was all so unreal.

During the second attack, however, I had the good fortune to be airborne and, from 15,000 feet, looked over the side of my cockpit to see my own airfield disappear beneath a silent scattering of crimson-centred shock-waves and a magical blossoming of brown smoke and earth. Again, there was the same feeling of total unreality. Was this all happening to me? To us? But, it was - apparently.

Minutes later I and others landed on the self-same area of grass, on which there were now a hundred mountainous mole-hills, each of us in his Spitfire, weaving between the craters with the dexterity of dirt-track riders. Foolhardy? Of course! But in war the impossible, the unthinkable, was common-place. There were no King's Regulations or Air Ministry Orders to cover such eventualities. So how were we to know?

September proceeded. The Huns gave up trying to ground us by crippling our airfields and turned their fury on London. Thrown against constant daylight attacks on the capital city our own particular battle area became the skies above the Thames Estuary and central and eastern Kent. Each day, all day, we would listen for the anticipated yet dreaded cry from the Airman-of-the Watch:

"Scramble! : Maidstone-Canterbury patrol line, 15,000 feet!" his cockney voice piercing our sleep-befuddled brains like spear-thrusts at all hours from four in the morning to nine at night. With leaden legs we ritually pounded across the grass towards our aircraft, engines bursting into life, slip-streams tearing at our faces as we strapped in, followed by wild taxying-out with lifting tails and the hectic, surging, howling, nudging, bouncing take-offs. Three minutes was the prescribed limit, but we invariably took less.

It was always the same. At, say, 17,000 feet, with the coastline of Kent from Margate, around Dover to Dungeness spread out like a map, it seems that nothing can prevent us from seeing even a single Hun, far less 100 plus. But it is seldom that the Ack-Ack does not point the way with faint erupting smudges on the horizon, in the midst of which the German formations gradually take shape -

wedges of 30 Dorniers in boxes of four or six, 20 Ju88s, or 30 He111s. And always the fighters. Like midges, behind and above, with others stepped up into oblivion. If we are lucky, they are the larger Me110 but, increasingly, as we come within their range, the shoals of minnows are 109s; pretty, yellow-nosed creatures which flit about and drop vertically on us, only to climb again like spiders on silken cords - threatening, parrying, always there.

We approach each armada, eyes fixed and tense, wings tilting almost to the vertical and pulling hard. Jostling with other Spitfires, elbowing, pushing, making space. Dark shapes swim into our windscreens and sights. More friendly

Ack-Ack bursting dangerously among us, then enemy tracer, white curling streamers - as though thrown from a child's hand - which suddenly become venomous, electric streaks of death. Finally, the shudder of my own guns. One second . . . two . . . three - if I'm lucky. The de Wilde incendiaries twinkling along an enemy fuselage and wings as my own smoking fingers feel about, then touch, the target. Then in an instant, a sudden wind-torn smear of crimson flame followed by a dark, developing, oil-laden trail. And occasionally, parachutes, whirling past with legs dangling. Followed by a stomach-wrenching break, with greying vision fading into red darkness. God Almighty! Am I still alive? Have I been hit?

Two 109s flash past silently, their coloured noses and black crosses close enough to be recognized. I hurl myself in pursuit, but in moments they are gone. More aircraft, this time friends. And more friends - three Hurricanes, turning. Two Spitfires, one on its side. But, there, crossing from left to right and a little below me, two less familiar dark shapes, Larger! Individual enemy bombers! Half-crippled? Possibly. But, after them! Quickly!

I follow one, hard, and come in fast and curving from the rear starboard quarter. The jarring shudder of my own guns once more and the exulting satisfaction of seeing an engine splutter fragments, an airscrew slowing as though by magic. More parachutes blossom. Ours or theirs? Garbled words over the RT and four brightly painted 109s with squarish extremities go winging across my forehead. After them! Now! But they curve away, diving steeply and are soon lost in mist and greyness beneath.

What's happening now? I look around. I'm alone, quite alone. In the whole of Kent, it seems. Not an aircraft in sight. After 50 desperate, violent, seconds it is as though there had been no enemy, no engagement – nothing. A distant coastline is exactly where and as it was. England! – Kent! - is still there, a green-brown smiling patchwork far below. Relief! Nothing has changed.

My engine still screams hysterically at 2,850 revs. I throttle back and look around, particularly to the rear. And turn to the north, checking my compass needle which is swimming about aimlessly in its liquid. I'm still on edge. Vigilant. My head turning as though on bearings. I remain belligerent and warlike, though; and wary. Very relieved and absurdly happy. I'm still alive and recovering my breath. But, where? I look down with searching eyes on the quiet countryside below. Detling, is it? A small grass airfield, anyway. Detling - I think.

For 27 days in September, the pattern of activity remained the same. Then, on the 28th day, we flew all the way to Dover and, from 22,000 feet, looked down on the harbour and its cluster of silver balloons. Some 109s passed swiftly overhead, their wings shining in the sun, but turned away as we chased after them. There was then a diving match over the Channel which nobody seemed to win, after which we flew back, seeing nothing. It was quiet. No bombers. Kent was empty. We returned to base.

The following day was much the same except that there were many roving bands of 109s above Kent. We caught a group in the Ashford area and sent two diving away streaming glycol. Forced-landings for them, either towards our own coast or in the Channel - 109s couldn't go for more than five minutes without coolant. Nor could Spits, for that matter.

We climbed again and cast around. There had been time to go higher these last several days - 25,000 feet about, and as high as 31,000 on several occasions – where it was dreadfully cold in our unheated cockpits. The Hurricanes were useless up there so we had the 109s to ourselves. Still no bombers, though. Had they given up? It rather looked like it.

October came in with clear skies. The 109s were carrying bombs now - some of them. Escorted by others. We dived on thirty or so in the area of Canterbury and scattered the bombers, who dropped their bombs, before having a melee with their escorting fighters. A wild party ensued with much diving, chasing and hard turning. I fired, but missed, a 109 squirming to safety before pulling up and leaving me standing - and marvelling!

With more time in hand, things were generally easier. We mostly gained height in comparatively leisurely fashion now and a Spit, once at altitude and given a little space, could make hay of a 109. With their direct-injection engines, the Huns might dive away initially but we could catch them given ten seconds or so to work up speed. The 109s wouldn't hesitate to jump a formation of Hurricanes and pick off the chaps at the back, but they thought twice about mixing it with Spitfires. Even so, it did happen from time to time and we lost several fellows that way - mostly their own fault, let it be said, for not keeping a proper look-out. Some of us argued that our formations were not best suited to immediate and flexible response; certainly the Huns appeared much more mobile in the air. In fact, in some respects, they were very good. And brave, most of them. I wouldn't have relished flying as far as North Weald from, say, St Omer or Poix, in a 109, with the limited amount of fuel they carried and knowing the likely opposition.

About this time, there were rumours of a new Spit - the Mark 2, with a more powerful engine, a few welcome embelishments and a better performance. Some squadrons, we learned, already had them. Yes, things were looking up. No sign of twin-engined bombers en masse these days, only a few singletons flitted in and out of the cloud on lone sorties - Dornier 17s mostly, and Ju88s. No trace of Heinkels now. Or Me110s. And no one had seen a Ju87 for ages. The Huns had obviously learned their lesson and withdrawn their more vulnerable aircraft. Apparently, there was to have been an invasion on about 15th September, but Hitler, apparently, had called it off, although we in the squadrons were not told. There were still 109s around though - bombers and fighters. Masses of them.

The Mark 2s arrived late one morning and during an afternoon, chaps in the ATA bringing them in. I claimed one - a sweetie - the engine as smooth as silk and with a lovely bouncy undercarriage. They could start up on their own, too, with the new Coffman cartridge starters. Most were 2as with eight machine guns, but several of us had 2bs which carried two 20mm cannons and four machine guns. How I wished I'd had the cannons to use against the massed formations of bombers a month earlier. Our new Spits did everything a bit quicker than the Mark Is - climb, speed on the straight, everything! Jolly nice aircraft, too, although one of my cannons would insist on stopping and throwing my aircraft off center. Even so, I was very pleased with my mount. And full of confidence.

October drifted to a conclusion. There was a good deal of activity in the month as a whole and I flew 58 times. As the days grew shorter and the weather worsened, we had slightly longer in bed and considerably more time to sit around the almost incandescent coke-stoves in the crew room. We were also able to eat regularly in the Mess too and sleep more in our rooms in the wooden huts alongside the Officers' Mess instead of at dispersal.

For reasons I always found difficult to comprehend, we younger pilots seemed only to qualify for quarters in the draughty, poorly insulated First World War huts adjacent to the main building. Important people such as Intelligence Officers, Equippers, Accountants and other 'key personnel' were granted the warm and comfortable bedrooms on the Mess proper. Clearly, heroism cut very little ice when it came to allocating accommodation at RAF North Weald. No doubt it was considered too administratively complicated to keep abreast of the comings and goings of those who were thoughtless enough to get themselves killed so regularly!

Throughout this arduous, exciting but sometimes trying three-month period, individual reactions and relationships within the squadron not only varied and developed, but underwent testing strains. Even so, I cannot recall anyone really rowing with a colleague, nor were there scenes so beloved of the film-makers in which nerves crack and pilots lose control and rush screaming out into the night crying 'I can't take it!'

Everyone 'took it' remarkably well; in fact the level of humour, merriment and good spirits abroad was very much a feature of the occasion. Even those who wilted a bit did so in a very composed and unobtrusive way, simply drifting partially, or completely, into the background and letting those who were less affected get on with the business of fighting. On the whole we enjoyed it, savouring the raw excitement of the occasion and the sheer, physical involvement - after all, a fighter squadron has more than once been likened to 'a rugger club in uniform'.

Although there were but a few occasions when the squadron could relax completely, there were periods when bad weather or other circumstances enabled our state of 'Readiness' to be reduced to 15, 30 or 60 minutes 'Available'. And, of course, occasionally we were 'Released', at which times we would return to the Mess, walk, read, or indulge in any private hobby or other pursuit and, in the evenings, go down to the pubs in Epping or the cinema, even venturing as far afield as London and the nightspots there.

In Epping, the two pubs favoured were The Thatched House and The Cock Hotel, the former being marginally in vogue during the latter part of 1940, possibly because it was just that little bit nearer. This presented me with a minor problem as I couldn't drink beer in those days, I can't very much now – it still makes me sick – and had to go through the ritual of accepting and stacking up pints of the stuff when my consumption rate flagged. Fortunately, the old Adj would come to my rescue when, with sly glances, he would surreptitiously move my brimming glasses towards his own and somehow dispose of them during the course of the evening. Once, when in desperation I had accepted whiskies in order to reduce the sheer volume of grog that was pushed in my direction, he had quietly placed himself at my shoulder and refused to let me drink it, adding quietly that spirits were not good for a chap my age.

The Adj was also the confidant and adviser for everyone in general; the few married officers who had wife or child difficulties, the ones in love who had heart and girl problems, and even the chaps who were on their uppers and who couldn't quite pay their mess bills at the end of the month. He was an expert on most things, financial matters in particular, knowing the City as he did like the back of his hand, and whilst in no way ostentatiously affluent, he was quietly generous with everyone, and particularly with me. Once, shortly after I had been complaining about being unable to get out as much as I would have liked, he appeared in my room in the Mess one evening and announced that he had managed to find an old car which might help with my transport difficulties. Old it was, but quite magnificent, being an enormous sit-up-and-beg Austin 18. I was quite overcome but he added sternly, though with a twinkle in his eye, that others, too, would have to share it, I should understand. He was a dear, dear man, the Adj, and I owe him so much.

It was during this period, too, that I came to be fairly close to Camel Elliot. Whilst I didn't consciously avoid going out with the pub-crawlers in the evenings, not being a drinking man or a naturally rowdy type, I preferred to stay in and read or chat around the fire in the ante-room, or make models - I was a great model enthusiast in those days. The result was that I would now and then find myself left behind in the Mess with several other officers of a like mind, Camel included.

Camel had survived the Battle of Britain, with two engine failures, without making either a reputation or even much of an impression. Still on the fringe of things, he had flown when required, without laying claim to any German aircraft destroyed or even damaged except when he flew as part of a section or formation which was credited with a shared victory. He was still regarded as our 'Maintenance Unit ferry pilot' and, strangely, I can't remember him much at dispersal - other faces I can see now, but never his.

I do recall, however, that he was always around the several animals we had acquired in the course of time - a puppy named Wimpy and a bigger French Poodle, each belonging to an owner killed or damaged sometime earlier. And, oddly enough, two ducks, hatched out from eggs under a broody hen we had borrowed, which spent their time in a local ditch. I remember him, too, walking about endlessly in the wood adjacent to dispersal with some sort of fowling piece over his shoulder and sitting for hours waiting for crows and pigeons to put in an appearance, which they seldom did I need hardly add, being no fools and observing Camel with a gun the size of a small telegraph pole. But it was in the Mess that I mostly came in touch with him when I would suddenly find him at my elbow.

"I say, Fitzgerald," I don't ever remember him calling me by my christian name, "care to be beaten up at snooker?" Or, "I say, could you face a walk in the fields? We might frighten a rabbit or two."

But when we did walk it would usually be in silence, with Camel nodding and smiling to himself as of old, sometimes walking ahead of me ten or twenty yards, at which times he would turn suddenly and shout, "I say, did I tell you - this, or that?" He was an unusual and remarkable boy, but likeable in a strange way. He clearly valued my companionship as I don't believe he had much in common with anyone else in the squadron; other than the Adj that is. From time to time I would see them huddled together in private conversation. I am sure that Van, like me, felt some sort of responsibility for the boy, knowing his family as he did and being acquainted with him since childhood.

But, what concerned me most was the thought that sooner or later Camel's unpredictability in the air would result in someone's death. I had in mind one occasion when he was flying as my No.2 in the area of Dover and, having done a wide detour at 20,000 feet in order to get behind and attack a dozen or more 109s which were shooting at the balloons, I had tumbled down on the enemy in fine style only to glance round in the dive to find myself alone. By that time, of course, I was committed and had to go through with the attack, nearly getting myself killed in the process. Later, when I had remonstrated pretty hotly with him about this particular lapse, he had looked worried in his usual agitated way and made some excuse which didn't seem to me at all convincing.

CHAPTER FOUR

November! What can I say? In the early days of the month a slow-moving high pressure area sat resolutely over eastern England, dominating the weather situation and bringing with it the briefest glimpses of hazy sunshine but, in the main, wet dripping fog. It was cold, clammy and utterly miserable. Flying was impossible. Our Spitfires, hooded and chocked, stood like silent scarecrows in their pens and around dispersal. A Hun bomber, perhaps mistakenly, flew right across the top of the airfield in broad daylight and at no more than 800 feet, but we neither saw it nor could we do anything to stop it. The aircraft was too low for the 3.7 inch guns and the 40mm airfield defence Bofors did not see a target to shoot at. Even so, to raise their spirits, two of them loosed off soaring streams of red balls which curved away into the fog ... and disappeared! I doubt that the Hun even noticed them.

In the evening of the same day, after killing time immediately before dinner by knocking a few balls around the billiard table, I met Camel on my way to the dining-room. He stopped me hesitantly. "I say, Fitzgerald, would you care to have dinner with me tonight?"

As I was in the act of pushing open the dining-room door, I looked at him in surprise. "All right," I said, "Let's go in together."

He shook his head. "No, I - I don't mean here. I thought we might go out. Eat at the Thatch. Couldn't we do that?"

"The Thatch!" I hesitated, not feeling in the least like roaming around in the fog and blackout in search of a five-shilling meal at the local pub. On the other hand, I didn't want to hurt his feelings and as he seemed so very anxious, his eyes large and appealing in his white angular face, I agreed without too much consideration and he bustled off immediately in search of his greatcoat. He returned a minute or so later, struggling into the sleeves.

"We can borrow the Adj's car, don't you think? Then I won't have to use my wreck."

I smiled to myself. He had obviously thought it all out; our trip was not entirely unpremeditated.

We climbed into the Adjutant's old Austin 18, rooting around in the darkness with the ignition key, and drove in silence the several miles through the Forest into Epping. After parking the car we did a blindman's bluff exercise through the car-park before pushing our way through the heavily blanketed door of the pub into the bright lights of the Lounge Bar and Dining-Room. Blinking, then looking around quickly, I was relieved to note the absence of Air Force blue.

After downing a couple of tomato-juice aperitifs and ordering dinner, we went in search of a table and sat down. I didn't much feel like conversation; in fact, I was more than a little peeved at being dragged away from my own dining-room and a quiet evening of agreeable conversation before a cheerful coal fire in the Mess ante-room. It was plain to see that Camel was very much on edge; he kept glancing over my shoulder, his great bony hands moving constantly. Meanwhile, he directed at me a continuous barrage of trivial and unrelated remarks.

I watched him for some time with growing impatience, making little or no contribution to the conversation, until I could stand it no longer. "Camel, what on earth's the matter with you? Is there something wrong?"

He stopped, feigning surprise. "Wrong? Good heavens, no! Why should there be?"

Seeing the look of pitying disbelief on my face he shrugged and gave a resigned smile. "Well . . . I suppose there is, really. Only. I don't see why I should trouble you with my worries."

"For Pete's sake, Camel, that's what were here for, isn't it?" And I was about to say more when the waitress arrived with the plates and we both watched without speaking; Camel grateful, I'm sure, for the interruption as she arranged the table and set out our soup.

We continued to drink in silence until, as though on impulse, Camel thrust his head in my direction. "Look, honestly Fitzgerald, do you think I'm cut out for this sort of thing?"

"What sort of thing?" I knew exactly what he meant but felt I had to play for time.

"Fighting. Flying Spitfires! Being in the squadron!"

When I made no comment and didn't even look up, he went on, "Don't you see? You have two gongs and all sorts of things to your credit and here am I with nothing to show after six months with the squadron, except a couple of bent Spitfires and a cut on the nose. What's more I seem to make a first-class job of annoying pretty well everyone I meet."

I found myself watching his soup-spoon poised in the air. Poor lad. I wanted so much to say something encouraging but couldn't bring myself to do so. After all, he had made a terrible ass of himself so many times. And there was that business over Dover a few weeks back. So, I'm afraid I hedged, more for my own purposes than for his peace of mind.

I said mildly, "Aren't you being a little too hard on yourself? After all, I've been pretty lucky one way and another and you seem to have had all the misfortune - you know, ropey engines, bushels of barley up the whatsit, that sort of thing. And who knows, perhaps your Huns were super-smart."

Camel shook his head. He was clearly not in the mood for levity or to be humoured.

"I don't think so. My trouble is, I never seem to do anything right. The CO thinks I'm pretty hopeless. So did 'Guinness' Garland, until he left. And now there's the Adj chivying me all the time, with all the others." He stared at me, his eyes wide with unhappiness. "I think I ought to ask to go, don't you?"

I shrugged, still feeling uncomfortable. "You know best, Camel. But are you sure that's the answer? After all, you'll have to find out why it is you're making such a nonsense of things. Until you do that, I don't think that moving on will help very much; you could have just as many problems at the next place."

There was a silence. Camel hung his head and toyed with his spoon.

I went on. "What's the difficulty? Is it the fighting that worries you - you know, the business of being clobbered or shot down? Or is it the flying? You've always seemed fairly capable to me - that is, when you've managed to keep the engine from boiling." I grinned in order to cheer him up. "Or is it something of everything?"

He shook his head sadly and for one terrible moment, I thought he was about to be tearful. "I - I really don't know. No, it's not the flying. It's the other. You see, I want to do well but as soon as we get into a mix-up, I seem to go to pieces. There's always so much going on that I never have time to settle to do anything. Then, when I've sorted myself out, it's all over - the sky's clear and the chance has gone. Time and time again. It always happens."

I nodded. "So, its the fighting you don't like." It was not so much a question as a statement.

Camel screwed up his face. "I don't think it worries me. Its just that I'm never really ready."

"Camel!" I said brusquely. "If your heart was really in it, you wouldn't have to keep readying yourself. You'd be mad keen to get to grips. Isn't that so? Come on, be honest."

Camel looked doubtful. "I really don't know. I don't think I really mind the Huns, you see its just that I'm always so unprepared." He looked at me defiantly. "You jolly well don't know."

"What d'you mean, I don't know?"

"Well ... you always seem so much at home; so infernally confident. When we run into some Huns, you're always the first to see them and I'm usually the last. And it's nothing to do with eyesight; its a sort of awareness that you seem to have. A sensitivity, if you like, that I just haven't got."

I said unsympathetically, "I think you're talking baloney, chum. Making excuses, in fact."

"Excuses?"

"Yes, excuses. I don't think you're being honest, either with me or with yourself. Look, if you're not worried about the Huns and you don't mind flying, then it's just a question of concentration - buckling-to and taking a grip of things. At the moment, you're just reacting and not taking the initiative. And if you can't take the initiative, you're never going to be any good at this game. What's more, if you go on as you are, you'll get yourself killed along with someone else. I'm sorry to be so blunt, Camel, but it's only a few weeks since you sugared off and left me with those Huns over Dover. The chaps shooting at the balloons, remember? That was criminal, Camel, and you ruddy well know it. And if you're thinking of playing the same trick again, I'd be glad if you'd arrange to fly with someone else when you decide."

Camel said nothing in reply and with bowed head, doodled idly with his spoon on the white cloth, so that I began to regret my vehemence. I said more gently, "Look, I'm sure you can work this out."

Silence.

I tried to be encouraging. "Listen. Have you ever seen a stoat take a rabbit from a whole pack of rabbits feeding above ground?" I watched the bowed head shake slightly. "Well, it picks one out - it could be the furthest one away - and it makes a bee-line for it, sometimes passing within a foot or so of several other rabbits. And the rabbit being hunted jolly well knows its number's up and just sits there, sometimes squealing, waiting to be killed."

I paused, warming to my subject. "It's the same with lions, I believe. They pick out one zebra or one antelope in a herd, to the exclusion of all the others, and unless that particular animal has something very special going for it, that's it - curtains! What's more, all the other zebras or antelopes seem to know they're not in danger and just go on feeding, totally unconcerned. Well, I believe it's rather the same in our business. You have to pick out the one chap on the other side that you're going to get, and you go for him bald-headed. You forget about all the others, although, obviously, you have to take precautions - watch out for number-twos and cross-fire and that sort of thing. The point is, it's the singling out that counts and the determination then to go through with the attack. If you could do that, I'm pretty sure you could get a Hun or two under your belt and feel a lot better."

Camel sat quietly, staring at the table, his food uneaten. I could see he was not convinced. Finally, he looked up and gave a wan smile. "So you think I ought to stay on?"

"No, I don't say that. But I do say there are right and wrong ways of doing anything. And if you try the method that suits me, you may have some success. Then, probably, the question wouldn't arise - you wouldn't want to move. However, you're the only chap who can provide the answers. And you're the one who has to make the decision"

Poor Camel. He shook his head slowly. "I really don't know. I really don't know."

And that was that. A moment later, the outer door and blankets were pushed aside and about a dozen officers of our own squadron with a few of 56, pushed their way in. Within moments, we were scooped up and in the middle of a noisy conversation so that the subject was dropped. Camel and I finished our meal and, joining the others, drifted apart. Shortly after, I lost sight of him and after hanging about so that we might return to the aerodrome together, I finally gave up and drove back alone.

During the week that followed the squadron was engaged largely on convoy patrols. The enemy regularly attacked the long lines of coastal and larger cargo vessels sailing up and down our eastern coast. For us, the routine was boringly repetitive. We would take-off in pairs, head off eastwards across Chelmsford and the Blackwater, crossing the coast usually at about 1,000 feet and heading out to sea. The ships, because they had to keep to well-defined navigational channels, were seldom more than five to ten miles out, a fact well known to us and, needless to say, to the enemy. After rendezvousing with the convoys, we would fly up and down for an hour or more, with only the occasional news of a lone Hun to quicken our interest. Then, with fuel gauges showing perhaps 25 gallons, we would return.

It was a dreary business and seldom very productive; we usually had little information of the enemy - until it was too late! - and always seemed to be at the wrong end of the convoy when the Hun popped out of the cloud to drop his bombs and nip back into obscurity. As Deputy Flight Commander, most of my seniors had been killed or wounded, I made a point of including Camel in my own section of two and I believe he profited from the arrangement. All told, he and I did about ten patrols in the course of a week, including one during which we sighted a Dornier 17 that sneaked out of the murk to drop a stick of bombs the far end of our convoy. Although we managed to close to within about 500 yards of it, the Hun climbed back into the mist before either of us had the opportunity to open fire.

The uneventful routine seemed to have a settling effect on Camel. He did not mention the possibility of leaving the squadron again and he seemed altogether more relaxed, both flying and in the Mess. Even so, he kept to himself and, as ever, always appeared to be on the fringe of things, constantly arriving or leaving hurriedly, never apparently able to spare more than a moment for a quick word with anyone. Then in the middle of the month he went on leave and if I didn't altogether forget about him, he was seldom in my thoughts.

At about the same time the weather cleared sufficiently for the Huns to resume their high-flying bombing attacks with 109s, so that day after day, we clambered aloft into the cold blue emptiness of 30,000 feet, thin pencil lines of white tracing both our and the Huns' movements across the skies. It seemed that we were constantly heading off or intercepting groups of 20 or 30 109s coming up from the south with the sun at their backs, after which they would unload their bombs and race for home.

I never ceased to admire their prettiness in the air as they flashed in the sunlight, their yellow noses easy to see and - when we were able to get sufficiently close - their black crosses prominent on pale wings and sides. Even with our new Mark 2s, unless we were able to get to height in time, they were not easy to catch, although over a period of 10 days we shot down four or five of them without loss to ourselves.

It was a cold clinical business, little more than breathless, vibrating climbs, long chases with throttles wide open and, occasionally, great curving, swooping dives. At anything much above 25,000 feet, the old-type dogfights were out of the question; in turns of anything more than three or four 'G', our Spits would give lady-like shudders in protest before falling away, and I dare say it was much the same for the Hun. The 109s never attempted to fight up there; they simply dropped down now and then in attempts to pick off chaps at the back of our formations, before scurrying off back into the sun, or go haring for home with their noses down and masses of boost. But, all in all, and despite the perishing cold, I believe I really enjoyed the knife-edged excitement of it all. Even with nothing to show for an aerial contest, I always landed back with a great feeling of personal achievement.

It was after one of these high altitude trips that, on letting down over Essex towards our home base, I suddenly experienced the dagger-like discomfort of sinus pains above my eyes. I was so badly afflicted that I had to pull out of formation and climb up again until the pain subsided, after which, with barely enough fuel to do so, I let down gradually and in stages before landing in considerable pain.

Once on the ground and finding myself deaf and my head like a balloon, I immediately sought the assistance of Sick Quarters and sat for some time draped in a towel, inhaling some aromatic vapour the Doctor had prescribed. Later, a thick head-cold developed but I hung around Flights, determined - very stupidly - to fly if at all possible.

For the next day or two, however, nothing much happened. Camel Elliot came back from leave and, with the weather wet, cold and miserable, we sat around the stoves in the crew-room, exchanging 'flu germs and playing endless games of Monopoly and L'Attaque.

It was, as I recall, the morning of 24th November, after waiting an hour or so to confirm Met. Section's forecast of 100 yards visibility and continuous low cloud for the rest of the day, that we discussed the weather situation with Sector and were instructed to 'Stand Down' shortly before 10 a.m.

Within minutes, it seemed, our Spitfires were covered and chocked and aircrew and ground-staff alike melted away to their respective quarters and Messes. My cold having developed nastily, and streaming mucus, I drove to the Mess to find most of the squadron officers preparing for an excursion into London. For me, however, it was a heaven-sent opportunity to enjoy a quiet after-noon and evening in bed. To this end, I instructed Round, my batman, to build up the fire in my hut and, after a quiet and solitary lunch, had a hot bath and slipped thankfully between stiff white sheets, thoughtfully warmed by Round with the aid of two flat-irons wrapped in a towel.

I lay for long time in the silence, deliciously cosy and half-way between sleep and consciousness, until I became aware of Round's face and his quiet voice together with the subdued chink of china as he placed tea and the inevitable fruit cake - standard British slab, we used to call it - on my bedside table. The light was almost gone despite the retention of Double Daylight Saving Time and I lay, warm and content, in the stillness of the darkening room, the flames of the coal fire flickering in the open stove, the lights and shadows playing on the walls and ceiling, dulling my senses with their hypnotic patterns.

I must have slept again for quite some time before, slowly and most unwillingly, I drifted back into consciousness in response to some gentle but persistent shaking. My eyes opened and focused on Round's face within inches of my own. I was so stupified with sleep that it took me a minute or two to comprehend what it was he was saying.

"Sir! Sir!" There was a quiet urgency in his voice. "You're wanted on the telephone. The telephone, sir. Now! On the telephone! The Sector Controller! He wants to speak to you. On the telephone!" He kept on shaking me but in a gentle and unobjectionable way.

I remember frowning, pulling my face in perplexity and thinking: Telephone? Me? It can't be! I heard myself asking, "What time is it?"

"It's ten-past-nine, sir. In the evening." Round's voice remained soft but compelling.

I closed my eyes again and said drowsily, "Tell him that I'm ill in bed and that we're all on Stand Down."

"I've already told him that, sir. But I'm afraid he still wants to speak to you. Now!"

I raised myself on to my elbow and said peevishly, "Why the bloody hell, me? There must be somebody else on this perishing station he can speak to."

"I've explained about the squadron, sir. But he keeps asking for you. Personally."

Poor Round. I can't exactly recall what it was I said to him but it can't have been very gracious and I can only offer sickness and a dulled and weary brain as an excuse for my boorishness. Because there seemed nothing else to do, I climbed slowly out of bed whilst he held my dressing-gown for me and stood aside as I shuffled out into the corridor and down towards the telephone. I picked up the receiver and placed it to my ear, my eyes still closed.

I was not allowed time to give a salutation before a voice came on, patient, slightly apologetic but urgent - noticeably so!

"This is the Sector Controller. Is that Pilot Officer Fitzgerald?"

"Yes sir." My voice was flat and barely above a whisper.

"Good: I'm sorry to drag you out of bed. I understand you're not feeling too well."

I replied thickly, "I'm all right."

"Can you get some of your chaps off the ground within an hour? I would like three aircraft off, if possible, by 22.30 at the latest."

For a moment I could scarcely believe my ears. The man must be joking, surely. It - It was a hoax! Someone was ringing from one of the dumps in London and pulling my leg. Some fool! By God, I'd - !

As my mind grappled with possible explanations, the man's voice came back to me again.

"Hello? Hello? Are you still there?"

I mumbled dully, "Yes . . . yes, I'm still here."

"Did you hear what I said? I want three aircraft off the ground by 22.30 at the latest!"

It was only at that point that I realised the fellow wasn't spoofing and that he was, without a shadow of doubt, giving me an order. But fly? At this time of night? In this weather? I was stunned, absolutely, and it was only in the brief silence that followed that I heard the thin drone of an aircraft high above and the mutter of guns in the distance.

Hoping desperately that a mistake had been made, I said petulantly, "But there's no one here. We're on 'Stand Down' and everyone has been away since noon. There are no aircraft, no people, no anything. And anyway, sir, I can't open up the airfield - just like that! I ... I mean, what about the Station Commander ... and everyone else. I -" My voice tailed off but, as the enormity of his instructions began to dawn on me, I began to wake up in earnest.

He cut in decisively, "Look, old chum! I'm aware of all that. I know that the Station Commander is not available, nor your Squadron Commander and Flight Commanders - that's why I'm speaking to you! I know too that the weather is miserable at present. However, it's due to improve and I have to tell you that three aircraft from North Weald - or two at the very least - must take-off within the hour. There's a heavy raid taking place this very moment on Central London and we have information that it will get worse as the night progresses. We have to get someone airborne and you have been selected. I can't make it any plainer than that. I take it you understand?" His voice rose a little at the end.

By this time, the seriousness of the situation had begun to dawn on me and I was very much awake despite a blocked and streaming nose. I heard my voice hardening.

"Look, sir. I honestly don't know what I can do. I'll get up and try to arrange something for you. But, to the best of my knowledge, I'm the only officer in our squadron left on the Station." I thought it best to make no mention of how miserably ill I felt. "You'll have to give me time to think. Can you leave it with me for 15 minutes?"

There was the briefest of pauses before the man replied. "All right. Ring me in 15 minutes. But understand this, my instructions are that you are to put three aircraft in the air, and it's your job somehow to DO JUST THAT. Do I make myself clear?" Then, a little more gently, he added. "Look, I'm sorry about all this, but there it is. We all have our instructions; I've had mine and I'm passing them on to you."

The 'phone then went dead and I was left standing in the corridor in bare feet and dressing gown, and in a mild state of shock. What in God's name did I do? And where did I start? The squadron was totally immobilised and there was blackness and fog everywhere. Walking forward to confirm this, I pulled down the blackout and peered into the night, my nose pressed against the streaming pane of glass in front of me. Then I leaned weakly against the wall and looked directly at Round who had followed me to the telephone. We were both barely twenty years of age, but the gap between my responsibilities and his was vast. Nice lad that he was, he saw the turmoil and hopelessness in my face and gave me a quiet but reassuring smile.

"Whilst you get dressed, sir, I'll make a cup of tea and see if I can find some of the others." Then, with a pat on my arm, "Don't worry, sir, it'll all turn out all right."

Within ten minutes I had established that almost all of the officers and NCO pilots were still away from the station. Completely dressed now, I scoured the almost empty public rooms in the Mess to find only 'Tommy' Thompson, the Engineer Officer, and Gibbs, our stand-in Intelligence Officer, chatting quietly in a corner. Both looked blank and uncomprehending as I explained the situation to them. Hurrying through the entrance hall I then bumped into a wild-eyed Camel Elliot, who had apparently been found by Round and despatched in my direction.

His voice was shrill. "I say, Fitzgerald, what's all this nonsense about flying?"

Not in the mood for any of Camel's histrionics I replied tersely, "I don't know what it is you've heard, Camel, but you and I are airborne within the hour unless we can find two others to take our places."

I well remember Camel's face registering total outrage.

"Look here, Fitzgerald! I'm not flying in this, now or at any time! It's quite nonsensical. Ridiculous! Have you seen the weather? Anyway, we're day fighters, not night fighters." His voice rose to a scream and his head began to nod violently. "Have you seen it, for heaven's sake? Go outside! Look, it really isn't on. It's just not fair."

I thought it best at that point to lower the temperature and replied more calmly and with a grin, "Camel, we're day and night fighters. Prestwick! Remember? Even if we are as effective at night as so many wet hens."

But Camel was not to be mollified and retorted hotly, "Well I can tell you, Fitzgerald, I'm jolly well not going to fly on a night like this. It just isn't fair. It isn't our job." His face and hands were working to such a degree that for a moment I thought his indignation would reduce him to tears.

"Well, anyway," I said, turning the conversation so that he would not be provoked into making remarks he might later regret, "I have to telephone Sector in a moment or two with a progress report. So, why don't we go down to dispersal and sort out the aircraft. After that, we'll look at the weather again and have another go at the Controller - if we want to, that is."

I then despatched 'Tommy' Thompson in search of as many NCOs and ground crews as he could find and rang the Transport Section for the Commer vans. After which, I contacted the Fire Section and Sick Quarters and finally located the Duty Pilot who was tucked away in the Sergeant's Mess. Camel, meanwhile, kept up a continuous barrage of protest, which I took for a time - God knew, I was much in sympathy with him - then, when I could stand no more of it, I turned on him sharply.

"Camel, for God's sake, stop belly-aching. I'm as upset about this as you are. But, we've been ordered to fly and that's the end of it. If you want to refuse, then upon your own head be it. I'm going down to dispersal and I suggest that it would be in your best interests if you did the same."

I turned on my heel and went back to my room in the hut, fuming and finding myself quite unusually disturbed in body and mind.

Within ten minutes I heard the Commer aircrew transport arrive, and walking out I climbed into the cab beside the driver. Before we moved off I heard Camel clambering through the tarpaulin screen and thumping about in the back. As the Commer moved off into the darkness and mist, I'm bound to say that my morale was as low as I had ever known it to be. I remember shivering convulsively in my seat, a mixture of fear and sickness I suppose, and I have no doubt there was rather more fear than sickness.

My spirits were in no way restored when, minutes later, the driver lost his way on the perimeter track and we found ourselves heading down the edge of the main runway. Ordering him to stop, I climbed out, recognised where we were, and turned him round - not without protest. After which, we resumed our snail-like progress and eventually reached dispersal.

It was a depressing sight. I found the crew-room in darkness, the coke-stoves dead and the surrounds grey with cold ashes. The place had an almost sepulchral air about it, damp and chilly. I had heard Camel dismount, but as he did not put in an appearance, I assumed he had gone off to attend to some unspecified task or other. Frankly, I was relieved not to have had him around.

In a quandary, I stood alone in the middle of the hut - the lockers, disordered beds and chairs, magazines, flying clothing, blackboard and notices - feeling desperately sorry for myself and very undecided. What did I do now? Call the Controller again? Argue? Plead? Try to persuade him? Or did I just wait for the aircraft to be made ready?

I went to the window and drew back the blackout. Thin beams from a couple of torches bobbed about in the darkness and I heard distant voices, one shouting. An engine burst into life and it was as though preparations for dawn 'Readiness' had started yet again for the hundredth - or was it the thousandth - time.

Walking into the empty room normally occupied by the Airman-of-the Watch, I was in the act of telephoning Sector when Camel appeared - noisily - the door banging behind him, his feet clumping on the boarded floor.

He started, "I say Fitzgerald." But I waved him into silence and asked to speak to the Controller. For some moments there were people speaking in the background then a man's voice came on.

I said, "Controller? Hello, sir. This is Pilot Officer Fitzgerald again. I thought I would report that we are now down at dispersal and I expect our aircraft to be ready in about twenty minutes. There are just two of us, Pilot Officer Elliot and me."

"Two! I see. Is that the best you can do?"

"There's no one else here!" I heard my voice hardening. I was beginning not to care what I said, and went on. "And I feel I ought to tell you that in my view the weather is totally unsuitable for flying. If you instruct me - us - to take off, we'll do so, but only under protest."

There was the briefest of hesitations as though the Controller was weighing up the likely repercussions of what he was about to say. Then he replied firmly and a little testily, "Is the weather good enough for you to get off the ground?"

I thought, Oh, God! but said, "I honestly don't know. All I can say is, our transport to dispersal lost its way on the aerodrome because of the fog. If we can find our way to the end of the runway, I daresay an instrument take-off might be possible. But, I'll be frank, I don't want to try it. I just don't want to go."

The voice came back, level and unfriendly. "You do understand, don't you, that at this very moment they're bombing hell out of Central London? And that you're saying you don't want take off?"

"Yes, I understand that, sir. And I'm very sorry about the bombing." The man was being grossly unfair and I found myself desperately trying to control my emotions and my responses. "But the situation is not going to improve if we're just needlessly sacrificed. Is it, sir? And you know very well that the prospect of our making any difference is just about nil."

"Are you saying you refuse to take off?" The voice was dangerously quiet.

I took a deep breath and heard my own voice trembling. "No, sir. If you say we must, then we will. But Elliot and I have only a few hours of night-flying to our credit and ... and frankly, I don't think we're up to it. Not in weather like this. There must be others better equipped to fly tonight. The Blenheims, for example. They're night fighters, we're not."

"Never mind the Blenheims! Do you refuse to fly? Yes or No!" I sensed that the man was trying to back me into a corner.

"No, sir. If you order me to, I will."

"Very well then, you may take it that I'm ordering you." There was a pause after which the tone became more friendly. "Look, old son. I'm sorry about all this. But, with things as they are, you - we - have no choice. Take your time about it, though. The weather is improving from the north. We'll get you down, if not at North Weald, somewhere else fairly close. Trust us. We'll manage. Believe me."

I felt myself as tense as a coiled spring, reasonably controlled, but shattered and almost in tears. I said, "This is waste of time, you know that, sir. We're just playing games. If I thought it worthwhile, I wouldn't mind so much. But it isn't, is it, sir?"

I received little sympathy. The voice when it came was coldly unemotional. "Get off as quickly as you can. Call me when you're airborne."

I replaced the telephone, breathed out tremulously, and turned to find Camel looking at me, his eyes fearful and staring.

"What did he say?"

I stood up and pushed past him roughly. "We have to go. I'll put the trips in the Authorisation Book. So just sign the bloody thing, Camel, and let's be off."

"Fitzgerald! I've told you, I'm not prepared to fly on a night like this."

Close to tears myself and writing down details of the flights, I said over my shoulder, "You please yourself. We've been ordered off. I've passed on that order. And I'm going. What you do is your business."

I felt my mouth quivering and, about to explode with the sheer, damned stupidity and injustice of the whole affair, I collected my Mae West, parachute and other equipment, and left in search of the Form 700. As I stepped out into the darkness, I felt as though I were walking over the edge of a cliff.

Moving forward cautiously in the blackness along the muddy path which led to the aircraft pens, I saw a torch waving about ahead of me and was soon confronted by a figure whose voice I recognised as 'Tommy's'. He stopped, his face ghostly in the reflected light.

"You can't be thinking of flying? This is madness!"

I replied, my voice shaking, "I have to. I've been ordered off."

"But - !"

"No buts, 'Tommy'." I detected the first shrill notes of hysteria in my voice. "We've been told to go and that's the end of it. Lambs to the slaughter! Is my aircraft ready?"

"Yes, your crew's there. With the Form 700. But is it too late, even now?"

I said, bitterly, almost shouting. "There's nothing more to be said. We have to go. So that's what's going to happen."

CHAPTER FIVE

Forty odd years later I can still recapture the feeling of total emptiness and cold naked fear that gripped me as I busied myself with the straps in that cheerless cockpit, searching for the triangular pin that would secure them at the level of my waist. The darkness loomed over me like a heavy enveloping shroud, impenetrable and wetly cold. I heard the voice of Jobson, the engine fitter on my crew, from somewhere to my left and saw the pale smudge of his face illuminated eerily by the diffused red glow of my port navigation light.

"Clear to start, sir."

From left to right around the cockpit, my practised fingers sought out the knurled rheostats which produced tiny glowing roses of pink light which grew in intensity as I rotated them one by one, the instruments and controls taking spectral shape and substance against the dark recesses of the cockpit. I checked the two fuel levers between my knees, examined the contents gauge, set the throttle and pitch controls and, unscrewing the ki-gas pump used to prime the engine, squirted six jets of fuel into the 12 cylinders of the big Merlin in front of me. As I screwed it up again, I felt petrol from a leaking gland, cool and wet on my ungloved fingers. I then flicked up the two ignition tumbler switches, pressed the starter and booster buttons simultaneously and felt, rather than saw, the airscrew jerk into motion as the cartridge fired with a serpent's hiss.

Ahead, in the darkness, the engine caught immediately with a rush of wind around my ears and the Spitfire reared forward minutely against the chocks as a small flick of pungent white smoke whipped into my face to disappear immediately over my shoulder. As the beat of the engine evened out, I adjusted the throttle so that 1,100 revs, showed on the rev-counter and, without conscious thought or effort, went mechanically through the motions of my cockpit drill; tightening straps, checking radio, switches, settings and instruments, adjusting the altimeter, the lubber-line of the compass, and the direction indicator.

I then waved away the chocks, anxious to get moving before the radiator temperature began to soar, released the brakes on the control column and rolled forward into the night.

Ahead, the darkness seemed an unscaleable wall. I jinked the long nose of my aircraft with its flickering blue and magenta exhaust flames, left and right, but could see next to nothing. The sunken lamps marking the perimeter track were barely visible so I switched on my landing light. The beam slowly developed but the broad, white swathe illuminated nothing more than a vast haloed semi-circle of dazzling grey, intensifying the blackness above and beyond and producing an eerie feeling of claustrophobia.

I switched it off promptly. The light faded slowly and died and I braked to a standstill to enable my eyes to readjust themselves to the blackness. I sat there tensely wondering how to proceed. This really was a fruitless task. I was aware that I was within 500 yards of the runway from which I would attempt a take-off. If I could negotiate the few bends ahead of me without coming to grief on the soft shoulders on either side of the perimeter track or inadvertently taxy into one of the dispersal pens, I could make a final decision at the threshold. With luck the Duty Pilot would be in position with his Aldis lamps and if I could orientate myself and line up on the first few flares, I could make a full instrument take-off, something I had never before attempted in a Spitfire, still less in almost total blackness and in fog.

I glanced at the dimly illuminated radiator temperature gauge; it showed 75 degrees. I had about four minutes maximum to get into position.

I was so engrossed with that jinking crawl to the end of the main runway that my fears and anxieties were, for the moment, forgotten. As I crept ahead a broad expanse of concrete opened out beyond my starboard wingtip with pin-prick lights curving away into the mist and I knew I had reached the threshold. Peering over the side and into the ground, I found the centre-line and turned so that my compass registered 240 degrees - the direction of take-off with which I was all too familiar. Braking, I reset the compass carefully, then the directional gyro, and methodically began to go through my cockpit drill yet again.

Suddenly, there was a series of thumps by my left shoulder and a disembodied face, white and pinched, appeared within inches of my own. It was an NCO pilot of 56 Squadron, acting as Duty Pilot. He was screaming above the noise of the engine and the wind was whipping his words away into the darkness.

I heard faintly: "You can't fly in this!" and as if to emphasise his words he shook his head violently.

Oh, God! How I wished then that I could turn back. But, at that precise moment, I knew I had to go on. There was no going back. I felt, in the strangest way, possessed. With my oxygen mask in place I could not speak to him so I, in turn, shook my head. He glared at me in disbelief. I can see his face now, his eyes and nose streamed in the icy slipstream. I glanced down. The radiator temperature was almost on the 100 mark; it was now or never. I nodded vigorously because it was all I could do and then, suddenly, he was gone.

I squeezed the brakes, opened the throttle until the boost gauge showed 0 lbs boost and tested the two magnetos in turn. The exhausts flared briefly as each of the switches was turned off and there was a faint but perceptible shudder as half the plugs were isolated. Then, I closed the throttle and, after a quick visual check around the cockpit, I breathed a prayer and set off carefully down the runway and into the blackness.

In retrospect, there was little extraordinary in what I was attempting; one of my sons, who now flies Boeing 747s, does a full instrument take-off almost every day and regards it as routine and commonplace. But to me, with a total flying time of little more than 350 hours, of which a mere 2 hours and 20 minutes had been spent on Spitfires at night - and clear or moonlit-nights at that! - it was a giant step into the unknown with a messy death as the penalty for error. Moreover, the Spit, a skittish, volatile creature, was much more at home in the air than on the ground and pulled powerfully to the left like a wayward filly if urged ahead too fiercely at the outset.

Concentrating hard on the directional indicator, therefore, I opened the throttle slowly, correcting immediately the slightest deviation. In a matter of moments I was up to 50 or so mph and I felt I had her moving straight and more or less under control. With growing confidence I pushed open the throttle fully, let the tail rise a little but not too much, and with my eyes glued to the instruments, committed myself absolutely to the fog and blank wall of blackness ahead.

To this day, I can feel that aircraft come to life and hear again the howl of the engine, its raucous snarl accentuated by the blanket of darkness around me, as we raced forward into the night. With my attention riveted to the dashboard I picked her carefully off the ground, the undercarriage came up cleanly with its characteristic 'clump' and I left the throttle wide open and waited until the speed had built up to 180 before raising the nose and climbing away. Resisting with all my concentration the temptation to look up into the blackness and risk disorientation, I kept my head buried in the cockpit and saw the finger on the altimeter-face wind rapidly towards the 1,000 feet mark, at which point I reduced power to 7lbs boost and heard the shrill scream of my racing engine moderate as I brought the revs, back to 2,850.

Breathing a little more freely, I climbed steadily ahead through the mercifully calm blackness, not daring to deviate or turn, until, with a mixture of satisfaction and mild shock, I realised I was heading directly towards the balloons on the northern outskirts of London. With a sharp and uncomfortable spasm of apprehension, visualising a hundred taut wires poised to snatch me out of the air, I gently coaxed the Spitfire into a turn to the left and, allowing my eyes to wander to the level of the cockpit coaming, caught sight of several pin-pricks of light somewhere above. Raising my head cautiously I observed a dull pink hue spread out before me like a huge pale stain. My heart bounded. I was through the fog and above the cloud. There were more pin-pricks ahead and I realised I was flying towards anti-aircraft fire, presumably directed against the raid over central London. The glare was obviously from the incendiary fires below the cloud but I blessed it with all my heart; it provided me with a horizon in the darkness and it was somehow comforting to know that I was not the only aircraft in the sky, even though my companions were German.

It was at that point that I became aware that my hood was still open and that my nose and eyes were streaming freely. I reached back for the handle above my head and pulled it forward. The perspex canopy slid closed with a thud, after which I settled myself in the cockpit, relishing the comparative silence and lack of buffeting wind. I then pulled back the throttle and revs, reduced the intensity of the lights playing on the instruments to the faintest of glows, and called Control. They answered promptly. I was to steer 140 degrees and to climb to 18,000 feet. I checked my instruments again and saw that I was at 6,000 feet and climbing at a fairly gentlemanly rate. I pinched my oxygen-tube, to make sure the flow was not impeded, then opened the throttle and turned my attention to the climb. The engine was smooth and regular, all the temperatures and pressures were normal and everything seemed to be working as it should. I felt altogether better; in fact, I was mildly elated that I had progressed as far I had in what were appalling weather conditions. For the briefest of periods, the future seemed unimportant.

I would like to be able to record that I made a dramatic and successful interception, at the end of which a German bomber went plunging to the ground in flames. Alas, it was not like that at all; indeed, it seldom was.

After climbing to the frozen heights of 20,000 feet and more, with only the stars as my companions in an unending cupola of blackness, I found myself wandering about the eastern edge of London looking down on a vast mottled carpet of the deepest of greys which, from time to time, was illuminated briefly by tinges of pink and the dull flicker of bursting bombs. Occasionally there would be wandering pools of light as searchlights below attempted to penetrate the fog and cloud, but these would invariably disappear quickly as though those below were reluctant to disclose their positions. The guns, however, were constantly in action, the bursting shells, some of them uncomfortably close at times, sparkling in clusters all around me. Although there must have been many Germans in my vicinity, I did not see a single enemy aircraft. With the long, black nose of the Spitfire ahead and the cherry-red glare from the engine's exhausts reducing my night vision almost to nil, it was hardly surprising.

Control did their best; they vectored me here and there and kept up an encouraging monologue but, after 55 minutes, I felt tired, dispirited and wretchedly cold. My head ached abominably, my nose streamed into my oxygen mask and two knifing sinus pains developed above my eyes.

I had used about 50 of the 87 gallons of fuel in my aircraft and I was dismayed when Control could speak of nothing more than a 'slight improvement' in weather conditions at Debden and further north. My own base, North Weald, was out completely it seemed, as were Duxford, Hornchurch and Rochford. There was nothing open immediately south of London and even Manston; which usually had the pick of the weather, was submerged in a thick fog. Suddenly, I found myself feeling very small and very alone. What good was all this? Why, in God's name, had they forced me into the air?

At that point, in a flash of rebelliousness, I decided I had had enough and demanded to be given a course for base. But, which base? I was already showing my IFF but I transmitted for a fix, even so, to provide a check, and was turned on to 345 degrees which, I estimated, would take me into the Cambridge area. Debden, it seemed, might just be able to accept me, and possibly Bassingbourn, a station I had never used before and which I knew to be a bomber airfield.

With drooping spirits I turned towards the north and began to descend, the sinus pains in my head stabbing like newly sharpened spears.

The flight north seemed endless though, in fact, it could not have been more than fifteen minutes. Control kept up a fairly breezy commentary but I noted they were careful not to tell me much about actual weather conditions at Debden and elsewhere, only about trends.

When I had descended by painful stages to 4,000 feet, I sensed I was in cloud again. I switched on my navigation lights briefly and two diffused coloured haloes confirmed that I was in something resembling a steam bath. I jogged around for a bit, then climbed up again until I could see the stars. Control was trying to get me into Debden and as I came closer to the airfield, the vectors began to change rapidly until there was a silence, after which I received a reciprocal heading and knew I had passed over the top. By that time my fuel gauge showed fifteen gallons and I realised only too clearly that I had to get down in fifteen minutes - or less!

Control and I then had a discussion and they took me away for several minutes, turned me round and, on their instructions, I reduced power and let-down once more into the cauldron of mist. With flaps down - it was all or nothing on a Spitfire - my nose well up in the air and the airscrew in fine pitch, I descended carefully, lower . . . lower . . . and lower, my eyes glued to the instruments, my nerves stretched to breaking point, hating every moment of it, expecting every second to be confronted by a wall of I-didn't-know-quite-what, but some obstacle that would put an end to my earthly existence in the briefest of explosive seconds. I watched the altimeter needle unwind past 800 feet, then 700, 600, 500. I felt myself to be on the edge of a precipice and about to step off into oblivion.

At 300 feet, I lost my nerve and levelled out, still totally enveloped in stinking fog. It was an eerie, unforgettable experience. It was as though I were tied up in a sack. There wasn't a chance and suddenly, with crystal clarity, I knew it and opened the throttle decisively. The engine gave the briefest of hesitations then roared like a Dervish and I surged upwards in a steep climb.

At 4,000 feet, tense and shivering, I was back again among the stars and Control came on, as calm as you like, to ask me whether or not I could see the flare path. Flare path! The fools! How the hell could I see anything in this endless cesspit of corruption! I replied abruptly, almost offensively, and flew in a gentle curve, tortured with indecision.

It was at that point that I knew I was going to have to bale out. I had been harbouring the thought for some time but had hoped it would never come to the point when I would have to. One thing was certain, I was not going down into that fog again. No, I would take my chance in a parachute.

I pressed my transmitter switch and told Control in half a sentence. That seemed to shake them somewhat because nothing was said for about twenty seconds. Then a new and more mature voice came on. They had me east of Saffron Walden, it explained. Would I not like another try?

Another try? Down there? Not bloody likely! I'd had enough of trying and being buggered about! They'd had their pound of flesh. To hell with them all! It was my life they were playing with - it wasn't much, but it was all I had!

In a savage mood, I made a succinct and not very complimentary response and switched off the radio in an impulsive gesture of defiance.

Alone again - and now it seemed completely so - I experienced a quite unusual feeling of calmness. The decision had been made. The rest was, if not easy, a matter of deliberate action. I checked my fuel state. About eight gallons. I throttled back and trimmed the aircraft to fly straight and level at 170 miles per hour and flew, hands off, for a few seconds. Then, for a moment, I sat there, cold and trembling but resolute, considering how best to abandon the aircraft.

I have never yet met a pilot who left his aircraft other than reluctantly - except, of course, when in dire straits. Fire is a powerful incentive and there is usually no hesitation in coming to a decision in such circumstances - anything is better than fire! But, even with a disabled aircraft, very often a pilot will hang on, clinging to the hope that, somehow, he will bring it to safety.

As I sat there my old Spit was purring away and responding almost pathetically to my every touch and whim. We had had some good times together. She had been a good friend and I could barely bring myself to leave her: it was like taking an old and faithful dog to be put down.

The approved method of baling out of a Spitfire was to turn the aircraft over and push on the control column. Then the pilot was shot out of the cockpit neatly and cleanly and without the risk of fouling the tail. Somehow, however, the prospect of doing something akin to aerobatics on a night of foggy and impenetrable darkness, did not appeal to me. So I carefully undid my oxygen pipe and disconnected my radio lead. I then thought about taking off my helmet, but decided against it. Finally I undid my straps and, after a second or two of breathless hesitation, I prised myself into a semi-standing position by pushing with my feet.

It was like advancing into the boiling cauldron of outer space. The slipstream tore at my face so that I found myself half-upright in an inferno of wind and noise and terrifying blackness. I pushed harder, almost frenziedly. What was happening? Would I never go? I kicked again, harder - violently - and in an instant I was plucked out and whirled about like a small bird caught by a passing car. I sensed rather than felt a blow on my right leg, then all was quiet . . . and still.

I seemed to be suspended in space, turning slowly, a gentle breeze making a pocket of air in the left side of my helmet. It was cool, caressing and very pleasant.

I was alive, that much I knew. But was the parachute open, or not? I tried to look upwards but could see nothing. Then, with a clarity of thought which has never ceased to astonish me, I explored with my right hand, first the tie at my neck, then the buttons and zip of my Sidcot suit, moving downwards to the quick-release box of my parachute and then, to the left, to the housing of the ripcord. It was still snugly in position! The parachute was not deployed. I was falling - free - like a stone. In a matter of seconds I would be dead.

Concentrating, I very deliberately and precisely pulled the 'D' ring and at once there was a brief flurry of activity behind and below me and I was jerked hard but not violently into an upright position. After that, even the breeze stopped and all around me was darkness and sighing silence. I even heard the harsh rasp of my own breath and suddenly, frightened that I might drop out of the parachute harness, I raised my arms and clung almost desperately to the thick linen straps above my head.

Hanging there I looked about. It was awesome, yet beautiful. I had no thoughts other than that of total and absolute relief. I was an interested onlooker in a dark, forbidding yet fascinating world.

My euphoria was soon interrupted, however, by a silent explosion of red light to my right and a small flowering burst of illumination which died away almost immediately to a small flicker of muted orange. It took me a moment or two to realise that my Spitfire had just exploded into flaming oblivion and that, there, but for the hand of providence, I would have met my own end. But, of more immediate concern, the explosion had appeared to be more or less at my own level, so that I could expect to hit the ground at any moment.

I had barely time to formulate this thought when something indefinable seemed to launch itself at me out of the darkness and I was struck a vast and crushing blow, so unexpected, so devastating, and so excruciatingly painful that the memory of it will live with me for ever.

For some moments, stupified with shock, I was beyond comprehending what had happened to me. As the first agonising paroxysms subsided, I then became aware that my face was pressed against cold, wet clay and some sort of vegetation and that the lower part of my body was so bathed in pain that all my muscles had clamped rigidly into spasm. I lay there for a while, like an animal run down by a car, conscious still yet oblivious of time or of anything other than the fact that I was alive and could think.

Gradually, I came-to sufficiently to attempt, gingerly and with trepidation, to identify my injuries, moving one by one my shoulders, neck and arms. But, in a dream almost, I sensed that the rest of me was dead - quite, quite dead! From the waist down I could not move ... not a limb ... not a foot ... not so much as a muscle - anywhere.

It was fortunate that, the night being so still, my parachute did not belly out and drag me around - like me it lay crushed and inert. As I lay there advice given months before by our, then, new squadron doctor, drifted into my mind. It was advisable, he had said, to lie still after an accident and, if possible, to sleep. Sleep? Recalling his words, which had seemed so ridiculous at the time, I lay on the cold wet earth, grateful to be alive but with no idea as to how I could possibly move or seek help. I was not consciously aware then of being cold but, after a time, I realised that I could not remain where I was throughout the night, otherwise I would die of exposure and shock. I calculated that it would be about 1 am and thought it unlikely that I could hang on until it was light, five or six hours hence.

I lay back, painfully, and looked up into the blackness. There was only silence - miserable, dripping, suffocating silence. Was this really me, lying there? I raised my head, but only an inch or so. More than anything else, the quiet stillness was overwhelming. I tried again to move my legs but found it impossible, after which I made a feeble but unsuccessful effort to pull my parachute cords in order to use the silk as a cover. Finally, I lay back exhausted and, staring into the darkness, allowed my mind to wander. Fifty miles away, my parents would be safe and warm in bed, completely unaware that their only son, aged twenty years and four months, was lying crippled and freezing in a field of stubble somewhere in Essex and likely to die of exposure. If only they knew!

Spurred on by this sombre thought, I made another effort to move, but with no success. If only someone . . . anyone . . . knew! Crushed by my helplessness I resolved to leave it for half-an-hour or so. I could wait that long. After that, I would try again. Attempt to drag myself somewhere - anywhere! Fields in Essex, I reasoned, couldn't be that large. If I crawled in the right direction I might reach a ditch, a road, a path - something. If I chose the wrong direction, well, I least I would have tried. I lay back again. And closed my eyes. In despair.

It would be an exaggeration to say that I slept; I don't think I did. I seemed, somehow, to submerge into a half-and-half world of fantasy and oblivion, a world in which my mind conjured up pictures and situations in total isolation from my body.

How long I remained in that euphoric state I shall never know. At one time I was convinced I was airborne again and the blue and brilliant glare of a searchlight was coming up at me from the ground. I remember turning my head this way and that, cursing the fools below who were exposing me and not recognising one of their own. Why in God's name did they persist in illuminating me when they should be concentrating on the enemy?

But the light kept on and on, until I wanted to scream that they were blinding me, God blast them! But no sound came from my throat and I remember putting up my hand feebly to shield my eyes. I remember, too, the surprise when my fingers, dead as they were with cold, touched the rough serge of someone's sleeve.

A voice said quietly, "He's alive, anyway. Shine your torch down below."

The light moved away and a disembodied voice said from out of the darkness, but with great gentleness, "Are you damaged?"

"Yes." My lips formed the word but there was only a dribble of sound.

"Whereabouts? Can you say?"

I wanted to reply that I didn't know, but I couldn't. Instead, I moved my hand towards my legs.

"All right." The voice was soft again and patient. "Don't say anything. I'll have a look." When he heard my swift intake of breath, the man added reassuringly, "Don't worry . . . I won't hurt."

I felt other hands exploring my body and then move towards my feet. There was whispering. I wanted to cry out, 'Be careful' but nothing came. There was a pause and the same voice came, "Look. Your legs have taken a bit of a knock. I'm going to send for some medical help and supplies. In the meantime, we'll cut off your parachute and cover you up."

Whoever it was stood up and I heard voices and feet moving about. I felt the parachute harness being cut and pulled away and wondered, stupidly, what sort of fuss there would be when the parachute section at North Weald got their 'brolly' back in pieces. Then there were more movements and quiet voices and the folded silk canopy was gently draped across my body and tucked in. Someone knelt by my side.

"Is that better?"

I nodded, shivering, then asked in a faint, thick voice, "Who are you?"

I heard a quiet chuckle. "Bloody pongos!"

I felt a sob rising to my throat and wanted to know how they'd found me and what time it was, but it was all too difficult, so I lay there quietly, shivering now and then in uncontrollable spasms. My companion said nothing but just put his hand on the side of my face to show me he was there still, and we remained like that for quite some time.

After what seemed an eternity, there were more flashing lights and footsteps and I heard the noise of a car engine in the background. A new voice said: "Hello. And how's the patient?"

My companion said quietly, "He's not feeling so good, I'm afraid."

The newcomer again, "Right. I'll have a look and give him something to ease the pain." The new voice was in my ear and I felt warm breath on my cheek.

"Hello, old chap. I'm the medicine man. I'm just going to look at you then make you a little more comfortable. After that, we'll get you into the warm somewhere. All right?"

I gave the smallest of nods. At that moment I didn't really care very much one way or the other - not even if I lived or died.

In the minutes that followed there were more voices and lights and hands. I heard many feet on the ground around me and the sound of a car moving slowly in my direction, the wheels slipping on the wet earth. Finally, someone lifted my arm and loosened my clothing.

A voice said gently, "Just a prick" and I felt the needle. After a time everything became more distant ... and relaxed ... and unimportant. Until, finally, there was only warmth and endless, endless grey, merging into blackness.

There is evidence, I'm told, that an animal in process of being killed by a predator experiences very little pain. In the same way, I suppose, the human nervous system reacts to any major accident in such a way that the pain and even the memory of it are mercifully erased so that, later, the victim recalls little or nothing of the dire moments.

My recollection of damaging myself and the hours that followed, are hazy. I was dimly aware of some sort of impact when leaving the aircraft, of being hurled very unpleasantly to the ground, and, later, of being bounced about in some vehicle or other and my clothing being removed. That I was partially stripped, strangely enough, remains clearest of all - I suppose there is some latent modesty in all of us which tends to resist such indignities, even for the best of reasons. Other than these recollections, however, very little has endured.

When eventually I awoke, the immediate past was an endless sequence of shadowy events and, in the silence of that white hospital room, the sight of ropes and pulleys around my bed was beyond my immediate comprehension. As I lay there, like a picture coming into focus, I gradually took stock. It seemed my entire body was rigidly stiff, and weighted, and tipped, and balanced, so that I was quite incapable of movement. I was later to learn that I was totally enclosed in plaster from my waist down. But, of far greater importance, I felt very, very sick and knew I was about to vomit. Which, to my distress, I did - many times - until I prayed for an end to it all.

An hour or so later, when I had been cleaned up and straightened with brisk efficiency, a young man in a white coat appeared and stood over me. He seemed little more than my own age with dark, curly hair and he had his hands in his pockets.

"Wotcher! Feeling better?"

I nodded. Then, in reply to my unasked question, he smiled and added, "Epping. The local hospital. A mile or so away from your own Station."

Epping? It was just too difficult to understand.

"You were brought here three days ago."

"Three days!" I found my voice and shook my head.

He saw my obvious exhaustion. "Right. Now that you've surfaced, it's important that you relax and sleep again - for as long as possible. We'll have another chat when you're a little stronger. All right?"

He moved away with a smile and I lay there quietly for a long time, my eyes half-closed and focused on the ceiling.

The following morning I was in rather better shape and learned that I had multiple fractures in both legs and had also been damaged about the pelvis. But, of far greater worry to the doctors, apparently, had been the likelihood of pneumonia, a threat which, I was relieved to be told, had since receded.

I had been picked up a mile or so to the north-east of Thaxted by a detachment from a local anti-aircraft battery, the unit having been warned - along with others in the area - of my crash and parachute descent. By the grace of God, in the fog and blackout, they had caught sight of a fragment of my parachute draped across a hedge bordering a back road leading to Finchingfield and had stopped to investigate. After that, I had been taken to sick-quarters at RAF Debden, thence to Epping, where I was operated on immediately. The prognosis was good; I would live to fight another day - but not for quite some time.

Within a day or two, I began to receive visitors from the squadron. The first was James Denby. He arrived in the late morning, limping and with his stick, looking relieved but serious.

"Junior! For God's sake! It's good to see you safe and well." He took off his hat and sat down. "What a night. I wanted to come and see you before but was warned off." His face became grave. "A bad business altogether, I'm afraid."

I nodded. "How did Camel get on?"

Denby hesitated and frowned. "Of course. You haven't heard." He drew in his breath and said carefully, "I'm afraid Camel bought it." When my eyes widened, he went on, "Poor chap. He took off directly after you and ... and, well, he just disappeared. There's been no trace of him since. So, sad to say, we had to list him as 'Missing believed Killed'."

I lowered my eyes and said simply, "Oh! ... I'm so very sorry. Poor old Camel! His heart really wasn't in it, I'm afraid."

Denby nodded in agreement. "Great shame, really. He was due to leave us anyway in a matter of days and be transferred to a Bomber OTU. He would probably have done better there. Not everyone is suited to our line of business, unfortunately."

We went on and after a few more remarks about Camel, we talked about my own injuries, my prospects of rejoining the squadron, and some personal details regarding my family and what I wished him to tell them. He obviously knew more about my condition than I did because he showed the kind of caution and sympathy which suggested to me immediately that I could not expect to return to active flying for many months to come. I was naturally disappointed, of course, but he was reassuring about my future prospects and after some further pleasantries and the excuse that he had only been permitted a few minutes with me, he stood up to leave.

He was in the act of moving away when he turned and said, almost as an after-thought, "By the way, you'll be sorry to learn that the old Adj has left us, too."

The news came so baldly and without preamble that I was quite stunned. My mouth fell open. "The Adj! Gone?" He saw the distress in my face.

"Yes. I'm afraid so. Air Ministry urgently wanted someone mature and reli-able for Canada. So, he's gone as part of the Empire Air Training Scheme. Sad for us, of course, but he's the sort of chap needed over there." He smiled. "But, don't let it upset you too much. He was due for promotion and would have gone within a month or two, anyway." He put on his hat in a gesture of farewell. "Nice to see you taking nourishment, as they say. Some of the others will be down to visit you, so you won't be short of company from now on. Get well soon, Junior." Nodding again, he turned away.

After he had gone, I just stared into space, crushed. The old Adj, posted! The Adj, who had been such a comfort and support to me over the months. God, I would miss him. The squadron would never be the same.

I lay back and reflected on the cruelties of war. Dear old Adj! For me, to lose him was about as bad as losing the squadron. And now I had lost both! Oh, what was the point?

Fortunately, with James Denby's departure, there commenced a good deal of activity around the ward so that I did not have time to dwell upon his news. Later that night, however, when the lights were dimmed and we all attempted to sleep, I remained awake for a long time, thinking about the squadron, my friends, and my own future. The aftermath of my accident and enforced confinement and, I suppose, some residual shock, all combined to give me a thorough-going misery. I kept seeing the Adj's face, his reassuring smile, and his eyes crinkling and full of understanding. Father-figure? Whatever he was, he was now no more. It barely seemed possible.

And Camel. Poor, dear Camel. Not much use, of course, but such a shame. A misfit, he had never been comfortable or at home in a fighter aircraft. Now he had gone, too. For ever. Not heroically, but indignantly, protesting and tearful. Killed for no reason other than to satisfy someone's unforgiveable self-indulgence in demonstrating that 'something was being done'. Such a waste. Such a wretched, squalid waste!

I lay there, well into the night, very close to tears, brought on, as much as anything, by a surfeit of self-pity. But, apart from being low in spirit, my bottom-half ached abominably and it was becoming clear that I had sustained the type of damage that was not easily going to be repaired. I pondered bitterly on the injustice of it all. Why, in God's name, did I have to be the only one around when the demand for action had been made? I was sick! Why the hell hadn't they 'phoned the Coconut Grove, or wherever? All the fit ones had been there – whooping it up with les girls! And what good had resulted, anyway? None! Not a damn thing! Savage and bitterly resentful, I then thought of Camel – and was ashamed of myself. And after him, the Adj. And round again, full circle. And again. The night seemed endless. I felt as low as ever I'd been in my life.

My intuitive fears about my injuries were confirmed a little later when I was suddenly parcelled off to the RAF Hospital at Halton where, over a period of nine weeks, I was in and out of the operating theatre no less than five times. My morale reached rock-bottom and there were occasions when I despaired that they would ever get me right. However, they persisted and finally announced themselves satisfied with their repair work.

After that, I was sent to the RAF Hospital at Ely - for reasons I never fully understood - where I stayed for almost three months, by which time, of course, I was up and about, although for most of the time in plaster and on crutches. Eventually, however, the day came when I was allowed home before moving on to the recuperation centre at Torquay.

My stay at Torquay was a cross between purgatory - there was a great deal of strenuous rehabilitation work to get through - and a holiday in a rather rowdy rest-camp. The place was full of officers such as myself with major crash injuries of one sort or another and, of course, those unfortunate victims with burns. At that stage of the war, the science of healing and repairing burn wounds was in its infancy and some of my companions were still in a horrifying state, so that, whenever I felt thoroughly depressed, it was the sight of their mutilated white faces, staring lidless eyes and scarecrow hands, that never failed to restore in me a sense of balance. Despite my legs, I really was a lot better off than most. It was just the frustration that I found so difficult to bear.

At long last, it all came to an end and I had, paradoxically, a rather trying and unsettled time at home before taking a last aircrew medical examination in London. The Board was a bit sniffy at first - it was almost as if they were granting me a favour! - but gave me the benefit of the doubt and I was passed fit for flying duties. I remember giving a relieved sigh. It was 11 months and four days precisely since that never-to-be-forgotten last flight in the fog and my subsequent parachute descent. By now the bastard who had ordered me off had either achieved Air rank or a seat in the Cabinet, God blast his soul! One day I would find out who he or they were! I still thought bitterly of the whole business.

News had long since filtered through that my old squadron had departed for the Middle East, so that hopes of returning to it were dashed once and for all. I was called to 'P' Staff at Air Ministry where it was suggested that I might like to join a high level Photographic Reconnaissance Unit flying the new Spit 5s. Excited by the prospects of a fresh career - and flying a blue aircraft! - I went down to RAF Benson and started training.

Unhappily it soon became apparent that high altitude flying in unpressurised cockpits was not for me. After about 30 minutes above 35,000 feet, I experienced the sort of pain in both legs that very soon became intolerable. Reluctantly, therefore, I had to ask for a transfer. There was then a further medical check-up and yet another discussion at Air Ministry, following which I was posted to a night-fighter squadron flying Beaufighters at RAF Valley in Anglesey. I'm bound to say, I went with some reluctance.

The first few weeks were not easy. After a Spit, flying a Beaufighter was like taking a spin - uphill - in a Matilda tank! Moreover, I still regarded myself as a day-fighter boy. Even so, it was nice to have two enormous engines bubbling away alongside one's ears and enough fuel to hang about for a month if the weather turned nasty. After a time, I actually came to like the brute. In fact when, shortly afterwards, we re-equipped with Mosquitos, I was sorry to see my old girl go. The Mossies were good, if a bit noisy, and for a chap my size, somewhat cramped. Also, having already made two unplanned parachute descents in my short career, I was not overly fond of the getting-out arrangements on the aircraft. But it was swings and roundabouts, I supposed.

It was about this time that we moved to the south of England and, although I thought it would never happen, I actually began to enjoy night-fighting. In part, of course, this was due to my navigator and me having some success, but also because I still regarded it as something of a luxury to have a mate to do all the navigating, with sufficient equipment at his disposal to lead me home in the worst of weather at the end of each flight. He was a splendid young man called Geoffrey Gunter, a little older than me and, in his own quiet way, as bright as a button. Together we flew 240 night interception and intruder sorties over a period of 17 months before we separated when our tour of duty ended. Although never entirely an adequate substitute for the sheer exhilaration of combat by day in a single-seater fighter, night work had its compensations. There was something especially fascinating and unearthly about those long, lonely patrols in the silent darkness, stealthily picking up and stalking an enemy invisible to the naked eye.

For me it was a strange, almost haunting, experience which seemed to take me out of this world and at least part of the way to God - although the business of killing could hardly be regarded as heavenly. I believe others were similarly affected as, after the war, a quite surprising number of successful night-fighter crews went into the Church.

Then in 1944, supposedly as a rest from flying, I was attached to the 9th USAAF as a liaison officer. In fact, I did as much flying with them as I had done in the various other squadrons in which I had served. And, I am happy to say, in a variety of new and interesting types ranging from the Thunderbolt to the Mustang, Lightning and others, even including the bigger Dakota, Mitchell and Marauder.

But flying, strangely enough, was not the greatest joy I associate with my stay with the Americans. More than anything, I was - and remain - grateful for the courtesy, the comradeship and the hospitality they showed me. Furthermore, it did wonders for my history as I was obliged to fight the 'War of Independence' - holding my own, I think - many times over during those twelve exciting months, during which we took part in the invasion of Europe and advanced to the borders of Germany.

When, in 1945, I returned to England, the end of the war was in sight. I joined the School of Air Support at RAF Old Sarum as an instructor and, with many of my colleagues, began to consider my future. Although I was attracted to the possibility of staying on in the Air Force, I was realistic enough to recognise that my legs were always likely to give me trouble and that, sooner or later, problems in that area would disqualify me from flying. I therefore decided to apply for a University place as a mature student and although Medicine was my first choice, I settled for Law.

In 1951, I left Cambridge and joined a firm of solicitors in Norwich - I won't reveal their name as, though now retired, I still do a little specialised work for them occasionally and they might not like it. And, of course, I made my home in Norfolk.

In these 40 odd post war years, I have led the life of an average county-town solicitor, a five day week - I'm not a compulsive worker by temperament - with gardening and golf at the week-ends and such other pursuits and interests that have appealed to me from time to time. I tried to keep up my flying but the expense of maintaining even a small light aircraft became prohibitive, and queuing up to fly the local Club Tiger Moth at considerable cost in time, effort and cash, soon lost its appeal.

All of which just about brings me up to date as far as my career is concerned. Except to add that I have always kept in touch with a small group of my American friends of 1944; in particular, Colonel Al Hill and his charming wife Genevieve who have been especially close. I visited them briefly in Virginia in 1948 and again in the '60s, and they have been across to Norfolk several times since. Somewhat older than me, they retired to Tucson, Arizona, some years ago and will spend the rest of their lives there, I have no doubt. We write, of course, but it matters not that we miss a year or so; we always manage to take-up where we left off and time does not seem to weaken the links between us.

CHAPTER SIX

It was in the late summer of 1982 that my wife and I – we had married in 1945 – received our usual annual letter from the Hills, this time with a pressing invitation to visit them in Green Valley, Arizona. If we came in November, they said, we would be spared the morale-sapping English winter and be able to bask in the sunshine and crystal-clean air of the Arizonan desert.

My spouse and I thought it over - but not for long! The prospect of a cloudless winter and breakfasts on the verandah in an area totally new to us was especially appealing and proved to be too great a lure. Without delay, therefore, we made two reservations on one of the new economy flights to Los Angeles in a DC-10.

We both found the trip across fascinating. It was a year at least since I had flown, either for pleasure or commercially, and it was my first trip in a wide-bodied jet. I sat in one of the window seats, as excited as a child, and looked down on the huge nacelle housing the starboard engine. According to the information folder I had taken from the pocket in front of me, it was a General Electric Fanjet developing 44,000 lbs of thrust. Together with the port and tail engines, that made 132,000 lbs of thrust - sufficient to lift a 60 ton aircraft vertically into the sky - theoretically, anyway.

I must have smiled to myself, thinking of the first Gloster Meteor jet that had become operational towards the end of the war, the one in which I had had the opportunity to fly briefly before I left the Service - quite the most miserably heavy aircraft on the controls I have ever experienced, incidentally - whose two engines, in total, produced something less than 6,000 lbs of push. How technology had advanced!

My wife noticing my expression, asked, "What's amusing you?"

I explained, keeping it pretty simple. "The power of these engines! It's quite overwhelming. Imagine a 60 ton airliner going straight up."

She thought for a moment. Then made the priceless remark: "But, how could it? What would happen to all the cups and saucers?" I recall shaking my head. The female mind defeated me!

We took off from Gatwick around midnight and, quietly and without fuss, climbed northward over central England with only the thin whine of the turbines to persuade us that we were not on some magic carpet. Below, moving ever more slowly as we rose into the cold void of the sub-stratosphere, the lights of the industrial Midlands and the North drifted by. Then, far, far below, a brief outline of the Scottish Lowlands and Arran before we turned and pointed our nose towards the distant shore of America. After that, all was blackness and dimmed lights.

Little more than five hours later, and still in total darkness, we began a slow descent, running down the northern coastline of Maine. As we slid gently into the more turbulent lower regions, isolated groups of lights began to appear and pass slowly beneath us. Eventually there were the clustered illuminations of Bangor beneath my window and after a slow, whispering curve in the darkness, we touched down and went racing between the runway lights and banks of heaped snow on either side. It was like a winter scene from the cover of an old Saturday Evening Post.

We stayed there for close on an hour and after refuelling and a fairly painless introduction to Immigration Control and Customs, were off again and climbing up into the cold, starlit darkness. And, throughout, there was the thin, almost inaudible whine of the turbines. As we were flying west and keeping pace with the sun - or, more obviously, the darkness - there was little to see and my wife and I slept. Towards dawn, however, we were over Nevada and the slow let down commenced into California and Los Angeles. Almost imperceptibly, the desert emerged in all its beauty, an endless landscape of delicate blues and browns which gradually was transformed into shadowed pinks and gold as the sun rose behind us. Then we were rocking and bouncing through a thin layer of convection cloud above California, whilst beneath us the green undulations of hill and valley gave way here and there to ordered rectangles of suburbia and urban sprawl. Finally, there was visible movement; endless crawling lines of cars which looked like a million ants moving purposefully in every direction.

Soon after, the whine of the turbines died once more to a whisper and we went into a wide curve, gradually losing speed and height, lifting our nose up - up and up, until suddenly there were roof tops, buildings and gardens. Finally, a flash of concrete, the aircraft was checked and there was the squeal of tires and the roar of reverse thrust as we touched down and gradually slowed to a halt.

We looked about with interest. The colours predominating were white, brown and green. A circle of jagged hills appeared almost to nod at us through the rising heat and haze of early morning. A natural basin, in which the vapourous effluent of several million human beings and almost as many cars produce a stagnant pool, it is small wonder that Los Angeles has a pollution problem. Even so, there was an excitement and a heady, warm beauty about the place that was quite breathtaking.

During our several hours in LA, we rediscovered the fascination of America; the throw-away opulence of the place, the glossy magazines, the bustling orderliness of their airports, the strange mixture of people - an amalgum of long-limbed sophisticates with blond hair, blue rinses and immaculate lightweight apparel, juxtaposed with the burly forms and dark, sweating faces of those of Negro and Mexican stock. But, above all, there were the fragrant odours of newly-made coffee, rich cigars and strange tobaccos. And there were blood-pressure testing machines! Everywhere! We immediately concluded that high blood-pressure was the fashionable ailment and that it seemed inconceivable that even one Californian should suffer from the low variety!

We booked two seats to Tucson with a pretty, coloured girl who consulted one of a battery of computers and bade us welcome to California and to 'have a nice day now', and a Boeing 737 whisked us at 30,000 feet across a starkly magnificent terrain of green hills and canyons, scrubland and desert. After little more than an hour we were once again letting down into the turbulence of the lower altitudes and preparing to land at the airport of Tucson, a wide-open grey-white space flanked by the now familiar jagged hills and a wilderness of scrub and cactus desert.

Al Hill and his wife were there to meet us, looking as sleek and as well-preserved as only Americans in late middle age seem able, after which, full of laughter and reminiscences, we drove in their Lincoln Continental down the 20-odd miles of through-way to Green Valley - Apache territory, as I teasingly referred to it - and a long, cool bungalow, sumptuously comfortable yet carefully sited in order to take full advantage of its desert setting. Alongside was a manicured golf course, the greens as bright at emeralds, whilst a mere mile away coyotes nosed surreptitiously through trash-cans in search of a succulent morsel - or a stray cat! The sky was the colour of blue steel, the sun a golden ball, and the air thin, clear and as freshly stimulating to the senses as a dry, white wine.

The next several weeks were a joy for us both. By car and on foot, we toured the desert hills with their bewildering abundance of cactus plants. Scarcely breathing, we stood and watched from a distance, coyotes, rattlesnakes and those fascinating clowns, the roadrunners. We visited the old frontier outposts, the cowboy Tom Mix's memorial, and trod the famous Apache Trail through the bleak mountains east of Phoenix. We then went northwards towards Grand Canyon, toured the Navajo homelands, crossed into New Mexico and then explored the local townships of Mexico proper, anaesthetising our palates with the hottest of chillis and reviving them with ice-cold beers and cool Californian wines.

Also, in the daytime, there was golf - with the golf-trolley clearly replacing the human leg as the principal means of locomotion! And, in the evening, an endless round of drinks and dinner engagements and 'visits' in the local country club. It seemed we met thousands of enquiring faces and shook almost as many hands. Ex-patriate British talked nostalgically of 'home' in mid-Atlantic accents, explaining as they did so, how it was that they never quite managed to return in 30 years. And all the time the sun shone brilliantly from a blue, blue sky, the distant hills were as sharp as cardboard cutouts, and the desert air as clean and as clear as a mountain stream.

And it was whilst we were there, and on Thanksgiving Day - 24th November - amid all the good fellowship and conversation, that an event occurred which, even now, I can scarcely credit. And, oh, so often, I wish that fate had not conspired to bring it about.

With our two American friends, we had been invited to another country-club of considerable reputation some miles to the north of Tucson. There, we were to be the guests of an elderly couple - whom we had never so much as heard of, far less met - to celebrate Thanksgiving Day with a score of more of their friends and prominent citizens of the area. This, it appeared, was a ritual gathering and one to which it was considered a great honour to be invited. And indeed, it was.

Shortly before noon on the Day, we drove out to an impressive low, ranch-style building, for all the world like a Hollywood version of a millionaire's retreat, and were admitted to an elegant drawing-room, richly furnished in the Spanish style but with more than an element of frontier folk-lore and Tom Mix thrown in. Our host and hostess, as bent and as lined as Apache Indians, extended to us a quite touching brand of geriatric courtesy, although, I suspect, they knew nothing of my wife or me beyond the fact that we were visiting British; furthermore, I doubted at the time that our presence as their guests would register with them for more than an hour thereafter. But their welcome was diminished not one iota by any such qualifications and we responded, we hoped, with suitable grace and dignity. Frankly, we greatly enjoyed the attention we were accorded.

After many introductions, much congenial talk and not a little wine, we were ushered into the dining-room and sat down to a meal that was extraordinary both in content and in the length of time it took to eat. Throughout this gargantuan repast of turkey and trimmings, the majority of which was left on the plates of most of our fellow diners, and possibly because of our accents and novelty value, my wife and I were bombarded with friendly comment and questions. On my right hand an elderly, quite charming and remarkably well-preserved old lady of at least 80, whom everyone referred to affectionately as Addie, directed a constant stream of slow-motion anecdotes in my direction, a one-sided conversation in which my only contribution was to provide a willing ear and an occasional appreciative noise. Addie, God bless her, was also a 'toucher', so that I found my hand being clasped at five-second intervals throughout the entire meal, even when holding my knife, all of which had my wife, seated not quite opposite, in carefully controlled hysterics.

After a good hour's concentration, my veneer of courtesy and patience was wearing a little thin and I caught more than one warning glance from my spouse, who could detect the fast approaching moment when she knew I would switch off and lapse totally into silence.

At that point, Addie was heavily committed to a monologue on the virtues of the country-club's priceless asset, its Social Secretary. This paragon, a man of great refinement and discretion, apparently, had been with them for twelve years and was responsible not only for the day's choice of menu, the presentation of the dinner as a whole and much else besides, but also the running of the club generally. No one had a bad word to say about the Social Secretary, it seemed; he was good-looking, efficient to a fault, and a man of the utmost integrity - in short, a treasure beyond price.

As Addie waxed eloquent about this most admirable of servants, my glance wandered idly around the room in the hope that I might observe this virtuous creature. Apart from the score or so others at our table, the room was filled to capacity with parties, large and small, so that possibly 70 or 80 people were enjoying the remains of their Thanksgiving meal. A chorus of laughter then focused my attention on a group in a far corner, where a tall and rather elegant-looking middle-aged man was bending over a woman, his hand on the back of her chair. I remember smiling. This, I surmised, was the redoubtable Social Secretary. However, I could see nothing of his face and my interest in the man was only such as to persuade me to give him a casual and amused glance.

With the serving of coffee and the announcement that dancing was to commence on the ball-room floor, I caught my wife's eye and made a silent appeal for help, anything to put distance between the formidable Addie and me. As we joined hands the band, excellent by any standard, struck up with a medley of Trini Lopez tunes and soon a dozen or more couples were stamping and laughing around the floor.

It was at the end of one of these sessions when, flushed and applauding, we waited for the music to recommence, that I found myself within several yards of Addie's Social Secretary. Again the man had his back to me, but I could see that he was a person of about my own age, slim and elegantly attired, with a good head of white hair and a small beard, a fraction darker than his hair and not unlike that of the gentleman who appears on Kentucky Fried Chicken advertisements. He was talking to a woman whose upturned face registered almost as much reverence as had Addie's conversation. He bent down again and, using his hands and shoulders to emphasise a point, carried on with his remarks.

I stopped, and stared. The movements struck a chord immediately and it was at that moment I knew I had seen him before.

When the music started again I moved off around the room, my eyes riveted on the man's bent figure. The set of the head and shoulders. But, above all, the hands. My mind went back 40-odd years. Yes, they were the same, of that I was almost sure. But ... no, it just couldn't be! I was mistaken. It was impossible. My God! I must be mistaken! But ... could there be two people in the world so alike? Not so much in appearance but in mannerisms?

For the next several minutes, I tried unsuccessfully to manoeuvre myself into a position where I could look at him directly. My wife, meanwhile, who had become aware that she was being pushed about more than was either customary or necessary, looked up and noticed my preoccupation.

"What's the matter, matey?"

I nodded. "That chap over there. With his back to us. I've seen him before. No, don't look round now. We'll dance in his direction."

We pushed against the flow of dancers and were within ten or twelve feet of him when our quarry straightened and, after nodding to his companions, moved away and disappeared through a door. I caught a glimpse of his face but it was

unremarkable though with a likeness that was vaguely familiar. But, the mannerisms, the nod of the head, and the quick and engaging smile - I stood there,
disturbed and frowning. No, there was no mistake. I most certainly knew him. It
was the old Camel. Camel Elliot, who was supposed to be dead!

I must have looked very serious because my wife shook me gently by the
elbow. "Oi! It's finished!" She put on her American voice. "Let's go, Buster!"

As we threaded our way back to our table, she said over her shoulder, "What's
the problem?"

"There's no problem. Just a bit of a mystery."

"What sort of a mystery?"

"That chap I was looking at. I've seen him before and, frankly, I'm trying hard
to persuade myself that I'm wrong."

My spouse was, as usual, uncomplicated and to the point. "Well, go and speak
to him, for Pete's sake. Then you'll know one way or the other."

I shook my head. "No, I don't want to do that now. It may cause a fuss." I gave
it some thought, smiling for the benefit of Addie and the rest. "I'll have a word
with Al a little later."

I was in the front of the car with Al and our two wives were in the back. We
were half way home when I broached the subject, "Al, what do you know about
that Social Secretary chap?"

"Who, John Grenville? Nothing very much, except that he's very well thought
of. In fact, his name is something of a household word around here."

"Do you happen to know if he's English?"

"English!" Al sounded surprised and looked up from his driving. "I don't
think so. He certainly doesn't sound English."

Genevieve spoke from the rear. "He's from Boston, Al. He told me so when
we first met him some years back."

I turned. "When was that?"

Al thought, "We've been here seven years and he's been around more than
ten, I believe. Perhaps longer. Why?"

I hesitated. I didn't want to embark on a long explanation, so I simply said,
"Oh . . . nothing, really. He's so very like someone I knew years ago. I thought
perhaps he might be a relation, that's all."

And, as that seemed to satisfy everyone, we said no more.

Arriving back we all changed quickly as we were out again to a small reception that evening. It was a pleasant, run-of-the-mill affair but my wife and I were so involved in the usual social chit-chat that neither of us had time to consider or speak of the events of the afternoon. They were never far away from my mind, however, and after retiring around midnight I did not sleep immediately but found myself wide awake in the small hours, my mind racing.

I lay there for quite some time. There was a moon which defied description, making it almost daylight in our bedroom, and the silence was the silence of the desert. I became aware that my wife's regular breathing had stopped and, a movement of her eyes catching my attention, I saw that she was looking at me in the darkness.

She whispered, "What's the matter, matey?"

I shifted slightly and shook my head. "I was just thinking about that chap we saw this afternoon."

"What about him?"

I thought for a moment and then faced her. "Look, that character, unless I'm mistaken, was in my squadron forty-odd years ago. During the war. The winter of 1940."

"All right, so what? If you're so sure, why don't you have a chat with him?"

I paused again, undecided. Did I go on with all this? I said quietly, "Why? Because, he's supposed to be dead, that's why."

My wife raised her head and echoed, "Dead!"

"That's right. Dead. We both took off one night, just before Christmas, 1940. And he crashed and was killed."

"Then how - ?"

"Precisely! How can a chap who was killed forty years earlier, come to life as the Social Secretary in a country-club in Arizona."

We both lay in silence for a minute or two.

"Are you absolutely sure?"

I sighed. "No, not absolutely. But, I'm pretty certain. You see, it's not so much his looks, it's his mannerisms, his hands, his shoulders, the way he holds himself when he talks - oh, everything."

A prolonged silence hung in the room as the significance began to sink in.

"What are you going to do?"

"I don't really know. If he's the man I think he is, it raises all sorts of questions. In fact, the mind boggles."

"All right, then. If it's so much of a problem, forget about it."

I pulled a face in the darkness and said with an edge to my voice, "How can I forget about it, you mutt? It's like trying to forget a broken leg!"

"Very well, then. If it upsets you, arrange to meet him again and have it out. But, think carefully about what you're going to do if you're right. And also, if you're wrong. You could destroy his life, you know. And don't forget what the lawyers are like in this country if you're wrong. A million dollar damages bill is not my idea of a happy holiday!"

"I know." I nodded and lay back. Thinking. She was absolutely right, of course. It could be a dangerous business. But I just couldn't leave without knowing one way or the other. Finally, I said, "All right. I'll speak to Al in the morning."

I raised the subject at breakfast. We had established a routine of meeting in the breakfast annex in our dressing gowns, usually about 7.30 am. The room had a beautiful view across the golf-course to the distant mountains. Each of us would eat as much or as little as he or she thought fit, reading the morning papers meanwhile, mostly in silence. Good, hot coffee would be consumed in pints to the accompaniment of brief and often caustic remarks about the Government and the state of the nation - Americans seldom talk about the weather unless it's extreme, one way or the other. The events of the previous

day were very much on my mind but I waited for some time before the opportunity to start a discussion presented itself.

"Al, do you remember my mentioning that Social Secretary chap yesterday? I was wondering, could you possibly arrange that I meet him again? Personally!"

Both Al and Gen, sensing that I was more than casually interested, put down their papers and gave me their attention. Al said, slowly, "Sure ... I guess so. If that's what you want."

I exchanged glances with my wife and chose my words carefully. "You see, I believe - in fact, I'm pretty sure - I've met him before. If I'm right, then it raises some very awkward questions, with the answers likely to be more awkward than the questions. All I want to say now is, to me it's very important."

There was a silence.

Gen's curiosity was aroused, "You mean he's a crook, or something?" I saw Al's eyebrows rise almost into his hairline.

"No, not in the ordinary sense. But, it does concern his past."

When I stopped, my wife put in impatiently, "Come on, matey. They're entitled to know more than you're telling them, for heaven's sake."

I thought about it, then nodded. "Fair enough. I'll explain."

I then spoke briefly of my suspicions. When I'd finished Gen summed up, "I think we've got to sort this one out, Al. Look, why don't we go and have lunch there today? Then, we can call into that Wildlife Park on the way back."

As the arrangement seemed to suit everyone, Al telephoned the club and reserved a table for lunch, making no mention of our reason for visiting.

We arrived at the Country Club a little before noon - Americans eat at very uncivilized hours. We had an aperitif before being shown to our table where we ordered our meal. I looked around casually. The Social Secretary was nowhere in evidence.

The lunch was excellent and the conversation light-hearted. By mutual consent, it seemed, we avoided talking about the main purpose of our visit. Even so, all four of us, I'm pretty sure, were thinking about the encounter that was shortly to come - I most of all.

When we had finished our coffee, somewhat to my amusement, I watched Al clear his throat, straighten his coat, and go in search of our quarry. After he had gone we moved into one of the lesser lounges and stood around talking and admiring the view across the desert from a large picture window. Several minutes passed, then I heard Al's raised voice in conversation and approaching our open door, after which he appeared in the threshold accompanied by the man I wished to meet. As he did so, I turned, raised my head and put on what I regarded as my most welcoming expression.

Although I had not seen him face to face for more than forty years, in an instant I knew it was the old Camel. He looked straight at me and, for the briefest of moments, I thought I detected first puzzlement then a flicker of recognition. His head gave the merest of bobs - the old habit returning under stress - after which his face immediately took on the bland look of courteous interest. However, it seemed to me that his eyes were just a little apprehensive.

Al introduced the man, "John, I'd like you to meet some friends from England."

Camel didn't attempt to shake hands, but bowed slightly. For a moment, his hands, as large as ever, began to wander in their familiar way but he controlled them almost immediately as if aware that his gesturing might betray him. In an attitude of apparent relaxation, he made the conventional remark that it was always nice to welcome guests from as far afield as England. I explained that we had been present at the Thanksgiving dinner the previous day and had been so impressed with the club and its standard of service that we had insisted on returning. I'm pretty sure he didn't believe me, but he inclined his head in appreciation of my compliment and for a moment or two there was a hiatus during which, I suspect, five minds were totally absorbed with similar thoughts.

I went on, "Mrs Hill tells me that you are from Boston, a place I know well. My company in England have associates with offices in State Street."

"Indeed? Well, yes and no." Camel's eyes were smiling, but wary and his voice had a slight New England intonation. "I lived in Lexington for many years. However, I came originally from Canada - driven south by the harsh winters." His smile broadened. "So you see, I'm a blood-brother, more or less."

I returned his gaze levelly, noting that he admitted coming from Canada, but not being born there.

I went on, pleasantly, "You have never been to England?"

Completely in control of himself now, Camel's eyes showed no apprehension.

"Unfortunately, no. I've been promising myself, of course. But ..." He shrugged as though acknowledging an almost unforgiveable oversight, but I thought I saw in a quick glance, a hint, just the faintest hint, of an appeal that I should not expose him. And I knew, at that moment, that nothing would persuade him to reveal his true identity and that I should probe no further.

I began to taper off. "You bear a most extraordinary likeness to somebody I knew many years ago in England. So much so, that I thought you must be related."

Camel shrugged again and spread his large hands. "Alas, I have no family, more's the pity. So, I fear it's a case of mistaken identity." He gave his old Gary Cooper grin. "Shame, really! It would have been nice to have had famous, or, better still, infamous English ancestors."

At that we all laughed politely and, the conversation almost concluded, we exchanged a few pleasantries before Camel excused himself. After wishing my wife and me a safe and pleasant journey home, he inclined his head to each of us in turn and left.

When he was out of earshot, Al said, "Well ... what d'you think?"

I let out a deep breath and was aware of a sudden release of tension. "That's him, all right. The old Camel." I shook my head. "Who'd have thought it? But, he's taken on a new identity and not about to give an inch. I knew him, though. And he knew me - I'm almost certain of that."

Gen frowned, "Junior, are you absolutely certain? After all, it's been a long, long time."

I turned to her more quickly that perhaps I need have done. "Sweetie, I'm sure! Forty years ago, I knew that man better than he knew himself." Pursing my lips I struck a fist into a palm. "That's Camel Elliot, all right. And he's supposed to be dead. My problem now, is what to do about it."

I did not have much opportunity to dwell on the matter for the next three days. A week or so earlier, we had arranged to drive up to the Grand Canyon and, in the brilliantly crisp early morning of the following day, we set off north on what was to prove one of the most fascinating trips I have ever undertaken.

The Grand Canyon represents a picture of the world's evolution over countless millions of years and although I would hesitate to be termed a fossil addict, I am sufficiently knowledgeable about that particular science to be enthralled with what I saw and was told. The breathtaking setting and the stillness and silence of the vast arena of rock, sky and desert were especially appealing to me and I was so absorbed that I doubt that I gave Camel Elliot more than a passing thought. As I sat quietly and wearily in the front seat of the big Lincoln on our long homeward journey, however, my mind turned towards the past. I thought about the war, the squadron, my friends - many long since dead and gone - and Camel. And I knew I could not leave the matter unresolved.

I brought up the subject yet again at dinner. I knew exactly what I wanted to do. "Al," I said, "I want to go across to the Country Club again and have another chat with our problem boy."

Al nodded. "I thought you might. In fact, I've been thinking about that, too. Look, if Gen and I go with you, that puts this guy on something of a hook; he might consider his job in jeopardy and clam up. If you go on your own - a chance visit, sort of thing - you could say what you want to in private. I was going to have a word with Joe Hechinger - he's the big chief over there - but on second thoughts I suggest you play it off the cuff. Why don't you take the car, drop in on your buddy, and see what happens?"

Which is what I resolved to do.

The following day, I drove north into Tucson and, skirting the town on the western side, headed off in the direction of the Santa Catalina foothills.

I had no trouble in finding the Country Club and, entering the big open gate, drove up the long gravelled drive. I parked the car and walked with studied nonchalance towards the main entrance. In the cool, spacious foyer, it seemed that no one was about and I was on the point of trying a few doors when an attractive middle-aged woman appeared and, with considerable charm, asked if she could help. I explained that I was from England and passing through and, should he be available, I would be glad of a brief chat with Mr. Grenville, the Social Secretary.

She hesitated, smiled very professionally, and after weighing me up in the nicest possible way, said she would be happy to try to help, inviting me, meanwhile, to be seated in one of the adjoining rooms. As she was gone for quite some time, I had ample opportunity to examine the furnishings, wall decorations and pictures and to stand gazing across a broad vista of cactus-clad desert.

Presently I heard the sound of footsteps approaching and braced myself mentally for another encounter with Camel Elliot. However I was surprised and, I'm almost ashamed to say, a little relieved, to find myself greeted by a burly, pleasant-looking man in his early 60s.

Joe Hechinger introduced himself and shook my hand warmly, adding that he was mighty glad to welcome anyone from England, after all, had he not recently returned from there after visiting with his son, daughter-in-law and family? Yes sir. Where was it now? Alconbury, Cambridgeshire, that was it. Yes, sir, he had enjoyed the lovely English countryside, though there was a bit too much rain for his liking. Still, you couldn't have all that green without a lot of water; no rain - no green, he guessed. Not a bit like Arizona, no sir.

Almost as an after-thought he took my arm and added proudly that his son was a Major and flew 'these high-level reconnaissance birds, all over, well ... everywhere!' directing a conspirator's glance in my direction which hinted of hush-hush missions to the most sinister of places. But, hell, he was forgetting his manners. Would I like to join him for a drink in his office? To which invitation I replied that I would be glad to and we walked off together down the corridor.

In his office, with bourbon and ice clinking in our glasses, we chatted pleasantly and I told him of my own background of flying and my association with the 9th USAAF. Credentials established, I could do no wrong and we conversed on a variety of subjects, my companion declaiming with great good-humour, and in the most picturesque of language which had the ice in my glass melting, I suspect, in embarrassment. When it became obvious that it was expected of me to give a more precise reason for my visit, I explained that I had been a guest several days earlier and that I was hoping to renew my acquaintance with Mr. Grenville, the Social Secretary. Almost immediately I saw Hechinger's eyes narrow, but he did not at once reveal his thoughts. Instead, he asked casually, "Is Mr. Grenville known to you, sir?"

I replied, equally off-handedly, "I ... er, I met him briefly a day or two ago. As a matter of fact, he bears a quite remarkable likeness to a friend of mine, some years back."

"Is that so?" Hechinger nodded, his eyes unblinking and I suddenly sensed a new caution and alertness in his attitude.

"Yes ... in fact, I was hoping to have had a chat with him. On that particular subject."

My companion slowly moved an ash-tray quite needlessly from left to right across his outsize desk, his mind obviously busy. "Yes ... well, I'm afraid I'm going to have to disappoint you." He looked at me directly. "Yes, sir. You see, Mr. Grenville's not here at the moment. He ... er, he left. At a moment's notice, in fact. Two days ago." He gave a snort. "Probably the first time he's been out of this building in almost ten years."

There was a silence at the end of which I said carefully, "I see. Is there something wrong?"

Hechinger shook his head as though suddenly waking up. "No ... no, not as far as I know, anyway - at this moment in time, that is." He gave a helpless shrug.

"To tell you the truth, I just got a three-line note. Yesterday. Saying that he was going back east for an unspecified time. Because of family trouble - sickness, apparently. Which is not so extraordinary, I guess, except that he's not supposed to have a family - or, not that we know of. Moreover, he didn't leave a forwarding address."

The man jerked to his feet and thrusting his hands into his pockets, began to walk about. "Goddam it! All hell's going to break loose in this place in the next four weeks - two big wedding receptions, a convention, and I don't know what else. And this guy walks out without so much as a telephone call." He turned abruptly and faced me squarely with a note of appeal in his voice. "Say, is there something you can tell me about this?"

I shook my head. "Nothing, I'm afraid. You see, I'm here purely by chance."

Hechinger eyed me doubtfully for a moment, then grinned. "Sure. For a moment, I thought you were going to give me some sort of explanation." He wagged his head. "Because, sure as heck, I need a little comfort from somewhere." He spread out his hands. "What do I do? Fire the guy? Hire someone else?" He shook his large grey head like a buffalo scattering flies. "Who'd have thought it, for Chrissake?"

Well, that was that. I stayed another ten or fifteen minutes, then drove back to Green Valley. Al telephoned the club the following day and was told blandly that Mr. Grenville was expected to be away at least a month - the Club hierarchy were keeping their cards close to their collective chests. But, the tone of voice suggested that Mr. Grenville was anything but popular. No sir! Not popular at all!

Needless to say, for the next day or so all four of us talked quite a bit about Camel Elliot and my visits to the club; then, by common consent, we let the matter drop. A week later, with fond memories of Arizona securely locked away in our minds, my wife and I returned to Los Angeles and boarded our DC-10 for home.

CHAPTER SEVEN

In the days and weeks that followed, I'm bound to admit that the memory of Camel Elliot drifted into the background. I meant to follow it up but, somehow, once at home, it was all very much 7,000 miles distant and, as one or two problems developed in connection with my business affairs, I procrastinated and did nothing.

And so it would have remained had I not been confronted one morning by several paragraphs in the Daily Telegraph which informed me that Air Marshal Sir James Denby had relinquished his post as Governor of somewhere-or-other and was returning to Britain with Jennifer his wife, by yacht. The report went on to describe his war activities, his later service on the Air Council, his appointments on retiring from the Air Force, and finally, his prowess as a yachtsman.

When I put the paper down, it was as though the whole Camel Elliot affair had emerged from cover and was there before me in a spotlight. I said nothing to my wife at the time, but mulled over the circumstances of the whole affair, attempting to push it below the surface, so to speak. But, try as I might, I did not succeed until finally I had to accept that I would never be content until I had been given some satisfactory explanation of Camel's apparent death and resurrection.

But, by what means? Over the years, I had lost touch with virtually everyone with whom I had served during the war, so that mention of James Denby in the paper seemed almost an act of fate. It was possible, even probable, that he would know something about Camel's fate - more, anyway, than I did - but, even assuming that to be true, would he be prepared to speak on the subject, particularly after such a time interval?

After a little heart-searching, I talked it over with my wife then wrote off a letter to Denby, care of the Royal Air Force Club. He was the eternal clubman, I recalled, and I was pretty confident my letter would reach him from there.

I must say, he was prompt in replying. Barely a week had passed before I received a letter in the familiar, bold hand-writing I so well remembered from his signatures in my flying log-book. He said that he was delighted to hear from me and would be happy to give me lunch at the RAF Club the following Wednesday.

So it was that, almost three months after my encounter with Camel Elliot in Arizona, and more than 40 years after his strange disappearance, I took the train from Norwich to London, intent on fitting together the final pieces in a most unusual and very complicated jigsaw picture.

I arrived at the Club shortly before 1 pm. and gave my name to a receptionist. I had not been a member for more than twenty years and was surprised and a little dismayed to observe that the place had changed considerably, appearing now much more of an hotel than before, with the female sex much in evidence - in my day ladies were let in at the back door – reluctantly!

I had not long to wait. Denby appeared almost immediately and greeted me effusively, hand outstreched. "Junior! For God's sake! How very nice to see you again after all this time and how splendid of you to come."

I winced. The term 'Junior' seemed wholly inappropriate for a man more than sixty years of age. But, I supposed, old habits died hard.

He led me by the arm, talking meanwhile at the top of his voice, for the benefit of London at large, I suspected, and we walked into the main bar. There we stopped briefly and, after introducing me to about six faces, the owners of which, I swear, were sitting on the same stools when I was last there twenty years earlier, we ordered drinks and chatted agreeably about old acquaintances and by-gone days. I had resolved not to mention the purpose of my visit until the first spate of conversation had been exhausted. But, if Denby was aware that I was little on edge, he gave not a sign and had the courtesy not to enquire about the reason for my sudden urge to meet him.

Meanwhile, I was able to study him at close quarters. He had certainly worn well; still the polished, dark hair - a little less of it, perhaps - the even white teeth and the infectious, ever-ready chuckle. A little heavier than in his youth, he was by no means fat and was obviously active, both physically and mentally. All the old charm was there, too, the sympathetic ear, the attentive expressions and observations, and the blatant flattering of some undistinguished and remarkably undeserving former colleagues.

Presently, at a sign from one of the Club servants, he ushered me into the dining-room and we sat down to an excellent meal complemented by a good wine. All the time, conversation flowed easily; family affairs, the past and present state of the Air Force, political events generally, and recent developments in NATO, about which he expressed considerable concern. I was able to voice my own fairly strong opinions on some of the subjects and issues and he did me the courtesy of listening intently, appearing genuinely interested in my layman's assessments and points of view. Throughout, he kept my glass replenished and, if I had not known gentleman James Denby of old, I would have been greatly flattered by his thoughtfulness and attention. Finally, he motioned to a steward and, after instructing him to bring our coffee into the ante-room, he looked at me directly, his eyes suddenly shrewd.

"Junior, I keep having this feeling that I'm about to be got at." He grinned disarmingly. "Would you like to put me out of my misery?"

I hesitated. I would have preferred to have spoken my mind in a little more comfort and in the privacy of a corner somewhere. However, I nodded and, without preamble, launched into my tale.

I said carefully. "Last November, my wife and I stayed with friends in Arizona. Whilst we were there, I ran into a man I recognised as Quentin Elliot - the old Camel of our squadron of 1940. He was acting as a sort of manager of a rather swept-up Country Club." I paused and looked at him directly, watching his face for any reaction. "The same Quentin Elliot you and I know only too well was killed forty-odd years ago."

For some moments Denby said nothing, his face blank, his emotions completely under control. He was thinking hard, I could see that, but he did not give a hint of what was passing through his mind. Then, he leaned back, his nostrils dilating slightly, and I watched his fingers tighten on the polished arms of the chair. Rather surprisingly, his gaze wandered slowly around the room before returning to my face. "You're absolutely sure?"

"As sure as I am of anything these days, yes. Although I'm bound to say, he did not admit it when I spoke to him."

"Then you can't be certain!" It was just a remark, there was no edge or malice in his voice.

"I'm certain - because I know!" I heard my own voice articulating clearly and emphatically. "Camel and I joined the squadron on almost the same day, you may recall. I was one of the few chaps he felt he could talk to; in fact, I daresay I knew him better than anyone." Then, to reinforce my explanation, "There was a likeness, of course; although, after forty years . . . ! But, it wasn't so much his looks, it was his mannerisms, his general demeanour, his ... his body language, if you like. You'll remember it well enough." I leaned back.

"Yes, it was the old Camel, all right. I knew it at the time, and he knew that I knew."

Denby nodded slowly as if accepting the fact. "Then, why come to me?"

I shrugged. "I'm unsettled . . . terribly unsettled. There could be a dozen explanations, a couple of them too unpleasant to contemplate. It seemed to me that you are the only one left who might be able to help."

Denby looked at me steadily before smiling and standing up. Putting a hand on my shoulder, "Let's find a quiet spot, should we?"

We sat in two armchairs by one of the tall windows looking out on to Piccadilly, our coffee between us. When there was no one obviously in earshot, he said quietly, "Junior, you've put me rather on a spot. To be perfectly frank, I'm in two minds whether or not to tell you anything. Not, I hasten to add, because I want to be secretive but because, even now, others might be affected. I'm sure you understand."

I returned his gaze but made no reply.

After a pause, he went on, "Tell me, if you did, in fact, see Quentin Elliot, and I tell you what I think you want to know, what will you do?"

I thought, then shook my head uncertainly. "It rather depends. If the old Camel turned out to be a German spy, or if he took off that night and defected - something like that - then, I believe I'd take the matter further. I don't know how, or with whom, but I'd manage by some means. If there's some other explanation, then I really don't know, I haven't thought it through."

Denby leaned back in his chair and looked at me for a while, thinking. Then, he bent forward decisively and said, "Very well. I'll try to satisfy your curiosity but, on one condition. That it positively goes no further than you." He stared at me. "Everyone else privy to the secret, as far as I know, is dead - you and I are the only one's left. Do I have your word?"

I hesitated.

He looked at me levelly. "I'm sorry, I must insist."

I nodded. "All right. I shan't say anything."

As though clearing the decks for action, Denby called a servant and, without consulting me, ordered more coffee and two brandies.

Then when the table had been replenished, James Denby mashalled his thoughts for a moment then commenced, his eyes on some distant point on the ceiling.

"You will remember, of course, that the day prior to the eventful night was a brute - drizzle, mist, and so on. The squadron was stood down about noon and I drove into London with a car-full of the chaps shortly after 2.30. I dropped them, I can't remember where exactly, and went on to Air Ministry where I had a session with some friends of mine in 'Plans'. I stayed with them for a meal so that I did not reach this place, the Club that is, until about 9.30 in the evening. As soon as I arrived, I was given a message to ring Henry Parsons. You'll remember him, of course: he was Sector Controller at North Weald when we first arrived there and he later moved on to Fighter Command."

I remembered the gentleman well and nodded, allowing Denby to proceed.

"Anyway, I returned his telephone call and he passed the word that I ought to get back to North Weald, hotfoot. Apparently, Churchill had been on to the C-in-C personally, wanting to know what action was being taken against the Huns over-head who were making a damned nuisance of themselves. As a result he - Henry Parsons, that is - had been instructed to press into the air anyone he could find from the airfields north of London, those to the immediate south being completely out. He then went on to tell me that the weather was marginal at best but that it was likely to improve from the north. In his view, if he could get one or two off the ground from North Weald, Hornchurch and possibly, Martlesham Heath, he could later divert them into the Cambridge area or even further afield. I learned later that you had spoken to him and that Camel Elliot had also added his not too helpful comments."

Denby paused and, very deliberately lifting up his brandy, took a little of it and rolled it round his tongue before returning the glass.

"Unfortunately for you and several others, political pressure tipped the balance against good sense. In all, five aircraft, two each from North Weald and Hornchurch and one from Rochford, were ordered into the air - against their better judgement, I may say - and four came to grief, you included. One from Hornchurch managed eventually to get down as far away as Coltishall in Norfolk."

He sipped his drink again and replaced the glass on the table.

"Well, I was on tenterhooks as I had to hang about in this place waiting for Charles Benbow, the Director of Plans, who had arranged to meet me here at 10.00 pm. He kept me for an hour so that it was close on eleven when I managed to get away. I then had to find my car in the blackout and crawl at a steady fifteen miles an hour through north London, with a few near misses for company. Then, after the 'piece-de-resistance' - a land-mine in the road around Edmonton - I finally arrived at North Weald at around 1 am.

When I got back to North Weald, I went straight across the airfield to dispersal. It was still very foggy. Arriving at the pilots' crew-room, there was no-one there other than Thompson, the Engineer Officer, who was as near to being demented as anyone I've ever seen. He was pacing up and down like a caged animal and almost dissolved into tears when I arrived. At that time, your's and the other aircraft, having taken off at about 10 pm, were both overdue and Thompson had already heard from Ops. that you had baled out. There was no news of our second aircraft. Then, in fits and starts, for reasons I understood later, 'Tommy' then told me a tale that I could scarcely believe. It went something like this."

"He, apparently, was in the Mess when you were casting about, trying to find members of the squadron left on the station. He followed you down to dispersal and arrived there shortly before Flight Sergeant Bennett and a handful of airmen appeared out of the night to prepare the aircraft. According to him, it was so black and foggy that the transport driver had the greatest difficulty in finding his way around the perimeter track; consequently, he never thought for a moment there was any prospect of flying. He supervised the removal of the covers and when the aircraft were fit and ready, he was returning to his own dispersal office when he bumped into you in the darkness. He apparently said that it was the worst weather he had ever seen in which to fly at night and that you should refuse to take-off. You replied, something to the effect that you had been ordered to do so and that there was no alternative. He then continued to the pilots' hut and entered to hear Camel Elliot on the telephone. According to 'Tommy' he was in a terrible state and was loudly telling someone the other end that conditions were impossible and that it was death for anyone who tried. Furthermore, neither he nor anyone else was likely to do any good if, and when, they did get off the ground, the whole thing, in short, being a suicide trip for no good reason."

"There then followed a one-sided conversation in which Elliot appeared to be defending his position very emotionally though with little success, as it seemed fairly clear that Ops. were being adamant. Finally, Camel threw down the telephone and ran out into the night in tears, mostly of frustration 'Tommy' thought, though they may have been for other reasons, too. Almost immediately 'Tommy' heard your engine start-up and your aircraft move off and, after a time, the noise of a second engine, which in turn died away. Several minutes later the Adjutant arrived out of the night to see what all the fuss was about. It seems he had just returned from an evening with his business partner who lived in Woodford Green and had heard the noise of engines from the Mess. Thompson told him what had happened and he, too, was very unhappy about the circumstances of the flight. Then, whilst they were in conversation, the door was flung open and Camel Elliot appeared, looking very wild and distraught, carrying his flying equipment and parachute which he threw down on a bed. He had, apparently set off and, whether by accident or design we shall never know, had taxied full tilt into a blast pen, damaging his propeller. The Adjutant tried to calm him down by being sympathetic, but Camel was in no mood to be comforted, becoming so unreasonable that Van started to chide him gently about his attitude, finally becoming very firm indeed and lecturing him about responsibility and an officer's obligation to obey orders. At this, Elliot went off at the deep end and 'Tommy' was so embarrassed he left them to it. Walking away in the darkness, he heard their voices raised to such an extent that he hoped that the NCOs and airmen would not overhear the very undignified row."

"Arriving at his own office, 'Tommy' thankfully closed his door on the quarrel. But within minutes the telephone rang and the Adjutant ordered him to return immediately. When he arrived at the pilots' hut, Camel was lying face-down on one of the beds, sobbing his heart out, and the Adjutant had taken on a completely new personality. He was white-faced and commanding and he ordered 'Tommy', his old friend 'Tommy' mind you, to assist him to get into a Spitfire. In order that the squadron should not be let down by an officer who was a coward and who did not know where his duty lay, he would replace him and do what he could."

Denby paused and shook his head as though in disbelief. Then, after sipping his brandy again in a careful movement, he continued. "I need hardly tell you that 'Tommy' could not believe his ears. He had been very close to the Adjutant since the squadron had been formed, as you well know. He was aware that Van could fly and knew also that he was a rational and reasonable man. But the person before him had been transformed into some latter-day zealot; his eyes blazed in a frightening manner and when 'Tommy' opened his mouth to protest, the Adjutant grabbed him by the collar and shook him so vigorously that the poor little chap thought his last moments had come. Van then threw him into a chair and, still standing, bent over one of the tables and wrote very quickly a few lines on the back of a stray combat report. This, he put into an envelope which he thrust into 'Tommy's' hand, instructing him to give it to me and to no one else if he did not return. Taking the Camel's parachute and other bits and pieces, he grabbed 'Tommy' by the arm and dragged him out into the night, leaving young Elliot howling on the bed."

At this point Denby paused again and, taking out his handkerchief, wiped his brow and face. His hands seemed steady enough but he was clearly very moved.

Frowning, I bent forward. "Are you really telling me that the Adjutant, with almost no flying experience, took off in a Spitfire, an aircraft he had never flown before, not only at night but in weather which even the best of us considered impossible?"

When he nodded, I went on, spreading my hands. "I simply don't believe it. I can't! And what about 'Tommy'? Surely, he could have stopped him by oh ... I don't know, putting the aircraft unserviceable, even kicking a hole in the back end - anything!"

Denby put on an expression of sad forebearance. "Aren't you being wise after the event? Also, you're wrong in one important respect: Van may have worn an Observer's flying badge but he was very much a pilot in his own right, having flown privately for hundreds of hours between the wars. Why, he had even competed in the King's Cup Race on three occasions. No, you're quite mistaken there. Only his age kept him out of the firing line."

He looked at me earnestly. "And put yourself in 'Tommy's' shoes: an ex-airman with twenty-odd years in the Service, used to taking orders, and absolutely dominated by the Adjutant's authority and personality. He certainly thought about putting the aircraft unserviceable, he told me so, and had the damn thing been anything other than a Mark 2, which had its own starting device, he could have faked a problem with the starter battery. But, for whatever reasons, he did none of these things. In fact, he helped the Adjutant into the cockpit, giving him as much information as he could about the lights and switches and things, and between them they started the engine and off Van went. Somehow, he found his way around the airfield and into the air. After which, of course, nothing!"

I frowned. I simply could not believe it. What would persuade even the most single-minded man into such madness? Van would know nothing about the radio, or procedures, or anything other than flying the aircraft straight and level. His prospects of success were nil, absolutely nil! And he must have known it. It simply did not ring true. Denby saw the doubt in my face and waited some moments for my response.

Finally I said, "Look, I simply cannot believe that the Adj could have done what you are suggesting he did."

Denby put up his hand and said, "Let me finish. Then you can decide. As I mentioned, when I arrived back, both of our aircraft had been airborne about three hours which meant, in fact, that they were down somewhere, whole or in pieces. I rang Ops. who confirmed that you had baled out but they had no news of Van."

He took a deep breath. "When it was obvious that both aircraft were lost, 'Tommy' passed across to me Van's letter. Camel Elliot, meanwhile, had disappeared and 'Tommy' was beside himself, worrying about his part in getting the Adj airborne. I read the letter and knew at once that I had to take some sort of action. So, I swore 'Tommy' to silence and went in search of Elliot."

"I found Camel in his room in one of the huts beside the Mess in an almost suicidal frame of mind. Without much in the way of explanation, I ordered him to pack immediately and to leave the station. He was to go home and to remain there until I, or Air Ministry, contacted him. Rather to my surprise, he did so without so much as a word. He was very deeply disturbed - in a trance almost. I then went to see the Station Commander but he was out and apparently delayed by fog. Eventually, he arrived back in the early hours and, after hearing me out, we discussed our next move. Finally, we decided to by-pass AOC, 11 Group and go straight to C-in-C, Fighter Command."

"So, at 3.30 in the morning, we set off by car for Bentley Priory. We dragged the C-in-C out of bed and spent an hour explaining the situation to him, after which we left, neither of us knowing exactly what action he took there and then. Nor, indeed, did I care very much; I'd had my fill of Quentin Elliot, Esquire!"

I took a deep breath and for the first time, I heard the silence in the ante-room and the ticking of one of the clocks. "So, the old Adj disappeared and Camel lived on?"

"That's about it."

"And I did see him in Arizona!"

Denby nodded. "You could have done; it's a chance in a million, but he did leave for Canada within days of the incident and, as far as I know, he's still that side of the Atlantic."

"And the Adj?"

"He crashed within a few miles of North Weald, probably going out of control shortly after take-off. Not far from Kelvedon Hatch. There was just a hole, the only means of identification being the numbers on several of the Browning guns that were eventually recovered. Unbelievably, the crash site was not found until twelve months later, and then by accident, his aircraft having gone vertically into a pond in the middle of an isolated copse."

Denby remained silent for a time, examining his hands. Then he looked up and gave a wan smile. "So there you are. I hope it helps. As you know, the C-in-C is now dead, the Station Commander was killed over the Channel a year or so later, and 'Tommy' died in the late 60s. You and I, therefore, are the only survivors with any knowledge of the affair."

For a long time I sat there silently, thinking of the past and of the night long ago which, at that moment, suddenly seemed so close. I was still uncertain. There were too many loose ends. Aircraft and people were not written-off, just like that. They didn't change identity or disappear, even in wartime. There were records, enquiries, parents, relations, posting notices, friends and colleagues likely to be affected - all manner of people and procedures.

No, it just didn't ring true.

Denby saw that I was troubled and, after gazing at me thoughtfully for a long time, said gently, "Perhaps it would help if I told you of the contents of Van's letter. I hadn't meant to, but I think it only right that you should know. I'll have to paraphrase it but the gist of it was:

I am taking Quentin's place to spare us all. Tidy things up if I don't come back. He is my only boy. It's the only way."

I can't describe how deeply I was surprised and affected by Denby's revelation, the more moving as it was conveyed in a low, monotone. For a time, I was unable to say anything. Then, I heard my own voice, hoarse with emotion.

"The Camel! Adj's only boy? But - !"

Denby nodded and went on. "The following day, I called on Van's wife - they had a house not far from Kew Gardens. She explained that, before they were married in 1921, Van had had a liaison with a girl in 1919, the girl who was Quentin Elliot's mother. Camel didn't know of his relationship to Van. In fact, the Adj didn't know either, until 1925 when he happened to run across his former girl-friend in London and learned, with considerable shock, that there had been a child. By this time, of course, Camel had been given the name Elliot, after his mother's husband. Naturally, in the years following, Van took a personal but very private interest in the boy, assisting the mother financially and putting Camel through school. But, Camel knew nothing of all this; until a few minutes before the Adj took to the air. Small wonder he was nearly suicidal!"

Denby spread his hands. "So you see, Camel should have been a Vandenburg - and it was arranged, and very fitting, that he should go to Canada under that name. In a sense, therefore, Quentin Elliot did die in 1940."

As I sat there I felt an overwhelming tide of sadness wash over me and a hundred incidents in the squadron forty years earlier, began to make sense.

"So" I reiterated, "the Adj gave his life for his only son."

"Yes, I'm sure that is so. It was a deliberate act of sacrifice. A brave man himself, he was deeply wounded by the sight of his own son lacking in morale fibre. And, of course, knowing that in all probability Camel would kill himself if he attempted to take-off on that dreadful night. Yes ... the sacrifice of a loving and, possibly, a guilt-ridden father. 'Greater love hath no man ... ' and so on."

We sat in silence for a time, each of us toying with the remains of his brandy. Then, Denby straightened and said, "So, for the second time, there you are. It's a secret that we, alone, share."

He stood up and put his hand on my shoulder so that I sensed he wished me to leave. "And I suggest that that is how it should remain."

As we walked slowly towards the door he added. "And, if you're still a little uncertain about your own attitude, perhaps I should tell you that on the night in question, about 200 people died in London during that air-raid and fifteen RAF aircraft and almost 100 aircrew were lost on bombing raids over Germany. In the light of those statistics, 'Junior', I don't think either of us should indulge in the luxury of breast-beating, or making a fuss about one man who meant well and made the ultimate sacrifice, and another who will have to live with his conscience for the rest of his life."

Reaching the door, we parted with a nod and a silent hand-shake and I walked back down Piccadilly, numbed by unhappiness.

Several days later I received a letter from Al Hill, which was a little unusual as Gen had for several years taken over the duties of scribe. The reason was clear enough, however. He started off:

"I don't know if you ever followed up that business of John Grenville. However, I think I should tell you that some weeks after you left, he wrote Joe Hechinger saying that he had personal problems and that he wouldn't be back. Joe was fit to be tied, of course. Then, a few days ago, and quite by chance, Joe's secretary, Nancy, came across a paragraph in the New York Times which said that a man, since identified as John Grenville and thought to be Canadian, or possibly British, had called at the British Consulate, New York, gone into the men's room, and hanged himself.

"Hanged himself, for God's sake! And in the men's room! Poor, poor guy. And what a terrible end to your holiday. We are crushed - as you must be too."

There was much more, of course, but I couldn't bring myself to read on at the time. Camel! Poor, dear, tragic Camel.

What had I done?

A WELCOME
IN THE
HILLSIDES

A Welcome in the Hillsides

*I*n 1942, the author, when Tactics Officer at Headquarters 81 Group, wrote to Jeffrey Quill, who was then one of the principal test pilots of the Supermarine Company, inviting him to make a contribution to the Group's training manual on the subject of 'The Spitfire'.

Jeffrey wrote: 'The Spitfire is a plain straight-forward piece of mechanical engineering, built to carefully calculated strengths and tolerances. In this respect, it differs little from the Forth Railway Bridge or the humblest motorcar, and can be bent or even broken if grossly misused.'

What is little known is that the Spitfire – there were 24 Marks and 22,000 of them built during the Second World War, incorporating more than 50 variations of engines, armament, wings, hoods and other bits and pieces – had an engine life when installed in fighters, of 240 hours. This equated to about 9 months' flying time in an operational squadron – if indeed the aircraft lasted that long! Like the Lancaster bomber, whose average service life was 40 flying hours, that of the Spitfire was about the same, some lasting no more than a week, or even a day.

A single Mark, such as the Mark 5, seldom lasted in active service for more than a year, before being superseded by a more modern, more powerful design. If it lasted for the full 240 hours, a Spitfire would then be withdrawn from squadron use and moved to a Maintenance Unit, where its engine would be removed and given a major overhaul before being installed in another airframe as a 'second life engine'. As a rule, new airframes and engines were given to the squadrons most often in combat, and the second life aircraft and engines, to those units not in daily contact with the enemy.

This story describes the experiences of a young man who commanded a Spitfire squadron not in a front line area, whose unit was equipped with what he would scornfully refer to as 'second-hand cripples'.

Squadron Leader Tom Burgoyne is a fictitious character but his problems were real enough. As were some members of his squadron!

CHAPTER ONE

Paddington Station. 2nd September, 1942.

Tom Burgoyne, clad unseasonably in RAF greatcoat, gloves and service dress hat - it was easier than carrying the wretched things - dropped the suitcase he held in his left hand and the raincoat, Moss Bros. carrier bag and covered tennis racquet he clutched in the other, to consult the train departure board.

Ruabon, the man had said. Change at Ruabon! Ruabon! Sounded like a Parisian street of ill-repute. Ah! There it was - 'Swindon-Cheltenham-Hereford.. '

He read out to himself the list of stops together with the relevant platform number before picking up his baggage. Beside him, the locomotive, King Henry IVth, dimly green beneath three years of war grime, began to move off backwards at walking pace, in slow pursuit of a train which had just pulled out, vestigial puffs breathing from her copper-topped funnel. Radiating heat, she 'tack-tacked' slowly past, the flanges of her big 6 feet 6 inch driving wheels squealing with the first pangs of movement.

Burgoyne stopped. He loved railway engines and everything about them from their looks to their pungent, sulphurous exhalations. Particularly the Great Western 'Kings'. Wonderful, elegant, four-cylindered brutes, full of leggy character and great barking puffs. But why did the Great Western always put the driver on the right-hand side of the cab? Were the signals on that side of the track? He'd never noticed! Came with always travelling to and from airfields in the centre or the east of England. He would have to watch out.

He found an empty first-class carriage and installed himself in a corner seat next to a window heavily protected with thick lace-curtain material glued to the glass. Sensible, admittedly. Trouble was, you could never see out of the damn things. What with that and the stations having their name-plates removed, travelling anywhere by train had become something of a mystery tour.

He had barely settled in and glanced through a book he had brought when the corridor door slid back with a thump and a middle-aged gentleman, fastidiously dressed with bowler-hat, brief-case and umbrella, pushed his way in behind a suitcase. When he had disposed of his impedimenta, he closely inspected the seat opposite before sitting down carefully. He smiled in Tom's direction. "Doesn't do to sit down too hard these days, otherwise the train's at Reading before the dust clears."

Tom smiled in response but said nothing, aware that the other man's eyes were on his uniform and decorations. Sooner or later, he decided, there was going to be a conversation.

It was not long in coming, "I hope you won't think I'm being too personal, but you look remarkably young to be a Squadron Leader."

Tom barely suppressed a groan. This really was old hat. Instead, he smiled and answered easily, "Thank you for the compliment. In fact, it's all part of a fiendish plot to fool the enemy. Their spies see me around and report back that Britain has run out of adults to fly their aircraft." Then, in case he should be seen to be too flippant, he grinned and added, "To tell you the truth, I'm not quite as juvenile as I appear. I've been in the Air Force since 1938 - four years and three months, to be exact."

"And most excellently you have done, as I see." The man was knowledgeable as well as observant. Then, bending down, he lowered his voice. "You must forgive my interest, but many years ago I was in 208 Squadron. At the back-end of the last war, in fact. We flew Sopwith Camels in those days and had previously been Naval 8, changing over on the creation of the RAF in the April of 1918. We had some very good chaps then - Bromet, who was the Commanding Officer, Compston, Little, Draper - oh, and many others. Most have gone now, of course, although Draper gets himself in the news from time to time doing all sorts of outrageous things and being fined. Bromet's alive, too, although he must be getting on a bit now - aren't we all?"

Tom's eyes widened, his interest aroused.

"How very interesting, sir. I came across 208 quite recently in the Middle East. Poor things, they used to fly Lysanders in the Western Desert, but I think they've since changed over to Hurricanes - as a sop to the 20th century!"

Feeling an obligation to make some further contribution to the conversation, he added, "I came back from that area a few months ago and I'm now off to Wales for my first command." He was about to reveal the number of his squadron when he suddenly thought better of it. The posters were full of warnings - 'Careless talk costs lives', and 'Be like Dad, keep Mum'. He checked himself and continued more circumspectly. "I shall be back on Spitfires for the first time since early 1941. I'm looking forward to it, of course." To himself, he thought vehemently, 'Am I not!'

"I'm sure you must be; you are entitled to be very proud." The man paused before nodding pleasantly. "Look, as we shall be cell-mates, so to speak, at least as far as the Midlands, perhaps we can have a chat over coffee a little later." Picking up his paper in a well-mannered and not too obvious gesture of dismissal, he gave a final nod and turned his attention to the financial pages. Tom sat back. 208, for heaven's sake. What a small world. He glanced at the man's hands grasping the edges of his paper. Big, square-cut fingers. Camel hands! Triplanes, too, he shouldn't wonder. What had he done in 1918? Von Richthofen was supposed to have been shot down by a Sopwith Camel of 20 . . . something, he couldn't recall which number exactly. Perhaps, too, he had come across Dallas. And Collishaw. Now there was a pilot, my goodness! Heaven knows how many victories and still in the Air Force, apparently. Yes, the ex-Naval squadrons were reputed to be among the best in the Service in those days.

Tom's reverie was rudely interrupted by a jolt as the train moved off. After that, his attention was concentrated on the moving panorama of bomb shattered London until, with gathering speed, they moved into the outer suburbs and finally into the countryside.

Shortly after 2 pm. Burgoyne let himself into a coach of a small train which sat in a side platform at Ruabon. A Border collie with one white eye, a ticket on its collar and tied to a luggage truck, gazed at him soulfully, and a crate of pigeons cooed at him from around his ankles. Otherwise, he seemed to have the place to himself.

Barmouth, on the west coast of Wales, was not that far off, but he knew that there was a journey of several hours ahead of him through the mountains. No complaint about that though. He loved the Welsh hills and the quiet informality of the country stations with their farm-yard odours, their clanging milk-churns and their private platform conversations, every word of which could be heard the length and breadth of the train. How the little locomotive in front, with a funnel like a clothes-peg, was going to lug the five coaches it had behind it over the several hills and passes en route, he would never know. Still, no doubt they had done it before - a thousand times. With a more gentlemanly start, they were off again, the little engine panting away in fine style and taking the first hill at a run. Llanbedr, here we come!

Tom sat back, savouring the pleasures of the sunshine and the journey, his blood tingling at the prospect of commanding a squadron of Spitfire Vbs. Not bad at all at barely 22 years of age. And Spits! After Hurricanes, in the Desert, all as old as God, with Vokes filters and bombs - built-in headwinds! And Tomahawks - ruddy streamlined bricks! What a relief to get on to something half-way decent. He wondered if the aircraft would be in good shape. Still, he couldn't go far wrong; Spit 5s had only come into service during the Spring of 1941, so they couldn't be that bad, whatever had happened to them in the meantime. He shivered deliciously. The future was loaded with promise.

At Barmouth, Burgoyne changed trains. Two coaches, pushed by an engine with an even taller funnel, limped in from a siding. From Barmouth to Llanbedr, the line ran northwards and parallel to the sea. They stopped at stations with such tongue-twisting names as Llanaber, Tal-y-bont and Dyffryn Ardudwy and the scenery was such that Burgoyne was reminded of the Altcar Rifle Range near his childhood home of Liverpool - scrub-tipped sandhills, wide skies and windblown silence. Then, Llanbedr. The train rattled in, slowed, and stopped with a squeal. Apart from a door banging and one other voice, utter stillness. The sun was a lowering golden ball in the western sky. This was it! His new command!

He stepped down to the platform, his arms full of baggage, clothing and bits.

Flying Officers Herbert Jenkins and Roger Lash, the Adjutant and Engineer Officer respectively of his new unit, were there to greet him. Introductions

completed and pleasantries passed, Burgoyne was conducted to a small Hillman
saloon car in the station yard.

"The Mess is up on the hill about a mile away," the Adjutant explained. "D'you
want to drive, sir, or shall I?"

Tom said that he would, and climbed in.

They set off briskly with Jenkins in the front seat, hanging on apprehensively
to a door-handle. He'd experienced the wild driving of some of these fly-boys
before and had a wife and kids to think about. Lash, with his arms bracing his
body left and right, sat in the back, silent and watchful.

Within fifty yards, Burgoyne recognised his inherited staff car as one of the
lemons of all time. A good Hillman was quite a nippy vehicle, but this one had all
the get-up-and-go of a three-legged tortoise - a real gutless wonder!

He remarked evenly but with just a trace of acidity, "By George! This has seen
better days."

His quip was met with a stony silence. He turned and offered what might have
been interpreted as a smile. "I hope the aircraft are in better shape than this
wreck." Had the driving mirror enabled them to do so, Jenkins and Lash would
have exchanged swift and meaningful glances.

The following day, having enjoyed a good breakfast within sight and sound of the
sea, Burgoyne, accompanied by the Adjutant, drove to his office.

The administrative element of the squadron occupied a wooden hut midway
between the two Flights, 'A' and 'B'. He had met most of the officers the previous
evening and they had seemed a nice enough group. He had, however, sensed an
air of quiet reservation. Everyone had been courteous and respectful but there
appeared to be a rather curious atmosphere of detachment as though, whilst
happy to welcome him, they were not absolutely sure that he was going to be
around for very long. Later that night, in the silence and privacy of his hutted
bedroom, he had thought about it carefully but had decided that he was being
altogether too sensitive.

Once in his office and introductions to the Orderly Room staff completed, he
waved the Adjutant to a chair.

"Sit down Adj, and let's have a chat."

Flying Officer Jenkins, aged 42, had been a junior executive in one of the
country's largest confectionery manufacturers; not to put too fine a point on it,

Jenkins had sold toffee! Traces of his cockney upbringing remained in his conversation and accent. He was an ordinary, unadventurous, run-of-the-mill salesman-cum-clerk who, at the outbreak of the war, had concluded that to volunteer for a job as Adjutant, Intelligence Officer, or some similar post, represented his best chance of serving throughout the conflict and emerging with some credit and a whole skin. He viewed his new Commanding Officer with interest but with no particular enthusiasm. They came and they went. This young chap looked promising enough but only time would tell. He had, however, detected a gimlety gleam in the youth's eye which had triggered an alarm signal which, though muted, was loud enough to be heard; and heeded! Flying Officer Jenkins's antennae was a finely tuned piece of apparatus and had seldom been found wanting in the past.

Burgoyne settled down in his chair, "Who was the last chap in charge here?"

Jenkins named the officer.

"What happened to him?"

"He was killed at Dieppe, sir. Only a week with the squadron and on his first operational trip. Ran into to some flak over Dieppe Harbour and was seen to crash just behind the town."

Tom nodded and made some conventional noises of sympathy.

"And what about the chap before him?"

Jenkins paused delicately, his face without expression. "He was with us a month, sir."

"A month! And what then?"

The Adjutant hesitated, then chose his words with care. "He was . . . er, removed, sir."

"Removed! What for?"

"He . . . er, he went on a low-level sortie - a Rhubarb - and knocked off a whole herd of cows."

"He what? You're joking!"

"I'm not. He shot a whole herd of cows - French cows." Jenkins shook his head sadly. "You could see the poor things in his camera-gun shots, leaping about like spring lambs and collapsing all over the place. Blimey!" The man swallowed in unhappy recollection of the event before recovering himself. "Anyway, the film went up to Group, as they all do, and he left almost the next day."

Burgoyne didn't know whether to laugh or be serious. A herd of cows! Whoever heard of such a thing? He glanced at Jenkins, whose face was anything but jolly, and decided that it would be wrong to be facetious. "I see. And what about the chap before him?"

"He pranged!"

"Pranged!" Burgoyne sat bolt upright in his seat. This was becoming ridiculous.

"Yes, sir. He flew into some power cables on the way from Tangmere to Manston. The boys were going up there low level to refuel before doing a sweep over Lille. Didn't kill himself, but was badly knocked about. Be in hospital for months."

Burgoyne subsided in his chair.

"Good God! This is like some horror story. And what about the chap before him?"

The Adjutant brightened. He had his favourites.

"He was with us a year. Squadron Leader D.J.M. Bundred. First class chap. Did a full tour then was promoted and went to Group. Great fellow. You probably know him."

Tom nodded. "Yes, I met him early on. He was with 73 in France. But, to go back. You've had, how many? Four Commanding Officers in, what, six months?"

"Five!" said Jenkins, who knew each one and to the day.

"And I'm the fifth?"

"That's right, sir."

Burgoyne stood up, his eyes glinting. "Well, I have news for you. I'm one of nature's survivors. I intend to be here for some time so I suggest you all get used to the idea." He turned in the Adjutant's direction and put on a shark's smile.

"Perhaps you'd be good enough to spread the word."

Later that morning Burgoyne interviewed the Engineer Officer, Roger Lash. He already had an inkling of the man's past. Late 30s, he judged. A commissioned airman, almost certainly - probably a Halton boy. Good at his job but, from the look of him, pretty humourless. Wise in the ways of the Service, though, and careful! Lash could be relied on not to take risks. No errors of commission for Flying Officer Lash. If in doubt, do nothing - or as little as you were likely to get away with. He knew the type only too well. Like the well-known egg of the curate - good, but only in parts!

The man was pleasant enough, however. "I've got a nice aircraft for you, sir." Lash had a trace of west country in his accent, "Been saving it specially. Wouldn't let anyone get near it when I knew you were coming. And it wasn't easy, I can tell you." He flexed his knees. 'Vee, Viceroy', he added, mutilating the phonetic alphabet. "I've had the chaps give it an extra kick on the tyres," he went on, by way of indicating his light-hearted approach to the war in general.

Burgoyne nodded approvingly but kept his face straight. "Well, you sound convincing enough, I must say. But, I warn you, good Lash, your neck is on the block. For the past year I've been on the receiving end, so to speak. I've had a belly-full of Hurricanes and Tommy-ruddy-hawks in the Western Desert, so, for the first time in an age, it rather looks as though I shall have an aircraft with a performance roughly similar to that of the Hun. Approximating, please note. I don't even demand parity, which shows how magnanimous I can be."

Lash flexed his knees again, like a policeman. "You'll have no trouble with this, mark my words. You've flown Spits before, I take it?"

"Indeed, yes. I was on Mark 1s and 2s in the Battle of Britain. Up until 1941, in fact, when I was hustled out to retrieve the situation in the Middle East. With Tedder and one or two others, I should add."

Lash smiled thinly. This chap looked and sounded the part. Probably was, too.

"I'm sure you'll do very well here, sir. We've had a few COs come and go recently."

Tom shot him a glance. "Yes ... well. The Adjutant will be speaking to you all on that particular subject."

For the rest of the day Burgoyne toured the Flights and interviewed his officers. After that, he spent some time with the senior NCOs and the staff of the Maintenance Section. Everyone was warily courteous and circumspect in their comments about the squadron's present situation. Recently removed to Wales from the Channel coast in order to recuperate, the unit had lost its front-line Spitfires and had been obliged to take-over eighteen or so others of the same mark, mostly from other squadrons. These, at best, could be described as second-hand and, at worst, thoroughly clapped out. Serviceability was barely tolerable and the zip and zing of operational flying with the prospect of enemy sightings every day had clearly gone.

Although nominally 'operational' at Llanbedr, the squadron was in a back-water. The German Air Force seldom intruded into the Irish Sea by day and, when it did, its aircraft came singly. In consequence, the tempo of life had slackened dramatically and practice flying and training had become the order of the day.

Deciding that his new squadron could operate well enough without him, at least for the immediate future, Burgoyne announced to the Adjutant that he would be away for several days.

"I shall be flying up to Scotland to collect my laundry and some other bits and pieces I was obliged to leave there," he explained. "I shall also drop into 9 Group Headquarters in Preston and have a word with the AOC."

Unsaid, but perfectly well understood, was his intention of parading evidence of his new appointment before his chums at his old OTU at RAF Tealing, near Dundee, whence he had recently departed. What, after all, was the point of been given an operational command - and a famous one at that - if you couldn't crow about it just a little?

The following morning Burgoyne inspected the Spitfire Lash had so carefully preserved for him. It certainly looked all right from a distance, with a quite remarkable gloss to its camouflaged exterior. Two members of his crew were in attendance, both about the same age as himself. Tom approached the first man,

"Hello, what's your name?"

"Parrish, sir. I'm your rigger."

"And yours?"

"Jones, sir."

"Jones! You're not responsible for all the ruddy sheep around here, are you? Particularly the brutes baaing themselves silly at 4 am. outside my bedroom window this morning?

" The boy grinned. "No, sir."

Tom smiled in response. They were mates now. He held out a hand. "Right. Let's have a look at the Form 700."

Parrish handed over the folded document which contained details of the history of the airframe and engine and the aircraft's serviceability record.

Burgoyne inspected it closely. "This is a new 700. Where's the old one?"

The two airmen exchanged uneasy glances. "The Engineer Officer's got it, sir. It was full up."

"Full up! I don't like the sound of that. Let's see, 178 hours on the engine. That's not so good. It's not my usual practice to fly behind anything older than 100 hours, you realise that?"

He glanced up quickly to see two worried faces wondering whether or not to

take him seriously. Seeing the humour in his eyes, the two relaxed and, shuffling their feet, grinned.

"Right-ho! Let's have a look round."

Burgoyne walked to the front and inspected the leading edges of the wings and then the cowlings. He ran his finger over the metal and it came away greasy.

"What's all this?"

The two airmen looked at each other uncertainly. Jones cleared his throat.

"Oil, sir. Just a bit. Gives it a gloss."

"Does it now! Well, it's pansy, I'll say that for it. But it's not very sensible. You've just knocked five miles an hour off my top speed with all that guck. And with these new Focke-Wulf 190s rushing about like March hares, we need all the speed we can get out of our old Spit 5s. You chaps are trying to get me killed off, I can see that at a glance"

The two airmen said, "Yes, sir," in unison then laughed sheepishly when they realised what they had said.

Completing his external checks and quick tour of the aeroplane, Burgoyne said, "Right. I'll sign up now but, when I come back, I want all the cracks in the leading edges filled in and sprayed, and the spinner taken off, repainted and polished until you can see your face in it. That goes for the hood, too. Can't afford to mistake a 190 for a scratch on the perspex, can we?"

"No, sir."

Burgoyne studied them solemnly for some moments, then winked. "Okay. Now, if you'll be good enough to strap my gear in the back, we'll get this show on the road."

Ten minutes later Burgoyne was in the air passing over Harlech Castle. He looked down. How on earth did the chaps in those days make that sort of building with the primitive tools they had at their disposal? Time was no object, of course, and there were no unions to cock things up, which was probably a major factor.

He smiled into his face mask. A new drawbridge by five o'clock, master carpenter, or into the boiling oil you go! A powerful incentive. Perhaps he could start something similar in the squadron, with the Engineer Officer first into the pot. He had a feeling that a little boiling oil would do Mr Lash no harm at all.

To his left, the water of Cardigan Bay was mirror smooth and, in the distance, Bardsey Island was a small lump on the horizon. On impulse he lowered the nose and headed for the gap between the Lleyn Penisular on his left and the uplands to his right which rose to become Snowdonia. Diving to ground level, he flashed across the coast a little east of Criccieth, Lloyd George territory, he recalled. He hoped the gentleman was not at home. Low flying, he decided, was one of the joys of aviation, particularly in a Spit. The aircraft was part of you, like a suit of clothing almost, responsive, mettlesome and eager.

He scooted over a road where someone waved a white arm at him and, keeping to the contours of the ground, climbed away gently over heather and scampering sheep, his heart singing in sheer exultation. The Spitfire was going well. Everything seemed to be working as it should and apart from a little left-wing heaviness, which could easily be rectified, the controls seemed nicely balanced. He studied the gauges carefully and his eye detected nothing that was other than normal.

With the engine running fairly hard, but sweetly, he twisted and meandered among the multi-shaded blue, green and purple hills until, catching sight of Caenarfon in the distance, he pulled up and soared to 3,000 feet, lowering the nose gently so that there should be no negative 'g' to upset either him or his engine. Then back on an even keel and with just under 260 mph on the airspeed indicator, he flew in the general direction of Llandudno and, further on, the grey pall that he knew was Liverpool.

Crossing the coast at Colwyn Bay he headed out across the water to where he estimated Southport would be. He felt utterly at home. The 5b, he decided, was much the same as the Mark 2, a little faster perhaps, but nothing really noticeable unless you were prepared to push things. The two cannons were novel, of course - he had only flown the Mark 2a, which had the eight machine guns - but the long nose, the stubby elliptical wings and the touchy elevator, were exactly as of old. Good old Spit! Nothing like her.

He was gently humming to himself, his voice resonant in his ears, when he realised he was flying over the artillery range a few miles to the north of Liverpool. Oh, heck! He would be popular! Too late now, though. In any case, whoever heard of an aircraft being shot down by an artillery shell? Although on second thoughts, perhaps it did happen from time to time; after all, those who had the misfortune to be clobbered were not likely to report the event! With visions of red-hot lumps of metal flying above, around and beneath him, he ducked out of the area as fast as he could.

Eight minutes later, Burgoyne was in sight of Preston. He let down to circuit height, reduced speed and banked gently around the airfield of Salmesbury.

Putting down his wheels and flaps, he curved in on his final approach, held off, and touched down. A real greaser! And after well over a year, too. He felt smugly content as the Spit rolled to the end of the runway and he stopped, turned and taxied in. But, which way to go? The place seemed deserted. He chose to go left and found himself taxiing between banks of high grass or some sort of crop on either side of the perimeter track. Ye Gods! What a wilderness!

He came to some hard-standings, veered to the left then found himself going the wrong way. The radiator temperature rose in sympathy with his annoyance. Blow these people! Why couldn't they put signs or markers or something?

He taxied a further 800 yards or so, jinking his nose left and right to avoid running into anything, before deciding that he would have to stop. The radiator temperature was over the 100 degree mark and he didn't want to boil the engine on his very first flight.

Turning in at the next hard-standing, he applied the brakes and switched off. The airscrew refused to stop, however, and kept flicking over until, with a sullen rumble of the reduction gear, it went round the other way and clanked to a standstill.

In the silence, the exhausts ticked like a clock and Tom sat there breathing hard. Damn and blast! Throwing off his straps, he climbed out. He'd have to walk. But which way, for heaven's sake? The nearest building was a mere dot on the horizon.

As he stood there fuming, a car appeared in the middle distance and, approaching him, slowed down. Inside was a man in a dark-blue uniform, his face vaguely familiar. Tom poked his head into the window space.

"Wotcher! Which way is civilisation?"

"Over in that direction." The man nodded. "I'm going across to the Watch Office. Would you care for a lift?"

Tom thanked him and climbed in.

Once inside he saw that the driver was a pilot in the ATA, the civilian ferry pilot organisation. He was small, plump, a little florid and seemingly very ill at ease. In fact, he seemed to be an unusually diffident gentleman altogether.

"I shall have to leave my Spit where it is." Burgoyne explained. "It's just about to explode. I daresay I can do without fuel. Don't know why they can't put markers in these ruddy wildernesses." He turned to the man beside him. "Have you just flown in?"

"Not exactly. I delivered an Oxford earlier on."

Tom nodded. As an afterthought he enquired, "Don't I know your face?"

The man's left eye gave a twitch as though someone had trodden on his toe.

"My name's Mollison. Jim Mollison."

Burgoyne looked blank, but only for a moment.

"You mean . . . ? Good Lord! My name's Burgoyne. Tom Burgoyne. How d'you do?"

Two hours later, Burgoyne was back at Salmesbury. He had been driven to 9 Group Headquarters and had met the AOC there. Air Vice Marshal William Dickson had seemed a nice sort of chap; small, balding, quietly friendly and with no obvious delusions of grandeur. Over after-lunch coffee they had perched themselves on the ante-room table and discussed training objectives, methods, and likely operational requirements in the near future. Tom had decided that the Air Marshal was all right. Better than some he knew; pompous, brain-pickers!

Back at the airfield, he discussed his departure with the NCO in charge of the Watch Office who appeared totally indifferent to Burgoyne, his destination or his future.

"I shall be going on to Grangemouth in Scotland," Tom explained. "I don't really need refuelling now and I shall try to start-up on internals. If there's no sign of life from my neck of the woods in, say, 15 minutes, perhaps you would tow out a starter battery to get me going. I have a feeling that this could be one of those days."

The NCO, an old sweat, hardly seemed interested, his only response being a more than audible sniff which set Burgoyne's back hair bristling; towing starter batteries, it seemed, was clearly outside his terms of reference. For a moment Tom thought of taking the fellow to task, but good nature overcame irritation and he turned on his heel and left - smouldering!

Once more in his Spitfire, and somewhat to his relief, he managed to start up without incident and taxied back the way he had come. He then took off and climbed away to the north.

Burgoyne remained below cloud and wandered in a north-easterly direction, avoiding the larger hills and the ragged patches of cumulus that barred his path. A patchwork of shadows, mist and open countryside drifted beneath him and he watched it idly, humming to himself and deeply content.

As he progressed, however, the cloud became thicker and the tops of the Pennines disappeared into dark, forbidding mists. He then decided, reluctantly, to climb through and, opening up to 6lbs boost he trimmed the aircraft into a climb at 180 mph, put his head into the office and concentrated on his instruments.

For some minutes he jogged on upwards, his aircraft bouncing solidly from time to time in the up currents, before coming out on top at 9,000 feet to bright sunshine and a sea of small white dumplings. Not exactly what he was hoping for but better by far than creeping about down below, frightening the life out of himself. Stuffed clouds! He had a horror of stuffed clouds!

After a further 20 minutes or so, he caught a glimpse far below of open coun-tryside and then part of a coastline. Thank the Lord! Not having refuelled, he didn't want to lose himself and be worried stiff trying to find somewhere to land with only a few gallons left. Wouldn't do to prang on his very first flight as squadron commander, by George! He suddenly found himself in a cold sweat and chided himself gently. He should have been more precise in his fight-planning and navigation. Perhaps he was becoming too much of a 'guess-and-by-God-pilot'. He would jolly well have to watch out.

He finally recognised the coastline of the Forth and, descending quickly, turned westward and flew in front of Edinburgh and over the top of the Forth Bridge. A train lugging a long plume of white smoke was half-way across and he watched it with the interest of a schoolboy as it crawled towards the northern bank of the river. With total lack of passion he wondered what chance he had of hitting it with a bomb, were he so inclined. Not much, probably. The Germans hadn't done so well at the outbreak of war!

Then, Grangemouth. He fitted himself into a queue of Spitfires and, with a green light winking at him from the caravan at the end of the runway, curved in, touched down and taxied in.

His ex-Squadron Commander, an old and valued friend who had recently been promoted, ran the Operational Training Unit at Grangemouth. They met cordially and, after some bantering exchanges, retired to the Wing Commander's office to yarn and await the refuelling of Tom's aircraft.

Reminiscences came thick and fast. Back in 1938, Tom's companion had been a Flying Officer in the squadron Burgoyne now commanded. The unit was then equipped with Hawker Fury biplanes which, splendid aircraft though they were, were totally outclassed by some of the bombers already in service. During the annual Redland versus Blueland exercises, the poor outdated Furies could not even keep up with, far less catch, the Blenheim bombers who were doing the attacking. Talk about pink faces! Old Chamberlain certainly did the right thing at Munich, misled though he might have been. In 1938, the RAF couldn't have taken on Iceland, far less Germany! Even now, some of the aircraft laughingly termed operational were heaps of obsolete junk. Look at the Battle and Lysander, for heaven's sake! And the Blenheim, too, for that matter. Useless! Coffins, most of 'em. Same as in the First World War when the RFC didn't have a decent aircraft until 1917. Ruddy politicians! And the British populace, too - thick as two planks! With no understanding of what went on in the air. Or anywhere else, for that matter! Never would face up to reality - if Britain ignored Hitler he would go away. Disarm and appeal to his better nature. Ye Gods!

And that Labour clown, Lansbury, carting his conscience around Europe right up to the outbreak of war. Many of 'em still at it, too, with their never-ending pressure for leaflet raids on 'the misguided but peace-loving German people'. And good lives being lost dropping them! Pacifism? Disarmament? Wetness and cowardice masquerading as principle. No, people in Britain didn't deserve the devotion and bravery of their armed forces. But then, it had always been the same, hadn't it? Look at old Sam Pepys and the Navy, donkey's years ago.

Things were changing, though, thank God. But, for how long? Come the peace - if there ever was a peace - it would be back to square one again. Everyone as wet as hell and full of forgiveness. It was no good, they'd have to emigrate. Get involved in a little profitable gun-running. If people wanted to kill themselves, let 'em get on with it. Roll on victory and a little private adventuring.

Tom loved jawing and working up a passion. He had a cooperative partner, too. An hour passed quickly.

Back at his aircraft Burgoyne examined the travelling Form 700. Full fuel and . . . what? Three-and-a-half gallons of oil? That just couldn't be right. He turned to the airman alongside, standing with his head askew, looking at the entries he had made and very much on the defensive. "You put in more than three gallons of oil?"

"Yes, sir."

"But, you couldn't have! I've only been airborne an hour and the tank only holds eight, full to the brim."

The man shrugged. "We put in three full jugs, sir, plus a bit more. And each jug holds a gallon."

Tom's brows gathered. Almost four gallons! He'd never heard of such a thing. Usually it took one at the most - a gallon an hour was the rule of thumb.

He bent down and inspected the concrete between the wheels of his Spit. A few drops, nothing more. Certainly not three gallons' worth. Where on earth had it gone to? No! It couldn't have been filled properly back at Llanbedr. That would be it. They'd made a mistake.

He gave a grudging nod. "All right. I'll sign up and take it. I've only 20 minutes or so to my next stop. Nothing much can happen in that time."

Burgoyne took off and climbed to 2,000 feet, watching the oil pressure and temperature gauges like a hawk. The pointers, however, sat comfortably on their marks and the engine sounded as sweet as a nut. Everything certainly seemed to

be all right. He relaxed on to his dinghy-pack seat, shifting a little so that the CO_2 bottle didn't impinge on the bone of his backside. Why couldn't they design something more comfortable?

He crossed the Forth and picked out Loch Leven in the distance, with its castle in the middle and the airfield of Balado Bridge on its western edge. Mary, Queen of Scots had been locked up there. Still, if she would bump off her husbands, he supposed. Or, was she in it for that? Anyway, he could think of far worse places.

Setting his compass and adjusting his directional indicator he flew roughly north-east and, after five minutes or so, dropped his nose and dived to ground level. He was in an authorised low-flying area and part of the country he knew like the back of his hand. Oil pressures and temperatures forgotten, he raced at tree-top height across the countryside, soaring over heather-clad hills with sheep scattering at the noise of his approach. Down then into the dips and crevasses, keeping a wary eye open for the occasional pylon, the space, the colours and the sheer joy of speed, intoxicating. God! Life was worth living. And Spits? Super! Nothing like 'em.

When, in the distance, he caught sight of the silver line of the Tay, he pulled up steeply and settled down to a more gentlemanly speed. Below, on his left, was the Tay railway bridge and beneath his starboard wing, the ferry ploughed across the river at the head of a pale green arrow.

He avoided Dundee and let himself cautiously into the circuit at RAF Tealing. Another OTU, there were at least half-a-dozen Hurricanes about. Burgoyne treated pupils in fighters much as he would nests of cobras - with the utmost care and suspicion. Especially suspicion!

There was a sizeable hill in the Tealing circuit so that Tom complied exactly with local rules and regulations, taking his turn soberly in a queue of Hurricanes about to land.

After touching down he taxied in and saw at least three people waving to him from the balcony of the control tower. Friends of his, he assumed. They would know he was coming. A Spitfire 5b from an operational squadron created quite a stir at a Hurricane OTU, as Burgoyne knew it would.

Small groups of course students appeared to gather around and touch it reverently. Tom felt mildly superior and put on his most casual air. He extracted his belongings and gave instructions for the aircraft to be refuelled and pushed into the hangar for the night. He would be taking off the following morning at 9 am.

Later, he collected his laundry and completed his other business. After a prolonged and convivial session in the new Officers' Mess bar, he had an agreeable dinner with friends, after which they all took root in the ante-room and fought the war several times over.

Burgoyne, fortified by liberal helpings of 'the malt', waxed eloquent on the iniquities of attempting to fight the war in the Middle East without the proper equipment. What on earth was the use of putting Matilda tanks with two-pounder pea-shooters against German Mark IVs with 88 mm blockbusters? Bravery was no substitute for bullets, large or small. And what about the air? Hurricanes and Tomahawks were the equivalent of bows and arrows; the Huns were laughing themselves sick in the Desert. Our only hope was that the Germans would die of sunburn! And even at home, we had allowed ourselves to be caught napping with the new Focke-Wulf 190s. Down south they were running rings around the Spit 5s so that, in desperation, the Air Force was cropping superchargers, clipping wings, and allowing umpteen pounds of boost in an effort to bridge the gap. Cropped, clipped and clapped! - that's what the chaps were saying. Small wonder the engines were beginning to hop out of the airframes. No, Air Ministry always seemed to have its finger in and the further you were from London, the worse off you became in terms of equipment. God help the chaps in the Far East! Why, they were even flying the old Hawker Audaxes somewhere out there. Biplane Audaxes, for heaven's sake!

And back home, the Trades Unions. Disgraceful! With the 'Tiffies' having engine trouble fit to be photographed, there was that communist shop-steward chap - what's his name? – Douglas Hyde, or something like that. Fomenting strikes at Napier's at the rate of one a week. One a week! And, getting away with it, too! Democracy? Political clap-trap! Nothing more than a theory! A system constantly being exploited and abused by the unscrupulous. Fire had to be fought with fire, by George. Bring on the revolution! By gum, he'd have his little black book ready, that was for sure. The Douglas Hydes of this world wouldn't last a morning out if he were in charge!

Wow! This grog was powerful stuff. Locally made? Probably using extinguisher fluid! 'Strord'nary how it made you sweat. Phew! What time was it now? Midnight? Lordy me! How the time flew.

Tom had difficulty keeping the walls in focus. Gosh, it was hot! He'd jolly well have to go to bed - while he could still find it!

CHAPTER TWO

The following morning, with his head feeling like a barrage balloon, Burgoyne presented himself at the hangar. His Spitfire was on the tarmac with two airmen in attendance. One of them said, "I'm afraid you can't fly this, sir. It's unserviceable."

Tom frowned. "What d'you mean, unserviceable? What's wrong with it?"

"It's got an oil problem, sir. The Engineer Officer wants you have a word with him in his office."

A Flight Lieutenant rose to his feet when Tom entered. "I'm sorry sir, but I'm afraid you need an engine change"

"An engine change?"

"Fraid so, sir. It's losing oil through the breather faster than we can pour it in the other end. You used almost three gallons in 25 minutes flying, which is something I've never heard of before. You must have a gremlin inside hoovering it all up," he added in an attempt at cheerfulness.

Burgoyne put on a hurt expression. "What's caused all this? It was going like a sewing machine yesterday."

The man shrugged. "It's hard to say. It's not that old. It's probably had a right old beating at some time in its life, added to which it could have been left hanging around. Probably most of the piston rings have gone, with the remainder not doing their job. Whatever the reason, the oil is piss . . . er, spewing out. You can't fly that. It's not safe. Anyway, its oil consumption is way beyond limits. In short, it's had it! Finished! Kaput!"

Burgoyne thought, a frown clouding his face. "What about a new engine? How quickly could you put one in?"

"Take some days, I'm afraid. We don't carry Merlin 45s on this station. We use 3s here and the occasional 20, as you well know. It would mean getting one from MU and, after that, it would take at least a day to fit. Say three or four days at best, possibly more."

Burgoyne sagged in resignation. "Heck! And I so wanted to get back today." He pursed his lips. "I'd better get on to Ken Bills and ask if I can use one of his Masters. May I use your 'phone?"

Flight Lieutenant Kenneth Bills was smallish, plump, self-effacing and possessed of a pair of twinkling blue eyes. The sort of man who might quite successfully have appeared in an advertisement for Christmas puddings, he was, in fact, a distinguished TT motor-cyclist whose name was legendary and who had won a string of international events. He was also Navigation Officer at No. 56 OTU. Burgoyne explained his predicament and it was arranged that a Miles Master should be placed at his disposal. Moreover, as there was little of importance for him to do that day, Bills would gild the lily and accompany the Squadron Leader himself in order to bring the aircraft back. Take-off was fixed for 10.30 am.

With his belongings safely stowed away, Tom joined Bills at the wingtip.

"You fly it and I'll sit in the back. And exercise discretion. I'm destined for greatness."

He climbed into the rear seat and pulled the lever which enabled him to be hoisted well above the level of the canopy roof - the instructor's position.

Bills strapped up and connected the intercom. "Have you flown in a Mark 3 before?"

"No," replied Tom. "Pratt and Whitney engine, isn't it?"

"That's right. A bit different but very nice. This is a brand new aircraft."

"That's a relief." Burgoyne spoke with feeling.

They started up and taxied out, Tom up on his perch, taking in the view. He didn't really mind being flown by someone he could trust, otherwise he was a thoroughly bad passenger.

They took off. The weather was fine and clear with little more than half cloud cover - a real Scottish summer. Climbing through the gaps, they set course for the south.

At 5,000 feet, in the smooth air above the cloud tops and nicely throttled back, the Master ambled along at a steady 160 mph, placidly and without fuss. Having lowered himself into his seat in the rear, Burgoyne had little to do other than admire the scenery and watch the instruments.

They crossed the Tay and then the Forth before running into some denser cloud over the Lowlands. Climbing up a little, they went across the top and lulled into a stupor by the dull beat of the engine and the sameness of the white expanse below, Tom nodded off.

After an hour or so, a little of the firewater he had consumed the previous evening began to stage a riot beneath his parachute harness and he experienced a powerful urge to get his feet on the ground.

He pressed the intercom button. "Let's land at Acklington, Kenneth, old son. There's a minor rebellion going on in my midriff."

Bills gave a chuckle. "Serves you right . . . sir."

They landed at Acklington and Burgoyne attended to his needs whilst the aircraft was being refuelled. Then, off again and back at 5,000 feet with the motor lulling him into a torpor. Lord! He really must put an end to these large nights.

With neither help nor comment from his passenger, Bills flew south until the grey mass of Leeds sat almost immediately beneath him before inclining to his right and crossing the smoke haze of industrial Lancashire. After checking his gauges, he switched on his microphone.

"We shall need to refuel again in about 20 minutes."

"Very well. Why don't we land at Hawarden, near Chester? There's a Spit OTU there and with a west wind we shall be away from all this filth underneath. After that, it's an easy 30 minutes to Llanbedr."

They let down over the Mersey and Tom looked down with interest on some of his old stamping grounds. Cricket in the Wirral with that fine batsman Patsy Hendren; rowing on the Dee; and a memorable night on the outbreak of war, singing with a highly vocal Welsh choir in an impromptu if somewhat inebri-ated patriotic performance in the ancient city of Chester. No. 5 FTS used to be at Sealand, too, and he wondered if it was still there. Ye Gods! The times he had sat as a child on the grass verges of that airfield in the early 30s with the Avro Tutors and Bristol Bulldogs floating over his head. Aircraft seemed different in those days, full of character and waspishly pretty to look at. All brand new, too, by the looks of them. The Air Force had only taken to flying wrecks since he had joined up!

Hawarden was surrounded by Spitfires doing circuits and bumps. Tom looked at them guardedly from a distance and decided that they must be part of a new course. Bills, who shared Burgoyne's suspicions of the uninitiated, approached warily and, having received a green wink, landed.

Whilst his pilot supervised the refuelling, Burgoyne called on the Chief Flying Instructor - an old acquaintance if not a friend - and passed the time of day until Bills could be seen waving. He then made his farewells and walked down towards the aircraft. Climbing into the rear seat again he levered himself into the raised position whilst Bills started the engine and taxied out.

Three-quarters way round the perimeter track there was a diversion, obliging them to taxi down one of the subsidiary runways to the intersection of the runway-in-use, pausing there to receive permission to backtrack to the point of take-off. There being three Spitfires ahead of them, they waited patiently for their turn, Burgoyne wondering idly meanwhile if the Spits were going to make it before they boiled. With the offset radiator on the earlier types of Spit, it was necessary to cut taxiing to a minimum, coming or going.

With two of the Spitfires gone, the third back-tracked to the start-point, swung round and opened up immediately. Stationary alongside the main runway, Bills and Burgoyne watched it with detached interest.

After running about 100 yards, the pupil pilot in the Spitfire began to lose control. At full throttle, he neglected to counter the left-hand swing and when the aircraft began to swerve and drop a wing, he allowed the engine to bellow away flat out and froze on the controls. The Spit, sensing a novice at the helm, planted its port wheel firmly on the grass verge, whereupon, the rate of turn was increased immeasurably by the added friction. Within seconds it had reached 60 mph and was totally out of control. More to the point, it was heading straight for Bills and Burgoyne in their Master.

From his exposed position up aloft, Tom watched it with growing concern. The wretched thing was heading straight for them; in a matter of seconds, he would have the whirling airscrew in his lap.

Bills in front was watching, too, but had made no move to take evasive action. In any case, which way to go? The big Pratt and Whitney engine was just ticking over, like a cow chewing cud, and much the same as that bovine creature, it could not that easily be jerked into activity.

Galvanised into action, Burgoyne threw off his straps and was just about to vault head-first from his raised seat when the Spitfire struck with a bang that could probably have been heard throughout Cheshire and much of Flintshire.

The Master was hurled backwards in a circle and the Spitfire bounced off, losing its legs immediately, its metal airscrew producing a firework display on the concrete before gouging great chunks out of the turf. It then bounded, legless, fifteen or twenty yards in one monstrous hiccup before engine, airframe and airscrew stopped - abruptly. In a dying gesture the tail reared up, as if in protest, before slowly falling back to earth. For five seconds there was a numbed and horrified silence. The whole airfield looked on aghast and three members of two crews checked to see if they were alive or dead.

Perched ridiculously in the air, Burgoyne saw only his own airscrew turning unconcernedly. He said quietly, "Switch off, Ken. We won't be going anywhere in this," adding almost as an after-thought, "Are you all right, by the way?"

Bills nodded his head wearily in front. Burgoyne let his breath whistle out between his teeth before looking over his shoulder. "Christmas! He's certainly put a dent in us."

And 'he' certainly had. The Spitfire's airscrew had hit the tail of the Master and its starboard wing had struck a secondary blow on the trainer's fuselage. Being a wooden aircraft, the Master had suffered badly. The elevators and rudder, with much of the fin and stabiliser, were wrecked and the fuselage itself badly holed. From about four feet to the rear of Burgoyne's seat, the aircraft was little more than matchwood.

Tom undid his parachute harness and, with no particular haste, climbed out and slid to the ground. He tasted salt in his mouth and remembered he had bitten his tongue when the collision had occurred. He felt drained and on edge. In front, Bills was sitting, head bowed, his elbows on the sides of the cockpit.

The pilot of the Spitfire was motionless in his cockpit. Tom walked across to him. The aircraft engine smelt very hot and there was liquid of some sort on the ground. The exhaust stubs were still contracting with loud and regular clicks.

"Are you all right?"

The boy in the cockpit still had his helmet on, but had removed his face mask. He looked up slowly. There was a lot of blood around his mouth and nose, some of it dripping. onto his lap.

Tom noticed his hands were shaking. "Have you damaged yourself badly?"

"Not really." The pilot shook his head. "I banged my face against the front here. My straps didn't seem to hold."

"Have you got your harness release catch in the right place?"

The boy looked down and, hesitating, said quietly, "No, I'm afraid I haven't."

An ambulance and fire-engine came racing up. They stopped abruptly on the grass and figures tumbled out.

"Anyone hurt?"

One of the two medical orderlies was fussing about and several firemen were hurrying around with their equipment, looking for flames or smoke. Two staff cars then drew up with skidding tires and the Chief Flying Instructor and an elderly Engineer Officer dismounted hastily. The CFI spoke tersely to Tom.

"What happened?"

"He swung on take-off and the aircraft ran away with him. We were jolly lucky to get away with just a fright."

The CFI glanced at the shattered Master. "That, I can see!"

The Spitfire pilot had climbed out of his aircraft with assistance and the ambulance men were supporting him and saying something. Presently, one of them came in Tom's direction. "Would you like to come along to Sick Quarters, sir, and have a check-up?" It was more of an order than a request.

Burgoyne said shortly, "I'm all right and there doesn't seem to be anything wrong with my pilot."

"I'm sorry, sir, but the rules say that whenever there's an accident –"

"I know all about the rules," replied Tom tightly. "But we haven't had an accident. We were just sitting there minding our own business when we were run into. The boy there certainly ought to go. We're not hurt. Just bloody annoyed."

Through the crush of people, Bills appeared carrying his parachute. "That's the end of that one, I'm afraid. Pity. D'you think they'll be able to lend us another aircraft?"

Tom examined his watch, giving it a shake before putting it to his ear. "If they do have anything available, I suggest you use it to get back to Scotland. I daresay I shall be able to find someone to take me on to Llanbedr. There's just my kit to get. At this rate, it'll all have to back to the laundry."

An hour later Burgoyne sat in the CFI's office drinking heavily sweetened tea from a not-too-wholesome mug. Flight Lieutenant Bills had just departed in a Martinet borrowed from the Target Towing Flight, having discovered he had an evening appointment.

Tom made known his thoughts to the CFI, "I shall never understand why it is that some pupils have such difficulty taking off in a Spit. It must be one of nature's most docile aircraft. It swings a bit, to be sure, but not that much. Possibly it's something to do with not being able to see over the nose."

The CFI was less charitable. "Some of the half-wits going through these days would crash a tea-trolley given half a chance. Trouble is, they're scared stiff of the aircraft. Why, I'll never know. If they had to fly a 109, then they'd have something to worry about. That aircraft is a right . . . . " The telephone rang at his elbow and he stopped to nod in Tom's direction. "That'll be your new mount. I've got a chap to fly with you to bring it back. Another Master, I fear. The Nav Section had one available. You don't know how lucky you are."

The young man who was to accompany Burgoyne turned out to be only a year or so younger than himself. Even so, Tom felt something of a father-figure. The boy was standing in front of the Master and saluted a little self-consciously when Burgoyne approached. "Hello," said Tom. "Are you the bloke who's going to fly with me?"

"Yes, sir."

"What are you? An instructor or a pupil?"

"Neither, sir. I'm a staff pilot. I was on the last course but one and was retained for dogsbody duties."

"Poor chap! Never mind. The Lord decides. Do you know how to fly these things?"

"I think so, sir." The boy grinned a little uncertainly.

"Right. You fly up front then, and I'll sit in the back. And a word in your ear. I've already had two false starts today, so treat me gently."

"I'll try, sir. And, one other thing, where are we going?"

Tom's eyes widened. "You don't know? To Llanbedr. A little north of Barmouth. Take off and go west along the coast until we hit Anglesey. Then, left down the west coast of Wales until we reach Harlech. From there, we should be able to see Llanbedr. You've a map, I take it?" He grinned. "The important thing is to go through the clouds and over the mountains: not the other way round! All right?"

Tom did a quick tour of the aircraft, which was an old Master I with a Kestrel engine. By George! This really was ancient. One of the original Masters, he suspected.

After they had both climbed in and strapped up, the boy started the engine and taxied out. Sensitive to the touch of all pilots with whom he flew, Tom felt reassured by the manner in which his chap handled the engine and moved around the airfield. Nothing harsh; everything smooth and with consideration.

Engine and take-off checks completed, on a green wink from the airfield caravan they turned into wind and took off.

The boy climbed up and, after completing a circuit of the airfield, headed off north-west to run along the coast. Throughout, Tom watched and listened carefully. Normally at ease when flying, he had a curious feeling of apprehension. In the privacy of the rear office, his brows gathered. He was far too much on edge and that wasn't like him at all. He chided himself inwardly: come on, settle down Burgoyne. He wriggled into his seat and, hands on knees, studied the instruments. Meanwhile the aircraft, climbing slowly, buzzed ahead with a rather disconcerting shudder and rattle which came and went in cycles as though it was experiencing a bout of ague.

Tom frowned. He hated aeroplanes which shook, shuddered, rattled or vibrated. And this one, by gum, was managing to do a bit of everything - and all at the same time!

They had been flying for about ten minutes when Burgoyne's eye was caught by a movement on the oil pressure gauge. The pointer dipped suddenly then rose slowly to its former position. His senses immediately alert he watched it carefully and, as he did so, after one or two practice totters, the indicator gradually fell away until it was registering about half its original amount.

Taking care to keep his voice level, Burgoyne asked, "What does your oil pressure gauge read?"

In front, he saw the boy's head incline as he looked more closely at his own instrument.

"About 30 lbs, sir."

"And your oil temperature?"

"Coming up to 60 degrees."

"Right. Now, I don't know whether you noticed it, but your oil pressure has just about halved in the last minute. As it isn't instrument error, that means we should go home - pronto!"

The boy sounded surprised. "You want me to turn back?"

"Right first time, laddie," said Tom emphatically. "And now!"

"Very well, sir." The youth in front didn't really sound convinced of the need.

They turned gently but firmly to the left and, as they did so, the 'g' force, small though it was, seemed to exercise some malign influence on the pointer because it gave a shimmy and sagged further towards the bottom of the instrument until it was barely visible.

In the back, Burgoyne indulged in a savage, silent soliloquy. "Damn and blast the thing!" Then, for the benefit of his pilot: "Reduce your revs, and throttle back. This brute of an engine is going to seize on us if we're not careful. Tell Hawarden we have an emergency and want to come straight in. What's your temperature now?"

"Still 60-ish, sir."

"Okay. When the pressure dies away completely - which it's just about to do - we shall have about five minutes before the engine stops. There! You see?" His voice rose a little. "The temperature's going up now. Throttle back further, if you can."

On tenterhooks in the back and fighting an almost overwhelming desire to take over the controls, Burgoyne craned his neck in order to catch sight of the airfield.

"Can you see Hawarden yet?"

"Not yet, sir. We're about 15 miles away."

"Right. Keep as much height as you possibly can and look around for decent fields to land in - ones without power cables, preferably. If you have to drop her in, don't forget to keep your wheels up; we don't want to turn over or go waltzing through the far hedge. What's your temperature now?"

"85 degrees, sir."

"Mine, too. Hell! There she goes! It's beginning to shoot up now. Damn and blast it to hell and back!" Tom struck his glove hand against the cockpit coaming in frustration.

At a speed of 150 mph, the Master was letting down fairly rapidly with the engine still smooth and showing little signs of distress. This, Tom found surprising. Bearing failures or piston trouble you could usually hear - if only briefly! A major oil leak and total loss of lubricant could, in his experience, result in a gradual loss of power, deteriorating to the point when either the engine just appeared to windmill; or it gave a heart-stopping shake and the airscrew stopped completely, that being the end of it. Blast and damn! Why couldn't they make engines that worked?

Whilst his mind was feverishly considering causes and effects and, not least, where they might have to put down, the boy said, "I can see Hawarden now, sir."

"Fine. Keep your wheels up until the last moment and don't rely on your engine to get you over the hedge. If you run out of urge before we get to the airfield, for God's sake don't try to stretch the glide. Land, wheels-up, short of the runway."

"Yes, sir." The boy sounded commendably calm but tense.

"Right. I'll shut up now and let you get on with it. Shout if you want help."

Two minutes passed in vibrating silence with Burgoyne being onlooker to the horizon canting this way and that. Then, ever watchful in the rear, he felt the nose rise a little and, hastily glancing at the airspeed indicator, noticed a reduction to 120 miles an hour. It remained there, steady, with the aircraft on a steepish let-down. Presently, the boy said, "I think I can make it now. I'll put the wheels down in a moment or two."

"As you wish." Tom concentrated on keeping his voice calm.

The boy selected 'wheels down' and there was a hollow roar as the undercar-riage emerged and descended. Some seconds later, two green lights appeared and the aircraft began to drop steeply. Thank God something was working!

Tom shot a quick glance at the engine instruments. There had been no oil pres-sure for several minutes now and the temperature was 'off the clock'. What on earth was keeping the engine going? He found himself jerking against his straps, urging the aircraft on. Speed up! Keep the speed up! Keep going, you brute! Around the pilot's left shoulder, he caught a glimpse of the perimeter track and the Master gave a hop and a wallow as the flaps were lowered and bit into the slipstream. Speed up! Don't lose flying speed! His body straining forward, he willed the Master to stay in the air.

They were falling steeply now. Then, an enormous change of attitude as the pilot dragged up the nose. A swift glimpse of concrete, then - Bang! All the windows crashed and shook, Burgoyne's teeth jolted together painfully for the second time within 90 minutes, and they were back on the ground on all three points racing erratically up the main runway. In front, the airscrew suddenly flicked to a standstill - the engine had obviously given up the ghost.

Phew! God given relief! But keep her straight. Straight, for Pete's sake! That's better!

Brakes screeching, the boy corrected the wander and the Master began to slow down, first to a walking pace, then to a stop. Seconds passed in silence. Burgoyne heard the lad breathing heavily over the intercom and picked up the tremors in his exhalations.

"Well done, up front! Did you have any engine at all on your final approach?"

"I didn't touch it, sir. It kept going more or less to the end. But I didn't need power to drag us in."

"Thank the Lord for that! I suspect it would have been too bad if we had have needed it."

"It's a goner now, I think. Rock solid."

"I think so, too." Back in his role of instructor, Tom added, "Good show! You did very well. Don't forget to switch everything off, will you?"

"No, sir."

Back in the CFI's office, his equable disposition noticeably less equable, Burgoyne considered his next course of action. His welcome at RAF Hawarden was clearly beginning to wear a bit thin. Nothing had been said, but he could sense the invisible barrier. His host, known to him 'off and on' for some years, was indeed starting to regard Tom as something of a Jonah. In barely three hours the whole airfield had been brought to a standstill twice and, as officer-in-charge of flying, he was already one Spitfire and two Masters up the spout - he would naturally have to take responsibility for the visiting Master from Tealing. Nothing to do with Burgoyne, of course. The collision on the ground was a nasty thing to have happened, after which it must have been very upsetting for him to have had an engine die on him in the air. Could have been much more serious, too, if the Master had crashed and two lives lost.

But it was undeniable that if Burgoyne had landed somewhere else en route for Llanbedr, none of this would have occurred. And now, he was after yet another aircraft. What other aircraft, for heaven's sake? Masters were as scarce as hen's teeth at the best of times. Still, courtesy demanded that he should try to oblige the chap, he supposed. The Chief Technical Officer might have something up his sleeve. He didn't like to ask, but . . . !

Half an hour later, Burgoyne, with a scowl on his face and his hands deep in his pockets, watched in silence as yet another Master was towed backwards around the perimeter track from an outlying hard-standing. Oh, Lord! Another Kestel-engined, Mark I! And no newer, it seemed, than the one in which he had just been a passenger.

He eyed it with distaste and stood around for 50 minutes, kicking his heels, whilst it was given a protracted daily inspection. When the final signature had been written in the Form 700, he collected his belongings and went in search of his staff pilot. That young man he found in an adjacent crew-room engrossed in a James Hadley Chase novel, clearly involved mentally if not physically with some scantily dressed blonde urgently in need of succour.

Burgoyne interrupted his fantasies.

"Are you ready to brave the elements in yet another Master?"

The boy, to his credit, jumped up immediately. "Of course, sir." His enthusiasm was touching.

They walked out together. Burgoyne said, "I'll fly it this time; you can sit in the back."

The boy nodded. "As you wish, sir."

Burgoyne stowed his kit seemingly for the umpteenth time and settled himself in the front seat. He had never been too enthusiastic about the old Mark I since a friend of his had had the throttle quadrant fall off into the well of the cockpit. At the time there had been a lot of merriment over the incident, everyone with a mental picture of the pilot rooting about on the floor looking for the throttle and other essential items. In fact it had not been quite like that, but tales circulated quickly and tended to be embellished in the telling.

He checked over the cockpit and instruments. Lord above! This really was senile! It smelt very farmyard-fruity, as though it had been in the fields for months. In the back the staff pilot unconcernedly fitted himself in, comforted by the back and shoulders of the man in front who was a squadron leader and had a chest full of medals. He ought to know what he was doing. This was going to be nothing but a joy-ride.

Burgoyne started up and taxied out gingerly to the point of take-off, his senses razor-edged. He then tested the engine carefully and went through his cockpit drill. After that, it was straight on to the runway and off.

As he pushed the throttle through the gate, the engine really entered into the spirit of things, howling and snarling deafeningly. The aircraft accelerated quickly, the widely-spaced legs setting up a rocking waddle immediately before the Master rose into the air. There was no doubt about it, the old Kestrel engine of the early 30s really had a bite to it.

Having carefully cleaned up the aircraft and adjusted the throttle, airscrew-pitch and trim, Burgoyne settled into a climb straight ahead and sat listening and watching. He had not long to wait!

At about 1,800 feet, a minute puff of white flicked from one of the starboard exhausts. For a moment he thought his eyes were deceiving him. Then there was another - and another. In exasperation he thumped his fists against the side of the canopy and, uncharacteristically, indulged in a bout of sophisticated profanity. Then he lowered the nose, throttled back, and turned to his left.

In the rear, the boy felt the reduction of power and saw the nose fall and the aircraft turn. He looked quickly at his instruments. They seemed to be all right. "Something wrong, sir?"

"Yes. We've got a coolant leak. It's coming from up-front. Probably internal. We shall have to go back immediately before we overheat and ruin another engine. Would you believe it? Three years of war and never a single engine problem, and now this - three on the trot! What have I ever done to deserve it?"

Within minutes, the CFI at Hawarden had been informed that Squadron Leader Burgoyne was returning with a duff engine. With his nose within an inch of his office window and his brow like a thunder-cloud, the man's language was not for a young ladies' dormitory.

An hour later Tom Burgoyne, with set face and clutching his belongings in a brown-paper parcel, left RAF Hawarden in a Hillman staff car bound for Chester railway station. He'd ruddy-well walk to Llanbedr before risking his neck in another of their flying bedsteads. Bedsteads, indeed! He was doing them an injustice! Bedsteads you could rely on!

In the wooden building that served as an Officers' Mess at RAF Llanbedr, Flying Officers Jenkins and Lash, their day's work concluded, were indulging in a quiet after-dinner drink and comparing notes.

Lash remarked, "Odd about the Boss. He left Tealing this morning, since when we've not heard a word. He did say he was coming back today, didn't he?"

"That's what I understood. Anyway, we wouldn't have heard from Tealing had he not started off." Jenkins paused to give the matter some thought, his mind running automatically to pessimism. "Might have gone in somewhere," he added dolefully. "Wouldn't be the first, by a long chalk."

Lash shook his head. "Bound to have heard from Group if there had been an accident."

Each officer drank his drink in silence considering the various possibilities, Jenkins's inner eye focusing on yet another face in the CO's chair.

Lash went on, "I hope nothing's happened to that Spit."

Jenkins was instantly alert. "Why should it?"

"Well . . . no particular reason." Lash didn't sound too convincing. "Just a thought. That was the one we got about a month ago, from that Polish squadron and . . . ."

"All right. Say no more!" Jenkins was grinning maliciously. "What you're really saying is, after a Polish squadron, all they're fit for is crop-spraying. True or false?"

Lash bridled. "Well, it seemed all right. Nothing obviously wrong with it. Nothing on paper, anyway."

"The two Flight Commanders wouldn't have it." Jenkins's grin widened. "Blimey! If it was the Spit, I'd take some leave if I were you. Double quick!"

Lash's face clouded over. "Why do you say that?"

"Well, he struck me as that sort of chap. Rub him up the wrong way and he could be a right bar-steward. Me? I'd rather meet up with Dracula on a dark night!" Jenkins glanced dramatically at his watch. "If you put a jerk on it, you might just catch the 8.50 train out of here." He winked. "It's your last chance."

At 10.30 that night, Flying Officer Lash was called to the telephone. Having imbibed well, but not too wisely, he was at his lugubrious best. He picked up the receiver and eventually found his ear. "Flying Officer Lash here."

"Is that you Lash?" The line was a bad one but, after one word, Lash was in no doubt as to the identity of his caller. Like a slate being wiped clean, his mind cleared magically.

"Yes, sir." Lash thought it would pay to be friendly. "Where are you speaking from?"

"You might well ask, Flying Officer Lash."

Lash, his morale plummeting, decided not to; he knew he was about to be told. Burgoyne's voice, articulating clearly, came through with menacing clarity.

"I'm ringing from a railway station the locals are pleased to call Pen-em-mour', although that's not what it says on the station sign. Not far from Conway, anyway.

"I see, sir." Lash felt it prudent to keep conversation to a minimum.

"And, d'you know why I'm here, Lash?"

"No, sir."

"Well, I'll tell you - in basic English. First, it's because that Spitfire you lumbered me with was a heap of junk, as I'm pretty sure you knew. Second, because I've been in three aircraft since then, each one of which, for reasons I will not go into, damn near killed me. And now, something else has happened to me, Lash, and I want you to guess what it is."

Lash had difficulty in clearing his throat. "What, sir?"

"Come on, Lash. Be a devil and have a guess."

"I'm afraid I can't." Lash's voice was barely audible.

"My train has broken down, Lash. For the first time in 22 years of travelling by rail, my train has broken down. And here I am, cold, miserable, extremely hungry, and sitting in the back of beyond, waiting for another steam engine to arrive from God knows where. It's all been happening to me, Lash, it really has."

"It seems so," said Lash faintly, wanting suddenly to sit down.

"Right. Are you still there, Lash?"

"Yes, sir."

"Now listen carefully." Burgoyne suddenly sounded very brisk. "I want you to get that gutless wonder of a car of mine - another of your presents, I recall - and I want you present yourself at Caenarfon railway station. Not a driver or some other flunkey, but you! There, brother Lash, you are to wait, sitting in the car, until I arrive. Which may be three hours from now or it could be five."

"Tonight, sir?" Lash's voice was a cracked falsetto. "It's getting on for eleven now!"

"You don't have to tell me, dear boy. I know it all too well. You see, I've been travelling - largely due to you - for over twelve hours already, accidents included, and I'm beginning to get my second wind. You, on the other hand, have the simplest of tasks. All you have to do is to get your backside to Caenarfon in two hours from now. Where you are to stay, repeat stay, moving not one jot or tittle, until I arrive. After which, there will be a two-hour drive in the opposite direction. In fact, I doubt that you need concern yourself with breakfast tomorrow, that is assuming you have an appetite by then. Oh, and Lash."

"Yes, sir?"

"Whilst you're driving to meet me, give some thought as to what you're going to tell me about that Spitfire. And think hard, because, if I'm not satisfied with your explanation in every respect, you're for the knacker's yard, dear boy. You have my solemn word on that!"

Flying Officer Lash swallowed noisily.

"Caenarfon, you said, sir?"

"Right, first time, Lash. Caenarfon. Where the castle is."

Back in the ante-room, Lash exhibited all the symptoms of shell-shock. Jenkins's eyes widened. "What's the matter?"

"That was the CO. I'm to meet him in Caenarfon."

"Caenarfon! What, tonight?"

"Tonight!"

"Is he all right?"

"All right! You must be pulling my leg. He's a survivor, that one. I should have taken your advice and caught the 8.50."

Jenkins looked blank, then burst into laughter. He motioned to a Mess servant. "Another whiskey for Mr Lash. He seems to have come over all queer."

A QUESTION
OF
RESPONSIBILITY

A Question of Responsibility

At the outbreak of the Second World War in 1939, the age of officers in command of RAF fighter squadrons was between 27 and 35. By 1942, the age had dropped to about 24, with some successful officers being as young as 22, and very exceptionally 21.

A commander was not only expected to lead his squadron in battle, but also supervise training, exercise discipline and at all times control what could be highly volatile groups of very young pilots.

In addition he had under his command up to 200 older and more experienced NCOs and airmen. At all times it was necessary for him to restrain his own emotions, act as a role model, and command their respect. Moreover, as the war continued, additional problems arose. A commander was under pressure, particularly if his unit was not in a 'frontline' area, to provide constantly his better and more experienced pilots to act as section leaders for squadrons based abroad in such hot spots as Malta, the Middle East and the Far East. Very importantly, too, he was expected to cope with the unending battle to keep the older aircraft of his squadron serviceable.

It was against this background that, in the autumn of 1942 and under the command of a Squadron Leader aged 22 years and one month, a flight of Spitfires took off from their base on the west coast of Wales - and disappeared!

This true story, slightly embellished for dramatic effect, describes almost exactly the events as they unfolded.

CHAPTER ONE

The four Spitfires of Starling Red Section were at 22,000 feet some 30 miles north-west of Liverpool. In the lead Squadron Leader Tom Burgoyne, aged 22 years and five days, watched with some unease as his number two, Sergeant Davies, not for the first time, made a disconcerting swoop in his direction as the aircraft commenced a rate-four turn to the right.

The section, in finger-four formation, was practising steep turns at something approaching combat speed and the sergeant, a new boy, was clearly having difficulty in maintaining station.

As the aircraft re-arranged themselves, with numbers three and four lifting tidily across the top of their leader, Tom following his number two with a wary, frowning gaze; poised to take evasive action if the youth made another fencing lunge in his direction. He resolved to have a sharp word with that youth when they got their feet on the ground. For the next few trips anyway, he could jolly well practise on his Flight Commander and not his Squadron Leader.

Some 8,000 feet beneath and stretching from horizon to horizon there was cloud, masses of it, in a series of broken layers so that only an occasional glimpse of a very grey and inhospitable Irish Sea was visible. High above was an unending ceiling of milk-white cirrus through which the sun, a hazy silver orb, bestowed little more than a pale gleam. From the aircraft themselves, pencil-thin trails of white vapour streamed from eight banks of open exhausts to trace gossamer curves across the sky.

The Spitfire pilots, listening out on the GCI frequency, were maintaining radio silence; in combat against the wily Hun, it was a golden rule to say as little as was absolutely necessary. However, a vigorous battle formation at altitude with the aircraft wheeling and turning without verbal instructions, demanded a good deal of concentration from both leader and led, together with skills developed only by constant practice. Starling Red Section had been at it for little more than half-an-hour and already the strain was beginning to tell. Against this background of silence and concentrated effort it came as something of a shock to Burgoyne, therefore, when a voice spoke very distinctly in his ears.

"Starling Red Leader. This is Cowslip."

Burgoyne responded: "Cowslip. Red Leader. Pass your message."

"Cowslip to Red Leader. Return to base immediately."

Tom glanced at the clock on his dashboard and frowned. What on earth were they on about, for heaven's sake? 42 minutes airborne! He had planned to stay up at least an hour.

"Cowslip from Red Leader. I will, but only if you insist. Can you say why?"

"Cowslip to Red Leader. Your unit wishes you to return without delay. No other information available except to say it is not, repeat not, because of weather."

Tom's brows gathered beneath his helmet. Trouble up't mill? But, what sort of trouble? Mildly perplexed, he pressed his transmit switch. "Cowslip from Red Leader. Returning to base. Request vector and distance to 'Tulip'. Transmitting for fix. Now."

He left his transmitter on for the statutory five or six seconds so that the plotters below could triangulate his position, if indeed they needed to, to check his radar plot. Cowslip came back almost immediately, suggesting that they didn't.

"Red Leader. Vector one-nine-four; distance 32 miles."

Burgoyne waggled his wings in slow-time and the three aircraft of his section converged until they were almost within touching distance. To descend through cloud they would have to be in close formation, the closer the better.

Tom kept a weather eye on Davies, who surged towards him menacingly, stopped abruptly like a nervous colt, then sat pointing his port wingtip at Tom's face. Damn the man! Why did he always have to formate above the lead aircraft and not below?

He motioned the boy down with a sharp gesture and the Spitfire dropped obligingly, porpoising slightly, until it sat in the correct position. Burgoyne then glanced to his left. No problem there; they were old hands on that side and were comfortably tucked in, gazing at him mutely, the spinners of their revolving airscrews duck-egg blue blurs of motion. What elegant aircraft Spitfires were. He never tired of admiring them.

On instructions from their leader, Starling Red Section changed to channel 'A' on their radios and throttled back as Burgoyne let down gently, intending to pass across the top of 'Tulip' (the code name for RAF Valley, in Anglesey) at 15,000 feet. The tops of the cloud were at 14,000 and he recalled there being three layers, the base of the lowest within 1,800 feet of the sea. He would continue south into Cardigan Bay, losing height after which, when below cloud, he would turn east for his own base of Llanbedr.

Timing himself carefully he crossed over 'Tulip', invisible in the murk below, and dropped gently into cloud. With his head in the office, he concentrated on his instruments aware that the three aircraft left and right of him were in close contact, bouncing a little in the turbulence of the cloud, the denser parts of which blurred and sometimes obscured their shadowy outlines in silent flashes of grey and white. Satisfied that everyone was keeping station he continued down ... down . . . down and down, coming into the clear now and then, and finding himself in endless galleries supported by ragged pillars of cumulus, for all the world like monstrous, brooding stalagmites. Then everything grew darker and he sensed he was emerging into the uniform gloom of the sea, the mist and the rain.

He checked his descent at 1,500 feet and lifted his head. He was below cloud and over water. It was darkly grey in every direction, the waves beneath him a sombre impasto of lead scumbled with white. His section intact, he gave the appropriate hand signal and turned left, the curved wings of the pale-nosed Spitfires tilting together, as though activated by a common control.

"Marigold control. Starling Red Leader. Request vector for base?"

"Red Leader. This is Marigold. Vector zero-eight-eight. Cloud eight tenths at 1,400 feet. Visibility three miles."

Burgoyne flew on for a time before responding. "Red Leader to Marigold. I have you in sight. Running in in two minutes."

"Red Leader. Runway two-four. Wind light and variable. QFE one-zero-zero-four millibars. Clear to join."

Burgoyne signalled his section into echelon starboard and dropped down to 500 feet, crossing first the line of waves and sand to the west of the airfield then the boundary of the aerodrome itself, before pulling up into a steep turn to the left. He gained height to 1,000 feet and lost speed. Then, hood open, the slipstream roared and buffeted around his head. Down with the wheels, at left centre a single green light, airscrew into fine pitch; a curving approach and now the flaps. The aircraft shimmied before settling down. He held off. The boundary slid beneath him with 85 showing on the clock. The nose well up now, blocking his view ahead, the runway rising to meet him. The merest jolt; the tyres squealed for an instant and the aircraft rocked on all three points. He let the Spitfire roll towards the end of the concrete. In the mirror above his head, he caught a glimpse of his section floating down behind him - three dark swans alighting on a lake.

Burgoyne walked across the mud and grass towards 'B' Flight dispersal hut. He saw with some surprise that his own car was parked outside together with one of the smaller ambulances and two other vehicles, each in the camouflage livery of dull brown. The Adjutant had obviously come across from the administration block and the presence of the doctor suggested something pretty ominous. With an effort, he tried to discipline his thoughts.

Clumping across the threshold in his flying boots and pausing to remove some of the larger pieces of clinging mud, he found himself confronted by half-a-dozen glum faces, their owners rising to greet him.

"Let me sign up first." He turned his attention to the authorisation book and the Form 700 which were being held by Flight Sergeant Burton, who was trying unsuccessfully to look inconspicuous in a corner. Signing completed, he selected a hard-backed chair and squatted so that he faced the rear, his arms resting on the curved wooden frame. Something was very wrong; he could sense the tension in the air. He looked at them calmly, his stomach a flutter of apprehension.

"Now. Problems, I take it?"

There was a silence during which glances were exchanged. The Adjutant then spoke up. "I'm afraid John Beazley and five others of 'A' Flight are overdue."

Burgoyne's insides contracted. He tried unsuccessfully not to swallow and lowered his head to conceal his dismay. "Six aircraft?"

Jenkins nodded.

"What happened?"

Jenkins turned to Peter James. "You'd better explain, Pete."

Flying Officer James, deputy Flight Commander of 'A' Flight, cleared his throat and in a nervous gesture began to fold his arms, but did not quite succeed.

"John took off at 9.35 leading three pairs. He was due up for an hour on fighter-attacks and camera-gun. He was heard on channels 'A' and 'B' for some time. Then, after about an hour, he gave an indication that he was coming home. He never returned. No RT. No sign. Nothing." He paused. "So, we had you brought back because we thought you ought to know."

Burgoyne nodded, his face expressionless, his mind stunned. He glanced down to consult his watch. "Quarter to twelve! They'd have been airborne two hours and ten minutes. Not impossible, but unlikely." He turned to Morris, the Air Traffic Controller. "Did John say definitely he was coming back here?"

"Not in so many words, sir. But, he did ask for a course to steer, although that could have been to position himself."

"Where was he?"

"They took off and climbed up on a westerly heading. They went across to button 'B' - the GCI frequency - but didn't use the GCI, which is not out of the ordinary as they didn't require close control, apparently. We listen out on button 'B', as you well know, and we heard them off and on for about half an hour. Then, they went over to channel 'A', possibly because they knew you were airborne and didn't want to clutter up a control frequency. They must have been some distance away as they didn't come through too well on 'A' - being local control our power on that channel is pretty low. Then they came through loud and clear and asked for a vector. John was given zero-six-four, which put him south-west of here."

"So, they were down south and over the Irish Sea?"

James took over the conversation. "It would seem so."

"Have you checked with GCI?"

"Yes, sir. They confirm it. They had six aircraft about halfway across to Ireland for some time."

"And now, nothing?"

James nodded. Burgoyne pursed his lips. "What height were they?"

"They were briefed for 20,000 feet."

"You know that?"

"Yes, sir. I was at the briefing."

"Have you got the authorisation book?"

"No, sir. It's back at 'A' Flight.

"Who was airborne?"

"There was John, leading; Scotty Pelham-Groom, James Farrell, Prentiss, and Sergeants Nolan and Dent."

Burgoyne closed his eyes. Christ! Pretty well the backbone of the squadron.

He rose wearily to his feet. "Does the Station Commander know?"

"Yes, sir. He wants you to contact him as soon as you can."

"And Group?"

"We're on to them, too. They're checking other airfields."

Burgoyne thought, frowning. "Ask them to get on to the Irish. They might just have had to land over there."

Jenkins broke in. "That's hardly likely, is it, sir?"

Tom rose, grim-faced. "That's what we thought about that fool Malinowski, who made a present of an aircraft to the Micks and is still walking about the Emerald Isle on parole, having a hell of a time."

His voice was sharp although he did not mean it to be. He took a deep breath.

"OK. Let's carry on. I'll go and see the Station Commander and check that there have been no developments." He turned on his heel. "Keep me informed."

Burgoyne went to his car and drove off. He had to get away, to think, to arrange his thoughts, to decide. He drove around the perimeter track, his mind churning. When on the western side of the airfield and well away from any buildings or people, he stopped and got out slowly. The area was deserted. There were only sand dunes between him and the flat shore, after that, the sea. The thud and hiss of the distant waves were muted and rhythmic. There was the clean smell of salt air. He walked aimlessly through the marram grass, his hands deep in his pockets, his shoes filling, unnoticed. Presently, he stopped. The wind was fresh on his face and cool. Sand particles, flicked by the breeze, brushed his cheeks. Six aircraft! Dear God! It was unthinkable. Where? Into the sea? Grafted on to some mountainside? He turned. The distant hills, dotted with the still, white spots of sheep, looked closer than they were. They climbed away silently, green and grey, merging into the lighter shades of mist and cloud. Always the mist and cloud. It had been like that for days. Sometimes the slate-coloured peaks nosed through towards the sun, but mostly they remained hidden. The clouds and mist sat motionless day after day. Either that, or they rolled ponderously, shifting, settling again; always there, biding their time, waiting - waiting and watching. Baited traps for the unwary. God! how he hated stuffed clouds.

He found himself shivering. Waiting! Everything and everyone seemed to be waiting. Jenkins, Lewis the doctor, James, all of them. Waiting! Waiting for him to do something; to take charge, to lead, to act. But what was he to do? Search? But where? A thousand square miles of sea? A hundred hills? Where did he start?

Six aircraft! Or, more to the point, six pilots: His friends. Around the table with him only that very morning. Breakfast, a quiet yet intimate meal. John Beazley - small, smiling, naturally retiring yet authoritative. Three weeks only with the squadron. An ex-patriate Englishman from Argentina. To come halfway round the world to fight, only to be needlessly drowned, or mutilated against a Welsh mountainside. And Scotty! Scotty Pelham-Groom; old Etonian, tall, graceful, articulate; with that natural flair and ability so often the hallmark of the privileged. Had he gone, too? Snuffed out like a light, a very brilliant light? And Farrell - solid, dependable, granite-faced James. No dash or flair about him. But there always; a tower of strength, a rock, impregnable. Prentiss - . little more than a schoolboy; uncertain but full of bubbling enthusiasm and promise. And Sergeant Nolan - older; a regular airman, another Farrell, without the gloss of education or sophistication but a sterling man, nevertheless. And Dent.- callow, spirited Dent; new and untried but full of promise. Six of them. Gone, all gone! He shook his head. It was unthinkable.

And what now? A Court of Inquiry for sure, even in war-time. Endless questions; books and orders examined, blame to be allocated, a scapegoat to be found. Had he failed them somehow? Ought he to have been at that briefing? Surely not? He couldn't be everywhere. Yet he was responsible. He was the man in charge. Responsible! Responsible! The word kept repeating itself in his mind with the persistence of a metronome. He felt sick and miserable. This morning, nothing but optimism. Now tragedy and gloom. Six aircraft, half the squadron. What was he to do?

A fine drizzle brought him to his senses. He looked up. A dark curtain of rain suspended from a slow-moving cloud was advancing towards him. He began to walk towards his car, quickly at first then breaking into a run, his feet digging into the sand of the shallow dunes, a plan forming in his head. He had to get airborne; to do something - anything. They could be in dinghies, wet and freezing, or dying on some mountainside. He was running hard now, the adrenalin flowing. Action! Anything to supplant the nagging self-criticism uppermost in his mind.

He reached his car and tumbled inside, starting the engine with uncharacteristic harshness and racing off. His tunic smelled of damp wool and his hands were wet on the steering-wheel. As he drove, his mind darted from subject to subject. Questions. Explanations. Arguments. Letters. Letters? Yet again, letters to parents, to wives, to girl-friends. Lord! How he hated it all. 'Dear Mr Beazley: I deeply regret to have to confirm that your son . . . !' Oh, God! How awful! Who'd be a parent these days? He thought of his own parents and the effect such a letter would have on them. But it was his duty; his responsibility!

He pressed the accelerator down to the floor and two walking airmen moved quickly to one side of the perimeter track and stared resentfully in the wake of his racing car. Damn the thing. Why didn't it go faster?

The Station Adjutant ushered Burgoyne into Squadron Leader Oliver Rhys-Davies's office. The Station Commander, Uncle Olly to Tom and indeed most of the Officers' Mess, rose and advanced to greet him, his face lined with concern. "Come in, do. What a wretched thing to happen. Any further news?"

Tom shook his head. "Not yet. I've asked Group to get in touch with the Irish."

Rhys-Davies's eyebrows rose. "D'you think there's a chance?"

"Not really. But we have to ask."

Rhys-Davies motioned him to a chair. He was a man of 50 or more with a pug-dog face, an accident in his youth having severely damaged his nose, which was now quite flat. In civilian life, 'Uncle Olly' was a South Wales businessman of some standing with many interests and a thousand contacts in all walks of life. There were no flies on Uncle when it came to wheeling and dealing in the Valleys! As an RAF administrator he was sound and knowledgeable and he arranged life at Llanbedr comfortably for everyone and, in particular, for himself. He lived off the station in ordered opulence, on his own, and with more than his entitlement of servants. Tom liked the man and had a grudging respect for his powers of organ-isation and his single-minded devotion to his own interests. He recognised Uncle Olly for what he was - something of a gentleman 'spiv', but capable, nevertheless, and someone who could be loyal and helpful.

Rhys-Davies was saying, "The AOC's been on whilst you were flying, inciden-tally. He wants you to have a word with him when you have a moment."

Tom frowned. "Can't you deal with him, Uncle? I'm not in the mood for AOCs at present. I want to get airborne again almost immediately. I have terrible visions of those chaps sitting in dinghies or alive but in pieces on some hillside." He moved towards the telephone. "May I use this?" The other made a gesture of consent.

Burgoyne asked for 'B' Flight dispersal. "Duggie? How many aircraft can we muster? Five? Right. I want three pairs to search an area 40 miles square to the south and west at low level. The hills are out in this weather but we can have a shot at the sea. I'll fly myself, making the sixth, and I want you to arrange for take-off within the hour. Draw up a search plan and warn Group and anyone else who needs to know. I think you'd better stay behind and take charge whilst I'm away." He glanced at his watch. "I'll be down in 30 minutes for briefing."

Rhys-Davies asked, "D'you think they're in the sea?"

"I doubt it. But, again, we're duty bound to search." He punched his open palm in frustration. "I know I sound as if there's not much hope, but we must do something if only to keep our own spirits up. I can't just sit around here marking time."

The Station Commander's eyes softened. "No, I can see that. On the other hand, it would only compound our problem if you came to grief with several others besides. The weather's not good. You should be careful."

Burgoyne turned to the window and lifted his eyes to the heavens. It was driz-zling a little heavier now and the light was failing. "All right, Uncle. Point made. I'll exercise caution, as they say." He grinned suddenly. "For both our sakes."

The Station Commander dropped his gaze. "And what do I say to the AOC?"

"Tell him that I had to get airborne again before the weather clamped and that I'll report to him immediately I get back."

Rhys-Davies nodded, not without misgivings. If this young hot-head crashed or damaged himself, the fat really would be in the fire and the AOC would hold him, the Station Commander, responsible - that much was clear to him if no one else. His mind clicked into gear, weighing up the pros and cons. He mustn't appear obstructive, but he had a lot to lose. It was a tricky situation.

Aloud he said, "Very well. I'll do as you say. But I don't like it very much I'm bound to add. So, for God's sake be careful and take no unnecessary risks. As you very rightly put it - for both our sakes!"

Burgoyne leaned over a map in 'B' Flight dispersal. There were eight of them round the table, six kitted out for flying.

"Right. We'll take off in pairs at one minute intervals. Individual search areas shown on this map. Check in on channel 'A' then go across to 'B' when airborne. Fly at lowish revs at 240 indicated, and at 250 feet. If we go any higher we shall miss anyone sitting in a dinghy, in fact we shall have to come a good deal lower than that if we are to pick out Mae Wests in the sea. Number ones to do the searching; number twos are there mainly for safety reasons and are to fly in loose formation, fifty or so yards away. Fly carefully on precise compass headings and time your legs to the second. All turns at rate one; to the left on your first leg then left and right alternately thereafter. If you see anyone or anything, climb to 1,000 feet, or as high as you can, and report. If you run into heavy rain or if the weather goes completely sour, return to base. Don't, whatever you do, have an accident. I don't think I could stand another accident and the Station Commander certainly couldn't. Anyone with an emergency should climb up and give a Mayday on channel 'C'. Any mechanical problem, don't attempt to ditch, bale out! If anyone drops in the sea it goes without saying that the other aircraft remains until help arrives or until it is relieved. Stay up for not more than one hour fifteen minutes. All right?" There was a general shuffling and gathering of equipment. "Right then. Let's be off."

Burgoyne strapped himself in, Parrish beside him handing him his shoulder-straps, his gloves and his leather helmet and goggles. The weather was worsening. There was now a steady drizzle and the clouds seemed even lower, darker and more threatening. With raised face and narrowed eyes he gazed aloft with sombre thoughts. Was it really worthwhile? Then the vision of the dinghies appeared and drove him on. What if he were out there, vomiting, drowning by degrees and freezing to death?

He checked his cockpit and controls, started up, and taxied out. Sergeant Davies turned into line behind him, his airscrew whirling a vortex of spray in his wake and over his ducking crew. With each pilot jinking as a safety measure, they made for the main runway.

After running his engine and checking switches, Burgoyne lined up carefully on the runway and set his compass and directional indicator, he also wound his altimeter to zero - the runway was actually fourteen feet above sea level so he comforted himself with the thought that he was a little on the safe side. He nodded to Davies who was tucked in on his right and opened the throttle gradually but firmly until both Spitfires were racing tail-high and at take-off power towards the sea. They lifted cleanly and without effort and headed out across the waves.

With wheels retracted and his hood closed, Tom throttled back and reduced engine speed. His Spitfire, rather unusually, vibrated at 2,000 revs, a setting he was in the habit of using, so he drew back on the pitch lever until the engine regained its smoothness at something over 1,900. He then slipped the radiator flap into trail, trimmed the elevator and rudder carefully, and took in all the temperatures and pressures at a glance. Flying low over the sea was a hazardous business at the best of times and nothing could be left to chance.

He settled down, wriggling more comfortably into the un-giving dinghy pack between him and his parachute, and looked ahead.

When he judged he had reached his area of search, Burgoyne turned on to his new heading, started his stop-watch, and flew carefully, adjusting his speed and height. The clouds seemed little more than his own altitude and the drizzle smeared itself along the side panels of his windscreen and collected in minute, shivering swirls in the depressions of his bubble canopy. Beneath him the sea was leaden grey, the waves stippled with white and very close, the horizon vast and empty. It was damp and cold and he had a sudden spasm of shivering. Thank God he wasn't sitting in the water below.

He flew on, searching, gazing, checking, intentionally altering the focus of his eyes so that they did not automatically adjust to the far horizon. From time to time his hand would fall unconsciously to the knurled wheel which controlled the elevator trimmer to adjust it fractionally and occasionally he glanced to his right to check on Sergeant Davies, about fifty yards away and almost abreast of his own aircraft.

Shortly before reaching the end of the first leg they ran into a heavy down-pour of rain. Visibility being reduced to a matter of yards, Burgoyne pulled up slightly and looked anxiously for his number two. He saw immediately that Davies had had the good sense to anticipate his action and was rising with him and drop-

ping to the rear. With the shower soon over and back again at their searching height, they turned left at the standard rate one speed of three degrees per second. Steady on their northward heading they faced again the endless expanse of sea, uniformly dull, a shifting waste of glinting grey varied only by the darker patches that marked slanting curtains of rain. No dinghies in this area, that was for sure; no pin-pricks of yellow denoting a floating Mae West, no soaring red curve of a distress flare. Nothing.

The seeds of hopelessness took root. On and on. Now southwards again. Then north. On and on. From time to time Burgoyne jerked himself into attentiveness. How easy it was to fly by instinct and allow the mind to coagulate even within a few feet of the sea. He remembered only too well the occasion when, in the winter of 1940 and warmly muffled in an old Sidcot suit, he had gone to sleep in a Hurricane whilst on convoy patrol and had come-to, horrified, to find the ships not only missing but a good five miles astern. God! He remembered that all right! Spurred on by the memory of it, he concentrated his thoughts on the possibility of his friends sitting in the water below, sodden, freezing and barely living. With renewed zeal and with narrowed eyes, he searched more diligently the slow-moving wilderness in methodical sweeps, ahead, left, right, then round again and again and again - endlessly.

The feeling of despair growing like a cancer, Burgoyne consulted his watch. They had been airborne 53 minutes. Three more legs and he would have to return. They were all wasting their time, he knew it deep down, yet they had to try. He pressed his transmit switch. "Starling Red Leader to Yellow One. Any luck?"

"Yellow One to Red Leader. No luck."

"Blue One?"

"Blue One. Nothing to report."

Then: "This is Red Leader. Returning to base in ten minutes from now."

His companions acknowledged his message without words but with clicks of their transmitters. No fuss. No drama. Just resignation.

With the shoreline approaching and the airfield hangars grey-brown match-boxes in the distance, Burgoyne saw two Spitfires flying low down in the opposite direction and heading out to sea. Good for them! It was nice to see everyone was trying. Counting the six that were missing, that meant 14 Spitfires serviceable and flying out of 18. Not bad. Immediately ashamed of his thoughts, he grunted bitterly to himself. Eight serviceable and flying? My God, what was he thinking about? He ran in and, losing speed in a tight climbing turn, curved towards the runway on his final approach. He touched down and felt rather than saw Davies alongside him. Then the others were in his rear-view mirror floating, then taxiing. Four matrons with their skirts trailing.

An hour later, Burgoyne, sitting in the Station Commander's office, replaced the telephone thoughtfully. Rhys-Davies broke the silence. "What did the AOC have to say?"

Tom returned a thin smile. "Much as I would have said myself, I suppose. Poor chap, he was in a bit of a cleft stick."

"Cleft stick?"

"Well, the first part was easy enough; where had we searched and with what success? Then the sympathy bit. He was sorry for the chaps, of course. And I think he was sorry for me, although he couldn't quite bring himself to say so."

"Why not, for heaven's sake?"

"Why not? Well, it stands to reason. If I'm judged to be responsible at some later date, he would look pretty silly weeping on my shoulder now and having to shoot me at dawn a week or two later after the result of a Court of Inquiry."

"But how can you possibly be judged responsible?"

"Oh, really Uncle?" Burgoyne's lip curled. "Six chaps disappear without trace but because the Flight Commander forgot to authorise the trip in the book or some clown failed to sign a Form 700, the Squadron Commander gets the chop. You've seen it often enough. It's variously called passing the buck, or, more grandly, allocating responsibility. If officialdom wants to pin it on someone they'll find a way, you can bet your boots."

Rhys-Davies shook his head. "I think you're exaggerating."

"You know it's true, Uncle." Burgoyne found his voice rising. "Look what happened to young Briggs when we were over in Ireland on detachment. Took off in a Spit, climbed through 2,000 feet of thick cloud; then, at 4,000 feet and going hard, there's a bloody great bang up front and half the con rods coming shooting out of the side of the engine. With the prop stopped, he comes floating down through cloud and, by the grace of God, sees Ballykelly underneath. Then, in an attempt to save the aircraft, he tries to land, wheels down, overshoots and piles up in the next field. After that, if you please, in spite of my saying on the 765c that he did a first class job in very difficult circumstances, Group insist on blaming him, Briggs, for pilot error and damaging a Spitfire. Not Mr Rolls-bloody-Royce and his duff piece of elastic, but Briggs!" Burgoyne snorted. "Don't talk to me about can-carrying and higher authority, Uncle. Pilots are the easiest of meat; guilty as charged unless they can prove themselves innocent. And Squadron Commanders run them a close second."

Burgoyne rose, put his hands in his pockets and went to the window. Raining still. Quite unbelievable! Did it never stop raining in this wilderness of a country?

He turned. "Sorry, Uncle. I'm not quite myself."

"I understand. I probably would be, too, in your situation. Look, go and get into a hot bath and come and have dinner with me tonight. Make it about seven and bring Douglas Hayman and that nice doctor fella of yours. We'll break open a bottle of something decent and dull a few nerve-ends."

Tom smiled a little sheepishly. "Uncle, you're too kind; I don't deserve such treatment. But, getting back to the AOC, he passed on the news that there's no trace of our Spits landing away and the Irish have had no reports, either."

He turned away, his mouth quivering. "They're goners, Uncle!. Everyone single one of them. Six aircraft and six pilots? Just vaporised. What an utter, tragic waste."

Later that evening, Burgoyne, in a calmer frame of mind, drove his senior Flight Commander, Douglas Hayman, and Richard Lewis, the Squadron doctor - a lowland Scot in spite of his name - out to Rhys-Davies's living accommodation a mile or so north of the village of Llanbedr.

The house, a splendid though somewhat inappropriate dwelling for the Welsh countryside, was perched on stilts in almost total isolation and little more than 200 yards above high-water mark. It would live in Burgoyne's memory not so much for its square and flat-roofed profile but for its precipitous steps leading from the rocks below and its oak panelling, included no doubt to remind its owner, a boat-crazy businessman from Birmingham, of his imagined sea-going heritage. Tom, on his occasional visits to the place, always felt that without brass buttons and a peaked yachting-cap, he was grossly underdressed. It certainly smelt of the sea; there were piles of seaweed everywhere and, more often than not, heaps of less wholesome debris.

Uncle Olly had discarded his uniform and was looking very 'pukka' in dark flannels, blazer, and bow tie. He greeted them effusively with bright conversation, clearly determined to lighten their load. Tom, still a dull ache inside, didn't much feel like being cheerful. However, he was grateful for his host's efforts and was, as always, appreciative of the ordered comfort of the place and the prospect of a good meal.

Corporal Owen, well turned out in blue and white mess steward's coat, served the drinks with practised deftness and the odours of something good wafted in from the kitchen. Tom smiled to himself. If you had to go to war, this was the way to do it. Damn sight better - and safer - than flying!

They had barely exchanged a few well-worn pleasantries when a telephone-bell rang in the background and Owen, after disappearing to answer it, returned to announce that Squadron Leader Burgoyne was required. Tom nodded in Rhys-Davies's direction. "I told them I would be down here with you, Uncle."

The telephone, hanging on the wall, had a distinctly pseudo-nautical appearance. Burgoyne took the receiver and gave his name. The accent was straight from East London, Stepney. " 'ello? Guard room 'ere, sir. Corp'l Johnson speaking. We have a man 'ere who says he may be able to help with news about our missin' aircraft."

Burgoyne's heart quickened and he suddenly found himself in need of a deep breath. But, how did 'a man' know? There had been no public announcement - or private, for that matter. The police? Possibly. The word could have leaked out. He said, cautiously, "I realise he's probably with you now, but can you tell me what sort of person he is? Does he look trustworthy?"

"Er . . . I think so, yes. It's a Mr Ned Hughes, sir. Says he's a farmer in the district."

"I see. Did the police send him?"

There was a brief muttered conversation in the background between the corporal and farmer Hughes. "No, sir. 'e came of is own accord. That is, his wife sent 'im."

Tom smiled in spite of himself. "Right. I'll send my car up for him immediately. Explain to him that I would like to have a chat with him down here and that I would much appreciate it if he could spare the time to come and see me."

"Right. I'll do that, sir."

Burgoyne returned to face three pairs of questioning eyes.

"Someone at the guardroom who says he knows something about our aircraft." There was a brief silence that could almost be felt. "Take my car, Duggie, and fetch him right away." Burgoyne glanced in the direction of Rhys-Davies. "With your permission, Uncle?"

Rhys-Davies nodded more vigorously than was necessary. "Of course! Of course! You can speak to him in the other room."

Hayman put down his drink and headed for the door and for one whole minute the three remaining officers, saying not a word, stared vacantly at their shoes.

Farmer Ned Hughes was about 50, a small, wiry, tough-looking man with the dark, sharp features of his race. Neatly dressed in rough tweeds, he carried a large flat cap which immediately brought to Tom's mind pictures of men standing about in the general strike of 1926. He was clearly ill at ease in his surroundings.

Burgoyne greeted him with studied courtesy. "It was good of you to come, Mr Hughes. If we step into this room, you can tell me what you know. Sit down, please. Would you care for a drink?"

Ned Hughes, seldom known to refuse alcohol, shook his head out of sheer nervousness and perched himself on the edge of a dining-room chair, gripping his cap. His voice was musically Welsh.

"Well . . . er." He cleared his throat. "I have a farm, see. Round behind Tal-y-bont. Sheep, mostly. They're in the hills as far back as Llyn Bodlyn." Tom didn't recognise the names as the man pronounced them but let him continue with a nod. "Well, this morning, it was. I was out, pretty high up, see. In the area of Moelfre - that's one of the hills up there - when I heard a big bang, like. Not the usual sort of bang, see, but different like, and bigger. More drawn out. Well, I was in a heavy mist at the time and things sound different in mist, see. Don't they?" He raised his eyes as though seeking confirmation. "Anyway, I didn't pay much attention - we're used to having bangs round here, see, because of the slate. When they're blasting, there's noise all around. It comes back from the hills. Everywhere."

For some moments the man stared at the table, as though collecting his thoughts. "Well, I didn't go back for dinner. Not today, because I had something to do at the railway. Then, later on, when I got back, I mentioned the noise, I don't know why, to my wife. She said that was strange as they were not blasting today. Her brother, see, is in the quarries and she knew through him. Then she told me that she'd heard there'd been an accident at the aerodrome and she asked me if I'd seen any aeroplanes."

"I said to her, 'Good God, woman, what would aeroplanes be doing flying about the hills in weather like this?' Well, anyway, we talked about it for a bit, then my wife said I should come and speak to someone as she had heard that some boys had probably been killed. Well, anyway, so I came and . . . ." At this point Ned Hughes petered out.

Burgoyne nodded courteously, his eyes bright. "What time was this, Mr Hughes?"

"Oh, 'bout quarter-to-eleven, I should think. About then, anyway. Difficult to say, really."

"And did you hear the sound of aircraft flying?"

The man thought, his brows gathered. "Not really. Not loud noises, anyway. Though I do remember a sort of . . . of whistle."

"What sort of whistle? A dog whistle?"

"Oh, no. Not that sort of whistle. A sort of cooin' whistle, if you know what I mean. Something like a cuckoo, without the wobble bit. Though I could have been mistaken. I was in cloud, see, and things sound different in cloud."

Burgoyne nodded encouragingly. "And have you any idea of how far away the bangs were? I mean, were they close, or a long way away?

Mr Hughes shook his head slowly. "Difficult to say, really. It was like a rumble. Like thunder, almost. And it seemed to come from all around. No, it wasn't close . . . like 100 yards or anything like that. But I couldn't say how far it was."

"And you heard no engine noises?" Tom's eyebrows were questioning. He paused. "You see, Mr Hughes, there were six aircraft, or so we think, and they would have made quite a bit of noise, even allowing for the fact that they were throttled back and descending."

The man thought again, obviously wishing to agree but unable to do so. "I can't say I heard engine noises, but I remember the whistle. Say for ten, twenty seconds; something like that. And another thing. I was standing by one of the streams which run down from the lake, see. It goes fairly fast about there, so there was this sound of water. To drown out other noise, see. But not the whistle. Or the bangs."

"And did the whistle end with the bangs?"

The man stared again at the table. He was clearly becoming embarrassed. "Oh, I don't know really. I wasn't paying a lot of attention to bangs at that time."

Burgoyne grimaced patiently. "Of course not. You're being very helpful Mr Hughes. Look. If I get you a map of the area, could you point out where you were and give me an idea of where the sounds came from? You see, if those aircraft crashed into the mountains, Mr Hughes, some of the pilots could still be alive and we have to get to them as quickly as possible."

The man nodded vigorously. "Yes, yes, I quite see that."

Tom rose quickly and walked into the next room. "Uncle. Have you an Ordnance Survey map of this area?"

"Ordnance Survey! I believe I have an old mile-to-an-inch somewhere." He rummaged in a drawer. "Here we are? Pretty old. But the mountains don't move around much, do they?" He looked up expectantly. "Are we getting anywhere?"

"We could be." Tom took it from him quickly and disappeared to spread it out on the dining-room table.

"Now, Mr Hughes. Would you show me approximately where you were when you heard the noises?"

The man stared at the map vacantly and Tom, with the first real spasm of impatience, realised that map-reading was going to present difficulties. After some moments, he pointed with his own finger. "Let me help you. There's Llanbedr. All right? You said you had a farm at the back of - where?"

The farmer placed a calloused finger over an area south of the airfield. "I'm there, about. Tal-y-bont. My farm, see. And I was walking off the mountain road that runs beneath this hill I was telling you about, Moelfre. It's getting on for 2,000 feet up there though I was nowhere near the top, you understand." He looked more closely, his eyes wrinkling. "Is the blue line a river, or something?"

"That's right. That would be the stream you were talking about, going to or coming from the lake. Lin, something."

"Llyn Bodlyn."

"Now. With this pencil, mark where you think you were."

Ned Hughes hesitated, then scratched a cross on the paper and Burgoyne found himself exhaling with relief. "Well done, Mr Hughes. Now, if you'll bear with me, we'll try to establish exactly where we go from here. Can you spare another fifteen minutes?"

Encouraged, the older man nodded and Burgoyne sat down beside him and became all brisk and to the point. Gently but firmly, and at times with barely concealed impatience, he guided and cajoled the farmer into revealing everything he knew of the area and the likely direction of the bangs and whistles. Finally, he threw down his pencil and leaned back.

"Fine! Now, Mr Hughes, I shall probably organise a search-party tonight which will move out first thing tomorrow morning." He raised his eyebrows. "I would be grateful if you would consider coming along with us. Would you be able to do that?"

"Of course, I'd be glad to."

"Splendid? Now, I'm going to write down your address and telephone number and when I've discussed this matter with my colleagues, I'll ring you later tonight. All right?"

Sensing that he was being dismissed, Ned Hughes stood up uncertainly, still clutching his cap. He was pleased his information had been of assistance. He was a nice young lad, this one, though he looked as though he could be a bit short-tempered if things didn't go his way. Very young, too, for all this responsibility and ordering about. Still, to fly these aeroplane things you had to be young, didn't you? He was glad it was all over though; his wife would be pleased. When he met them on the hills tomorrow, he would feel better. On his own ground then. Which made all the difference.

Then Burgoyne was shaking his hand. "Thank you for all your trouble, Mr Hughes. You have been most helpful. It's a sad day for all of us here, but at least we have a possible lead on where to look for our missing aircraft. You're sure I can't offer you a drink? Coffee, perhaps?"

A little after nine that evening Burgoyne stood with his back to a blackboard in 'B' Flight dispersal. Outside, the airfield was dark and desolate and it was raining still, slowly now, but with a soul-destroying persistence. In front of him sat Jenkins the Adjutant, Roger Lash the Engineer Officer, Richard Lewis the Doctor, the senior Flight Commander Douglas Hayman, James of 'A' Flight and, perched on a table in the rear, Hawkins the civilian Met. Officer.

Tom began. "The situation as I see it is this; with no news of John and the rest, we must assume they have gone in somewhere, either in the sea or, more likely, in the hills. Tonight we had a farmer who reported hearing unusual noises about five miles inland, a little to the south of here. He didn't hear the engines but he did hear whistles, Spitfire whistles it would appear, which sounds pretty ominous. He also heard bangs which he described as being like thunder."

Burgoyne turned to the map behind him. "The farmer was here, where the cross is drawn, when he heard the noises. However, he couldn't say from which direction they came. They weren't close, apparently; on the other hand, they weren't far away, either. The usual conundrum." He looked more closely at the board. "In that immediate area there are three peaks. This one here, the closest, is just under 2,000 feet and is known as Moelfre. These other two, Diffwys and Y Llethr, each around 2,500 feet, are about five to six miles inland. My view is that our aircraft are on the top of one of those three peaks, in pieces probably with everyone dead, but with just a possibility that someone might still be alive - which, in this weather, is a terrible thought. Tomorrow morning at first light I want to go out and find them and we are here now to discuss how best to do it."

Jenkins asked the first and most obvious question. "Will the weather be flyable tomorrow, sir?"

"I don't think so." Burgoyne looked towards Hawkins. "Can you confirm that?"

"Yes, sir, I can. There'll be a fair amount of rain about with the hills covered and visibility right down, as today, to about 1,000 yards in places. Non-flying weather, without a doubt."

Tom nodded and continued. "Anything we do will have to be done on foot. We can take transport and equipment to the general area but there'll be a hell of a lot of walking, climbing and carrying. The three points we have to consider now are where do we go, what do we take with us, and what do we do when we get there. Don't forget, we shall be looking for half-a-dozen scratches on a mountainside in an area of about 64 square miles. In fact, if I think about it too much, I'm almost persuaded that it's hardly worth setting out."

"What sort of medical team do you have in mind, sir," said Richard Lewis, "assuming there's a faint possibility of one or more being alive?"

Burgoyne gave a resigned shrug. "You're the expert, Richard, but it seems to me that we shall have to take sufficient men and equipment to give emergency treatment - enough to keep them breathing, anyway. The dead are dead; there's nothing we can do for them other than stand guard until a full rescue team can take over and bring them down."

He turned to Lash. "What do we do about the aircraft, Roger? Do we leave them up there in bits or attempt to bring everything down?"

"As a rule, we clean up the place as best we can although, strictly speaking, it's not our job." Roger Lash clearly welcomed the opportunity to give his opinion. "If they're really difficult to get at, then we leave the bigger items where they are and dig in everything we can't move. I think we shall have to make an assessment on the spot. Anyway, I'll get advice from Group. Incidentally, there are aircraft in the Scottish Highlands that have been there since the last war. An old Bristol Fighter was found up there only the other day - with the pilot still sitting in the seat!"

There was a brief and uncomfortable silence during which glances were exchanged. Then Burgoyne turned to the doctor again. "Richard, you'll have to come, of course, and I suggest at least two medical orderlies with stretchers and emergency equipment. I'll accept your advice on what to bring." He addressed himself to Lash. "I want eight men from you, Roger, plus two pretty active senior NCOs, together with what you consider to be the appropriate rescue equipment - cutters, ropes, spades and so on. If anything is found, four of those chaps must be prepared to stay on the mountainside whilst the second stage of the rescue is being organised." He turned again. "And from you, Adj, I need transport for everyone including the injured; also emergency clothing, blankets, rations, distress flares, marker flags, compasses - all that sort of stuff. We shall be away for a minimum of 24 hours with four men possibly staying out for an additional two days and nights."

Burgoyne took a deep breath; he was beginning to feel wretchedly tired. It had been a long day; more than two hours flying in miserable weather conditions plus all the extra mental wear and tear. He went on, "I shall lead the party and you, Duggie, will look after things in my absence. Peter, you'd better come; and you Richard, as I've said."

Roger Lash said stiffly, "I'd like to come too, sir, if you think I could help." Tom was reminded of a small boy, hurt that he was being excluded.

"Of course. Silly of me, Roger. More than anyone, you'll be needed. And now," Burgoyne examined his watch, "it's 9.25. I want you all to make detailed arrangements even if it means staying up all night. Meanwhile, I'll have another session with Uncle and tell Group what we intend to do. I'll be back in an hour, by which time I expect you all to be in a position to tell me what you have fixed up." He nodded a little brusquely. "Thank you for turning out. We're going to find those blokes if we break our necks in the process." He winked at Lash whose face still bore the traces of a sulk. "Your neck too, Roger - probably the first to be broken, in fact."

Chapter Two

Burgoyne spent a restless night. He was conscious of tossing about endlessly, the surging patter of rain against his window constantly in his ears, so that when his watch showed 4.15 am, he felt mentally and physically drained. In the feverish twilight period between sleeping and waking, his mind reeled from problem to problem, the difficulties of the search assuming exaggerated and frightening proportions. Then, as if to reinforce his apprehensions, a heavy shower beat a tattoo on the roof and window of his hut and the wind set something clattering wildly outside. My God! What a time to fall into the sea or run into a hill. He forced his eyes open and lay there, staring at the darkened ceiling.

Presently, without waiting for his batman's call, he arose shivering in the damp blackness. He washed and shaved briefly, struggled into string-vest, long underwear, and much of the heavier flying equipment he possessed but seldom wore. Then he put on his flying boots but immediately had second thoughts; they were fleece-lined and probably too hot in which to walk any distance. He sat down again and pulled them off with difficulty, choosing instead some stout civilian walking shoes, which seemed pretty inadequate. He was going to have problems, he knew it. He hoped he wouldn't turn an ankle on the loose shale he suspected would be lying about in masses on the hills.

After stamping about to encourage the circulation, he donned his fur-lined Irving jacket, the ubiquitous 'goon-skin', the only damn thing they were good for; that and keeping the car radiator from freezing!

He joined the party gathering at the guardroom, everyone muffled against the damp chill of the morning and showing few signs of conviviality. The rain had stopped, thank God, but there were pools everywhere and it was uniformly dark with a great deal of moisture in the air despite a turbulent breeze. Dawns! He had seen enough dawns to last him a lifetime!

Burgoyne had his own car and there was an ambulance and three Commer aircrew transports, the latter stoutly-built vehicles with tarpaulin hoods, one loaded to the roof-line with equipment.

In the darkness he bumped into the Adjutant heavily disguised as an Arctic explorer. "Hello, Adj. What are you doing here?"

"Just checking that everything's in order, sir."

Tom put his hand on the man's shoulder. "You should be in bed. You're much too old for this sort of lark. We'll find them, never fear." The words were said more as encouragement than as a prediction.

"I hope so. We have to know one way or the other. By the way, the champagne and smoked salmon - marked tea and wads - are in the boot of your car. Just thought you'd like to know."

Tom grinned. 'Sadist!"

Burgoyne climbed into his own car, the gutless wonder, and motioned Lewis and James to accompany him. Lash was fussing about with the airmen and had declared his intention of riding in the leading Commer. The Engineer Officer, a small man, was a great fusser. There was always an element of high drama with Roger, who could transform the handing over of a pencil into something resembling a Royal investiture.

They reached the Hughes farm within the hour, by which time it was reasonably light. It was a solidly-built two-storey building at the end of a long, rutted path. Having left the ambulance and other vehicles on the side of the public highway half a mile to the rear, Tom advanced cautiously, wondering meanwhile if the springs of his Hillman would be equal to the task. Farmers didn't seem to

worry too much about mud and potholes; or about their farm machinery either, it appeared. Perhaps it was because it was all tax-deductable, or whatever the term was.

As they approached, the farmer advanced towards them from the shadows carrying a long stick and accompanied by two black-and-white Border Collies, which serpented around his legs in herding formation, their tails trailing.

"Good morning to you." The man's voice seemed more Welsh than ever. "I'll lead the way in my own car, if you don't mind."

Burgoyne nodded. "Anything you say. If you'll take us to the exact spot at which your heard the bangs, we'll take it from there. Are your dogs coming too?"

"Where I go, they go. They're much more sensible than I am, anyway."

Ned Hughes moved towards a high-standing open van and the two collies leapt in the back without a word of command and stood watching, their eyes bright with intelligence.

The small convoy drove slowly along the mountain road for several miles. Tom looked up dubiously at the green slopes heavily shrouded in mist. It was even worse than he had expected although the rain was keeping off. Someone was going to get lost, he felt it in his bones. Then there would be a search-party looking for a search-party! He began to have second thoughts yet again about the wisdom of pressing ahead. Beside him, Lewis and James, jolted into silence by the lumpy ride, thought their own thoughts with pensive faces.

Presently the lead van veered off to the left and ran up a grassy track for some hundreds of yards before turning and halting. The farmer climbed out and Tom drew up beside him. He looked out from the open window. They were pretty high up and it was raw and miserable. What a hell-fire place to have an accident.

"Is this it?" The tone of Burgoyne's voice was indicative of his lack of enthusiasm.

The farmer nodded, the two collies circling around his feet eager for a word. "Not far from here."

As the five other vehicles lurched to a standstill in a rough circle, Tom was tempted to make a facetious remark about repelling Indians, but refrained when it occurred to him that it might be regarded as being in bad taste. He rebuked himself mentally and turned his attention to business.

With the whole group gathered round, he spread out the map and orientated himself. "Right. We have four compasses between us and mine says that we are now facing due east. The mountain, Moelfre, is up here to our left, somewhere in the murk. The lake, or reservoir, called Bodlyn, is straight ahead and the higher mountain, Diffwys, is about two-o'clock".

"We're going to have a go at Diffwys first, using this as our base camp. The top is about two miles away and we'll split into two parties, going approximately left and right of the summit. I'll take the first party and Flying Officer James will lead the second. We'll walk for 90 minutes, each group on a different heading. If the visibility gets really bad, we'll mark our trails with flagged sticks - each party should have a dozen. At the end of 90 minutes, both parties will return, which means that we should all be back here in three hours. After that, we'll have a bite of something and another think. Anyone finding anything will fire a red distress flare, each party has twelve although they may not be seen in all the muck further up the mountain. The flares mean, in plain terms, come and assist. If the aircraft are found - well, you know what to do; we've discussed it sufficiently. The aim is to preserve life should there be any life to preserve. Keep a careful note of your compass headings, particularly if you have to skirt something you can't cross and, for God's sake - and for my future - don't get yourselves lost. Mark your trails and if anyone is injured, someone is to stay with that particular person until help arrives. It may even be necessary to abandon the search. Right. We'll now split up and each party will have a more detailed briefing. Kick-off is at 7.55, which is in - 16 minutes time."

Tom walked over to where the farmer was standing alone, his dogs lying in watchful silence. "Anything you would like to add, Mr Hughes?"

The man looked thoughtful. "I don't think so, really. It's a pity we can't see more."

Burgoyne shrugged. "We'll just have to do the best we can. Are you going to stay here, go back, or come with us?"

"I'll come with you, if you don't mind."

"Pleased to have you, Mr Hughes." Burgoyne nodded in Lewis's direction. "Richard, if you'll gather your people, we'll have a further discush."

An hour later Burgoyne brought his party to a halt and took stock of his position. His heart was beating a tattoo somewhere inside amid all the perspiration and he was wet and very uncomfortable. As he had suspected, his shoes had been unequal to the task, giving too little support to his ankles and offering almost no resistance to water. Visibility was down to several hundred yards and hills which looked attractively green and smooth from a distance, turned out to be viciously corrugated with rocky overhangs, shale by the acre, dips, ridges and – amazingly - bogs.

During their ascent they had slipped, stumbled, clambered with clawing fingers and waded. Tom's knees were skinned and his feet awash. What a squalid place! The sheep were welcome to this part of Wales, he decided.

He had found himself in the lead throughout, studying his compass carefully. Lewis and the farmer had followed ten or so yards behind, with the rest in Indian file. The exertion of struggling up a one-in-four ascent had reduced conversation to monosyllables. All around was wetness and mist and an unearthly silence. He felt like Moses climbing up into a moisture-laden, very inhospitable heaven. The summit on his side of the mountain couldn't be that far off and the other party, long since lost to sight, must be approaching their own objective. There was, however, no sign of any summit. There was no sign of any aircraft. There was no sign of anything, not even of sheep. What a wild-goose chase this was turning out to be. He was a fool to have believed it might be otherwise.

With his hands on his hips, Burgoyne waited until Lewis and the farmer had drawn level. "I think we must be somewhere near the top now. Another 25 minutes before we turn back."

His chest heaving, Lewis nodded and bared his teeth - it was easier than replying. Beneath them and spread out over a distance of 100 yards, the rest of the party toiled up and the yellow flags marking the trail disappeared into the mist. Burgoyne took out the field-glasses he was carrying and scanned the slopes around him. It was hopeless; the naked eye could see five times further than the visibility permitted. The two dogs stretched out patiently beside them with lolling tongues, eyeing their master with doleful interest. Nothing much doing today! They were clearly disappointed. Overhead, the faint sound of an aircraft engine filtered through to them. Tom cocked his head and listened. "He's pretty high."

Lewis retorted grimly, "If he has any sense, he is!"

Within ten minutes they had reached a ridge which appeared to stretch away evenly left and right. Ahead the ground began to slope away until it disappeared into grey oblivion.

Burgoyne propped himself against a rock, his breast heaving, and the others gathered round welcoming a respite. "Five minutes rest. After that, I want two chaps each to walk left and right, keeping to this top ridge. Time yourselves. Ten minutes at the most, then back again. If the ground becomes impossible, turn round immediately. I know you're tired but we're here to find aircraft and, more important, people - people who might need us desperately. And don't forget, unlike us, they've already be up here for almost a whole day." He gave a brief encouraging smile. "When you're ready."

An hour later Burgoyne came in sight of the circle of vehicles and breathed a sigh of relief. Thank God! Coming down the mountain after the fruitless search along the ridge had been almost as wearing as going up. His thigh and calf muscles ached abominably and his whole body trembled with fatigue and stress. This was a damn-fool expedition. What chance had they of finding anything in this blasted weather and in this vast expanse of damn-all? He was a half-wit to have suggested it.

He stopped wearily and looked around. His party was spread out behind him but were all there. Poor chaps; most were older than himself, some considerably so, and unlike him they were carrying equipment of one sort or another. He wondered what they must be feeling. Probably cursing him to hell and gone! Still, it had to be done. He saw John Beazley's face in his mind's eye, and his eyes creased in a smile. Was it only yesterday? He widened his gaze. There was no sign of James and his party. He hoped to heaven they had not run into any sort of trouble.

When Burgoyne had calculated that James and his group were 20 minutes overdue, he got to his feet and paced about like a caged animal. Eaten up with concern, he tried to keep his fears under control and his face from mirroring his feelings. He examined his watch for the twentieth time and peered into the mist. Had they found anything? There had been no flares, or none that they had seen. He sighed. God knew, they could do without any further mishaps. He glanced at an uneaten sandwich in his hand. No appetite for anything. Blast the bloody weather. They should be conducting a search by air not creeping about the countryside like so many lame snails. He peered into the mist praying for some sign, some movement.

It was Lewis who saw them first. "There they are, sir."

Tom looked round. A group in single file, their figures blurred by the mist, was approaching slowly. Someone was being carried. James was in the lead.

With Burgoyne and the doctor advancing towards him, James smiled painfully in greeting. "Sorry we're late, sir." He looked tired and drawn. "Corporal Cadwallader has either broken or sprained an ankle. Fell off one of those bloody crags back there. I thought for a time we would have to leave him behind, but he's weathered the journey, poor chap. He's in a good deal of pain. Carried him all the way. Heavens! Am I glad to be back."

Burgoyne sighed, "No sign of any aircraft?"

James shook his head. "Nothing, I'm afraid. Nothing but boulders, shale, and a mass of boggy, bugger-all! I wish I did have something to report. On the other hand, perhaps I don't." He flopped down. "Lord, what a business."

Lewis handed round tea and sandwiches whilst Tom looked about. Everyone was tired and dispirited, that was clear enough. Farmer Hughes was standing to one side gazing into space, his dogs beside him. What now? They couldn't go on like this. Corporal Cadwallader was stretched out on the ground, his foot swollen and discoloured. Lewis had put down the food he was carrying and was attending to him with others gathered around, idly watching and silent.

Tom walked off, his hands in his pockets. Ahead, to the north, the ground rose steeply into the mist. There were sheep dotted about, their voices echoing plaintively between the sloping sides of the valley. This was the hill the farmer had mentioned first. He examined the chart he was carrying. Pretty high - 1,932 feet and, what . . . three to four miles from the airfield? If they had gone in, this is where they would probably be. Perhaps he should have tried this place first. The mountain they had climbed was too far away, he was pretty certain of that. On the other hand it was 500 feet higher, and the farmer had said. . . . but, what the heck? There were scores of blasted hills and tens of miles of nothing in every direction. What was so special about this little bit of Wales? They were wasting their time. They would have to go back. Yet; he walked across to where Lewis, James and Lash were in a silent, exhausted group, James sitting, the other two standing and leaning. "Well, what do you think?"

James raised his head. "Looks pretty hopeless, sir."

"Richard?"

"I agree. Where do we start?"

"Roger?"

"I don't think it's on, sir. Wait until the weather clears then make a search by air."

"And what if there's someone alive still? Are you happy to leave him? Them?"

All three returned his gaze without answering. There was a pause whilst Burgoyne studied his feet. "You're absolutely right, of course. But, as the fisherman said, "You only catch fish when your hook's in the water." No good us talking about helping - from the bottom of the hill."

He paused again and they each saw conflict in his face. A sudden smile spread across his face. "Look. I have a thing about this hill ahead of us. I want to have a go at it. Just one. If we draw a blank, we'll go home. Peter here has had enough for the moment. Who'll volunteer to come with me?"

After the briefest of hesitations, Lewis spoke up, "Of course, sir. If you say so."

"I don't want pressed men, Richard." Burgoyne was unsmiling.

Lewis grinned. "Always a volunteer, sir."

"And you, Roger?"

"I'm with you, sir. I'd never live it down if I wasn't."

Tom smiled. It all sounded like something out of Boys' Own Paper. Nice to hear, even so. "Fine. We'll take a party of six and I'll tell farmer Hughes he can go home. Whilst I'm doing that, go and spread the word."

With Burgoyne in the lead the party climbed painfully back into the mist. In parts it was so steep that they were obliged to move diagonally, slipping and scrambling over shale and wet turf. There was a good deal of what Tom took to be fern – he was no expert on plant-life – which soaked them chillingly up to their thighs. From time to time they stopped, panting like animals, their leg muscles shaking with the unaccustomed exertion.

Burgoyne consulted his watch; thirty minutes. He'd give it another half hour. As they ascended, it began to rain and the heavy drizzle dampened their spirits almost as much as their garments. Above his head Tom saw daunting outcrops of rock. The occasional indigo-smeared sheep, startled from its feeding, would go scampering away, its tiny feet thudding, its bleating echoing eerily in the mist. They were near cloud now, there was no doubt about that, visibility was down to little more than thirty paces. He hoped to God they wouldn't stumble over a precipice of any sort. He consulted his watch again. Not long now. Another ten minutes.

They came to a point where the ground levelled off briefly. Burgoyne stopped and Lewis rested beside him. Bent double, the blood pounding in their ears, they recovered their breath. Lewis held his side. "Pretty hopeless, I'm afraid."

Tom nodded, his mouth agape, making a mental note that two of the party were below them, climbing laboriously. He looked round for the others. No sign. Lash and one of the corporals were missing. He stifled a groan. Surely the fools had not missed the way.

He was about to remark on their absence when a cry, blanketed by moisture and distance, reached him. It was formless, but had a note of urgency. Instantly on the alert, Burgoyne listened again, tilting his head. Very dimly, the call came again. "Here, sir? Over here!"

With Lewis beside him, Tom began to run haltingly towards the voice, his feet slipping on the treacherous wetness of the stunted grass. A figure, two figures, emerged like spooks from the opaque blanket, both motionless, one pointing.

Burgoyne followed the outstretched arm. The outline of an aircraft rudder was above them some twenty yards distant, a dark mass silhouetted against the grey. He recognised at once the tail of a Spitfire. My God, they had found them. They were here. They had succeeded. It was a miracle! Burgoyne put his hand on Lash's shoulder and breathed quietly, "Well done! Well done, that man." He turned to Lewis gulping air beside him. "Richard, it's them. It's them, for heaven's sake."

Lewis paused. Recovering, he said in an undertone, "Look, sir . . . let me go first. It may not be very pleasant."

Burgoyne shook his head emphatically, his face set. "I know. But it's the least I can do. And it won't be the first time." He moved forward. "Come on."

The single aircraft they approached had disintegrated completely, but had not caught fire. There was a shallow crater, more a depression in the earth, from which a deep scar ran forward for ten or fifteen yards. There, the Spitfire had finally stopped. It had struck at a point where the ground was rising at an angle of about 40 degrees. The wings and tail were recognisable and broken apart, but the fuselage was mutilated almost beyond description. The engine and propeller were missing.

About ten paces from the wreck Tom stopped and drew in his breath. The pilot was there, he could see, a brownish-grey pulverised mess in what had been the cockpit. Lewis said quietly in his ear, "No chance, I'm afraid," and walked forward.

"Who is it? Can you see?"

"Not yet. Can you read the letter or number?"

Burgoyne stooped to examine the fuselage, but the metal was so shattered that only part of the roundel was recognisable. Lewis was bending over, a medical orderly in attendance. "It's a Sergeant. I can't say which one at the moment."

Tom looked around and nodded. "Let's spread out and find the others."

As Burgoyne moved off slowly, his eyes searching, he found himself damply cold and trembling but with a quite inexplicable sense of relief. He knew he was about to come face to face with five more shattered bodies, comrades he had known only hours before, laughing and talking. Five obscene hulks, butchered as the result of one trifling miscalculation in time and distance. Yet, somehow, he felt he had honoured a pledge. They were no longer waste matter strewn about a hillside, but individuals with names and personalities, back with their own squadron, back among their friends. Their bodies would be handled tenderly and with compassion, their deeds recounted, their memory cherished.

Shivering suddenly, he stopped to compose himself. It was so unreal. The silence. The mountain scents and the tugging breeze. Was this really happening to him? He began to feel sick, his stomach fluttering. He walked on, breathing deeply in an attempt to control the nausea that was threatening to overwhelm him.

Another wreck appeared ahead and slightly beneath him, a black mound in the mist. And beyond that, another. He looked about and tried to visualize how they had been flying when they had struck. Probably in a close vic of five with a man in the box. Possibly the one they had found would be Sergeant Dent. John Beazley would be somewhere ahead and Pelham-Groom to his right. Or, perhaps Scotty as section leader, would be on his left, he just didn't know. Anyway, what difference did it make now?

He approached the first blackened hulk, forcing himself to walk with measured steps. This one had burned and the stench of conflagration remained in the air despite the moisture-laden atmosphere, the wind, and the time interval. It was impossible to pick out the pilot clearly, but he was there right enough, a charred doll-like mummy, totally unrecognisable as a human being. His features contorting unconsciously in distaste, Burgoyne gazed silently at the tragic scene. In the blackened debris the fire-streaked bones of a hand were visible. And teeth, a row of white teeth, somehow miraculously preserved. Christ! How awful. And yet how tragically pathetic. Someone's son. A brother. A loved one, certainly. Life one moment, then, in an instant, violent, bludgeoning death amid searing flames. He turned away, trembling and week-kneed.

When Burgoyne returned, Lewis, his sleeves rolled back and his hands blackened, was in discussion with his men. Tom said quietly, "There are two back there. I imagine there is at least one ahead and there should be more to our left. They obviously went in in formation, letting down, presumably.

An airman approached from above. "There's one up here, sir - burned out."

"How many does that make?"

"Don't know exactly, sir. But it doesn't seem to add up to six. Another fifty feet and they would have been over the top. Perhaps one struck and went over the edge. We'll have to look down below a little later."

Lewis said gently, "What d'you want us to do now, sir?"

Burgoyne gave a fluttering sigh. "I'm afraid we'll have to check every body, Richard, and collect the remains. After we've covered them up, I suggest we go back down leaving everything as it is. I don't think my stomach will stand much more of this."

"Don't upset yourself, sir. This is not your job." Lewis's face was compassionate. "This is medical work. We'll look after everything up here. Why don't you go down? We'll follow as soon as we've finished."

Burgoyne shook his head, his voice unsteady. "I have to stay. I wouldn't feel right if I left them now. I'll give you a hand. Come on, the sooner we start, the sooner we finish."

He turned away quickly and stumbled off. Unable to prevent it, he felt a sob rising like a huge bubble and there were tears on his cheeks. Lordy! This would never do. Momentarily, he was savagely cross with himself. Come on Burgoyne, for God's sake! Pull yourself together. He found himself swallowing, head bowed. After a time, he turned round, his face composed; crisis over. He'd be all right now. He looked up. Lewis was looking in his direction, thoughtfully, and nodding.

Tom Burgoyne sat writing at his office desk, half his mind contemplating the imminent arrival of Oliver Rhys-Davies who, he had been informed, was heading in his direction. News of some sort, he supposed, and, if things ran true to form, bad news at that.

Two days had elapsed since he and his search-party had trudged painfully over the mountains; two days of trauma, signals, enquiries, letters, explanations, 765cs, discussions and heart-searching. What it was to be a Squadron Commander - fighting the Germans was the least of his problems. In the First World War, they didn't allow Commanding Officers to take an active part in day-to-day operations - for most of the time, anyway. Still, he supposed he couldn't have it all ways. On the whole, he preferred things as they were.

There was a knock on his door and Jenkins appeared leading Uncle Olly. "The Station Commander, sir."

Burgoyne rose in greeting. "Hello, Uncle." He motioned his visitor to a chair. "Will you have some sort of wetness?"

Rhys-Davies grinned, his battered face hideous. "Must I?"

"If you don't, I shall have to drink on my own. What's more, if you can correctly identify it as coffee, tea or cocoa, you could be entitled to a free holiday for two in the Western Desert, clearing minefields."

Uncle Olly sat down, pleased that Burgoyne seemed to be recovering some of his good spirits. The boy had shown real signs of stress lately. A direct young man at the best of times, he could ruin his future if he lashed out as he tended to do when faced with injustice or official stupidity, real or imagined. He drew a signal from his pocket. "Court of Inquiry, I'm afraid. Friday next. Group Captain Lloyd from Fighter Command."

Burgoyne wrinkled his nose. "Him alone? I thought there had to be two or more."

"Not necessarily - at times like this. Anyway, do you know him?"

Burgoyne shook his head and Rhys-Davies continued. "Decent chap. Rhodesian. He'll give you a fair hearing. In any case, you have nothing to worry about. Group seem fairly happy that the accident was purely mischance. It'll be all right, you see."

Burgoyne put on a sceptical look and the older man changed the subject. "The bodies are all down, I hear."

"Yes. The last party got in at midnight. We've now recovered everything other than some of the larger pieces of the aircraft. There's nothing much we can do about them at the moment. All told, it was a very unpleasant job, I can tell you. Poor old Richard Lewis, who takes most things in his stride, was very blue."

"Did . . . did, er, did you see the remains?"

"Most of what there was, yes. I'm afraid we shall have to put everything in a heap and divide by six, adding a few bricks to make the weight respectable." His lip curled. "There's your son, Mr Beazley. That half-spade-full over there"

Rhys-Davies lowered his head. He didn't like to hear this sort of talk. Nor did he like the boy's tone.

Burgoyne went on tightly. "And another thing, Uncle. When we have the funeral, could you persuade our God-bothering gentleman to lay off the platitudes about sacrifice and duty and the rest of the pious claptrap he normally comes out with? These chaps were killed by mistake and unnecessarily, in my view; it had nothing to do with honour and sacrifice and I'm sure all of them would have bitterly resented going the way they did. They wouldn't have thought it the least bit noble or worthwhile. Nor indeed do I."

Rhys-Davies replied quietly, "No, I don't suppose they would. But they all knew it was a possibility. Everyone did, and does. Including you."

Burgoyne shrugged, his face hard. "Anyway, the funeral's on Sunday. I only hope we can find someone on the camp who can play the 'Last Post' decently." After a pause he went on. "Scotty Pelham-Groom's parents say they want to attend. I heard by 'phone today. They're the only ones, thank heaven. I'm afraid I'm not exactly overjoyed at the prospect of meeting them. Bad enough losing the chaps themselves and having to write the letters without the business of consoling the parents, face to face."

He gave a grim smile. "How are your religious beliefs, Uncle? Are you able to interpret events like this as being uplifting for the soul? I have difficulty, I'm bound to say. If something good is supposed to emerge, I wish I could be told what it is, who is likely to benefit, and when."

The Station Commander, shifting uncomfortably, gazed at his shoes. "It's all very difficult I know. But, these things have happened before and they'll happen again."

He was about to continue when he saw Burgoyne's face tighten and heard the boy's voice carrying on. "When an accident like this happens, Uncle, you suddenly feel terribly naked; as though all your defences have been stripped away at a stroke. Most chaps, very conveniently, get themselves killed on someone else's doorstep. They just don't come back - no bullets, no blood, no black, cremated dolls to ruin your lunch. Then, all of a sudden, it happens. Not only do your mates die, but it's all there before your eyes; blood, broken pieces, fire, the lot. And it takes weeks, sometimes months, to build up that very personal and private cocoon of impregnability, which everyone has to some degree and which is absolutely essential if chaps like us are to survive. It's all in the mind, I know, but if you don't have it you go dotty and very soon become a casualty yourself. The best example I can give is Major Mick Mannock in the last war. He was the big ace of his day, with over 70 victories to his credit, when the loss of some of his closest friends and, in particular, some of the flamers he saw, all at once got to him. His cocoon disintegrated and, unfortunately for him, he'd been going for so long he didn't have the resistance or the time to build up another defence mechanism. So he became morbid, foretold his own death, and almost immediately after, was killed in the most horrible way. So terribly sad. So near the end of the war, too."

Rhys-Davies nodded. "I well remember. In fact, one of his protégés is a friend of mine. Ira T. Jones - the famous, or infamous, 'Taffy'. Have you heard of him?"

Burgoyne hesitated then admitted that he had, in a manner so casual that the Station Commander looked up in surprise. "Have you met him? He commanded RAF Llandow until quite recently."

Tom nodded. "Yes, I've met him. As a matter of fact, I had the unhappy task of delivering an official letter to him, after which he left the Service."

Rhys-Davies stared. "Good Lord! I didn"t know that."

"In fact, it rather proves a point, Uncle; the one I was making earlier about responsibility and the unfeeling attitude of authority. 'Taffy' Jones shot down - what? - 40 odd aircraft in the last war. A big hero, all the decorations in the world. Then, in 1942, he offends his Lords and Masters in some comparatively trivial way and is hoofed out of the Air Force quicker than that. That's gratitude for you. No, Uncle. Officialdom has a pretty short memory when its own interests are served; decorations count for very little, believe me. Betray your country by disarming the nation and encouraging invasion and you get elected to Parliament with a seat in the Lords at the end of it. Neglect to say the right words at a briefing or forget to sign the Form 700 and you're put on the scrap heap and blighted for life."

For some moments there was an uncomfortable silence. Realising that his uncompromising outburst had embarrassed the older man, Burgoyne suddenly grinned. "Well, anyway, there it is. A fortnight hence, the dead will have been buried and everything forgotten; the ripples will have died away and the pool will be mirror-smooth again. But, within a year, I've not the slightest doubt, six other poor mutts will graft themselves on to a mountain-side, after which some goon at Air Ministry will spend a sleepless week trying to pin it on the poor, unfortunate blighter of a squadron commander - who was probably away on leave at the time, anyway. Responsibility, Uncle! That's the operative word. Someone must always carry the can. And always someone else!"

Rhys-Davies stood up, smiling bleakly and thin-lipped. It was best he made himself scarce. The conversation was becoming altogether too near the knuckle for his liking. He decided to change the subject. "What arrangements have you made for Scotty's parents?"

"They're coming by train, his father, mother and sister. I plan to meet them at the station and take them to the Mess. I doubt that they'll feel much like eating before the funeral so we shall arrange a meal for later. After that, I don't know what they have in mind. We'll just have to play it by ear."

"What does Pellham-Groom senior do, by the way?"

"He's a diplomat. Foreign Office. A First Secretary, whatever that may mean."

Rhys-Davies nodded thoughtfully. He'd never dealt with the Foreign Office before. It would be a new and interesting experience. Aloud, he said. "If they're not pressed for time, I'd be happy to have them for dinner. Even give them a bed, if they want to stay, that is." He turned away. "I'll mention it to them."

When the Station Commander had gone, Burgoyne leaned back in his chair, some of the tension evaporating. Even so, he still felt on edge and deeply disturbed. He should not have been so outspoken. He had been rambling on a bit, too, an upsurge of emotion, nothing more. Perhaps he had been more deeply affected by the sight of those bodies than he cared to admit. Air Ministry, Fighter Command, Group - they were no more to blame than he was and he knew that. Despite the impending Court of Inquiry, he was unlikely to be held accountable for the accident, although they might catch him out on some technicality or other. But, what the heck. With six chaps dead, criticism and reproof amounted to nothing by comparison. No, the whole affair was just an ugly and tragic mishap, one that was bound to occur from time to time however tight an organisation. The important thing was to get events into perspective. He mustn't do a Mannock. Control! Self-control! That was the secret. He'd be more careful next time.

He took up his pen, but the words would not flow and in the middle of all the mental turmoil and self-reproach, there came a knock on the door and Jenkins ushered in Roger Lash.

"A new Flight Commander posted in, sir. Flight Lieutenant J.D.A. Braithwaite from 53 OTU. Arrives Monday next. Also," he read from a signal, "Pilot Officers P.L. Tomkins, J.D.P. Squire, and Sergeant N.F. Stone, all new boys." He glanced up. "Not wasting much time, are they? And - wait for it - we are to offer up two experienced section leaders for posting to Malta and a third for the Far East. Volunteers to be called for, but if there are no volunteers, we are to nominate three officers anyway."

As the words fell like stones, Burgoyne felt the blood surge to his face and recognised the start of an eruption. For some seconds he was totally lost for words. Then the storm broke.

"I . . . I really don't think I'm hearing this. Are they all mad? Is it possible that 'P' Staff are genuinely demented? Six pilots lost and before they are even buried, they want a further three experienced officers as section leaders. What the hell are they trying to do to us? What are we, a squadron or a kindergarten? How in God's name are we to maintain any sort squadron spirit if all they do is poach our most experienced officers? Have they heard what has just happened to us? Have they?"

His voice rising almost to a cry, he jerked himself to his feet and stalked to the window trying to control himself. Bloody half wits! He was very near to tears. Had they no feelings at all?

Behind his back, Jenkins and Lash exchanged glances. Lash said: "A bit of better news, sir. Warning notice of six new aircraft".

"New?" Burgoyne, his voice shrill, didn't even turn.

"Well ... new to us. Four from MU and one each from Treble One and 41 Squadrons."

Burgoyne said bitterly, "Reconditioned hulks from MU I dare say, and clapped out rejects from the other squadrons. Are there no new Mark 5s these days?"

Lash lowered his gaze. "I don't think they're producing any more now. They're busy with 8s and 9s, and other types."

Tom turned quickly and glared at his subordinates. Christ! He'd strike someone soon. He had to get out. Out! Out - before he exploded.

With a supreme effort he controlled himself, but could not entirely eliminate the thickness or quaver from his voice. "Thank you both, anyway. It's not your fault." He took up his hat with an abrupt gesture and jammed it on his head. "And now, if you don't mind, I'm going to walk round and round the airfield. Endlessly; until I'm fit to be spoken to. And if anyone wants me, the AOC included, tell them I've bloody gone. To China! On foot!"

As the door closed with a thud that shook the building, Jenkins and Lash remained standing in the middle of the room, signals dangling from their fingers.

Jenkins shrugged, "Poor fella! I feel for him. I sometimes think we ask too much of kids of 22."

He paced slowly towards his own office. "All we need now is a good funeral. And six-to-four it'll rain like the clappers!"

A RICHER DUST

A Richer Dust

*F*or most of the war, Fighter Command aircraft were controlled from Sector Operations Rooms, each room linked to a main airfield - Biggin Hill, Kenley, North Weald, etc. Each main airfield had a number of lesser airfields associated with it; these were termed 'satellites' and usually there were up to three to each major airfield.

The Sector Operations Rooms were largely manned by members of the Women's Auxiliary Air Force, who plotted the aircraft on large table maps, watched by the Controller and his staff from a raised balcony.

These girls, officers and airwomen alike, were invariably young, often attractive, all of them very much aware of the pilots flying the aircraft they were controlling. They frequently met them at station functions and elsewhere and often, regardless of rank, formed friendships which developed into close relationships. Although many such liaisons turned out to be happy events there was often a reluctance to form committed friendships. All were well aware of the high casualty rate among pilots, it being especially upsetting when a WAAF watched her boyfriend disappear from the board she was working on, or heard of his loss over the radio.

'A Richer Dust' describes one such liaison which took place at RAF Biggin Hill in the Spring of 1943, when the Luftwaffe was making frequent attacks on coastal towns such as Eastbourne. The facts of this story are substantially correct, only the final outcome has been changed.

Chapter One

They turned at the crossroad into the lane which climbed away to the right. There were two adults in the front of the car; the driver, a young woman of thirty, or thereabouts, and her companion, older by a generation but still with much of the beauty and colouring of her youth. In the rear seat three young children chattered and fidgeted and a Gordon Setter, with a face registering infinite gloom, rested her head on the front seat and drooled reflectively.

The older of the two girls remarked, "Mummy, Sheba's making candlesticks again."

The younger woman, with the serenity of disposition bequeath only to a few, replied, "Wipe her chops, darling. No, not with your handkerchief, matey! Use a tissue, there's an angel."

The cleansing of Sheba was, however, only a fleeting diversion and within moments Christopher, aged seven, had voiced the frustrations of the entire back seat. "How long now, Mummy?"

"How long? Let's see. About eleven-and-a-half very deep breaths away. So begin counting. Slowly mind. Five whoppers to the top of the hill then another six-and-a-half to our very special picnic field. Right? Ready; Steady; Go!"

After changing down, the younger woman glanced into the driving mirror to be faced with the image of Susan, the eldest, frowning and cross-eyed with the effort of harnessing an eruption of air which struggled to escape. "How many breaths, Susie?"

But Susan, of the bulging cheeks, on her second and not about to be thwarted, remained silent.

The older woman, 'Grandma' and mother-in-law, observed quietly, "If we turn at the tee-junction ahead there's a fork to the right which drops us down into Westerham."

"Ma, how could I possibly forget? You're the expert on these parts, I should have remembered. Heavens! Look at this lunatic." She braked for a cyclist and yelled a cheerful 'Roadhog!' at him as he passed, causing the unfortunate man to lift his head in astonishment before wobbling crazily into a ditch. With a triumphant 'Gotcha!', the young woman grinned impishly and, hunching her shoulders, carried on the conversation as though nothing had happened. "So, how long is it since you were here at Biggin Hill?"

"Oh, Lord! More than forty years. '41 to '44, anyway. Ye Gods! It hardly bears thinking about." She smiled reflectively. "I don't think I could quite get into my uniform now. I had an 18 inch waist then, believe it or not."

"You mean you still have it - your uniform, that is?

"Of course!" The older woman looked away and stared, adding quietly, "Wouldn't part with it for the world. Ever!"

They reached the tee-junction and there was much looking left and right and a chorus of instruction. When they moved off the older woman said with a nod, "There it is! You'll have to watch out; there's only room for one car."

They dropped down into the valley, moving slowly with squealing brakes, until a broad expanse of green meadow opened out on their right. Immediately, deep breaths forgotten, the children became ecstatic and the dog, responding to their enthusiasm, shook herself vigorously scattering a shower of saliva throughout the car.

"Sheba!" Condemnation was loud, shrill and unanimous.

From the rear seat came, "Oh, Mummy, please stop here. Please. This is super! Look at those trees. Bags I put the picnic out!"

When the car had finally drawn to a halt, the older woman did not move. Gently but earnestly she suggested, "Can't we go on a little further?"

Her daughter-in-law glanced up in surprise. "If you want to, Ma. I thought this place looked rather special."

"Oh, Grandma, let's stop here. Please Grandma? This is a super field."

The older woman hesitated, then gave an almost inaudible sigh before reaching for the door handle. The three children and the dog piled out from the back and the two women followed, opening the boot and distributing rugs, picnic basket and folding chairs. There was a confusion of flying limbs and some self-conscious laughter as they all climbed over a five-bar gate into the field.

A shriek came from Christopher. "Mummy's showing her knickers! They're frilly."

"You're not supposed to be looking, young man. And they're not frilly!" His mother winked at the older woman. "What it is to have a seven-year-old sex-fiend!"

With everyone loaded down and the dog bounding ahead, they all pushed their way through the thick, summer grass. Presently, the younger woman called

a halt. "Right! Everything down!" She turned to the children. "I suggest you chaps buzz off until Grandma and I sort out the eats." She raised a warning finger. "But no climbing, mind. And Christopher, keep Sheba out of the water. We can't have her smelling of roses all the way home in the back of the car, can we?"

Julia, aged five, said gravely, "Christopher doesn't smell of roses, Mummy."

As Christopher, perplexed, considered this female barb, his mother bent down and hitched up the little girl's pants. "Just watch it, young lady. Otherwise it's no buns for someone. Right?"

With the sheer exuberance of youth that comes from total release, the three children then scampered down the hill with the black-and-tan dog leaping and barking beside them like an animated cartoon Pluto.

When the voices had died away the two women busied themselves with the rugs and picnic basket. "You don't seem too keen on this place, Ma."

The older woman straightened. "Oh ... I'm just being silly. I thought somewhere further on might have been better, that's all. But ... as we're here."

"We can still move on if you wish."

"No, really! The children are happy. Anyway, I doubt that I could manage that gate again without complete loss of dignity."

The other grinned affectionately. "Nonsense, Ma! Sherpa Tensing had nothing on you!"

****

After night duty especially, she always liked to walk in the late afternoon. The Commer transport would bring them back to the airfield from the Operations Room in Bromley shortly after 8 am. Then, she would have breakfast in the Officers' Mess before taking a bath and sleeping until tea-time. The walk had become something of a ritual, partly because she enjoyed walking and needed the exercise but also because it was a means of getting rid of some of Meg's ginger. Meg was her dog - almost an Alsatian, but not quite, she would explain - and unless she had her 'walks' the animal was liable to jump through windows, open or closed, bringing odium in no small measure on her mistress. Dogs were tolerated, but not officially approved of, on RAF stations. For this reason she was obliged to watch her 'Ps and Qs' and see that Meg was given every opportunity to work off at least some of her high spirits. So, it was either the airfield or, more frequently, the long sloping path behind the Mess leading to the Westerham valley.

The airfield, though, presented problems, particularly when the two resident squadrons were 'on call.' Moreover, there was always the possibility of unheralded visitors dropping in. In summertime when the ground was firm the Spitfires were able to use the grass and it was unnerving, to say the least, to find half-a-dozen aircraft racing towards you on take-off or landing on top of your head!

Normally, she would cross in front of the Watch Office and Jack Shepherd, the officer-in-charge there, would either give her the thumbs-up sign from his window or warn her to keep to the perimeter track. In that event, the walk was rather spoiled as it was the endless acres of green pasture she so enjoyed, with the white and yellow meadow flowers, the fresh sweet smells and, in the early autumn, the mushrooms.

Often, in the silence and the sultry warmth of summer, she would sit for hours watching the larks and listening to their song as they climbed their invisible ladders before tumbling lightly to earth, whilst beside her, Meg would be stretched out, her tongue lolling. On this occasion however she knew that the squadrons, one of them French, had been released from duty, so she was a little surprised when Jack Shepherd had shouted to her through cupped hands from the Watch Office balcony.

"629 are due in from Hawkinge in five minutes. They'll be landing east to west, so keep out of the way, won't you old love?"

To this, she had grinned and waved in acknowledgement.

At first she had considered cutting short her walk but then, reluctant to waste so beautiful an afternoon, she decided to wait and watch the aircraft land. She then remembered the gossip in the Mess of 629's impending arrival and the surprise it had caused. It seemed they flew a new and different type of Spitfire and were not likely to be easily absorbed into the Biggin Hill Wing. So, why were they coming? It hardly seemed sensible to experiment with so successful and well-established a fighting unit.

She took off her cap and sat down on the grass facing south. Savouring the silence, she raised her head to the sun. Then, on impulse, she shaded her eyes and gazed into the distance.

She saw the formation a long way off, a wedge of dots moving almost imperceptibly across the line of the horizon. For a long time there was no sound as the aircraft were well downwind but, as they approached and swept overhead, the noise of their engines became a pulsating roar. Following them round and squinting against the sun, she counted 18 in three rows of six, then watched them divide and drift apart.

Within moments they were moving round in a wide circle before approaching with their noses up and wheels and flaps extended, to touch down and balloon with slow-motion grace across the uneven grass, their exhausts spitting and crackling. With bursts of engine and tiny puffs of blue smoke they turned and taxied slowly towards some far distant dispersal pens. The engines died away one by one and only the subdued mutter and beat of the petrol bowsers broke the warm and scented silence as the fuel tanks were replenished.

Returning to the Mess that evening, she had quite forgotten about the new arrivals until she was confronted by a dozen or so unfamiliar faces in the ante-room. They seemed a pleasant if rather noisy and juvenile group, most of them apparently a little younger than herself. Each was dressed in the customary tunic and slacks with a white rolled-neck jersey and flying boots. Dress regulations forbade such sartorial extravagances in the Mess but, in the daytime anyway, some eccentricities were tolerated.

She joined a group of WAAF Officers and other friends at the hatch which served as a bar and, having received her drink, turned to find herself facing a young man who was sitting on one of the tables swinging his legs. Observing that he wore the rank-stripes of Squadron Leader - something that surprised her because of his obvious youth - she deduced that he must be the Commander of the incoming unit. Her interest was quickened, not only by his generally attractive appearance, but also because, in breach of every regulation, he was wearing brown suede desert shoes - known locally and irreverently, she was aware, as 'brothel-creepers'.

Sipping her drink she continued to watch him covertly, taking in the dark hair and eyebrows which contrasted sharply with his unusually fair skin and two remarkably blue eyes. To her fascination and mild amusement the eyes appeared to speak a language of their own as he conversed with some animation with another squadron member.

For some time he continued, unaware of her scrutiny, until a little to her embarrassment, he looked up suddenly, catching her eye. After a moment's hesitation he smiled, then winked.

A little later, and not entirely by accident, she followed him into the dining-room, carefully sitting apart from him but close enough to hear some of his conversation and laughter. Somewhat to her own surprise and concern she found herself glancing at his back throughout the meal and was a little disappointed when he rose to leave and did so without so much as a glance in her direction.

She did not see him for the next several days as his squadron was busy settling into its new accommodation on the airfield and flying about in formations of various sizes. She started a week of morning duties and, from time to time, saw the new call-signs entered on the state-board in front of her. She found herself watching especially for 'Starling 14', which would be his particular call-sign and number.

A little later still she saw him in the Mess after tea. A fortuitous moment, she decided, as the WAAF Officers had planned a party that evening in the Married Quarter they used as sleeping accommodation and as a private ante-room to which they usually retired when 'things became difficult' in the Mess proper. As they had so recently arrived 629 had not been invited; an omission, she decided, that ought to be rectified. After a discussion with her colleagues she volunteered, with a promptness that did not go entirely unnoticed, to speak to the new Commanding Officer.

He was sitting in a corner engrossed in a newspaper when she moved in his direction, a little conscious of the occasion, but presenting her most composed 'coun-tey' face. She half bent over him, aware of a sudden warmth. "Sir. I wonder if you and your squadron would care to join us at the WAAFery tonight?"

He did not look up, she noted, and felt her back stiffen. "It was arranged some time ago, which is why you've not been invited. No slight intended, or anything like that." She gave a little laugh more in nervousness than cordiality and despised herself for it. "We felt you ought to know."

He looked up suddenly and she sensed the blue gaze taking in the copper-auburn hair, the green eyes and the red mobile mouth, twisted slightly in the grin that was betraying her uncertainty. "It all sounds exciting." The smile was there but the voice casual. "Thank you all very much. I'll gather the clan. What time, incidentally?"

"Any time. But not before 8 o'clock. The later you come, though, the less grog there'll be to share out!" She saw his smile widen and then his white teeth.

"T'was ever thus!"

There must have been 60 of them crowded into the small space that served as an ante-room. Each squadron and department was represented. Drinks were dispensed, nudged, spilled then consumed and the noise of conversation and laughter rose in proportion to the glasses emptying. There were many accents; Canadian, French, Australian, Scottish and English and a number falling some-where in between.

As joint hostess she had welcomed him at the door, shaking his hand and making the usual formal but friendly noises. She was in her 'best blue', her hair as casually correct as Kings Regulations would allow and, had she been accused of paying special attention to her appearance, she would have admitted it frankly.

Later, and still in her hostess role, she kept seeing him in the distance but, try as she might, their paths stubbornly refused to cross. She noted, too, with some dismay, that he seemed quite oblivious to her presence. Twice she contrived to manoeuvre herself shoulder-to-shoulder with him only to be thwarted or dragged away. A direct approach? Certainly not! That would never do.

The evening progressed amid an atmosphere tinged with a deepening blue haze and a crescendo of noise. One or two couples tried to dance, a development she welcomed as hopeful. But there was too little space and after a few hilarious attempts to push through the throng, the dancers retired, defeated. Then the telephone kept ringing and there was much to-ing and fro-ing and passing of messages. Finally, the party took on a more settled appearance with groups sitting around on the floor and up the stairs, most in quiet and earnest conversation.

As it grew dark one of the French officers produced a guitar and proceeded to sing some mournful songs in his own tongue whilst she and others sat around him and made their not-too-expert contributions. To the less perceptive she was contentedly engaged with her friends. The more observant might have noticed that her glances kept straying in one direction, but glances were not sufficient, it seemed. Although he appeared congenial enough, he did not come near her.

Towards midnight there was much laughter and shouting in the hallway and someone pushed past saying there was talk of a debagging and that one WAAF Officer, to be on the safe side, had gone upstairs to put on her best pants! Amid all the noise and hilarity she suddenly found him standing alongside.

He held out his hand. "Goodnight, ma'am, and thank you for the party. My morale is restored." His blue eyes were full of innocence, "I trust your pants are in good order?"

With that, and accompanied by most members of his squadron, he left - and for her the evening was finished.

CHAPTER TWO

The following morning she was on duty in the Operations Room. As Ops. 'B', she sat on the high dais next to the Sector Controller. She was his mouthpiece, his link with the squadrons, the radars, Group Headquarters at Uxbridge and Fighter Command at Bentley Priory, Stanmore, indeed everyone in any way concerned with their part of the war.

Normally she was obliged to work very hard, the job being demanding both mentally and physically. She was meticulous, efficient, cool-headed and a much-valued crutch for her Controller. There were no 'committee' decisions in an Ops Room. It was 'do this now!' and, 'Lo' it was done! It was said that a good Ops 'B' was a treasure beyond price. There were very few poor ones; those found wanting disappeared overnight.

Below her, around a large table-map of the South of England and Northern France, a dozen WAAF airwomen plotters, armed with long 'wands', dexterously shifted plaques showing the position, height, and direction of flight of all aircraft in the Sector. In front of her, from floor to ceiling, were the stateboards showing the details of the squadrons and their activities and of every defence resource on the ground and in the air. In all, there were more than fifty men and women working quietly and methodically, controlling the defence of more than three million citizens living in the Biggin Hill Sector.

Shortly before 11 am, the three squadrons took off, their intention being to carry out a 'sweep' some twenty miles inland from the French coast. It was the practice to conduct this type of operation regularly in order to lure the German fighters into combat but, on this occasion, the exercise was more in the nature of an experiment as 629 Squadron was equipped with the Mark 12 Spitfire, whereas the other squadrons flew the Mark 9. With the performance of each considerably different at various heights, it was important to establish whether or not the two were sufficiently compatible to operate successfully together.

As the 36 fighters climbed away to the south, the first plots appeared on the board below. In her mind's eye she saw them rocking and shuddering in the turbulence as they burst through the clouds like salmon breasting their way into

the spray of a fast-moving river, before ascending purposefully into a vast inverted bowl of endless, deepening blue. The twelve aircraft of 629 would be in the lead with the others higher and behind. She knew he would be up there in front and felt a strange and unaccustomed tenseness even though she had watched her friends and acquaintances fly off towards the enemy a hundred times before.

As the aircraft levelled out more than five miles above the English Channel, the plots began to move more quickly and the first enemy reaction appeared. Small groups began to show up in Northern France as German fighters took off. Soon plaques marked 'H' for hostile were indicating twelve plus, eight plus and sixteen plus at various altitudes. Then, like medieval knights of old, the several groups gradually merged until there were two major formations which began to take up position before coldly and inexorably moving towards each other.

The Biggin Hill Wing crossed the French coast at Le Touquet and began to execute a slow turn to the left which would bring it over Amiens and St.Omer. From the radio hissing gently on the Controller's desk next to her, came brief and sometimes unintelligible comments and acknowledgements from the leaders high above. She tried to pick out his voice but little was said and, apart from one terse remark, he contributed nothing. The Controller meanwhile passed on information of the enemy's activities and gave new headings from time to time as there was complete cloud cover over France and the pilots would be unable to see the ground.

Around Amiens, the wing ran into some heavy anti-aircraft fire which pecked away at them doggedly, smudging the atmosphere with a mass of seemingly innocuous brown blossoms, soon to feather and drift away into oblivion. The Spitfires ploughed on through the disturbed, shrapnel-laden air as imperturbably as swans. Apart from a brief mention of the barrage, nothing was said.

Then, a metallic voice shouting briefly 'Bandits above!' jerked the whole Operations Room into a new tenseness as it, almost as much as the pilots themselves, prepared for combat.

On the map beneath her she watched the plots converge until they were side by side and she knew that 120 miles to the south, more than 70 British and German aircraft - or more importantly, 70 superior, virile and intelligent young men - were poised to attack and kill each other.

Most unusually she found it difficult to concentrate on her duties and became so intent on listening to the now rapid exchanges on the hissing radio that she found the Controller, an old friend, regarding her with raised eyebrows when she did not respond with her customary promptness to one of his instructions.

"What's the matter, dear? Something hurting?" The remark was half jocular, half a reprimand but it had the effect of bringing her round immediately.

A little sheepish at being caught out, she gathered herself and set about her business with renewed zeal. Behind her she heard a new voice and, turning, saw the Station Commander, Group Captain 'Sailor' Malan, a solid, well-built man of about thirty, handsome, tanned, and with a faint South African accent.

He was looking at the table. "Have they made contact yet?"

The Controller, still concentrating on the picture below him, said over his shoulder, "Yes, but the Huns don't want to mix it." He turned. "I think there may be too many of us." He then conveyed a message over the radio before leaning back and raising his head. "629 went ahead on the climb and the others had difficulty in keeping up. Now they're all together but with 629 complaining that they are being left behind! They do seem a bit oil and water, I'm afraid."

As they all watched, the plots moved northwards parallel to the coast. The Germans kept their distance and, after a time, the Spitfires continued their slow turn to the left and came out at Gravellines before turning for home.

As the plots separated a more relaxed atmosphere prevailed in the Operations Room until everyone was brought up sharply by a voice reporting engine trouble.

Immediately she became her old efficient self, organising the Air Sea Rescue boats and getting the Walrus seaplane in the air from Hawkinge. The aircraft in difficulty was detached from the formation with a companion and directed towards Lympne, whilst two additional fighters from Hawkinge were ordered off to shadow them during the last stages of their journey.

For some time she worked at top pressure so that when it became clear that the crippled Spitfire would reach the coast of England, the Biggin Hill Wing was letting down over Sussex towards the landmarks of Sevenoaks and Westerham and their airfield on the hill.

At 12.18 hours, the last of the 34 aircraft landed without incident and she was able to relax. As she pushed back her seat and reached for a now-tepid mug of tea, she felt both exalted and exhausted. Why had this trip been so different? She well knew the answer but refused to allow her thoughts to dwell on the matter.

She had not expected to see him until the evening when he would almost certainly be dining in the Mess. It came as a pleasant surprise, therefore, when in the early afternoon and with Meg on a lead, she saw him ahead of her and about to cross the road leading to the main gate and Station Headquarters. She saw him glance to his left before stepping off the curb at which time he caught sight of her. To her considerable satisfaction he stopped and waited for her to draw abreast, which she did with all the calculated nonchalance of someone aware that she was being scrutinised.

She wondered if she should salute whilst holding on to a straining dog with one hand - it seemed a little inappropriate in the circumstances even though his rank entitled him to such a courtesy. She compromised with a smile, at the same time touching her hat with a gloved finger.

He greeted her with, "Wotcher!" stooping to pat Meg's head. "Who's this, Fido? Or does his blue blood entitle him to something more exotic? It is a he, isn't it?" He smiled up at her. "I'm not very good at recognising the signs without becoming too obviously inquisitive."

She said a little primly, "He's a lady. Her name's Meg and she usually bites anyone calling her Fido."

"Does she now!" He was rubbing the dog's ears. "Then she's very badly brought up. Probably takes after her mistress." He smiled and winked. "If we're going to have a lasting friendship, she'll have to improve, you know."

She laughed. "Don't bank on it."

"What, the friendship? Or the improvement?"

"Both, I would say."

There was a moment's hesitation and, sensing her discomfort, he smiled again. "You know, of course, that I have paid informers who report your every movement?"

She laughed again, this time relaxing. "What nonsense you talk! You were on your way to SHQ and I was probably the last person in the world you had in mind."

"You're wrong. About everything. You were next to last, actually." He grinned to rob his remark of any offence. "Sad, though, that I should appear so transparent."

They fell into step as they walked, "I watched you go this morning."

"You were on duty?"

She nodded. "Did you see anything?"

The blue eyes lit up. "Indeed we did. We sat there like lumps of suet looking up at thirty Huns for close on ten minutes. But, as they weren't particularly warlike and as we were too low to get at them, it was stalemate. In that respect it was a flop. In fact, it was a flop in every respect."

"Why so?"

"Why? Well, our aircraft are much too fast for the others low down and they're a bit too good for us high up. In addition to which, they can stay up for longer than we can - and I hate running out of 'essence'."

"I can imagine." She frowned. "So, what now? Does this mean you will be leaving?" She tried to keep her voice unconcerned.

"That depends on 'Sailor'. If he and Group decide that we should go, then that's what will happen. And it might make sense, too. If the Huns keep hitting the coastal towns with their tip-and-run raids, it would be better that we were down on the edge somewhere. After all, apart from the 'Tiffies' we're the only chaps who can catch the varmints low down."

They approached the gate in the fence which she habitually used and she slowed and smiled. "I normally go down here, then walk along the valley."

For one fleeting moment she hoped that he might say he would join her. But, apart from asking where the valley went to and making a comment about the mud and getting her feet dirty, he did not offer. For a second they looked at each other before he said, "Well, as we can't very well shake hands in the road, it's goodbye from me and have a nice walk." He glanced down. "And you too Fido." He stooped to pat the dog again then turned away only to stop. "Oh, now that I think of it, are you going to the Victory Bonds 'do' tonight? It's somewhere on the Station, I don't know where, exactly"

Before she had time to admit that she had not even considered it, he was adding, "If you are, perhaps I'll see you there."

Her eyes smiled, but with a hint of mischief. "I'll have to look at my engagement book."

"Your engagement book! I see. Well, do that."

He coolly returned her smile, raised his hand and walked off.

She opened the gate, fiddling with the catch in order to make as much a meal of it as possible, watching him meanwhile through lowered eyes in the hope that he would turn round. But, he didn't, and suddenly the road seemed very empty.

The dance that evening was a station function, the purpose of which was to solicit pledges to buy Victory Bonds. At least, that was the official excuse. Among the mass of airmen, airwomen, nurses and others, however, Victory Bonds were probably the last things most of them had in mind.

The officers, led by the Station Commander, were normally expected to arrive half-way through the proceedings before leaving en masse an hour or so later. In practice, however, this was seldom the case. There was an unusual camaraderie at RAF Biggin Hill and the relationship between officers - male and female - and non-commissioned officers and others was sometimes very close. There was little of the division that often existed on other stations between those who flew and those who didn't. Biggin Hill fought the war together, and occasionally died together, as had happened several times in the past. When the opportunity arose, they enjoyed their pleasures together in much the same spirit.

She arrived with about twenty other officers, about a third of whom were WAAFs. The party was in full swing, the enormous hall gay with bunting, colour and noise and, by the flushed and animated faces around her, she guessed that much had gone on before.

As they entered, De la Torre, the Station Intelligence Officer, was auctioning some of the bonds and there was noisy bidding, some of it clearly the result of a surfeit of good spirits, alcoholic as well as the other variety. Finally, a winner was announced, an airman mounting the platform, head down and pink around the ears, to claim his reward - a kiss from a young woman especially attired for the occasion in evening dress. The embrace was enacted with great drama to cheers, clapping and not a few improper suggestions from the rear of the crowd. When it was all over, the band struck up again and the room became a seething mass of moving bodies.

It took her some time to find him. She picked him out, dancing with a tall airwoman, one she recognised. Immediately, she felt concern. His partner, besides being attractive, was a member of high society - slumming it! - the languid, spirited and pampered daughter of a prominent race-horse owning family. For a moment she experienced a shaft of jealousy; the girl was not the sort of person to have as a competitor in anything. To her relief they parted at the end of the dance and he was claimed by an officer of his own squadron who led him away deep in conversation.

When the inevitable Paul Jones started, she was pulled onto the floor by one of the Air Traffic Controllers, a face she barely knew. After enduring an un-enter-prising shuffle around the four corners of the room, she joined hands and, at the change of partners, found herself opposite a sergeant colleague from the Ops Room, who clutched her with such ferocity that she had to concentrate hard to avoid being trodden on and smothered.

It was with some relief, therefore, that she heard the music stop, enabling her to smile her thanks then pull away and move on around the circle. She looked over the heads of her near companions and saw the back of his dark head across the room. She moved around, praying that the music would not stop, until he saw her and raised his eyebrows in recognition.

When they were still some five or six paces apart the tune and tempo changed again and she resigned herself to the arms of an older airman who barely came up to her chin. She was about to step off when he was by her side saying politely to her partner, "May I butt in?" Smiling, he carried on, "Would you think me terribly rude if I asked to dance with my auntie?"

The man's mouth dropped open. Then he grinned in return. "Carry on, sir, and the best of British! I wish I had an auntie like her!"

In the middle of the crowded floor there was little they could do other than rock to and fro. She was conscious of his height, but he held her lightly so that she had no feeling of being possessed. He looked down and whispered quietly.

"Wotcher! Enjoy the walk?"

She nodded in return, smiling with her eyes.

"And Fido?"

She nodded again and they continued to dance in silence.

"You dance like a gazelle."

"My cloven hooves?" She gave a stage grimace.

"Right first time! But you're very light on my feet."

With that they both laughed and she felt his arm tighten around her waist. At that moment the music stopped, but he still held on to her. "Don't move!"

Someone pushed past shouting; "Cheat!" at which they both grinned before ignoring the remark, moving off again when the music recommenced. "So, what's your name?"

"You know my name."

"I know your rank and your surname. What does your Mum call you."

She laughed suddenly, her mouth curving, showing her teeth. "If only you knew!"

"Come on, don't muck abart!"

She hesitated."Eileen."

"Eileen."

"You 'eard!"

"That's a nice name.

"I'm glad you like it. It's the only one I've got."

"Mine's Tom."

She cocked her head, then gave an almost secret smile. "I know it is."

"How did you know?"

"Never you mind."

They moved around slowly and she began to feel a subtle warmth as though she were a part of him. Fitting in, everywhere. She was just the right height - her shoulder and his armpit. Just ... oh, everything.! Comfortable. That was the word. Nice and comfortable.

His voice shook her out of her trance. "I've got something to tell you."

She raised her head, enquiringly. "What?"

"We shall be moving on down to Friston tomorrow."

"Friston!" She didn't have the presence of mind to stop her face falling; or to keep dancing. "You mean you've spoken to Sailor?"

He nodded. "I flew down there this afternoon, after I'd left you. It's a grass strip and a bit lumpy for Spits, but I daresay we'll manage. Right on the tip of Beachy Head, which puts us in the best possible position for a raid on Eastbourne." He smiled. "Trouble is we shall be taking off right over the cliffs. I did it today and nearly lost my meat-and-two-veg."

She said nothing for quite some time so that he had to bend a little to peer into her face. "Lost your tongue?

She shook her head then, looking up, wrinkled her nose. "All of a sudden I've gone right off Friston."

He made no reply but squeezed her waist slightly as they continued to dance. After some moments he rested his chin on her hair and, sensing her mood, said in a Noel Coward voice, "Do you come here often?"

Surprised, she looked up then laughed in spite of herself. "You really are a nut."

"Sir, if you please." He was sternly waggish.

"All right, Sir Nut!"

"That's more like it!"

629 Squadron took off next morning whilst she was on duty. She watched details of the movement go up on the stateboard, but they did not bother to put the plots on the table as it was only a thirty mile journey and hardly in the next county. Nor was there any radio conversation or fuss. They just went! Quietly yet completely.

No one around her seemed to care or even to notice, yet she herself felt a deep sense of loss.

For some time she was so unusually quiet that the Controller, thinking it might be her 'time of the month', asked if she were unwell. She tried to reassure him with a bright smile, but knew she had not been very convincing.

In the afternoon she took Meg onto the airfield. 629's dispersal pens were empty and the hardstandings vacant. Standing there, she suddenly experienced a great feeling of loneliness and chided herself for coming. How silly she was being; she had only known him a week or so after all. But being reasonable didn't help very much. She sighed and turned away. She just felt downright miserable, her gloom almost an enjoyable sensation. She was moping, she recognised, like a school-girl. Decently, though, and in a way that no one would notice or bring commiserations. No, hers was a private grief. A very personal thing. But, why, oh why? Life was so unjust!

In the Mess that evening, she sat among her friends at dinner, having little to say. She heard one of her colleagues lamenting the fact that duty would result in a missed party in London, and she heard herself volunteering to stand in.

She spent the night 'down the hole' and, though tired next day, felt somewhat better. She told herself firmly that things could only improve. After all, Friston was still in the Biggin Hill Sector; they would still be able to talk together on business if nothing else.

But as the day wore on her spirits flagged and her heart felt like lead. She found she could not face another walk on the airfield and even the valley had somehow lost its attraction. Meg eyed her with concern; the atmosphere to her acute canine sensors was heavy with gloom and inaction

Then she had a brainwave. Perhaps one of the Controllers, most of whom were pilots, would fly her down to Friston. It would be quite legal and in the line of duty. Yes, that was it! She would enquire about the Tiger Moth - she had flown in that several times before - and charm one of her colleagues into spending a day on 'liaison duties'. Immediately, the prospect of doing something positive made her feel better. Why had she not thought of it before?

On the fifth day after his departure she arrived on duty in the early evening to find action taking place over the South Coast. About a dozen Focke Wulf 190 fighters carrying bombs had raided Eastbourne and she saw that eight of 629 were airborne with other aircraft from Lympne and Hawkinge. Two Germans had been shot down; one pilot, apparently, was in a dinghy and a group of hostile and other plots were fast retreating across the Channel.

She slipped into her Ops 'B' position and began organising the Air Sea Rescue Walrus and the boats. She was relieved to hear that there had been no casualties among the Spitfires and wondered if he had been airborne, with half an eye scanning the stateboards for his call-sign.

Then her telephone rang. It was him. Joy of joys, he was on the 'phone, a bit excited and abrupt, but him none the less. Couldn't she sort out the Walrus immediately? There was a Hun sitting in a dinghy eight miles off-shore and it was vital that he should be picked up before dark. If not, the Hun E-boats would have him in the night and no one wanted that, did they? What about Peter Scott and his MTBs at Newhaven? Couldn't she persuade him to put down his paintbrush for an hour or two and do a bit of searching? Four of his own aircraft were out there now, sitting over the top of the Hun, but they would have to return for fuel very shortly.

She began to explain that the Walrus was already airborne and he recognised her voice at once. He said quietly, "Wotcher! I didn't realise it was you. Have you just come on duty?"

"Yes. Did you shoot at anything?" She asked.

She heard him give a short laugh and imagined his blue eyes dancing. "You're joking. In fact, I was sitting at the end of the runway on 'standby', like the proverbial lemon I may add, when a dozen of them appeared over the hedge, nearly knocking my head off. By the time I was airborne they had all gone. Fortunately, they ran into four of my chaps returning from Manston. They knew nothing of any raid until they were suddenly confronted by twelve Huns going like the clappers. Gave them a nasty turn, I can tell you!"

They both laughed, more as a reflex action than signifying a response to humour, and there was a moment's silence. She glanced around quickly and lowered her voice; "I'm glad that nothing dreadful happened to you. We all miss you back here, you know."

An awkward silence fell between them. Had she said something out of place? Panicking, she spoke at the same time as he did.

"Are you still … ?"

They both laughed simultaneously, but he went on, "You do? Well, that's nice to know."

She wanted to ask him, 'Can you fly up and see me, perhaps?' But her courage failed her and she heard herself saying, "Are you likely to be this way again, any time? Calling on 'Sailor', maybe?"

His short responding laugh made her smile again. "Not Pygmalion likely! Otherwise, I should have to ask him what his Ops Staff were doing whilst a dozen Huns were on a Cook's tour of Southern England, scaring the daylights out of us poor, honest pilot boys."

"We do our best, sir."

A perfectly timed pause had her waiting expectantly, until his quiet voice broke the silence, "Are you still as lovely?"

She smiled. "Of course."

"And the cloven hooves?"

"Never in better shape."

She waited for his response, hardly daring to breath. "Tell you what, then. I'll fly up on Thursday next, which is our stand-down day. We can take Fido for a run and, who knows, we may be able to plan something for next week."

Her heart gave a bound, but she managed to reply calmly and primly, "That would be nice."

"Will you be free?"

"I could arrange to be."

"Fine. Thursday, then."

"Thursday. I shall look forward to it."

She replaced the telephone and glanced quickly around the room. No one had noticed, apparently. She was obliged to take a very deep breath. Goodness! Everything - but everything! - began to look better.

She took Meg on to the airfield to meet him. She knew that she was early but persuaded herself that it was because she would not know where he would park his aircraft. She decided to wait at the Watch Office and, as she approached, Jack Shepherd appeared on his balcony in his shirt-sleeves to shout down to her. "Be here in about five minutes, old love."

She waved in acknowledgement and, looking towards the south, saw the single dot of his aeroplane in the distance and watched it grow until the noise of it reached her and it circled the airfield. It curved towards her gracefully on its final approach and touched down.

She walked towards him as he taxied in, her heart light, her face smiling. He threw off his straps and parachute harness and, fitting on his side-cap, stepped down to meet her. "Wotcher! How nice to be greeted with the red carpet."

She smiled and shrugged. "We do it for almost everyone!"

They stood briefly in silence, before he took the initiative. "Well, here I am. All booted and spurred. Are we ready for the off?"

She knuckled her forelock in a stage gesture. "All ready for starting, sir."

He bent down and rubbed the dog's ears. "Nice to see you again, Fido? Has your mistress been behaving herself?"

As though on cue, Meg put her head between her front paws and stuck her rump in the air. After a brief 'Whuff!' she began to race around in a circle, barking and causing them both to laugh and break the tension of the moment. "She's trying to change the subject, wouldn't you say?"

They left the station by the main gate and walked together down the road to where a stile led them into the valley.

She climbed over, laughing a little self-consciously as her tight skirt rode above her knees so that he made a pretence of not looking as he helped her down, holding her hand firmly as she jumped.

The path being narrow and soft in places, they moved off in single file, the dog running ahead over what was for her, familiar ground. Finally they emerged into an open meadow which fell away before them revealing an expanse of rolling, sun-bathed countryside. He stopped and took in the view, breathing deeply several times.

"Kent! How lovely it is, this England of ours." He turned and smiled. "What lucky people we are. None of the mud and filth of trench-warfare for us. We should count our blessings." He held out his hand and, a little surprised but moved by his sudden emotion, she took it - gladly and with a strange feeling of contentment. They walked off down the hill, their joined arms swinging in unison.

For more than an hour they wandered, two young people brought together by the circumstances of war. Had it not been so, he would probably have left Cambridge and returned to the hills of Cumberland whence he sprang, whilst she would have remained among her New Forest villages. They talked of families, schools and universities, of friends, of home life and of holidays and places visited. He threw sticks for the dog and spoke to her of history in amusing and fascinating terms; of Quebec and General Wolfe, near whose home they were walking, of the Indian Mutiny, of which she knew absolutely nothing other than the name, and of his forebears who had fought with Howe and Burgoyne in America during the

War of Independence. Always a good listener, she was quietly intrigued and delighted by his anecdotes and his light-hearted manner of describing events.

She asked, "Do you like it at Friston?" Hoping he would say that he preferred Biggin Hill.

Instead, he was full of boyish enthusiasm. "Heavens, yes! We're right on the top of Beachy Head with the sea, the hills, and infinite space in every direction. Wonderful. The take-off still bothers me, though. Straight over the cliff edge and each time praying that the old fan will keep on turning." He grinned. "I've halted more lunches just on the point of seeing daylight for the second time … ." an unfinished remark at which she pulled a face and looked away saying, "Don't! Please. I see it all."

"But, Friston isn't a permanent aerodrome, surely? Where do you live?"

"Live? Oh, there's a private house on the airfield boundary. Very elegant. The family who own it live in three rooms and we chaps use the rest. Patriotic self-denial in its most practical form. Also there's a super garden. Full of lilies. Do you know there are over seventy different kinds of lily?" He shook his head in disbelief. "I'm hopeless with flowers - the complete ignoramus! I could write a book on what I don't know on the subject!"

She smiled fondly at his unaffected delight. She knew all about lilies but allowed her face to register polite astonishment in order to encourage him.

He was going on. "The scent of them is beyond belief, particularly in the evening. I have a mass of them in my room, too. The girl who looks after me picks them especially each day."

"How nice for you." She heard her own voice, flatly restrained. "Who does look after you, incidentally?"

He replied guilelessly, "Oh, a WAAF Corporal. Nice girl. Came from here, I believe. Daphne something or other - I don't recall her second name. Everyone likes her. She's one of four in the Mess."

She frowned, trying to remembered the 'Daphnes' who had served in the Mess at Biggin but could not place her. Probably some designing minx taking advantage of her scarcity value to make sheep's eyes at the pilots. What fools men were! She would find out about Daphne. And after that, for a moment or two, she was silent.

Within minutes, however, his good spirits had swept away her brief bout of dejection and they continued to walk in cheerful harmony until they were several miles away from the aerodrome.

They had breasted a steep rise when he turned to her, a little breathless. "Shall we rest for a while before turning back?"

They sat down on the grass after removing their hats, she with her legs decorously tucked beneath her, he with his arms about his knees, each of them silent in quiet contemplation of the scenery. He played contemplatively with a stem of long grass for what seemd an age.

Without looking in her direction he asked suddenly, "What does the future hold for us?"

She shrugged. "Does anyone know? Particularly those of you who fly?"

"We have to think ahead, though, don't we? Otherwise, what is the point of all these terrible goings-on ... unless something good is born of them?" He turned and looked at her directly, his eyes serious.

She was watching his face. It was as though a cloud had passed over an area formerly bathed in sunshine. She became aware, not for the first time, of the wistful eyes, the sensitive mouth, and the clean line of his chin, not feminine in any way but not heavily masculine either. Boyish, rather than that of a man. And appealing. Oh, so appealing. Her protective instincts were aroused in a way she had never known before. She felt her heart reach out to him and it was at that moment, like an act of religious conversion, that she knew she loved him.

Controlling herself with an effort, she steadied her voice, "I suppose so. But we're all such small people in a very big war. Pawns in a highly complicated game of chess. Expendable, if we faced reality."

"But all of us with a purpose, wouldn't you agree?"

She was still trembling inside. "I don't know." It was difficult to concentrate.

"It's nice to think so. But, sometimes ... I wonder."

"We have to believe so. Otherwise, what is the point?"

"Our paths are charted, you mean?" She was a little better now.

"We each have something to do, surely. Something to achieve. Some impression to make. Something."

She smiled. "Perhaps you're right. I wonder, though, what I'm achieving."

"You're doing a worthwhile job, for a start. And you're making me happy."

She glanced up quickly, but from his blandly innocent look could not decide whether or not he was serious. She gave a little snort to relieve her emotions.

"You're a romantic. Or, a bit naughty. Or both, I'm not quite sure." She smiled to cover her uncertainty, then put out a hand. "I'm sorry, I don't mean to be facetious."

He regarded her thoughtfully and grinned, the sunshine returning to their private world. "You're a wary old morsel, aren't you?"

She put on a mock frown. "Not so much of the 'old', young sir!"

The pair fell silent and he tossed a few stones idly at a fallen twig. She felt obliged to make some contribution. "Will you stay on in the Air Force?"

"Probably, God willing. I can't imagine doing anything else now." He shrugged. "That's if they'll have me, of course. What will you do?"

"Oh, I don't know, really. Marry eventually, I suppose. I've never given it much thought." Hearing her own words, she knew she was lying. She watched him throw another small stone before he replied in contemplation. "Promise not to give it too much thought, will you? Not yet, anyway."

She was trying hard to keep her voice level. "If you insist. But, there not exactly being a queue at my door, it's not a decision I have to make at the moment." She smiled in his direction, reducing the conversation to banter, "I'll tell you when it is, though."

There was a long silence during which her gaze followed cloud shadows drifting slowly over the nearby hills, the whole forming a patchwork of greens, blues and greys, intermingled with the yellows of ripening crops. All so different yet all combined by nature into a balanced and matching whole. Part of a scheme? A grand design? She was churning inside still. If only she knew. If only it were true.

His voice shook her out of her daze. "How long have you been here?"

"Biggin, you mean? Almost two years, now. I came here after I was commissioned. Before that, I was a Corporal at Kenley. In 1940."

"So it was you who won the Battle of Britain?"

"Of course! Single-handed!" She smiled. "I thought you would have known."

They walked back up the valley, Slowly, often without speaking, always comfortably.

"If I asked you, would you come up to London with me?" He was speaking over his shoulder. "On my next stand-down. We could do something madly exciting like ... like feeding the ducks, or going to Westminster Abbey, or visiting the Chamber of Horrors, that sort of thing. I might even buy you a bun - that coffee stall at Hyde Park Corner, or even Lyons Corner House; the big one at Charing Cross."

She grinned derisively. "You make it sound irresistible. I'm overwhelmed!" She put a finger to her brow, frowning. "I'd certainly give it some thought - if you asked me, of course. Subject to my other engagements, you understand." She gave a mischievous glance. "I could be absolutely sure of a meal?"

"Almost! Not absolutely."

"And.," She looked at him calmly, "I wouldn't be expected to stay the night, would I?"

His eyes smiled gently in return. "No, you wouldn't be staying the night."

"Then why don't you ask me?"

He nodded, purposely inscrutable. "I'll give it some thought!"

It was arranged for Thursday, at 2 pm., and she had asked especially that he called for her at the WAAF Officers' Quarters and not the Mess proper.

He arrived, punctual to the minute, and was climbing out of his blue and black 1937 Morris Ten when she walked quickly down the small drive to meet him, her heels tapping.

"Goodness!" She was speaking before she even reached him. "I didn't know you were so affluent. Sunshine roof, too! Does it open?"

"Open! It doesn't close! If it rains, we get wet, and there's nothing I can do about it." He eyed her appraisingly and with some surprise. "Civvies, I see. My word, you do look - different."

"Illegal, I know." She pulled a face. "That's why it would be a good idea if you opened the door so that I can disappear from public view."

He started. "Sorry! I was rooted to the ground by the spectacle."

Inside, he turned to her admiringly. "I'm spellbound! You're a different person. You really are a very beautiful woman."

She was obliged to lower her gaze. "Yes . . . well." Then she added more brightly, "And a little less of the 'woman', if you don't mind." To cover her embarrassment she blew a plume of air from her lower lip so that a lock of her auburn hair shook.   "Less of everything, in fact; otherwise, I shall be bright pink for the rest of the afternoon." She smiled mischievously. "That doesn't rule out the occasional compliment, though."

"Right, I'll remember that."

They drove off towards Bromley, then into London, comfortable in each other's presence, chatting, relaxed and carefree. From time to time, some word or phrase would bring them face to face, laughing, appraising, appreciating, new to each other yet settled in companionship. Often she felt an almost overwhelming urge to reach out and touch him, his hand, his arm, anywhere. And his glances, she saw, were on her hair, her mouth, her hands, her body ... everywhere! And she was pleasing him, she knew. She recognised it in his face, sensing it with a pleasure totally unsullied by embarrassment. She wanted to be beautiful for him. Oh God! She was so happy.

They crossed the river at London Bridge and he jinked through the traffic with such determination that she was obliged to hang on, trying hard not to show signs of apprehension. He drew up with a squeal in Birdcage Walk in the West-End and backed into a parking space.

As he locked the car he grinned in her direction. "I know what you're thinking. But I always park in Birdcage Walk because it's near to Scotland Yard." He was walking round the car towards her. "I did a broadcast once and they kept me so long, the police towed my car away. It took me an hour to find out where it was; an hour to get to Scotland Yard, and another hour to persuade them to hand it back. All between midnight and 3 am. Now," he grinned, "I take the precaution of cutting out at least one stage of the exercise." He offered his arm. "Across St James Park for a start. All set?"

As they walked towards the lake, she suddenly hugged his arm tightly. "You see, if I were in uniform I shouldn't be able to do this. You've no idea how different I feel; another person entirely, no saluting, no ... . Oh, I'm prattling on! Take no notice. I'm just, just very, very happy."

"I'm only moderately impressed. Happiness is mostly to do with the stomach! It's that bun I promised you at Lyons Corner House that's cheering you up."

She laughed. "How like a man. No, come on, where are you taking me?" Her red mouth curved bewitchingly.

He gave her a sidelong glance. "Madame Tussauds to kick off with."

"Madame Tussauds!" Her face showed dismay and disbelief. "Walking? But it's miles away." She lifted a foot. "No, look! I can't in these, really I can't"

"There you are, you see. No sooner do we start, than you want to change the programme immediately." He began to fish in his pocket. "Here, I got this stuff from the Mess kitchen. Item one. Feed the ducks." He handed her some bread. "That one over there looks terribly thin."

Laughing, she began to toss the food to the gathering flotilla. "You really are a nut!"

"Sir!"

"No, I'm not going to say, sir. It's my day off." She smirked. "And anyway, I'm older than you."

He turned in surprise. "You've been checking up!"

"Well, what if I have?"

"Rank insubordination, that's what it is." He made a sudden grab and gathered her to him so that, crushed into his side, her face pressed against his wings and medal ribbons, she felt as childishly and as ridiculously light-hearted as ever she had been in her life.

"Watch my lipstick! If it goes on your wings, you really will have some explaining to do."

"Blow the lipstick! And it's no use wriggling, either. I don't care who's watching." He held her breathless body gently.

An hour later they were seated at tea in the Mayfair Hotel. She hesitated as the waitress smoothed a wrinkle from their table cloth. "I still think I'm dreaming. I was absolutely sure I was going to have the Execution of Charles the First as the forerunner to a Lyons Corner House doughnut. Instead of which, here I am, cucumber sandwiches, China tea, et al."

"D'you like China tea?"

"Not really. But I thought it would be worth my life to say so when you were ordering it."

"Very tactful of you, but you can have Indian if you want. No, on second thoughts, you can't. We must all cultivate more sophisticated tastes, don't you think?"

"If you say so."

"I do. Now, shall I tell you what I have in mind for later on?"

She paused, her eyes amused but knowing. "What you have in mind and what's actually going to happen may not necessarily be the same thing. If you see what I mean."

She saw him hesitate a fraction and instantly regretted her remark.

"Only too well do I see what you mean. Your virginity, however, is of no concern to me tonight, nor need you mention it again." He looked at her directly, the corners of his mouth twitching. "And well might you go pink, young lady - which is what you are doing - because you jolly well deserve to be embarrassed."

She stretched out a hand, penitent. "Please! I'm sorry. I shouldn't have said it. Let's ... let's go back to where we were a minute ago. Please?"

He touched her fingers in reconciliation. "Now, where were we? Yes, I remember. First, we'll do an Ivor Novello musical. And so that you can't quibble, I've already booked."

"Quibble!" Her face was radiant. "Who'd want to quibble with that? Which one, by the way?"

"I don't know, to tell you the truth. All I do know is that Mary Ellis is in it. And I'd go anywhere to see and hear Mary Ellis. So that's that! After which, we'll dine at the Lansdowne."

"Lansdowne! I don't know it."

"Very special. We'll probably fall over Noel Coward and Diana Wynyarde; it's that sort of a place. But nice. You'll like it."

She put on a stage frown. "First Mary Ellis then Diana Wynyarde! I'm not so sure."

But he was going on with his itinerary. "After which, you have a choice. It's either Chappie d'Amato at the Cafe de Paris or Don Marino Barretto at the Embassy Club, whichever you prefer."

She hesitated again, this time with fondness and concern in her eyes. "Please, please, you're spoiling me." Her voice fell to a hushed whisper. "I don't really need all this, you know. It'll be, well, terribly, terribly expensive. Won't it?"

But his eyes were dancing. "You'd like to go, though?"

"Yes, but." She reached out and grasped his fingers. "Look, it's you I want to be with, not all these, these other people. If I could just stand in a corner with you somewhere for the rest of the evening, I'd be happy. Or dance, perhaps, anywhere, I don't mind. Then I'd be much, much more than happy. Please?"

She saw his eyes again, as she had seen them on that first day she had met him at Biggin Hill, bright, challenging, imperious, and she knew her protest would come to nothing.

"The first principle of war! D'you remember it?" His voice was firm and faintly contemptuous. "Maintain the aim! Right? So that's what we'll do. And if we're home by dawn, we'll be lucky." He grinned. "Why d'you think I parked my car where I did? Anyway," he closed one eye slowly, "this is to be a very special occasion."

And so, indeed, it became; an occasion she was to remember all her life, a time of tenderness, of laughter, of merriment and of quiet contemplation. A time, too, of sadness mingled with fear as she allowed her mind to dwell, if only briefly, on the miracle of good fortune that had brought them together and how short-lived her happiness might be.

Her heart had filled more than once when her glances and touches of affection were reciprocated in full measure and she radiated pride when those nearby looked with admiration at his wings and decorations as they took their seats in the theatre. She knew they would be thinking and remarking quietly between themselves how attractive and obviously well-suited the two of them were, a thought to which she responded by becoming even more radiant herself.

Their visit to the theatre had been a joyful experience. In the fourth row from the stage it seemed that the whole production, play and players, was there for their personal benefit. He had seemed unaccountably a little on edge at first, so much so that she had surreptitiously touched his hand and, in a whisper, asked why. He had shaken his head. "It's always the same. For the first act, I'm always in a tizzy waiting for them to forget their lines." He grinned and whispered back. "Don't fret, I shall be all right in a moment."

The Lansdowne had also caused some laughs. They had bundled into a cab and the driver had asked, "Lansdowne, Guv? Which one d'yer mean?"

And he hadn't known. Rising to the occasion, however, he had said cheerfully, "Try 'em all in turn and I'll shout when we arrive at the right one." Adding, as he held her hand in the dark confines of the rear seat, "I've only been to it in the blackout and usually when I've been very-nice-thank-you! But, I'll know when I'm there - I've never been that far gone!"

At the Lansdowne, the atmosphere had been just right. As had been the meal, a long drawn out period of bliss, with good food, quiet music, the most elegant of company - even without Diana Wynyarde and Noel Coward - and dancing.

Dancing, when they had drifted around sedately in a warm, pleasurable haze of good wine and love, in such harmony of body and spirit that her feet seemed to melt away into nothingness and she was able to imagine herself floating off on an endless expanse of white cloud. But she had remained sufficiently alert to whisper once whilst they were on the floor. "Are you quite sure we're not going to have to wash the dishes after all this?" To which he had looked down at her and solemnly closed one eye.

Midnight came and went before they were out once more in the velvety darkness. An air-raid was in progress, the fingers of the searchlights rippling silently across the base of the clouds and, in the distance, the hollow 'tonk-tonk-tonk' of the guns as they fired, followed by the far-off 'crumps' of the bursting shells and the more solid explosions of bombs. And throughout it all, the thin drone of the

German bombers, strangely discordant and unlike the noise of British aircraft.

For a time they stood and watched, invisible in the blackness, wrapped in each others arms. With her head buried in his shoulder, aware of the faint wool odour of his uniform, she felt warm and comfortable and safe, so that, despite the turmoil around her, it all seemed an unreal fantasy, the sombre sounds of the war serving only to heighten their awareness of companionship and love. She heard him asking quietly, "Scared?"

And she had shaken her head. "Not a bit. Not with you,' and she had raised her mouth so that he could touch her lips with his own.

"Tired, then?"

"No. Just gloriously ... relaxed ... and floating ...and drifting. Wonderful!"

"To our night-club, then? The Embassy?"

"Anything. Anywhere."

In the Embassy Club it was barely light and they sat in a rose-tinted corner in silent company, their hands and bodies touching. The dance floor was minuscule and the dancers, few in number, moved hardly at all, their apparent lethargy and the slow muffled thudding of a drum amid the background of soft music, contributing to the almost unreal atmosphere of some primitive love ceremony.

In front, Don Marino, his copper face glistening with sweat, fingered the keys, grinning and nodding and pausing only with one hand to push back erring strands of glistening black hair from his forehead.

They danced again and again, doing little more than sway to the rhythm, often without speaking, their bodies moulded together, cocooned in an aura of affection, occasionally touching lips unselfconsciously, aware of each other with an almost frightening intensity. Once, with her eyes closed, she suddenly became stricken with fear. What if ... ? But when she looked at him wide-eyed, she was comforted by his presence, breathing deeply several times and hugging him so tightly that he had asked, "All right?" And she had nodded with a wan smile. "Someone walking on my grave."

Back at their table she noticed a sudden restlessness in him. "Do you like champagne?"

"Champagne!" Her eyes were soft again. "No, really. You shouldn't." She took his hand. "In any case, it's wasted on me. Please?"

"All right. But we need something to celebrate. I'll get some more wine."

"Very well, if you must." She leaned forward, lips parted, her eyes teasing. "Tell me, what particularly are we celebrating?"

"Celebrating?" He paused to stroke her nose gently with a forefinger. "I'll tell you what we're celebrating. I'm just about to ask you to marry me. That's what!"

Although some deep-seated female instinct had in some way prepared her, the impact of his offhand remark left her stunned and speechless so that she could only put a hand to her throat and return a half-blank, half-surprised stare. He looked at her, his eyes moving slowly about her face with the smallest of questioning smiles. "Well? Am I to go on?"

It seemed an age before she could summon the composure to say: "Oh, dear!" She laughed uncertainly. "I'm thrown! Utterly thrown! My dear, this has never happened before. I just don't know what to say. Or do." She took his hands and looked into his eyes. "You must know that every fibre in my body wants to say Yes! Yes! Yes! A thousand Yesses! But ... ."

"But, what?"

"Oh, so many things." She paused, her eyes searching. "Are you really serious? Or, are you just being ... being smartly amusing? Giving me the opportunity of saying something terribly witty in reply?"

His face broke into a grin. "Of course I'm serious, you mutt. I never joke about important things. Such as flying, my mess bill and getting married. Believe me, it all amounts to high drama in my book." His eyes softening, he touched her nose again with a finger. "I've decided to marry you. Not this week, or next month, or even next year – life's a bit too uncertain at the moment. But, some day. When times are better. Or look as though they're going to be better. So, I thought I should let you know. So that you could get used to the idea." When she shook her head in disbelief, he laughed at her silent confusion. "Cheer up! It's not as bad as that. With my superior education, I could well be useful about the house - you know, paint a wall, mend a tap, who knows? Besides rendering a few more personal services, of course!" He was grinning again. "Well, do I go on?"

She felt a sob rising in her throat but somehow managed a kind of laugh. "Go on? Yes, go on, please! Please, go on?"

"All right, then." He took her hands. "I do ask. Now. Making it as real and as earnest as I possibly can." He looked away and felt carefully in the small slit pocket beneath his uniform belt. "Here. This was especially designed to cope with this sort of occasion." He proffered a ring, slim, dully gold in the half-light, with several small stones. "We'll put it on now - with your agreement. But let's make symbolic only, at the moment, should we? Then, later, when we both decide, we can do the thing proper-like. In fact, no one else need know yet. Our private secret."

She watched him slide the ring on her finger with much the same feelings she imagined she would have witnessing some terribly dramatic incident from afar - those of helpless awe. Everything inside her was churning about, but with a difference; it was a glorious, warm and thrilling turmoil. Yet she was not without uncertainty, not entirely without a niggling fear.

Reaching up and kissing him lightly on the mouth she said softly, "You are a chump; a wonderful, lovely, romantic chump. And I do so love you. Yes, I really do. And it's because I love you so much that I have this terrible inner something. I can't explain it. But it's there. A little malevolent worm among all the wonderful things that are going on inside me."

"Then we'll have to winkle it out, won't we?"

She paused and smiled fondly. Did he understand, she wondered? Did men ever understand? But he was going on, his eyes alight.

"Look, in two weeks time I shall take ten days leave and - you may not know it yet - so shall you. I've saved up six months' petrol coupons - let's see, that's 36 gallons - which will take us up to the Lakes and at least half the way back. There we'll walk among the hills, eat cream teas, and search for Wordsworth's daffodils." His face became serious. "You will come, won't you?"

Her eyes brimming, she squeezed his hands. "I'm not sure my Mum's going to approve."

"She can come, too, if you insist!"

She laughed then put on a solemn face. "My last scruple is demolished! Have your wicked way with me!" Her eyes explored his face. "Oh dear God! I'm so happy. I don't think you'll ever understand how happy."

Sensing her emotion, he said, "Then let's enjoy the experience. The worrying and the less nice bits will come without our inviting them. It's all meant, you know. Part of the grand plan. Do you remember me saying?"

"You really think so?" She so wanted reassurance.

"Why else would we have been brought to Biggin when it was so obvious that we wouldn't fit in? No, I'm convinced the Lord looks down. What's the old adage?

'There's a destiny which shapes our ends, rough hew them as we will.' Something like that anyway."

To her surprise but without embarrassment, she felt her face begin to crumble.

"Oh, my dear, you shouldn't do this to me. Just ... just hold me."

Which he was happy to do. For some time.

The night was fine and clear when they emerged from the Embassy, the air raid over. They wandered in the darkness of the blackout for a long time, their arms clasped around each other's waists and mostly silent with fatigue, emotion and a glorious contentment. Finally, when they reached the top of Whitehall and with Trafalgar Square eerily deserted and quiet, he said, "D'you realise, it's almost 3 am?"

She looked up. "Time! What is time? I could be in another century."

"I could be too, except that I have to be on standby at seven. Which gives me precisely four hours to get you home and drive down to the south coast."

She giggled. "If we still have a car."

"You are so right! If we still have a car."

But the car was there and soon they were crossing London Bridge on their way to the south east. Silent and motionless in her seat, she suddenly cuddled against him and as she relaxed and leaned more heavily, he knew she was nearly asleep. Guiding her head with his arm, he allowed her to fall gently into his lap until she was lying across him, her body warm and softly inert.

Cramped and restricted himself, he drove with one hand on the steering wheel and, his eyes drooping, missed the turning that would take them to Bromley, so committing himself to the Maidstone Road. Savagely but silently annoyed with himself, he decided not to turn round. He would carry on and go through Sevenoaks.

By the time the little car finally drew up outside the WAAF Officers' Quarters at Biggin Hill, the eastern sky was full of the dawn's arrival. She awoke without prompting and straightened sleepily.

"Where are we?"

"Home. Your home, anyway."

"And I've let you drive all the way without company." She took his hands as they sat in the car. "Fine old partner in life's eternal struggle I'm going to make!"

He smiled, weariness in his eyes. "You haven't changed your mind?"

"Not in a thousand years. And you?"

"Need you ask? It would be interfering with the grand design, anyway." He grinned. "Which isn't allowed."

A robin trilled from the bushes in the dawn light, the only sound as they held each other. "I don't want you to leave me." Her voice was childishly petulant.

"I don't want to go. But I must."

She squeezed his hands. "Then hold me, and kiss me, and tell me that you'll drive carefully." She sat watching him with fond eyes. "And keep thinking of me all the time, as I shall be thinking of you. And praying for both of us. Goodnight, my darling. And thank you, thank you for a wonderful, memorable evening."

When she had finally slid out of the car, she came round the other side and bent to his open window. "I would never forgive myself if anything happened to you. So drive carefully because you must be worn out. Then telephone me, tomorrow. Or, I will call you, which may be better. I'm on duty between four and midnight."
She then let him clasp her hand briefly before he moved off.

Shortly before 7 am. he drove into dispersal on the airstrip at Friston, and examined the squadron stateboard through tired, burning eyes. "What time have you got me down for?"

"We left you off until eight, sir. As you were not here, that is." He detected a faint air of amused conspiracy in the voice.

"You needn't be so diplomatic. I'm ready now, if you want me. Is my aircraft serviceable?"

"All ready to go, sir."

"Then I'll relieve the others in half-an-hour. And just hope to God nothing comes our way!"

"As you wish, sir."

CHAPTER THREE

For the next several days she walked on air. On duty she was willing, cheerful but preoccupied. At all other times she greeted the world with a new serenity and a knowing amiability. But there were brief periods of doubt and uncertainty, particularly in the small hours of the morning when she was tired and alone. She would be stricken by sudden, disturbing bouts of melancholy, periods of naked fear when she felt that somehow her happiness was unmerited and therefore something that could be torn away from her in an instant.

But these were momentary lapses and her new attitude, although not markedly different from her old agreeable self, did not go unnoticed, resulting in a few raised eyebrows and some sage deductions as to why, not all of them wide of the mark. She did not wear her ring nor did she discuss her new-found love with anyone. Hers was a private joy; public rejoicing would come later.

It was when she had awakened earlier than usual, before going on night duty, and was staring at the darkened ceiling, her mind racing, that she had become obsessed with the need to make some tangible, reciprocal gesture for the ring he had given her. Something masculine, of course, and useful, and of real and lasting value, naturally. What could she get him? She was not without resources but there were limits. Something gold? Well! Silver perhaps? That was more like it. She would go into London and see what she could find.

The following day, in a minor fever of excitement, she obtained permission to change her times of duty and took the bus into Bromley and the train and tube to the centre of London. She surfaced in Piccadilly Circus and set off up Regent Street. Garrards was the place she had decided on; she couldn't do better than Garrards.

The interior of that famous establishment never failed to impress her but, having been there several times before, she remained undaunted by the display of wealth that lay around. She approached an elderly, elegantly turned-out gentleman assistant who, without her knowledge, had been eyeing her discreetly and with appreciative interest.

"Good morning. I'm looking for a gift. For a friend. Something silver; something that he would find useful as well as being decorative."

She smiled and the man's eyes took in her face, alight with feeling, the shining auburn hair beneath her cap and the slim curves of her uniformed figure, his gaze lasting for rather longer than either convention or politeness normally allowed.

"Of course, Madame. Did you have anything particular in mind?"

"I haven't, I'm afraid. I was hoping you might be able to help me."

"Silver, you say. Well ... a cigarette case? Or, what about a flask? For brandy, or indeed any sort of spirit. Is the gentleman a rugger enthusiast? Or given to standing about in the cold? A racing man, perhaps?"

Her smile broadened. "I don't know if he's any of those things, but your second suggestion sounds very sensible. May I see some?

"Of course, Madame." The man bowed and turned away to return shortly but unhurriedly with several flasks of different sizes and values. After examining them all at length she selected one that appealed to her most and asked the price. The man scrutinized the ticket attached to it with the devout air of a connoisseur and gave a figure which made her insides shrivel. Two months' pay, at least! But, with aplomb, she maintained her outward calm and nodded in acceptance.

"I shall need it engraved, though. Would you be able to do that immediately?"

The man tilted his head and looked doubtful. "Well Madame, we normally ask for the article to be left. But ... . He eyed her enquiringly.

"I'm afraid I can't do that. I'm happy to wait for an hour or so, but no longer."

She looked at the man directly and he noted, not without a spasm of admiration, the firmness in her face and the open frankness of her hazel-green eyes.

He smiled. "Of course. It's unusual, Madame, but I'll see what I can do. I imagine there's a degree of urgency involved?"

"You could say that, yes."

"Then, could I suggest you leave it for about 90 minutes? If I can't have it done on the premises, well ... there are always ways and means."

She grinned broadly, "Thank you, you are very kind," and handed over a paper with his printed initials.

Two hours later she was on her way back to Biggin Hill with the flask, gleaming, inscribed, and carefully wrapped in tissue paper, safe in a recess of her blue WAAF handbag. More than two months' pay! What was she going to live on? Still, she begrudged not a penny of it. Moreover, the act of giving kindled a pleasurably warm glow within her. Now, all that remained was to arrange for someone to take her down to Friston in the Tiger Moth. Everything was to be a surprise; not only the gift but the visit itself.

Once back, she lost no time in speaking to Jack Shepherd, the Air Traffic Control Officer, who in turn consulted a close acquaintance in the Communications Flight. Within minutes an arrangement was concluded. Not only would the Tiger Moth be made available but a pilot would also be provided to take her. It was a condition, however, that she would have to wear trousers - how else would she be able to strap on the seat-type parachute harness?

This particular aspect of the trip she viewed with some misgivings. A little sensitive about the dimensions of her seat - an imperfection more imagined than real - she preferred it not to be exhibited more than was absolutely necessary. Even so, she concluded that it was a small price to pay for such an eagerly anticipated meeting.

In the event, however, she was to be disappointed. Arriving at the Communications Flight at the agreed time, she was dismayed to see the engine panels of the Tiger Moth on the hangar floor and two overall-clad airmen inspecting the aircraft's interior.

Her pilot, hands in pockets, explained the circumstances. "I'm afraid we have a problem. They found some metal fragments in the main oil filter, which could mean bearing trouble. Even if it doesn't, it rather looks as though our trip is off, as we shall have to do a full exploratory inspection anyway." He shrugged. "I'm sorry, but that's the way things are."

She was crushed. "Is there no other aircraft we could use?"

"There's the Oxford, but unfortunately the Station Commander is using that later on to go to Fighter Command Headquarters." He rolled his eyes. "I don't think I dare ask him to use something else. Or go by road!"

She sighed. "No, of course not. And there's absolutely nothing else."

"Not unless you're willing to fly a Spitfire - solo!"

She gave a wan smile before turning away. Why did people have to be humorous at such terribly disappointing moments?

After several minutes hesitation, however, she entered the Communications Flight office and asked to use the telephone. Having been put through to Friston via the Operations Room and noting that she was alone, she waited for the ringing tone to be answered.

"Crew Room." She heard a voice, brief and to the point. The airman-of-the-watch, she guessed.

"Is the Commanding Officer there?"

"Squadron Commander, you mean?"

"Yes."

"Just a moment. Who is that?"

She hesitated briefly. "Sector Ops."

"Hold on, please."

Within seconds a brisk voice answered. "Hello?"

She knew his voice immediately. "My goodness, you were quick."

There was a pause and she sensed that he had recognised her own voice and that he would have to be discreet.

"Can I help you?" His tone was politely flat.

"Can I speak?"

"Up to a point, yes."

"I was just on my way down to see you by air but my aircraft has gone unserviceable."

"You were coming here?" She heard his voice rise.

"Yes. By Tiger Moth. It was to be today's big event. A surprise. I wanted to see you so very much. To give you something, actually. And now it looks as though I can't."

"I see. An insurmountable problem?"

"It rather looks like it. I'm absolutely deflated and feel like crying."

"Well, we can't have that, can we? So, now what?"

"I don't know." There was a brief silence. "You couldn't come up here, I suppose?"

"Now, you mean?"

"Yes."

"Very difficult, I'm afraid. I'm all booted and spurred and in the crew-room. I'm next pair on stand-by, in fact."

He heard her sigh. "Oh, dear! Well ... that's that, I reckon." There was a pause. "I was so looking forward to seeing you. Are you still there?"

"Yes. I was thinking."

"You were so quiet."

"Look, if I come up in about two hours time, would that do? I could do my stint on the end of the runway for an hour, then fly across. Only take me ten minutes. It would have to be very important, though. Special dispensation, and all that."

She could imagine him grinning and said. "It is very important. Almost a national emergency, in fact. It seems that way to me, anyway."

"In that case, I shall have to come, won't I?"

"Are you sure?" Her heart was bounding.

"I'll come, sure or unsure. Two hours from now. All right?"

"Two hours from now." She lowered her voice. "And I do so love you. Especially now."

"Naturally! I would have expected no less!" And she thought she heard him chuckle as she replaced the receiver.

After her telephone call, she walked back to the Mess and changed - she had no intention of being seen in anything so unglamorous as battle-dress trousers.

She killed time for more than an hour, first with a book - finding it impossible to read - then in the garden where, with the approval of the Mess Secretary, she picked some flowers for the Ladies' Room.

As the hour of his arrival approached, she put on a new face with more than usual care before settling her service-dress hat precisely on her head and walking across to the airfield.

She was standing outside the Communications Flight office when his aircraft slipped quietly into the circuit and sank like an alighting swan, its wheels and flaps extended, to touch down, run for a while, then slowly wend its way towards her.

She found herself smiling and excited, thinking at the same time how ungainly the Spitfire - so beautiful and graceful in the air - suddenly became on landing; ungainly and venomous, with its protruding cannons, its rocking, dipping wings and its raucous, spitting exhausts.

As she watched, the noise ceased as the engine was switched off and the big four-bladed airscrew clanked to a standstill. Then he was throwing off his straps, removing his helmet and face-mask and, in the act of tucking away his gloves into a crevasse by the windscreen, waving to her - a small, very personal ripple of his fingers.

She walked forward, a very correct WAAF Officer, hat just so, gloves, the seams of her stocking immaculately straight, aware of a small audience.

"Hello!" She felt her heart beating. "You're dead on time."

He was straightening his tunic and smiling. "Of course!"

Conscious that there were several airmen near at hand, placing chocks in position and standing on the wing to attend to the refuelling, she said very quietly and with a blankly polite face, "It's just not fair! I want to throw my arms around you, but I can't, can I?"

"I should think not, my goodness!" His voice equally quiet, he put a hand on her elbow and gently propelled her forward. "And I didn't get a salute, either."

"Oh! You! You embarrassing creature! All right, I'm sorry. I forgot."

"Scandalous! See that it doesn't happen again!" His eyes were mischievous. "Now, what have you in mind?"

"How long can you stay?"

"About an hour."

"Then, may we walk for 30 minutes?"

"If you think it will help."

They left the station by the main gate, walking silently side by side, their faces formally composed until they had crossed the stile and let them themselves down into the meadow which led to the valley. In the shelter and cover of some high elms and shielded from view by hawthorne bushes, she turned and held him gently so that he was obliged to stop.

"Just hold me. Please? I want you to."

They stood together for a long time.

"Is something wrong? Something worrying you?"

"I don't know." She looked up at him, her eyes soft yet troubled. "These last several days, I've never been so happy. Or so unsettled. Life has been one exciting but sick-making turmoil and I've hardly been able to do my work." She removed her cap and pressed her head against him. "Then, today, I just had to see you. I felt I had to! Had to, more than anything else in the world. And then, when all my plans fell flat . . . well" She shrugged and he felt her shudder in his arms. "Am I really being silly? You must be thinking you have a very neurotic female on your hands."

"I'm unhappy to see you upset." He looked down at her and put his finger on the end of her nose, affectionately. "Love shouldn't be like this, you know."

"But don't you ...?"

He interrupted her. "You're in my thoughts all the time. But I'm not worried, only impatient. To see you. To be with you. To hold you, as I'm doing now. Because I know that all this is meant to happen. As I have explained. It will happen. Don't you feel that?"

She was silent for a long time. "Yes, I suppose you're right. Somehow, when you're with me, it all seems different." She raised her head, her eyes suddenly bright. "And you're the young one, too."

He responded to her better spirits. "Come on, by how much?"

"I'm not going to tell you - you might throw me over."

"I certainly will if you don't, here and now!"

"Don't you dare! Not in my second best blue!" She seemed happier now.

"Look, I've something for you." With shy yet shining eyes, she produced her gift and pressed it into his hand. "Nothing very much. Just a little something from me to you. In exchange for ... Oh, everything." She smiled, embarrassed. "Just take it and don't look. Do that when you get back. Then you can telephone me and, well telephone me, anyway."

He was smiling at her. "You shouldn't have. It wasn't necessary. But, thank you." He bent and kissed her gently, lingeringly, but without passion, conscious of her slim curving figure against him and the softness of her bosom; the kiss of a parent for a dearly-loved child.

They strolled together down the hill but the conversation was stilted as though the briefness of his visit had formed a barrier between them. He was anxious to reassure her. "Only another week now before our long trek northwards. It'll be fun. Have you made your arrangements?"

She nodded, preoccupied. "I can't bring myself to think about it. It just seems too unreal to be true." In a spontaneous surge of enthusiasm added urgently, "Oh, but I shall! It's just ... ." Her voice faded into silence. "You're sure? Of everything? Tell me that you're quite, quite sure?"

He took her hand. "I'm sure. Quite, quite sure. Everything will be fine. You see."

His aircraft was refuelled and ready for take-off when they returned. As they walked across the grass towards it, the air-raid siren started its mournful dirge. He looked to the sky. "Probably some 190s beating up Eastbourne again, the rascals." But he stared carefully into the distance, his eyes slitted against the lowering afternoon sun. "The boys are probably making hay down at Friston and here am I, poodle-faking."

They stopped, the air-raid siren forgotten, on the far side of the Spitfire. They were shielded from the buildings and the two airmen waiting for him to start up had their backs to them. He faced her, his eyes wary but smiling. "Do you think it would be prejudicial to good order and Service discipline if I kissed you in front of all these people?"

She shook her head and, bending slowly, he brushed her lips very lightly and quickly with his own. Then, with the back of one of his fingers, he gently touched the auburn hair peeping from her cap. "You are very, very lovely, you know. So, take good care. Won't you? For my sake?"

She watched him strap himself in and adjust his helmet with the help of an airman standing alongside. The engine burst into life with a lick of flame from the exhausts and a plume of blue smoke. The chocks were pulled away from the wheels and he turned his aircraft and taxied towards her. Masked and goggled, she could not see his face but he raised one ungloved hand as he

passed, his fingers, slightly spread, pale against the shadow of the cockpit. She stood, again with that strange and uncomfortable feeling of loneliness and apprehension, as the aircraft slowly jinked its way to the far side of the airfield. There was a pause before it turned into wind and, almost immediately, she saw the airscrew dissolve into a blur and the Spitfire begin to move, gathering speed at once and lifting its tail.

CHAPTER FOUR

K arl-Heinz Kircheis was born on 14th July, 1921, in a village outside Koblenz. He was a small, good-looking, flaxen-haired young man; grave, disciplined and courteous. In 1936, when he was fifteen, he had joined the Hitler Youth and had excelled at sports and athletics. In the same year he had also been introduced to gliding, an experience which had so excited him that at 18, he had volunteered for the Luftwaffe and had begun training as a pilot.

Four years later, in 1943, he was stationed at Poix, a little to the south and west of Amiens, flying the latest German fighter, the Focke Wulf 190. Karl-Heinz's Gruppe had only recently been re-equipped with the 190 and although his new aircraft had a better performance than the Messerschmitt 109F, with which he was more familiar, he was not entirely happy with his new and formidable mount. The big 1,700 horse-power BMW radial engine in the 190 had shown itself to be a little temperamental at times, which made flying over the sea an unpopular exercise. It was with mixed feelings, therefore, that he sat in dispersal listening to his friend and immediate senior, Heinrich Steinhauser, who was holding the floor.

A dark, rather spare man of 26, Steinhauser bore little resemblance to the fashionable image of the fair-complexioned, blue-eyed Aryan hero. Holding the rank of Hauptmann, he would have been described as a Flight Commander in the Royal Air Force, and it was in this capacity that he was addressing nine other pilots together with a dozen or so other officers, including his Gruppe Commander and various other specialists. Pointer in hand, he half sat on the corner of a table, surrounded by maps and a well-chalked blackboard.

"Right! We shall be taking off at 16.30 hours local time and our target is the railway junction at Sevenoaks, on the southern outskirts of London." He pointed out Sevenoaks on the map beside him and there were several subdued expressions of dismay from his audience.

Ignoring the interruption, Steinhauser went on, speaking with a studied lack of emotion. "As you see, it's not going to be easy. Thus far, we have gone for coastal towns in what Tommy chooses to call Baedeker raids. This one, however, is different." He paused, conscious that the room was silent, each man drinking in every word. "As we all know, the Abbeville boys bombed the railway station in

Eastbourne several days ago and lost a couple of aircraft in the process. Our target, which is more than 50 kilometres inland, means that for us the risks are a good deal greater."

Steinhauser stood up and straightened in an exaggerated movement before picking up the pointer and going to the blackboard. "On the credit side weatherman Kurt, we'll hear from him in a moment, is forecasting good visibility but complete cloud-cover throughout, so that, although we shall go in low, we can always nip up into cloud in an emergency. If we are intercepted before we get there, we shall have a crack at a secondary target on the way out - if at all possible, that is. But more of that later."

He paused to chalk two formations of crosses on the blackboard.

"I will lead six aircraft, each of us carrying one 250 kilo bomb, fused eleven seconds delay - so that we don't demolish each other! The remaining four aircraft, led by Karl-Heinz, will act as close escort and will not carry bombs. Their task is to head off the enemy, or at least try to, should we be caught on the way to the target." He leaned on the pointer and said with careful emphasis, "It has been decided not to use a larger force in the hope that ten aircraft might get through whereas twenty or more would undoubtedly arouse more attention over the other side and perhaps provoke an overwhelming response. His face creased into a caricature of a smile and he shot a glance at his Gruppe Commander. "That's the official view, anyway. I'm bound to say, it's not an opinion which impresses me very much or one that is widely shared!"

Aware of the impact his words were having on the nine pilots sitting mutely in front of him, Steinhauser returned slowly to perch himself carefully on the corner of the table.

"We shall go in at ground-level along the route shown on the map. We have taken account of most of the known flak positions but we can't do much about the fighter stations. As you see, we shall have at least five of them around us; Hawkinge, Lympne, where we know there are Typhoons, Biggin Hill, and Kenley. Further afield there are Manston and Tangmere and we can't exclude the night fighters at West Malling. Finally," his pointer described a large circle encompassing Brighton and Hastings, "the Abbeville boys say they were caught, without too much difficulty apparently, by a new type of Spitfire with clipped wings and a much larger nose, believed to be based somewhere in this area. All of which adds up to danger."

He paused, weighing his words. "One more possibility, as we get close to London we shall be moving into balloon country. We have no reports of balloons in the target area but they are, of course, mobile and their sites can be changed quickly enough if the area is considered to be especially sensitive. This is a point worth making as, and make no mistake, the target we're going for is important. It's a main rail junction for traffic from the south-east into London and if we can hit it hard enough, it will cause chaos for a month. What's more, the morale effect will be considerable. It will bring home to the three million or so people living around and about, the fact that they are a good deal more vulnerable to this type of attack than they have so far believed."

Steinhauser stood up, laid down his pointer and took a deep breath. "That, then, is the long and short of it. All we have to do now is consider the detail."

Forty minutes later Steinhauser and Kircheis walked together across the grass to where their Staffel Mercedes was parked. The former put his arm around his companion's shoulder. "Karl-Heinz, you're going to have to see things today as you've never done before." His smile was without humour. "If we stir up a hornets' nest, old mate, we're going to have a very rough ride indeed and I doubt that many of us will come back. The best we can hope for is surprise. And as I see it, they're bound to be surprised. After all, who in their right mind would attack a target within sight of London, in broad daylight, and right slap-bang in the middle of a whole clutch of fighter bases?" His mouth turned down in a cynical curve. "We must be demented - all of us. But chiefly one or two who can't be named!"

They took off in pairs, the leading six aircraft heavy with bombs. Keeping at tree-top height, they set course for Dieppe. There was a regular pattern of activity in that area; if Tommy saw them on radar - which was unlikely - he would probably not attach too much importance to their formation.

Once over the coast the 190s dropped down to sea level and, turning a little to their right, in a broad vee of five pairs raced towards England, skimming the waves.

On the left of the formation Karl-Heinz kept half an eye on the second hand of the clock down on his right. It clicked on remorselessly but with agonising slowness. Underneath him the grey, white-flecked waters of the Channel streaked past. Ahead the huge BMW radial thundered and shook making the gunsight before his face tremble.

After less than nine minutes he saw in the distance the pale irregular outline of the chalk cliffs at Beachy Head, his stomach contracting almost to the point of pain as he anxiously scanned the horizon for signs of enemy aircraft. Then, low down and to the left, some radio masts appeared, four thin pencil line marks on a grey canvas. So far, so good! They were dead on course.

They flashed across the English coast almost at the point where, 900 years earlier, Duke William and his Norman army had struggled ashore before forming up and marching towards the site of the fateful battle, later to be known as Hastings. Within seconds they were racing among the hills and villages of Sussex, with woods and hills surging past on either side. Not a shot had been fired. Karl-Heinz, rigidly tense, was mightily relieved. This was surprise, indeed. In those fleeting seconds when he allowed his mind to relax sufficiently he thought how beautiful the countryside looked. And hilly. He had not expected the hills. Or so many woods and trees.

For interminable minutes they flew, hugging the patchwork landscape, the formation rising and falling like the undulating wings of a great flat fish as the aircraft negotiated the contours of the countryside. Then they were streaking between higher hills after which the buildings, roofs and gardens of a small town appeared, a town which Karl-Heinz recalled from his briefing as being Tunbridge Wells. Forty kilometres inland already! Fifteen to go. They were well and truly committed.

Crouching in his cockpit, a bedlam of noise and vibration, Karl-Heinz was at fever pitch. Steinhauser was slightly in front, on his right and fractionally lower, his black-crossed aircraft heavy with bomb, racing like a lethal grey-green dart within metres of the ground. One minute and twenty seconds to go before the target would appear! It was not going to be easy; there was a gathering smoke haze which they had not bargained for and the visibility was deteriorating rapidly.

He flashed a glance at his clock. Twenty-eight seconds to go. He began to count and peered anxiously ahead through the disc of the airscrew for the concentration of houses that would signify Sevenoaks.

Then, in an instant, catastrophe!

Both Steinhauser and Kircheis saw the balloons at precisely the same moment. Like silver-grey phantoms, they sat motionless and almost invisible beneath the ragged edges of the cloud. Neither had time to speak nor even to register fully what he had seen before the ten aircraft were among the wires.

Steinhauser, horrified, wrenched his aircraft upwards and to the right, throwing his formation into wild and instant confusion. Kircheis, suddenly aware that he was directly below one enormous sagging shape, saw the vertical hair-line tendril that was a wire whip past his port wing with barely feet to spare before he, too, snatched at his controls sending his aircraft lurching and skidding to the left. In an instant, he was down among house-tops and chimneys and railway lines that seemed to curve in every direction.

Ahead were more balloons with the vicious, slicing wires he knew to be there but could not see. Jinking like a hare pursued by dogs he weaved and banked and pushed, thrusting all the time the nose of his aircraft downwards, ever more down towards the ground, the animal instinct for self-preservation all-powerful and compelling. He was almost touching the tops of the buildings, now in the middle of a pall of smoke with roofs flashing by, then pylons with more wires and a factory with car parks and stationary vehicles. White-faced people gaped in his direction, some staring aghast, others ducking and running and falling. And throughout, the wild, drumming bellow of the engine in front of him and the savage buffeting and gravity forces as he was hurled around the cockpit by his own manoeuvres.

After what seemed to be a life-time, he found himself in the clear and among open fields and hills. The balloons had disappeared. His mouth dry with fear beneath his oxygen mask and still in a fever of excitement, he craned his neck left and right, then upwards and to the rear and all the way round again - several times. He was quite alone; his formation had vanished!

He continued to turn instinctively to the left, sinking below the level of the hills to remain inconspicuous. There were more house-tops, red and some green, followed by a lake, then trees, and more open spaces with black and white cattle.

South. 'He must go south'. But, which way was south? There was no sun and his gyroscopic instruments had toppled with the violence of his manoeuvres. Instinct, however, again persuaded him to continue with his slow turn to the left and, darting quick and anxious glances around the cockpit, he lifted the 190 over the lip of a hill which came surging towards him and peered yet again over the blunt nose of his aircraft.

It was at that point that it seemed his bowels would melt. He was flying straight towards an airfield situated on the top of a hill and surrounded by trees.

Horror-stricken, Karl-Heinz saw that he was approaching in line with what appeared to be the main runway and that nothing he could do would prevent him crossing the boundary. Within seconds, he knew, he would be shot to pieces. His only slim chance was the cloud. He must at all costs get into cloud. Now!

He was on the point of leaving the protection of the ground and soaring into the grey layer above him when an aircraft he did not immediately recognise rose slowly from the runway as though suspended on an invisible wire. It had just raised its undercarriage and was climbing away to the south - alone, naked, unsuspecting.

It sat there, totally unaware of his presence, growing rapidly in size in the centre of his windscreen. As he was closing, it seemed at almost the speed of sound, Karl-Heinz had less than two seconds to decide what he should do. His reaction was instantaneous and predictable. He raised his nose a fraction so that the other aircraft sat squarely in the middle of his gunsight and he pressed the triggers on his control column.

The 190 shuddered briefly as both cannons and machine guns launched four lethal grey streamers which streaked ahead, curling and writhing about the silhouette in front. As the shells and bullets struck home, they sparkled prettily like a child's firework. The target seemed first to flinch, then stagger and lurch, like a running animal mortally wounded by a hunter's gun, before toppling over slowly onto its side. In a moment it had fallen beneath Karl-Heinz's wing and had gone so that he saw it no more.

****

She was looking in the opposite direction and did not see the German until the harsh scream of his racing aircraft made her turn. The shape of the 190 was unfamiliar to her and, perplexed initially, it was only when she saw the single black cross on the side of the fuselage that she experienced the first spasm of doubt and fear.

Almost immediately little trails of smoke detached themselves from the under-side of the wings and with them came a strange sound, as of someone tearing calico, but magnified a thousand times. In silence, then in horror and disbelief, she watched the Spitfire falter, turn briefly and hesitantly to the right, then fall away nose-first until it disappeared into the valley.

She did not hear the explosion but saw the rising column of dark smoke, at which point, she gave an anguished moan before putting her hand to her throat and running, not because she knew what she was doing, but because some violent, unseen force made her body react.

In later years she had no recollection of leaving the airfield, or of crossing the road and descending into the valley. She must have fallen several times for her stockings were badly torn and her uniform soiled with mud and slime. But, of that terrible, sobbing, gasping mile, she remembered nothing.

When at last she reached the field where the smoke, now only a thick haze, was still rising, the gate had been thrown back and the entrance rutted with the wheels-marks of heavy vehicles. She continued to stagger on, her heart bursting, the breath rasping from her tortured lungs. Ahead and to the left was an ambulance and some figures.

There were also two fire-engines with hoses and other figures hurrying about and shouting. A man in shirt-sleeves with blackened arms and face was laboriously climbing the hill with urgent strides. He altered course in her direction and she barely recognised him as Jack Shepherd, her friend from the Watch Office.

Seeing her, he put up his arm and shouted brokenly and almost hysterically, "Don't go! For Christ's sake, don't go! Don't go down there, love. Please?" Lumbering heavily towards her he clutched at her arm, but she threw him off and stumbled on down the hill. In the distance and behind her, she heard him cry again and again. But his words meant nothing.

She came eventually to the crater. The fire had been quenched and there were only bits, twisted and burnt and strewn about amid wisps of smoke and steam. The remains of one wing with its red and blue roundel lay to the right and the tail, miraculously intact, stood tilted on the side of the hole. She saw the pale-blue band around the torn edges of the rear of the fuselage and the aircraft number, unblemished, MB748.

In the centre of the crater the ground had been pulverised by the explosion. There were remnants everywhere, things she did not recognise - mutilated, twisted, and shattered. But there were also things she knew and understood - the sleeve of a blue tunic, charred and smoking; the bright yellow snake of an intestine; and alone, palely waxen and infinitely pathetic, the final obscenity, a single, severed hand, the fingers spread as though in supplication. And above it all, hanging like an evil cloud, was the foul stench of death.

For some moments she stood transfixed, a sense of total unreality paralysing her body and mind. Then, her face contorted in horror and with her hands to her head, she turned and stumbled blindly away. A figure cannoning into her, she clutched at it with talon-like fingers, sobbing and shaking. Then her stomach revolted and she vomited - again and again - until finally, her spirit and body broken, she collapsed.

Jack Shepherd held her tightly so that she did not fall. With tears furrowing his blackened face, he cried over and over, "I told you not to come, love. I told you! Didn't I tell you? Oh my dear, dear love. God help you. Oh, God, please, please help this lovely girl."

The Sergeant-in-charge of the fire-engines approached, his face a mask of shock and embarrassment. "For Christ's sake, take her away, sir." His voice broke. "She shouldn't be here. Take away, please. For all our sakes!" As though exhausted by his outburst he stood irresolutely before slowly turning aside, his face crumpling with anguish.

Ignoring the man, Jack Shepherd stood with his blackened head lifted and his eyes closed, holding her shaking body and patting her gently like a child. "I tried to tell you, old love. Didn't I tell you? Why did you have to come? Why, oh why, did you have to come?"

Karl-Heinz experienced the fierce exultation of victory when he saw the aircraft in front of him fall away to destruction. He had overtaken it so quickly that there was no question of recognition. The identity of the occupant did not concern him for a moment, nor did the consequences likely to arise from the aircraft's sudden obliteration. Nor even that a man had been killed, brutally, by an unseen hand and without knowing of his assailant. All such considerations were merely the 'fortunes of war' and all was fair in love and war, was it not? How else did one fight?

But, these issues he had little time to reflect upon as he was immediately confronted by a hill, which he was obliged to negotiate swiftly and positively, after which the ground fell away steeply. He pushed forward sharply on his control column and his head thumped uncomfortably against the canopy roof as he was lifted bodily out of his seat. He glanced at his airspeed indicator. Close on 540 kilometres per hour. No Spitfire he knew of could catch him at this speed.

The countryside continued to race beneath his wings - fields, woods, roads, cottages and farms. Every now and then he would lift the 190 over pylon wires draped in gentle curves across his path. He felt wildly elated. Five minutes more and he would be over the coast and away. He wondered where the others were and looked around methodically; behind, left, right, then upwards. Again. And again. But, nothing. Always nothing.

There were larger hills ahead now and, away to the left on flatter ground, he picked out the masts he had first seen when approaching the English coast and which he knew were near Eastbourne. His heart singing he hugged the contours of the ground and, with a final prayer of thanksgiving for deliverance, he shot over the cliffs at Beachy Head like a porpoise and headed out across the Channel.

But Karl-Heinz's rejoicings were premature. Four Spitfires of 629 Squadron patrolling over the water a mile off Eastbourne saw his aircraft quite by accident as it left the land, a dark grey projectile. Twenty seconds later they would have commenced their routine turn to the left and had their backs to him. By sheer coincidence they happened to be the same four who had been surprised by the twelve German fighters a week or so earlier.

They were just as surprised by the appearance of Karl-Heinz as they were expecting intruders from the sea and not a single German aircraft from the land.

But they did not allow their astonishment to affect their response for more than a moment. They raced in pursuit, cutting the corners, trails of dark smoke streaming from their straining engines.

They caught Karl-Heinz Kircheis in mid-Channel and they killed him. His body, torn by cannon fire, was pulped into oblivion before his aircraft dipped suddenly and hit the sea. It struck once, skimming like a flat stone thrown by a child, before striking again and disintegrating in a chaos of whirling wings and fragments. It sank immediately, leaving nothing more than a small, pale-green smudge on the gently-heaving, leaden waters.

The four Spitfire pilots circled once, looked down, and when they saw no sign of life, flew off northwards. Unhurriedly. Without fuss. Unaware of the significance of their bloody act.

CHAPTER FIVE

At the sound of running feet the younger woman straightened up and turned. "Oh, Ma! For heaven's sake, look at these two!" One small dishevelled boy halted, too breathless to speak. Beside him a Gordon Setter stood with lolling tongue, caked from paws to shoulder with mud and slime - grinning! "Christopher, darling! Where on earth have you been with Sheba? Just look at her! It'll take us a week to get her presentable!"

"Mummy, Sheba jumped into the stream before we could stop her." The child swallowed noisily. "But, I've really come to tell you about Julia. She's stuck up a tree and can't get down."

His mother bent over him, gently admonishing. "Look, matey. Little girls aged five are not supposed to be up trees; far less stuck up trees! Anyway, where's Susan?"

"Mummy, that's the point. She's stuck up the tree, too. You see, she went up first, then Julia went up, though I told her not to. Then Julia couldn't get down and Susan can't get past her. Now, they are both there. And Mummy," the child lowered his voice, "Julia says she wants to 'go'!"

The Grandmother asked innocently, "Go where?"

The younger woman sighed in resignation. "She just wants to 'go'." Whenever there's a crisis in our family it goes straight to Julia's bladder! A walking sprinkler, that child!' She bent to pick up her cardigan. "Lead on MacDuff. Let's get the cavewomen down from the trees!"

But the small boy remained, reluctant to accompany her. "Grandma, you'd better come too. I think Mummy will need help."

The older woman turned away, head lowered. "Oh, I doubt it, darling. You go on and I'll sort things out here."

"No, Grandma; you've got to come! Julia's asking for you." He grasped the woman's arm and pulled her into motion.

Resisting the child, she looked up to see her daughter-in-law's eyes mildly surprised and querying. She paused a moment and finally tilted her head resignedly. "All right then. Off you go. I'll follow in a while."

She walked slowly down the hill, knowing instinctively where to tread, some inner compulsion guiding her steps. And, as she went, forty long years and more stole past on silent feet.

Approaching the place, she felt as though she were moving towards a cliff-edge; aware, too, of her drumming heart-beats and that her legs were trembling and losing their strength.

But, there was no stopping. No stopping, now. She was there; and all was tranquillity. The hole, mercifully, was gone; only a shallow depression remained, a gentle slope with rushes and sweet-smelling grasses.

For more than forty seasons ploughmen had guided, first their horses, then their tractors around the spot as though they had known it to be hallowed ground. She looked about in silence, vaguely conscious of the smallest breeze which touched her cheek and moved a strand of her now greying auburn hair across her brow. Everything, so much the same, yet different. How still it was. No death now. No violence. No stench of destruction. Only peace and life, and a scar healed by nature and by time.

As though carefully and uncertainly unveiling the past, she allowed herself to recall the scene which had etched so indelible an imprint of horror on her memory. She saw his face again; and he was smiling. And his pale hand, as he had moved away in those final moments. No, she must not torture herself. He was here still, that much she felt and knew. Not dead, but here: For always. This was the place. The place were he, where they, had parted. Her place, too. Their own private place.

Looking down, her eyes brimming, from some recess in her mind came words practised in her childhood:

> *There shall be in that rich earth a richer dust concealed;*
> *A dust whom England bore, shaped, made aware,*
> *Gave, once, her flowers to love, her ways to roam,*
> *A body of England's breathing English air ... .*

There was more. But ... what? Her memory struggled to recall the forgotten lines. No, there was nothing . Only mist. Mist and time. A richer dust? Oh, yes! A richer dust. A dust rich beyond compare.

It was then that she saw the lilies. Were they truly her lilies; the lilies she had planted with her own hands? A year later, when she had found the strength to return? And had some compassionate Deity decreed that her flowers should bloom for all time?

She sank slowly to touch the silken petals and smell the fragrance. The past welled up within her so that her eyes filled with tears and, with bowed head, she sobbed silently, her body shaking in anguish as had happened so many years before.

The rapid thud of feet, of tiny, eager feet, startled her The feet of a small boy, a joyous, living, blue-eyed child. A child who knew nothing of war, of death, or of things long past. A child only of the present, of the sun, the clean air and the scents and beauty of nature. The beauty of England. The beauty of his England. Their England.

She stood up quickly, composing herself as best she could, a smile struggling to supplant the sorrow in her face. The child halted, his eyes wide with concern. "Grandma! You don't have to cry. Julia's all right. And Susan, too. Mummy helped them down"

Seeing she could not reply he added consolingly, "You come with me, Grandma. I'll take you to them. Everything's all right. Everything will be fine. You see."

And then, as she felt herself being filled with both sadness and rejoicing at the rebirth and continuity of all things; the child took her hand and led her away.

About the Author

Tom Neil was born, brought up and educated in Lancashire. In the summer of 1938 he joined the RAF Volunteer Reserve in Manchester and carried out his ab inito training there before moving on to No.8 FTS in Scotland where he completed his flying instruction, all of it on biplanes.

In May 1940, he became the first officer pilot to join the newly forming 249 Squadron at RAF Church Fenton, the unit first being equipped with Spitfires before changing to Hurricanes.

With 249 he flew throughout the Battle of Britain, becoming one of the most successful pilots to take part with 13 confirmed victories, and later, in the latter part of the year becoming senior Flight Commander of that unit at the age of 20.

Ordered to the Middle East in May 1941, 249 flew off the aircraft carrier HMS Ark Royal in the Mediterranean, Neil leading his half of the squadron for almost six hours before landing on Malta, then the longest trip by Hurricanes ever recorded.

Serving with his unit in Malta – 249 Squadron being retained there for its defence – he left eight months later and returned to England to be promoted and given command of No. 41 Fighter Squadron flying first, Spitfire Mk5s, then the new Griffon-engined Mark 12s, a post he held for a year, flying mainly from airfields along the Channel coast.

Tom Neil's next operational posting was as a flying liaison officer with the 100th Fighter Wing of the 9th USAAF, an appointment he held for a further year, flying mainly P-47s and P-51s, before, during and after the Invasion of Europe in June 1944.

Returning to the RAF in January 1945, he became an instructor at the School of Air Support at RAF Old Sarum, was sent briefly to Burma for operational experience, after which he attended the Test Pilot's Course at Cranfield and served as a Service Test Pilot for five years, at home, in the United States, and other areas abroad, flying as part of A&AEE, Boscombe Down

His next flying appointment was as Commander of 208 (Meteor) Squadron and also OC Flying, RAF Abu Sueir, Egypt, from which he returned in 1956.

At various times, Neil also attended Staff College, the War College and Empire Central Flying School and served in other roles which included a quasi diplomatic post in the British Embassy, Washington, and as a junior Delegate to the Untied Nations, New York, appointments he held for more than 3 years.

Neil retired from the RAF in 1963, having flown more than 115 types of aircraft in war and peace, and having been awarded the Distinguished Flying Cross with Bar, the Air Force Cross, the American Bronze Star and other decorations.

Intending to emigrate with his family to America, he took up an appointment with a British Consultancy Company in Boston and headed the American element of that organisation for some years before returning to Britain to join a company in the same field in Norfolk, where he finally retired.

A gifted lecturer on flying subjects, he has also written a number of books and many stories and articles for more than 30 years, and is among the most popular authors writing for various aviation magazines but principally 'Aeroplane Monthly'.

Tom Neil and his wife, who also served in the RAF, have three sons, all of whom have distinguished themselves in their various fields, two of them in aviation.